DEMON HATE

A human-shine swept past the spot where the demon floated curled about himself, and he winced. But it was not the one, and it passed by unawares. Still, it would not be long before the one would return and question him, and the demon knew it was time to prepare himself for that contact. To conceal his hatred and smoldering anger of the human and his species. To present himself as a willing and trustworthy servant, eager to do the foolish human's bidding.

It was a role Astaroth detested, a role most of his race would never have accepted and put up with. But he had more patience than they did; or perhaps he saw the potential of the situation more clearly. Soon, he knew, all of this pain and bitter humiliation would be turned back onto humankind and repaid a thousand times over.

Very soon.

TIMOTHY ZAHN
TRIPLET

science fiction

Distributed in Canada by PaperJacks Ltd., a Licensee
of the trademarks of Simon & Schuster, Inc.

TRIPLET

This is a work of fiction. All the characters and events portrayed in this book are fictional, and any resemblance to real people or incidents is purely coincidental.

Copyright © 1987 by Timothy Zahn

A Baen Books Original

In Canada distributed by PaperJacks Ltd., 330 Steelcase Road, Markham, Ontario

First printing, August 1987

ISBN: 0-671-65341-5

Cover art by Alan Gutierrez

Printed in Canada

Distributed by
SIMON & SCHUSTER
1230 Avenue of the Americas
New York, N.Y. 10020

For Dan and Kathy,
and Don and Kathe:

who, in their own individual ways,
have scotched the rumor that writing is by
necessity a lonely occupation.

Prologue

The world was a mass of garish color, surrounding him like splotches of light thrown into a whirlpool. The faint background haze of plant life, the brighter and more localized bits that were animals and insects, the almost painful shining that bespoke a member of humankind—it was a far cry from the grays and blacks of his proper abode.

Astaroth hated it all.

He hated the humans most, of course, but none of it totally escaped his resentment. Not even the plant life, for useless and innocent it might be by itself, without it none of the rest could exist . . . and then the demon's own kind would not be in such a hateful position. Mortal life was both the enemy and the prize in this war, and the resulting combination of lust and fury was often almost more than he could bear. So incredibly frail and foolish, it was incredible that humankind could be at the same time so impossibly strong. The demon didn't understand it—none of the Powers truly understood it—and the frustration of that paradox merely added to his determination to destroy it all.

A human-shine swept past the spot where the demon floated curled about himself, and he winced. But it was not the one, and it passed by unawares. Still, it would not be long before the one would return and question him, and the demon knew it was time to prepare himself for that contact. To conceal his hatred and smoldering anger

1

of the human and his species. To present himself as a willing and trustworthy servant, eager to do the foolish human's bidding. To hide the truth of which of them was truly the master here.

It was a role Astaroth detested, a role most of his race would never have accepted and put up with. But he had more patience than they did; or perhaps he saw the potential of the situation more clearly. Soon, he knew, all of this pain and bitter humiliation would be turned back onto humankind and repaid a thousand times over.

Very soon.

Chapter 1

The housecomp's trilling was quiet but persistent, and the machine itself of course had infinite patience . . . and eventually Danae mal ce Taeger dragged herself out of her leaden sleep to answer it. "Yes, Rax, what is it?" she mumbled.

"You had a call this morning from Dean Hsiu, Danae," the housecomp's soft voice said. "I'm sorry to wake you, but he asked for you to call him back by eleven at the latest."

Danae forced her eyes open enough to focus on the holoclock at her side of the floatbed. Five minutes till. "Did he say what he wanted?" she sighed, shifting tired muscles under the sheet and cautioning a suddenly rebellious stomach.

"No, but from his tone I would say he was pleased about something."

"With Dean Hsiu that could mean practically anything," she said dryly, sitting up and scratching vigorously at her hair. A belated glance beside her . . . but Pirro wasn't lying there trying to sleep through the conversation. In fact, from the looks of it, he hadn't come to bed at all. "Pirro up and gone already?" she asked with forced casualness, sliding off onto the floor and padding to her closet for a robe.

"I believe he left the house shortly after you went to bed last night," Rax answered.

3

"This morning, you mean." Danae glared back at the bed. For a moment she was tempted to search Pirro's half of the closet, to see whether he'd left in his work clothes or had simply gone off in search of another party after theirs folded up. But Dean Hsiu was waiting . . . and checking up on Pirro was a waste of effort, anyway. She'd known for a long time now that this one was over and done with. "Code out Dean Hsiu for me, will you, Rax?" she sighed.

She was seated at the phone by the time the older man's holoimage appeared in front of her. "Ah—Ms. Panya," Hsiu beamed. "Thank you for returning my call. I hope I didn't disturb you?"

"Not at all, sir," Danae told him. "I'm afraid I was helping some friends celebrate their graduate assignments last night and it got a bit late."

"Well, you'll just have to call them all back tonight to return the favor," the other smiled. "Your own assignment request has just come back in—" he paused dramatically— "marked *approved*."

Danae felt her mouth fall open. "You mean . . . Triplet?"

"Triplet it is," Hsiu nodded. "Threshold, Shamsheer, and Karyx—you've been approved for all three worlds. And to the best of my knowledge this is the first time anyone from Autaris has been so honored. My heartiest congratulations to you."

Danae started to breathe again. "Thank you, sir. It's . . . a lot more than I expected myself."

"Yes, I can tell," the other said, a twinkle in his eye. "But you've got a lot of work ahead of you, so get your heart restarted and get to it. First of all, you'll need to get a full high-retention mnemonic treatment; after that'll come a three-week language course. Then—let's see—then you'll have another three-weeker on the cultures of Shamsheer and Karyx; and finally, there'll be a lab on voice commands and the more common spells."

"Yes. Right. Uh, was there anything about the Courier I asked for?"

"Courier? I didn't realize you'd made a specific request . . ." Hsiu peered somewhere off-camera. "Oh, yes, here

it is. Most experienced Courier . . . name given here is
Ravagin."

"Am I getting him?"

Hsiu frowned slightly. "It's a little hard to tell from the
wording . . . but it looks like if he agrees to it Triplet
Control itself is willing. He a friend of yours?"

"Never met him. But getting the most experienced
Courier is important to the project proposal I made."

"Ah." Hsiu shrugged, apparently dismissing it as none
of his business. "Well, anyway, I've already begun making the arrangements with the various departments involved. Why don't you check back with my office tomorrow
for the final schedule?"

Danae's jaw clenched momentarily; but there was nothing of her father's casual arrogance in either Hsiu's face or
voice. *He's just trying to help*, she told herself, sitting
hard on the automatic rebellion the other had inadver-
tently triggered. Not *trying to take over; not treating me
like a child who can't handle her own life. Just offering
assistance and common courtesy.* It helped a little. "That
would be fine, sir," she told him, managing to keep her
voice civil. "Thank you for taking the time out of your
busy schedule."

"Oh, no problem at all, Ms. Panya. Well, I'll let you go
now. Once again, congratulations."

"Thank you, Dean Hsiu."

Hsiu's image smiled and vanished. Danae leaned back
in her chair, eyes gazing unseeingly around the room as
she tried to absorb the magnitude of her triumph. Permits
to visit either of the Hidden Worlds of Triplet were as
scarce as honest men . . . and or her—for *her*—to actually
have been awarded one of them was—

Was suspicious in the extreme.

She bit at her lip, the glow within her fading before the
sudden doubt. If he had traced her here—and if he had,
he would certainly have learned of her application to Triplet. . . .

All right, Danae—stop emoting and think. She'd sent in
the application . . . when? Three months ago? About that.
Okay: one-way spaceflight to Triplet would have been perhaps a week; evaluation would have included a check with

Earth's master records for possible psychological, political, or legal problems. Another four to five weeks' round trip for that one, with handling and all; and of course at the very end there would be another week to get the approval back here to Autaris. Which left . . . six or seven weeks at the most. Six weeks for them to shuffle her application out of the sacks and sacks of similar requests; to study it, evaluate it, pass it around to everyone in sight and up the decision-making hierarchy, and to approve it.

No way. There was simply no way.

"Damn," she said, very quietly. "Damn. *Damn!*"

"Danae, are you all right?"

"No, Rax, I am *not* all right," she snarled. "Where is he?"

"Pirro? I believe—"

"The hell with Pirro. I mean Hart. Where is he?"

There was a slight pause. "I don't believe I know anyone by that name."

"Check again," she snapped. "He's here somewhere—next door, down the street, maybe under a rock in the yard." Abruptly, she raised her voice. "Hart? I know you can hear me, you bastard. Get your butt in here, now. You hear me? *Now.*"

There was no answer . . . but she hadn't really expected one. Tightening her robe sash savagely, she stomped out of the room and downstairs to the foyer. There she waited, glaring at the front door.

There was a gentle, almost diffident rap on the steel-core wood. "Come in," Danae gritted, making no move to unlock it. A short pause . . . and with a click the electronic lock disengaged and the door swung open. A medium-nondescript man stepped quietly into the foyer, slipping a small electronic scrambler back into his pocket.

For a moment they just eyed each other in silence. Then Danae took a deep breath. "You did it, didn't you," she said. "You got me that slot on Triplet. You and Daddy Dear and a hell of a lot of money."

Hart shrugged fractionally. "I only make reports," he told her. "What your father does with the information I couldn't say."

"Sure." She closed her eyes briefly, all her earlier excitement turning to ashes in her mouth. "What if I turn it down? I can do that, you know. What would Daddy Dear do to you if he knew I'd caught on to you and his little interference-running?"

"My job isn't to stay hidden forever, Ms. mal ce Taeger. You're far too intelligent for that, and your father knows it. I'm here to guard you. That's all."

"And to help him interfere with every aspect of my life he can get his hands on. Right?"

Hart didn't answer. "How long have you been on to me?" Danae asked, for lack of anything better to say.

"Almost since you started at the university," Hart answered. "The 'Danae Panya' cover was one of your more transparent ones." He cocked a speculative eyebrow. "Almost as if you knew you'd never get to Triplet without some help."

She very nearly spat in his face for that one. What stopped her was the gnawing suspicion that he might just be right. "You think that, do you?" she snarled at him instead. "You think all this is just Daddy Dear's little girl nibbling on both ends of the pie? Trying to have things both ways?"

Hart's lip twitched, just noticeably. "I couldn't say, Ms. mal ce Taeger. If that'll be all . . . ?"

Danae snorted. "As if my orders meant a damn to you. Sure, go on—get out of here."

He started to go, but then hesitated. "Ms. mal ce Taeger . . . will your friend be accompanying you to Triplet?"

"Who, Pirro?" She smiled lopsidedly. "Ah, yes —I suppose Daddy Dear's pretty annoyed by him, isn't he? His sweet, innocent daughter living with an ambitionless, borderline bum. Well, you tell him, yes, I'll certainly be taking him to Threshold with me. Maybe even into Shamsheer and Karyx if you've bribed the officials there adequately."

"As you wish," Hart said evenly. "I presume you'll want to give Pirro the good news personally. I believe he's still in the apartment building at the corner with the woman he escorted home from your party last night."

At her side, Danae's right hand curled into an impotent fist. "Get out," she whispered.

Hart nodded and slipped quietly outside, locking the door electronically behind him. Closing her eyes, Danae sagged against the wall beside her as the steel of her resolve turned to water and drained away. Pirro's tomcatting behavior was no real surprise—she was honest enough to admit that to herself—but the bluntness of the revelation had still hurt. As Hart had no doubt meant it to. The bastard.

She stood there for a long minute, pressing the fresh bruises on her psyche. Then, taking a deep breath, she straightened up. The University of Autaris was no longer a haven for her . . . but then, she'd had no intention of staying here forever, anyway. Hart was here; Pirro was on his way out—and to hell with both of them.

Because whatever his own reasons, Daddy Dear had finally outsmarted himself. For as long as she could remember he'd been pulling on her strings, refusing to let her live her own life or to accept the fact that she was an adult now and—she had to admit it—embittering her in the process. But now, by opening this particular door for her, he'd just possibly given her the way out of the cocoon that was smothering her.

Triplet.

Buying her way to Threshold was one thing; but Shamsheer and Karyx were another story entirely. Money didn't reach through the Tunnels—not money, not connections, not Hart and his private spy network. Once inside the Hidden Worlds she could do anything she pleased . . . and there wasn't a damn thing Daddy Dear could do about it.

And there was a good chance he'd live to regret letting her in there.

Chapter 2

It was rare that the area around Reingold Crater was treated to more than a brief glimpse of the sun, but today was one of those rare occasions. Sunny and warm, the usual winds moderated to gentle breezes, it was the sort of morning that reminded Ravagin of the more carefree days of his childhood, tempting him to hike out into the surrounding hills and put off finishing his report. No one seriously cared about the damn things unless something went wrong, anyway, and God knew he'd earned himself an extra day off.

But duty called with its damned Siren song . . . and anyway, it would be Corah Lea who took it in the neck if the stupid busywork was too late. In the end he compromised, skipping the usual shuttle service and instead walking the two kilometers from his house to his Crosspoint Building office.

The Courier wing of the sprawling structure was, as usual, a haven from the controlled pandemonium that always seemed to fill the rest of the building. With supervisors and planners continually rushing to meetings, new groups preparing for their sorties into the Hidden Worlds scrambling madly with last-minute details, and bone-weary returning groups slogging toward debrief rooms at half the speed of everyone else, Ravagin had often felt that getting through the Crosspoint Building was the most dangerous part of any trip. Today was no exception, and he breathed

9

a sigh of relief when the Courier wing door sealed with its solid *thunk* behind him.

Only to discover he'd relaxed too soon. Keying onto his terminal, he was confronted with a red-lettered message plastered across his screen:

RAVAGIN: PLEASE REPORT TO ME AS SOON AS YOU COME IN.

CORAH

"Great," he muttered. "Just great." Lea didn't call Couriers to her office just for the hell of it. If she wanted to see him in person, it was almost guaranteed to be bad news. Grimacing, he got to his feet and headed out again into the pandemonium.

Supervisor Corah Lea was waiting for him, the neutral expression he knew so well plastered across her face. "Ravagin," she nodded in greeting, waving him to a chair in front of her desk. "I expected you here rather earlier."

"I took the long way in," he said mildly. "You can dock my pay if you want to."

That got him a harrumph and an almost reluctant smile. "You never were one to try with intimidation gambits, were you? All right; let's get down to business. This application you've filed for a leave of absence, for starters. Are you really serious about leaving?"

Ravagin nodded. "It's not a ploy for more money or vacation time, if that's what you mean. If I'd wanted something like that I would have asked for it directly. You know that."

"I know." Her face and voice softened a bit. "Mind telling me why?"

He sighed. "You've seen the test results. I'm *tired*, Corah. Just tired. I've been shuttling people through the Tunnels for sixteen years now—that's two to three years longer than any other Courier you've got, and a year longer than the supposed maximum."

"You're good at what you do," Lea said. "Damned good. We wouldn't have finagled the rules so hard to keep you on this long if you weren't."

"I appreciate the compliment," he nodded. "If I wasn't

so good at it I'd have left long ago with or without your help."

She snorted wryly. "Not much for false modesty, are you?"

"False modesty is for politicians," he shrugged.

There was a moment of silence. "Well," Lea said at last. "Is there anything I can offer that might change your mind? You *did* mention extra money and vacation time."

He smiled. "Not unless you've got some kind of magic salve for the terminally burned-out psyche."

"Sorry—all the technological miracles are down the Tunnel a ways in Shamsheer. I don't suppose . . . ?"

"If they had something like that, I would have used it long ago," he said dryly. "Probably. Was there anything else?"

"As a matter of fact, there was." The neutral expression was back in place, with a twinge of discomfort hovering at its edges. "I've had a . . . let's call it an unusual request come down from an unnamed source—unnamed because no one will tell *me* where the hell it came from, either. It asks specifically that our most experienced Courier be assigned to take a female graduate student from the University of Autaris into the Hidden Worlds for her field assignment."

Ravagin frowned. "A single student? *One*?"

"That's what it says."

"What the hell do they think we're running here, a personal guided tour service?"

Lea shrugged. "I don't know any more than I've just given you . . . except that there are distinct hints that pressure is going to be brought to bear on your neck if you don't agree to take her in."

"Whoa—freeze that frame, huh? What does this have to do with *me*? I'm leaving, remember?"

"Maybe, maybe not." Lea took a deep breath. "It isn't like we can pretend someone else is more experienced than you are—it's an on-record fact we can't hide. The higher-ups have already made it clear they want you to stay on for this one last trip. If you don't . . . it's entirely possible your leave of absence might not be approved."

"Well, I'm sure that's a triumph for *some* branch of

human stupidity," Ravagin snorted. "I presume you offered my last med/psych test results for their reading
enjoyment?"

"*And* I told them you were suffering the entire Courier
burnout syndrome," she sighed. "None of it did a scrap of
good. Most experienced is what they want, most experienced is what they're determined to get."

"All right, then. If that's how they want to play I'll quit
outright. Then I'm out of their grasp entirely."

"Yeah. Well . . ." Lea looked acutely uncomfortable. "I
would presume, though, that you're not ready to retire at
the ripe old age of thirty-eight."

Ravagin felt his eyes narrow. "Are you suggesting," he
said slowly, "that they might blackmark my records if I
refuse to roll over for them?"

Lea spread her hands. "I don't know *what* they've got in
mind upstairs—God's truth. All I know is that I haven't
seen everyone this nervous since the Proloc of Vandahl
ignored all the warnings and horror stories and demanded
we take his children into Shamsheer to ride the flying
carpets."

Ravagin felt a shiver run up his spine. "Just who the hell
is this grad student, anyway—the Presidio's daughter?"

"All I've got is a name: Danae Panya. Currently on
Autaris; no other data given. Mean anything to you?"

"Not a thing." He didn't add that the politics and business affairs of the Twenty Worlds were somewhat outside
his usual field of interest.

"Not to me, either." Lea twisted her mouth sourly.
"Look, Ravagin, I know you probably hate giving in to
pressure about as much as I do . . . but, really, would it
be so bad? Really? It would be only a single person—"

"An inexperienced kid."

"They're *all* inexperienced—that's what we need Couriers for, remember? So it's a single person, not one of those
group zoos you all hate, and on a university field research
assignment besides. Which means a short trip, and she'll
be out of your hair puttering around on her own most of
the time, anyway. *And* she won't be here for several more
weeks, which'll give you a good stretch of rest/rec time to
get ready for her."

"Oh, it's just a Courier's fondest dream," Ravagin said sardonically, a sudden thought souring his mouth. "Tell me, Corah: what are they threatening you with if you don't talk me into this?"

Her eyes slipped away from his gaze. "That's irrelevant. It's also none of your business."

"Uh-huh." In other words, if he cut out she'd wind up bearing the full weight of this official elephant by herself. *Damn them all,* he thought bitterly. It took a particularly low class of vermin to hit a man through his friends . . . and a particularly stupid class of man to give in to such tactics.

A class of which he was, unfortunately, a member. And there were times he hated himself for it.

"All right," he sighed. "I'll do it—not for your boss, and sure as hell not for this Panya kid and her political connections. I'll do it as a personal favor to you, Corah . . . and you're to damn well make sure they know it. Understand? They owe you a Big One."

Lea nodded, trying not entirely successfully to keep the moisture out of her eyes. "I understand, Ravagin. I'll make them pay it back, too, in some way that'll benefit the entire Corps. Count on it."

"Yeah." He got to his feet. "If that's all, then, I still have a report to fill out."

"The hell with the report," she said. "It's a beautiful day out there—go out and enjoy it while it lasts."

He pursed his lips. "All right. Yes, I think I will."

She attempted a smile. "It's the least I can do. And Ravagin . . . thanks. They owe you a Big One, too."

"Sure." A Big One, he knew, that he would probably never get around to collecting. But it was the thought that counted. "Talk to you later. Bye-and-luck."

Chapter 3

Triplet, on first impression, was a distinct disappointment.

The minor-class starport they came down at was bad enough, in Danae's opinion; haphazardly designed and stuck twenty-five kilometers away from the nearest real city like an architectural leper. But the nearby buildings of Triplet Control that were visible through the starport lounge's window were even worse. She'd seen military camps before, but even by those dubious standards this one didn't measure up. The main Triplet Defense building was a massive chunk of masonry that looked like it had been thrown together under combat conditions. A half kilometer further north, the Crosspoint Building was a little better; but any improvement in design was more than made up for by the fenced-in perimeter surrounding it . . .

Involuntarily, Danae shivered. The three-hundred-meter-wide defensive ring around Threshold's Tunnel was called the Dead Zone, and was allegedly the most airtight perimeter anywhere in the Twenty Worlds. She didn't know any of the details . . . and gazing at the oddly indistinct view beyond the Dead Zone's outer fence, she decided she didn't want to.

"Ms. Danae Panya?"

She started, shifting her eyes from the window to the two men approaching from behind her. "Yes?" she acknowledged cautiously.

14

"Welcome to Triplet," the older of the men smiled. "I'm Liaison Director Hamen DorLexis. I must say, you caught us a little by surprise, coming in early like this."

She relaxed a bit. "I had a chance at an earlier flight than I'd originally planned," she explained, striving to sound offhanded about it. In truth, it had cost her a run through Hell's own bureaucracy to get her flight switched at the last minute. "I thought I could use the extra time to look around Threshold a little."

"You're on the wrong side of the planet to do any sightseeing," DorLexis said. "Everything around here is strictly geared to support and defense of the Tunnel."

"I see." The second man was still standing quietly in the background, and Danae caught his eye. "And you are . . . ?"

"Oh, excuse me," DorLexis jumped in before the other could answer. "Ms. Panya, this is Courier Ravagin, the man who'll be taking you into the Hidden Worlds."

"Indeed?" She looked at the second man with new interest. Medium height and build, dark eyes in a quiet face—there was nothing especially noteworthy about him. Certainly nothing that immediately marked him as a veteran of travel in the Hidden Worlds. "Pleased to meet you, Mr. Ravagin."

"Just Ravagin, Ms. Panya," he told her. The quiet of his voice matched that of his face. "It's a single, all-purpose name."

"Ah," she said, not really understanding. "Well . . . please call me Danae, then."

He nodded, and DorLexis jumped back into the conversation. "I've already arranged for your luggage to be transfered to the Checkpoint Building, Ms. Panya; whenever you're ready we can head there ourselves and start your processing."

"Already? I assumed that with my early arrival and all I'd have to wait a few days."

DorLexis smiled, almost smugly. "We're well accustomed to dealing with the unexpected here. I started things rolling as soon as the ship's captain lasered his passenger list to us. If you'll come this way . . . ?"

Together, they headed toward the exit. "About how long will all this take?" Danae asked.

"Oh, the processing itself will only take a couple of hours," DorLexis assured her. "We need to check you for any diseases you might be carrying, give you some broad-spectrum immunity injections and check for reactions to them—that sort of thing."

"And also make sure you know what you're getting into," Ravagin put in.

"I read all the material you sent to me," Danae told him. "Are you saying it was inaccurate?"

"Of course not," DorLexis said quickly. "It's just that—well, the Couriers tend to think our information packets are incomplete."

Danae looked at Ravagin. "Are they?"

"Of course," he said. "You can't put everything about two entire worlds on a few pages, especially when they're not meant to be anything but a general overview in the first place."

"So why don't the packets include more?"

"What would be the point? Most travelers wouldn't bother to read them anyway. They'd just do what they do now: rely on the Courier to do all the major thinking and worrying for them inside."

"Ravagin—" DorLexis began warningly.

"No, let him continue, please," Danae interrupted. "If you think so little of your clients, why do you continue to put up with the job?"

"Who said I thought little of them?" Ravagin growled. "I said most of them wouldn't prepare themselves any more than they do now, regardless of what material we gave them."

"Be assured, Ms. Panya," DorLexis cut in, "that Ravagin and all our other Couriers are strongly dedicated to their work, no matter how they may talk on occasion." He flicked a glare at Ravagin. "You have nothing at all to fear going into the Hidden Worlds with anyone from the Corps."

"Of course," Danae nodded, hiding with an effort her annoyance at the other's well-meant interference. Her first clean shot at seeing what made Ravagin tick, and DorLexis had just fouled it up. But there would be plenty of time for that later. "So when will we actually be heading into Shamsheer?"

"Tomorrow morning, if you'd like," DorLexis said, clearly glad to be on safe ground again. "We prefer you to have a good night's sleep before you go in."

Danae nodded. "Sounds good. I'm anxious to get started. If that's all right with you, Ravagin?"

He shrugged, back inside his shell again. "You're the boss."

They walked in silence for another minute, reaching the exit and walking into the shifting winds outside. They were halfway to the car DorLexis had pointed out when the faint pop of a sonic boom drifted in from the distance. Danae looked up, but the low clouds hid the approaching starship from sight. "How often do you get off-world ships in here?" she asked, keeping her voice casual.

"Oh, once or twice a week, usually," DorLexis said, glancing at the sky himself. "As I said, there's not much in this part of Threshold except the Tunnel, and as you know there are strict limitations on the number of people who are allowed inside."

"Um." But that *had* been a starship's deceleration boom— Danae was almost sure of it. Which meant the respite she'd gained by finagling the earlier flight was about due to end.

Whatever that ship was—commercial, military, or private—she could almost guarantee that Hart would be on it.

They reached the car and climbed in . . . and as DorLexis threaded them through the other parked vehicles toward the exit road, she caught a glimpse of the sleek rich man's skimmer settling into its approach glide over the starport's landway.

Hart, for sure.

Damn. But there was nothing she could do about it now. Settling back against the cushions, she closed her eyes and tried unsuccessfully to relax.

His copy of the test results tracked their way across his display, and Ravagin paused in his route planning for a quick look at the bottom line. A green light, as expected.

Which meant Danae Panya had cleared the last hurdle standing between her and her two fun-filled months on the Hidden Worlds.

Damn.

With a sigh, he erased the information from the screen. He'd been feeling ambivalent enough about this trip before the trip to the starport this morning—and now, having spent much of the day with his client, his mood was even worse. From the sort of questions she'd plied him with it was clear that she was the type who thought Courier and client should be best friends right from the starting gun, and there were few types Ravagin hated more. It was indeed going to be a fun couple of months.

The click of his phone interrupted his brooding. "Ravagin, this is Kyle Grey at the main entrance guard station. Do you know anyone by the name of Hart?"

"No," Ravagin answered. "Should I?"

"I wouldn't if I were you. He wants to see you about joining your tour tomorrow."

Ravagin snorted. "Sure thing. I'll just pack him in my trunk and smuggle him across the telefold. Tell him to take a hike in the Dead Zone, will you?"

"Wait, you haven't heard the best part. When I told him I couldn't let him in to see you without a permit, he tried to buy one. From me."

Ravagin felt his eyebrows go up. "You mean a bribe?"

"Uh-huh. A *big* one, too. Makes me almost wish I didn't have any scruples."

"Or monitor cameras pointed at your station?" Ravagin added acidly.

"That too. Anyway, I've already sealed the foyer and pushed the panic button, but I thought you might want to come take a look at this character before they haul him away."

Why not? "On my way."

The reinforcements were in the process of frisking Hart down when Ravagin arrived; and judging from the pile on the foyer table, he was carrying more than his fair share of illegal or suspicious gear. But if the man was worried the emotion didn't show anywhere in face or stance. In fact, from his almost bored expression, Ravagin might almost guess he broke into restricted areas twice a week.

"You must be Ravagin," the man said as Ravagin walked into the room. "My name is Hart. I'd like to discuss your trip tomorrow, if I may."

The man had poise; Ravagin had to give him that. "Sorry, but I usually make it a point not to take blithering idiots into the Hidden Worlds with me—not good for one's health. Whatever made you think you could offer such a blatant bribe here and get away with it?"

"Oh, the bribe was just a conversation piece," Hart shrugged. "I thought the guard might call and let you know about it. I see I was right."

"Good for you," the guard captain standing nearby grunted. "First prize is a few years in a very deep hole somewhere. Congratulations."

"Not at all—I'll be out in a matter of hours," Hart said calmly. "I have—let us say—well-placed friends."

"Fine—you can call them when you get to Gateway City," the captain told him.

"I will. Meanwhile—" his eyes bored into Ravagin's— "perhaps I may discuss with Mr. Ravagin the possibility of joining his party tomorrow."

"There isn't any possibility," Ravagin said flatly. "The roster is set, and there's nothing I can do about it."

"Not strictly true," Hart shook his head. "A Courier has considerable power over the makeup of his group—including the power to add someone. Even at this late date, if you didn't mind postponing your departure a day or two. Which is also within your authority."

Ravagin pursed his lips, intrigued in spite of himself. Danae Panya was here through official and probably money-based pressure; now Hart was implying a similar backing. Connection? "You're correct, at least in principle," he admitted, "but in this case it's irrelevant. My client has gone to great lengths to ensure a private trip into the Hidden Worlds, and I've found that when money fights with money the first batch in usually wins."

Hart cocked an eyebrow. "Would it help if I told you that her money and my money were from the same person?"

"It might . . . if you could also explain why he didn't arrange it as a joint package in the first place."

"It was done that way for reasons I'd rather not go into," the other said with a shrug. "Be assured, though, that I *can* easily prove what I'm saying."

A motion outside caught Ravagin's eye: a heavy prisoner transport pulling up to the door. "If I were you, I wouldn't waste the time. By the time you get anyone to believe you we'll be in Shamsheer and long out of your reach."

Hart eyed him coolly. "I see. Well, I suppose I should take some comfort in the fact that you're not easily corruptible. Let me try a different tack, then, for the—" he glanced out the door at the transport—"few seconds I have left here. The Hidden Worlds are an extremely dangerous place, even for a Courier of your experience and reputation. If something should happen to your client in there, you could be in severe trouble."

"Is that a threat?"

"Not at all—just a statement of reality. For all your undoubted skills, you're not trained as a professional bodyguard. I am. If you allow me to accompany you, you'll be taking far less risk, both of serious injury to your client and of possible legal fallout upon your return."

And with that Ravagin's simmering dislike of Hart finally passed the fine line into disgust. "I don't know where you learned how to deal with people, Hart," he said, controlling himself with a supreme effort. "But I suggest you never again try suggesting to a Triplet Courier that he can't do his job. Captain, I'd appreciate it if you'd make sure the authorities at Gateway City hold your prisoner here until my client and I are in Shamsheer. If you need more charges against him to do that, let me know—I've got a few I'd be happy to file."

The other nodded grimly. "You got it, Ravgin. Come on, Hart—let's not keep the cells waiting."

Ravagin watched from inside as they bundled Hart into the transport and drove away. "Guy's a real winner, isn't he?" Grey commented from the guard station.

"This whole trip is starting to look that way," Ravagin growled. "Listen, Grey, I'd like you to alert the rest of the Couriers to this guy. If he's really got the pull to get out of the mess he's in he might try to talk someone else into taking him in behind me."

"Right," Grey nodded. "You think all that talk about danger meant anything sinister?"

"As in Danae Panya is somehow marked for trouble?" Ravagin shook his head. "At this point nothing would surprise me. Keep a good eye on that door, okay?"

"Sure. Don't worry; anyone who wants into the Tunnel tonight'll have to go through the Dead Zone to get to it."

"I almost hope Hart tries it. Talk to you later."

Still seething inside, he headed back to his office and his waiting maps.

Chapter 4

Hart was, unfortunately, almost as good as his word. By morning he was out of custody; and though the authorities in Gateway City assured Ravagin that he'd been "strongly warned" to stay away from the entire Reingold Crater area, it was with a nagging sense of being watched that Ravagin climbed into an autocar with Danae for the short drive to the Tunnel.

It was a typical Threshold day: cool, cloudy, and generally unpleasant—the sort of departure day, according to Courier superstition, that boded well for a trip to the Hidden Worlds. Not that Ravagin believed any of that nonsense . . . not really. But he'd spent a great deal of time traveling on Karyx, and no one who'd been there could ever again take a completely cavalier attitude toward the concepts of luck and fate. And with the trouble this whole trip had already generated. . . . Furtively, feeling more than a little foolish, he made the prescribed good-luck sign toward the gray clouds above. Just in case.

There was actually little danger of the gesture being seen. Danae's eyes, like everyone else's who came this way, were glued to the window, though what visitors saw in the remnants of an ancient nuclear bomb crater Ravagin would never know. That Reingold Crater had been the site of a tremendous blast was abundantly clear; even after some eight centuries of erosion, it was nearly two hundred kilometers across and easily visible from low orbit on a

22

clear day. The biggest crater on Threshold; but at ground level it wasn't particularly impressive. There was little to see, in fact, but the same sterile gray-brown dirt that covered most of the rest of the world.

"I understand the whole planet's basically like this," Danae commented, still gazing out the window.

"Uh—?" he managed, momentarily startled at the way her thoughts had paralleled his. "You mean the ground?"

"And the giant craters and the lousy weather," she nodded, turning to look curiously at him. "All of it from the war?"

He shrugged. "Presumably, though we're hardly in a position to know what the place was like before they blew themselves to gray dust."

"I tried to look up information about the war before I came here," she said, turning back to the window. "No one's written much about it."

"That's because no one knows a hell of a lot about it," he retorted. "We know the civilization was composed of humanoids—probably true humans like ourselves and those of the Hidden Worlds—and that it did a first-class job of wiping itself out. Everything else is pure speculation."

She made a face. "Including the theory that the Tunnel was one of their prime targets?"

Ravagin made a face. "It *could* be just coincidence that this part of Threshold was bombed the most. It may have nothing at all to do with the Tunnel."

And as if on cue, the autocar topped a slight rise and the Tunnel came into view.

It wasn't particularly impressive, in and of itself, almost certainly by deliberate design of its unknown builders. A few small hills surrounding a longer mound, the latter with a small cave-like opening facing west. The prewar Threshold landscape had probably been riddled with similarly unremarkable hills, with these not worth a second glance . . . until after the war, when the mounds could be seen to have survived a near-direct nuclear blast. . . .

Danae let out a long, wondering breath. "Incredible," she murmured. "It doesn't even look deformed."

"Not noticeably, anyway," Ravagin nodded. "Have you ever read Reingold's original log entry of its discovery?

You'll have to when we get back. Poor woman nearly went nuts trying to explain how it could still be standing out here—and the crewman who first figured out the Tunnel itself really *did* slip his programming for awhile."

"I don't blame him. Shamsheer must have been a real shock."

The autocar negotiated the gentle ramp that had been built up to the mounds and rolled to a stop. "Last chance to change your mind," Ravagin warned as they got out.

"Don't be silly," Danae retorted, striding ahead of him into the Tunnel mouth. Ravagin took a careful look at the landscape behind them and then followed, feeling marginally better. Hart could still be skulking around the background somewhere; but from here on he'd have a hell of a time keeping up with them.

For the first fifty meters or so the Tunnel went straight into the mound with only a slight slope downward, and by the time it began its lefthanded circular bend the last traces of light from the entrance had been left behind. The faint glow of Danae's dimlight waited for him at the bend; lighting his own, Ravagin caught up with her. "Stay clear of the walls," he warned her as he brushed past and took the lead. "They're rough in places—and the material is just as unyielding as the stuff the outside is made of, so you can get a bruise you'll long remember."

"It would help if you people would give us decent lights," she grumbled as they walked. "Even fire matches would be brighter than these things."

"And would be very noticeable to anyone from Shamsheer who happened to be wandering around the Tunnel. We try to discourage travel from that end."

"But—oh." She fell silent. Perhaps, Ravagin thought, the other reason for the dim lighting had suddenly occurred to her.

The trip, taken in near-absolute darkness, always seemed longer than it really was, and Ravagin was beginning to sense restlessness in his client when the first of the marker dots came into view along the wall. Standard procedure was to immediately point them out to newcomers . . . but nothing yet about this trip had been particularly standard, and just for the hell of it he decided to give Danae a more direct introduction to what Reingold had dubbed the Unwelcome Mat. They passed the camouflaged lockers . . . the triangle marker loomed just ahead . . . Ravagin increased his lead a step—

And abruptly he was five meters behind her.

The shock of his disappearance kept her feet moving another two steps; and by the time she gasped and twisted around it was too late. Her motion brought her elbow across the invisible line of the telefold—

And abruptly she was a meter behind *him* again.

She spun again to face him, and he heard the breath go out of her in a *wumph*. "That was a rotten trick," she muttered, sounding more awed than angry. "Your information packet doesn't nearly do the thing justice."

"I don't think anything can," he agreed, vaguely disappointed she'd recovered so fast. "You have to experience it to really believe it."

"I don't even believe it now." She took another deep breath. "The really scary part is that I didn't feel a thing. You could keep crossing that same five meters of Tunnel forever trying to reach the other end."

"Reingold's people damn near did that. It was sheer desperate inspiration that anyone thought about trying it naked."

He could almost hear her wince. ". . . right. Well. We ought to get started on that ourselves, I suppose. Shouldn't we."

"Yeah. The lockers are over here, built to look like part of the wall . . ."

He showed her how to open them, and in the dim light they stripped off their coveralls and stowed them on the hooks provided. Ravagin had long since stopped being embarrassed by the necessity of crossing the telefold naked, but a surprising percentage of his clients—even though they knew what to expect—got their backs up at this point and tried like hell to bend the rules. Usually it took several trips across that same five meters, as Danae had put it, to convince them that *nothing* but their own personal bodies could make the trip through from Threshold to Shamsheer. No one knew exactly why the Tunnel's builders had set things up that way, but it was abundantly clear that there was nothing anyone could do about it.

"Okay, I'm ready," Danae said at last, flipping off her dimlight and closing the locker door. "Now what?"

"Take my hand," Ravagin said, reaching it out toward her voice in the darkness. "Crossing the telefold sometimes plays tricks with your balance."

Her hand was stiff and unwilling, but at least she didn't argue the point. Walking carefully, taking both balance and direction cues from the faintly luminous marker dots, he led her forward . . . and abruptly, for just an instant, the floor seemed to tilt sideways.

Danae gasped and lost her balance, falling heavily against him. He caught her, and for a moment they were pressed together—

She got her feet under her again and jerked away, pulling her hand out of his in the process. "Sorry," she muttered, sounding both angry and embarrassed.

"That's all right," he assured her, the words somehow coming out a lot more sincere than he'd planned them to. "That generally happens during a person's first time," he added, a bit lamely. Her skin had felt extraordinarily good against his. . . . "Come on—the next set of lockers are down the tunnel a ways. Give me your hand and I'll lead you."

"I'm all right, thank you," she said, a bit tartly.

"Up to you." He headed off down the tunnel, leaving her to find her own way as best she could. The pathway continued to curve to the left, and he let his fingertips graze the righthand wall until he felt the gentle swelling that was one end of this set of camouflaged lockers. The bulge swelled further and further out into the passageway, and a few steps later Ravagin's fingers found the hidden catch and swung open the door. A handful of firefly rings sat on the top shelf; picking one up, he slipped it onto his left hand. "Let there be light," he said, cupping his palm . . . and a glowing ball of hazy light appeared. "Now," he said, glancing back at Danae, "let's get dressed and get out of here. Here—try this on for starters." He handed her a flowing dress of the sort worn by the minor Shamsheer nobility.

"Thanks," she said, hugging the dress close to her against

her nudity and the firefly's light. "What was that you said?—'let there be light'?"

"All you really have to say to a firefly is 'be light,' or 'be lighted,'" he shrugged, searching through the locker for the garb he wanted for himself. "I was just being a little theatrical."

"But you need to give these commands in Shamahni, don't you?" she asked.

"What do you think we're speaking now?" he countered.

"We're—? Oh! I didn't—I mean. . . ."

She stopped short, in confusion or embarrassment, and Ravagin smiled to himself in the dim light. Deep implant language training was far more thorough than most people realized. "Don't let it bother you—I've had clients go halfway across Shamsheer before they realized the rest of the population wasn't speaking Standard. Do you need more light?"

"This is fine," she said, her words muffled as she fought with the unfamiliar clothing style.

He smiled again to himself, and they finished getting dressed in silence. Afterwards, he brought the firefly's light up a few lumens and studied the various tools and weapons stored on the equipment shelf. The selection was always more limited than he liked, a problem that was normally more an annoyance than anything else. But with Hart's veiled threats echoing in the back of his mind—and Hart himself God only knew where—the lack of weaponry especially was feeling a lot more critical than usual. But there was nothing he could do about it, at least not until they could get to one of the way houses.

"Well?" Danae asked impatiently as he hesitated in indecision. "What're we waiting for?"

"Just relax," Ravagin growled back at her. "We're not on any schedule here." Gritting his teeth, he picked up the largest sheath knife available—an ordinary one, unfortunately, not a target-seeking watchblade—and his own personal favorite, a scorpion glove. Both weapons went onto his belt; scooping up another firefly and a prayer stick, he slammed the locker closed and started down the Tunnel. "Come on," he called over his shoulder.

She caught up with him within a few steps. "Here," he

said, thrusting the extra firefly into her hand. "You might as well have your own light."

"Thank you," she said, sounding almost subdued.

Ravagin glanced at her, noting with mild surprise the tightness in her face. "You getting nervous?"

"Me? No. Why?"

He felt his lip twitch. "Never mind."

The half of the Tunnel they were in now was exactly the same length as that on Threshold's side of the telefold, but already Ravagin could smell the subtle aromas of Shamsheer's plant life wafting through the passageway toward them. It brought back memories, not all of them pleasant, of all the visits he'd made to this world. *I'm getting old,* he thought morosely. *Only thirty-eight, and already I'm getting old.*

The curved section of the Tunnel came to an end and they started up the slight slope toward the mouth. After the relative darkness the light pouring through the opening ahead was blindingly bright, but by the time they actually reached it their eyes had had sufficient time to adjust. Ravagin, a cautious step in the lead, they stepped through onto Shamsheer.

Danae gasped, a long exhalation of pure wonder Ravagin had heard from countless clients over the years. "Ravagin," she breathed. "It's *beautiful.*"

He nodded silently, drinking in the view himself with unashamed eagerness. There was never a mood so low, or an anger so burning, that this first view of Shamsheer's countryside couldn't make a severe dent in it in short order. The brilliant blue sky, the equally brilliant flowers and plants dotting the green hills surrounding the Tunnel site, the darting insects and trilling birds—it was a section of paradise transplanted onto another world.

For several minutes they just looked about them, Danae moving a few steps away from the Tunnel mouth at one point to peer northward at the Maiandros River wending its twisted path across the landscape. "Beautiful," she repeated, turning in a slow circle with almost child-wide eyes taking it all in. "Is all of Shamsheer like this?"

"Most of the countryside sections are," he said absently, doing his own three-sixty turn with something other than sightseeing in mind. To the south and east, the Harrian

Hills rose up in a half-cirle around the Tunnel mouth—good visual protection from the villages around Castle Numanteal to the east, but also ideal hiding places for anyone bent on ambush.

But if anyone was up there, he wasn't giving his presence away. "I'm sorry," Ravagin said, suddenly realizing Danae was speaking again. "What did you say?"

"I was asking how far away Castle Numanteal was," she repeated.

"It's about ten kilometers east-northeast as the birdine flies," he told her.

"Over all those hills?"

He snorted gently. "Don't worry—no one has to walk anywhere on Shamsheer that they don't want to. And you're right; let's get moving."

Taking one last look around, he pulled the prayer stick from his belt and raised it to his lips. "I pray thee, deliver unto me a sky-plane."

Chapter 5

For a long minute nothing happened. Danae kept her eyes on the eastern sky, watching for the transport Ravagin had just ordered. But aside from a sprinkling of birds, nothing seemed to be moving over that way. *Might not have any available at the castle just now,* she thought. Reconstructing the map of this part of Shamsheer in her mind, she searched it for the next nearest place a sky-plane might be kept.

"Here it comes," Ravagin announced, pointing northward.

Danae turned and shaded her eyes. Sure enough, a tiny rectangular shape was skimming the treetops directly toward them. Visualizing her map again . . . "From the village of Phamyr?" she asked, frowning.

"Probably," Ravagin nodded. "It's closer than Castle Numanteal."

"Pretty small place to have any extra sky-planes on hand, isn't it? I thought it only had a population of—"

"Size doesn't make any difference," he interrupted with the same forced patience she'd heard in the Tunnel. "A sky-plane sitting idle is available for use by anyone—pure and simple. They're one item of property no one owns."

The sky-plane was a lot faster than Danae had expected it to be, and barely two minutes later it settled to the ground in front of them . . . and she found that the drawings and descriptions she'd seen of this machine had indeed been completely accurate.

It was the spitting image of a flying carpet.

Two meters by perhaps three, its upper surface apparently rough-woven and decorated by intricate designs and arabesques, its edge sporting a delicate fringe, it could have come straight out of the old Earth myths. And just like those flying carpets, it had nothing remotely resembling safety restraints. Or, for that matter, any kind of control mechanism.

Ravagin had already seated himself cross-legged near the skyplane's center. "Any time you're ready," he said, cocking an eyebrow up at her.

Swallowing, she stepped gingerly onto the carpet and sat down behind him. It yielded to her weight just like ordinary cloth would have, and she had to force herself to remember that visitors to Shamsheer had been using these things safely for over a century. To say nothing of the world's inhabitants themselves, of course, who'd been using them a lot longer.

"Sky-plane: to Kelaine City," Ravagin said . . . and without so much as a lurch, the carpet stiffened around her and lifted smoothly into the sky.

Carefully, Danae let out the breath she'd been holding and concentrated on Ravagin's back. Never before in her life had she suffered even a twinge of acrophobia . . . but never before had she been five hundred meters up on something that had no business flying in the first place. Licking her lips, she tried another calming breath and kept her eyes away from the blue sky surrounding them on all sides.

"How're you doing?" Ravagin called over his shoulder.

"Fine," she said, too quickly.

His head twisted around for a look. "Yeah, you *look* fine," he growled. "Your profile said you didn't have any fear of heights."

"They never tested me on an open-air rug," she returned tightly.

He sighed. "You didn't believe the info packet either, huh? Amazing how many don't. All right: stick your hand over the edge of the sky-plane."

"What?" she said.

"You heard me. Reach out over the edge."

She opened her mouth to say no . . . and then clamped it shut. If she could fight her father, she could fight this, too. "All right." She reached gingerly out . . . and right where the fringe began ran into a solid wall.

An invisible wall, but no less real for that. She poked at it again and again, trying different spots along the side and rear edges of the sky-plane, eventually building up enough courage to put some real muscle into her jabs. Nothing.

"You can try kicking it, if you want to, or even poking my knife at it," Ravagin offered when she finally gave up. "Wouldn't bother the field at all—whoever designed these things had a healthy respect for safety. I'd have thought the lack of wind up here would've clued you in."

She frowned, realizing for the first time that the air around them was indeed perfectly still. "I . . . yes, I guess I should have noticed that. I'm sorry."

He waved a hand in dismissal. "Like I said, it happens a lot. Most visitors seem to have trouble believing in something they can't see. Which can be a real problem when they get to Karyx."

"It's not just that," Danae told him, feeling an obscure need to explain her reaction. "I *did* remember that sky-planes were supposed to have an edge barrier, but all the force-fields I've ever seen have been milky white or totally opaque. I guess I just made the assumption that this one was out of order."

"Sky-planes don't fly when something's out of order," he shook his head. "They go to one of the Dark Towers for repair, either under their own power or another sky-plane's."

Danae grimaced. She was already feeling like a fool over the irrational fear that was only slowly ebbing, and Ravagin's condescending attitude toward her was doing nothing to help. "I'm sorry I'm not perfect," she snapped with more vehemence than she'd intended. "If you people would put together better information packets—or if you bothered to include some real photos—"

His eyebrows went up, and she clamped down her jaw in utter disgust at herself. "Damn. What am I *saying*?"

Ravagin sighed. "Hey, look, just try to relax, okay? You're right—the Hidden Worlds *are* a big shock and the packets don't really prepare newcomers for them. So just settle back and learn. And don't be afraid to ask questions."

She turned her head away from him, forcing her eyes to shift downward over the sky-plane's edge. Passing a ways off to the right was a hexagonal wall surrounded by several large clumps of houses. "Is that Castle Numanteal down there?" she asked grudgingly.

"Right," he nodded. "Would you like a closer look?" Without waiting for an answer he turned back toward the front edge of the sky-plane. "Sky-plane: stop."

Obediently, the carpet glided to a halt and sat hovering in midair. "Sky-plane: to Castle Numanteal," Ravagin said, and they turned and headed downward.

"We're going to land *in* the castle?" Danae asked uneasily, the descriptions of Shamsheer's guardian trolls flashing through her mind.

"No, I'll cancel the course again before we get there," he assured her. "This is the best way to see the place, though."

She pursed her lips, acrophobia evaporating as she studied the stronghold they were approaching. "Are all those houses clustered around the wall inside the troll perimeter?" she asked.

"The inner perimeter, yes. You can see that they form a rough hexagon, too, like the castle wall and the outer protectorate boundary."

Danae nodded again. "The info packet seemed to talk a lot about hexagons when describing the Shamsheer landscape."

"Oh, the obsession is definitely there. The Dark Towers are also six-sided, as are the forest and desert areas surrounding them. No one knows why."

"Sounds like a giant game board," Danae said, only half jokingly.

"Don't laugh—there are people who take that theory

seriously," Ravagin said, an oddly grim note to his voice. "*Some*one built the Tunnels, after all—why couldn't they have built both of the Hidden Worlds, too? And made Shamsheer into a giant game?"

Danae shivered. "I don't like that idea at all. Two complete worlds, just for a game?"

"I don't buy it myself," Ravagin shrugged. "Where's the gamemaster, for instance, if that's what's happening? And if Shamsheer's a game, what's Karyx supposed to be? There are other theories that make more sense." He leaned over toward the sky-plane's side. "We're coming up on the castle."

Danae followed his gaze. They were no more than half a kilometer from the outer wall now and perhaps two hundred meters above it. A half-dozen buildings were visible inside the wall, and she tried to match them up with the sketches she'd seen. The manor house itself was easy— looking vaguely like a huge inverted mushroom with four rocket fin-shaped entrance halls anchoring it to the ground, it dominated the space near the center of the enclosure. In one corner of the hexagon was a smaller hex-shaped building that was probably the local House of Healing; in another corner was the Giantsword power generator/broadcaster. Near the manor house, in the exact center of the enclosure, was a small geodesic dome. "The Shrine of Knowledge?" she asked, pointing to it.

"Right," Ravagin nodded. "It'll be where the castle-lord's crystal eye is kept."

"I'd think he'd put it inside the house where he could get at it more easily."

He shrugged. "The villagers can petition the castle-lord to use the eye for information on what's happening elsewhere on Shamsheer, and this way he doesn't have to let them into the manor house itself. And you have to remember that none of these people understand these gadgets, not even the ones they use every day. Once tradition has the crystal eye in a shrine of knowledge, who's going to risk moving it into the manor house?"

Danae grimaced. "No one, I suppose." They were starting to come around in a wide circle now, and she could

see another building and a flat area set against the closer
parts of the castle wall: the horse/vehicle stable and the
sky-plane landing area, respectively.

And they were aiming directly toward the latter.
"Shouldn't we be getting out of here?" she asked, starting
to feel a bit nervous. Trying to explain an unauthorized
landing inside a castle enclosure wasn't the way she really
wanted to start her trip.

"In a minute," Ravagin said calmly. "Castle-lord Simrahi's
used to people buzzing his castle—half the visitors through
the Tunnel come by here and want to take a look."

"I'm sure he loves the attention," Danae retorted. "Don't
you think it's possible he might get tired of it one of these
days?"

"And do what? As long as we're not actually bothering
anyone he's not going to have his soldiers or trolls try and
shoot us down." He pointed ahead and upward. "Besides,
it doesn't look like he's even home at the moment."

Danae followed his finger. Moving against a mottling of
high cirrus clouds she could see a tiny golden ball. "A
bubble?" she hazarded, though there wasn't much else it
could be.

Ravagin nodded anyway. "Sure is. Take a good look—
you probably won't see one of these things again. Most of
the visitors I've brought in here never even get this
close."

Danae reached a hand up to shade her eyes. A crystal
throne surrounded by a translucent, golden-hued force-
field sphere was the way the Triplet information packet
had described the thing. It had further added that, seen
close up, bubbles were possibly the most dramatic piece of
technology on Shamsheer. "How do you know it's Simrahi's
bubble, though?" she asked. "I mean, it could be any
castle-lord up there, couldn't it?"

"Sure; but after all we *are* right in the center of the
Numant Protectorate. For all the pomp and relative plush-
ness bubbles allow them, castle-lords really don't travel all
that much outside their own territories."

The bubble disappeared behind the clouds, and Danae
returned her attention to the castle enclosure, her eyes

flicking to the tower rising from the wide circular roof of
the lower manor house. At the tower's top a crystaline
dome glittered in the sunlight . . . "How does the bubble
get out of the sky room?" she asked. "Does the dome split
or what?"

"No idea," Ravagin said. "I've never been invited aboard
one for a ride. Ah, look—there's someone wearing the
livery of the castle-lord's guard: red, silver, and black."

And the man in question was looking directly up at
them. Danae's mouth went dry; in her interest over the
bubble she'd almost forgotten they were still headed straight
for a castle landing. "Hadn't we better be changing course?"
she asked, as calmly as possible. "Even if the castle-lord's
gone, there are still a lot of people down there who might
take exception to our flying over them."

"Why?" he asked. "You have to remember, Danae, that
Shamsheer's only partly a feudalistic society, and that that
part isn't really like the Earth types you're probably thinking about. There's no interprotectorate warfare here, for
starters, and correspondingly no regal paranoia."

"I understand all that," Danae gritted. The castle was
close enough now for her to make out the individual
bushes lining the roadway from gate to manor house . . .
and to see that the faces of the troll guards were also
lifted in their direction. "I would still like to get *out of
here.*"

"If you insist. Sky-plane: stop. Sky-plane: to Kelaine
City."

The carpet's descent reversed, and as it rose back into
the sky and headed eastward again Danae took a deep
breath. Her hands were beginning to tremble with reaction to what she still considered to have been a close call.
She turned to glare at Ravagin . . . and found he was
already watching her. Watching her entirely too closely. . . .

"You did that on purpose," she accused him coldly.
"Didn't you? You wanted to see how easily I got rattled."

His expression remained calm. "I like to know what sort
of person I'm going to be traveling with. The Hidden
Worlds can be dangerous at times."

"Isn't that *your* job?—to protect me?" she retorted. "I
noticed I wasn't offered any weapons back at the Tunnel."

"Women of your station in life don't carry weapons."

Something cold tickled her back. "What do you mean, my station in life?"

He gestured at her clothing. "You're dressed as a minor noblelady. Nobleladies don't carry weapons—they have men like me to fight for them if and when necessary."

Danae grimaced, a sour taste rising into her mouth. "I'm perfectly capable of fighting on my own if I have to," she told him stiffly. "I've had training in both armed and unarmed combat styles—"

"Wonderful," Ravagin interrupted. "If you have to fight for your life and I'm not around, you have my permission to rip his ears off. Otherwise yell for help and let someone else take care of him. Fighting is out of character for women here, and we don't want to draw unnecessary attention to ourselves. Understood?"

"I suppose so." She gestured to the black glove with its tightly coiled spiral hanging beside the dagger on his belt. "Though if we're going to talk about attracting attention, isn't that scorpion glove a little out of place in this part of Shamsheer?"

"It's somewhat rare, but perfectly acceptable," he shrugged. "They're underused mainly because it takes less training to learn how to hack at someone with a sword and people here have no more patience than any other human beings you're likely to meet. Translation: don't grab for the glove if something happens to me and you need to defend yourself. You're more likely to gift-wrap yourself than to damage your opponent."

"I'll keep that in mind," she said icily.

Ravagin nodded and turned back toward the front of the sky-plane, apparently missing the sarcasm completely. Danae scowled at his back, feeling her aleady ebbing excitement toward this trip sink a point or two further. Here she'd finally escaped from her father and Hart, only to find another man who wanted to run her life for her—worse, one who was apparently determined to treat her like a child in the process.

Damn him. Damn them all.

Still . . .

Shaking her head, she put the irritation firmly out of her

mind. She was here to do some work, and to do some study, and Ravagin was an unavoidable part of that project. She would ignore his patronizing attitude as much as she could, recognizing that she would be having the last laugh in the end. And she would remember that there was always one final resort available to her here, one that would put her beyond reach of them all, forever.

Taking a calming breath, she directed her gaze at the landscape passing beneath them, studying the world that would be her home for two months. Or perhaps longer.

Chapter 6

They passed over the edge of the Numant Protectorate about half an hour later and entered the hundred-fifty-kilometer-wide strip of territory between Numant and the Ordarl Protectorate to the east. The edge of the Numant Protectorate was more sharply defined than Danae had expected it to be, with villages and even sections of farmland breaking off abruptly at the border.

"Seems rather extreme," she commented to Ravagin. "Are the Tweens really that dangerous?"

"Some of them are, certainly," he shrugged. "You have to remember that a castle-lord's trolls can't go even a meter outside their protectorate and most of the robber gangs take full advantage of that. But a village like the one back there on the border probably doesn't see a troll more than twice a year unless there's trouble. Mostly I suspect that it's psychological, that if you choose to live under a castle-lord's rule and laws you do so whole-heartedly, without any fence straddling."

"And there aren't any corresponding villages just outside the border because it's not safe to live in anything that small in the Tweens?"

"Partly that; partly that if you're going to live in this part of the Tweens anyway, you might as well be closer to the Giantsword in Kelaine City."

Danae digested that. "I thought the power broadcast

from the Giantsword network reached everywhere on Shamsheer. What does living near one do for you?"

"You're thinking about it like someone from a technological culture," Ravagin said. "Why don't you try pretending all this stuff is pure magic instead and see if you can come up with anything."

Danae gritted her teeth. Just when she'd started feeling more relaxed in Ravagin's presence, here he was being condescending again. "I presume it has something to do with the fact that Giantswords are associated with the castle-lords and are therefore a symbol of authority?"

"Basically," he nodded. "That's presumably why the major Tween cities got started around them, anyway. That and the belief that Giantswords were where a castle's troll protectors lived."

Danae frowned. "I thought there aren't any trolls outside the protectorates."

"There aren't. But that doesn't stop people from believing that they're safer in the shadow of a Giantsword—*any* Giantsword—than they would be elsewhere. Pure sympathetic magic."

Danae shook her head, caught somewhere between disbelief and contempt. To live in a world fairly dripping with technology and yet have no concept of how or why any of it worked—it seemed incomprehensible.

And yet. . . .

Her eyes fell on the scorpion glove at Ravagin's belt . . . traced the tightly coiled four-meter whip attached to its back . . . drifted to the wide wrist strap and the incredibly sophisticated neural sensors it somehow contained . . . and an old, old saying quoted in the Triplet information packet came to mind: *A sufficiently advanced technology is indistinguishable from magic.*

Perhaps, she decided, the people of Shamsheer could be forgiven for their ignorance, after all.

Castle Numanteal and the surrounding villages had been solidly locked into the hexagonal pattern that dominated every protectorate Ravagin had ever seen. Kelaine City, situated dead center in the Tween strip between Numant and Ordarl, had no such built-in constraints. The city was a sprawling mass of houses, shops, small industries, stables, and even scatterings of cultivated land, all of it clustered around the only hexagon in the place, the plot of land around the Giantsword's base.

"Is that Kelaine City?" Danae asked from behind him. "It's bigger than I was expecting."

"That's it," he nodded. "It's actually only about the twentieth largest city on Shamsheer, but it's got a lot of cottage industries and that spreads it out more than some of the others that have a larger population." They were over the city's westward edge now, and Ravagin leaned as close to the sky-plane's edge barrier as he could to peer at the ground below. An oversized gap between buildings caught his eye, and he thought he could see the tiny rectangles of other sky-planes there. "Sky-plane: stop," he ordered. "Sky-plane: descend."

"Can you see the way house from here?" Danae asked, leaning uncomfortably close as she tried to follow his gaze.

"It's actually a couple of kilometers north of here," he told her, easing back from her a few centimeters. "But these cities are continually changing, and when you find a good place to set down, you're usually smart to go ahead and take it."

"Why—? Oh, right. The sky-planes can't fly closer than ten meters or so to buildings, can they?"

"That's it," Ravagin nodded, vaguely surprised she'd picked up on that so quickly. "And they can't hover directly over one, either. Anti-burglar protection, presumably, though with the edge barrier always running it'd be hard to use for second-story work anyway. Sky-plane: forward slowly."

It was a little tricky to pinpoint a sky-plane onto so small a plot of ground, but Ravagin had had lots of practice and within a couple of minutes they were safely down. Danae, he noticed, poked a hand over the edge before standing up and stepping off the carpet. "Unh," she grunted, stretching carefully. "Left foot's gone to sleep. Do we walk or ride?"

"Up to you," he told her, easing his own stiff leg muscles as he took a careful look around them. "Most of the local people would walk such a short in-city distance, but I can call a carriage if you want."

"No, let's walk," she said, her voice almost dreamy.

He glanced back. She was gazing around her at the colorfully dressed people filling the streets, head turning this way and that as one thing or another caught her eye or ear. It was, he realized, the same way she'd reacted to her first look at Shamsheer. An almost sad twinge of cynicism tugged at him, and he hoped she wouldn't have to run into the darker side of the storybook city before her. "Let's go, then," he said. "This way. And stay close to me."

They headed off, threading their way through the bustling crowds. Shamsheer had often been described as a society of contradictions, and the contrasts were nowhere more strongly in evidence than in cities like Kelaine. They passed a smoking armorer's shop and a sweating smith tending the fires of a computerized Forge Beast metal-working machine while, right across the narrow street, a skinner sewed his animal-hide garments together by hand. Danae had to sidestep at one point to avoid a fruit grower and his ox-like beast of burden as they carried their oranges to market—oranges, Ravagin knew, that would be protected from the early frosts of this part of Shamsheer by a small obelisk that somehow kept the entire grove at a safe temperature until the fruit was completely harvested. Further along, they passed a baker whose oven consisted of simple fire-heated rock and iron, just as a customer called via prayer stick for a carriage to help carry away her purchase. Simple people, casually using technology totally beyond their comprehension . . . or, for that matter, the comprehension of anyone in the Twenty Worlds.

Magic, by any other name. Small wonder that visitors so often treated Shamsheer as a storybook kingdom . . . at least until the harsher realities came crashing down onto the facade.

For this trip the expected crash came all too quickly.

They were barely halfway to the way house and had just left the market place for a residential area when Danae suddenly gripped his arm. "Look—over there," she hissed, nodding across the street.

Ravagin followed her gaze to see a veiled woman backed

up against a building by three fairly grubby-looking men. "What of it?" he asked.

"What do you mean, what of it?" Danae snapped back "She's being assaulted—shouldn't we do something about it?"

"No," he told her flatly, keeping his voice low, his eyes flicking around to make sure none of the passers-by were listening in.

"Ravagin—"

"We leave them alone," he insisted. A portly man looked curiously in his direction; Ravagin glared back and the other gulped and looked quickly away. "They won't hurt her out in the open, and defending her honor's the job of her men—"

He looked back to find Danae gone.

"Damn!" he spat. "Danae!—get back here!"

He was too late. Already she had made it through the streams of pedestrians ignoring the situation and glided up behind one of the three men . . . and even as Ravagin belatedly set off after her she jabbed her fist hard beneath the man's shoulderblade.

He bellowed and spun around, and Ravagin snarled a curse under his breath. There was no way to avoid it now; he'd either have to fight, risking the wrath of Kelaine City law, or else stand by and watch his client get herself carved into fish bait. Shoving through the crowd that was already beginning to form, he snatched the scorpion glove from his belt and jabbed it onto his right hand, fastening the wrist strap snugly as he moved. The familiar tingle told him the neural sensors were functioning, but there would be no time to double-check their positioning. Against three armed men, he was going to need whatever advantages surprise could give him.

The man Danae had hit had his sword out now and Ravagin gritted his teeth hard enough to hurt as the blade slashed out at her abdomen. But she had already dropped into a crouch beneath the arc, her foot snapping out toward his knee. The kick missed, her foot caught up short by the unfamiliar length of her Shamsheer dress. The man raised his sword over his head—

"Halt!" Ravagin shouted, stepping into view behind Danae.

The man paused, his companions drawing their own swords and stepping up to flank him. "You protect this *carhrat?*" the first man growled the insult, his left hand twisting up behind him to rub his back.

Ravagin fought down a flush of anger. "I protect this *noblelady*, yes," he returned evenly. "Do you in turn make your livelihood assaulting helpless women like the one yonder?"

"It is a private family affair," one of the others snapped. "No concern of yours."

"Perhaps," Ravagin said. "Perhaps not. I had not heard it said that private family business was carried out on the streets of Kelaine City."

"For an outlander with no weapon," the first man said, eyes flicking to the empty glove on Ravagin's right hand, "you show amazing foolishness. Kelaine law permits an attacked citizen the right of equal response; and if you interfere you and she will both suffer worse."

"Equal response to a blow of a hand does not require the use of a sword," Ravagin pointed out, feeling beads of sweat breaking out on his forehead. The man was right about the law, unfortunately, and Ravagin knew most of the crowd behind him would have a similar dislike for interfering strangers. On the other hand, he could sense that the three men weren't held in the highest esteem among their neighbors, either. It probably worked out to a fairly neutral audience—better than might be expected, worse than might be hoped. The men themselves were probably competent enough with their swords, but their clear unfamiliarity with his scorpion glove might balance that somewhat.

He had, in other words, an even chance of getting them out of this alive. Maybe. "If you wish to invoke the equal response law," he continued to the other, "you may strike the noblelady a single blow with your empty hand." Danae, still crouched in front of the man, threw him an astonished look; he ignored it, concentrating on the other's expression. It was beginning to waver—perhaps he'd cooled down enough to realize that Ravagin wouldn't be standing against three armed men without some kind of unseen and potentially lethal protection. The bluff was actually going to work. . . .

"Are you mad, Maruch?" one of the man's companions snarled abruptly. "Are you going to let a stranger push your face into the dust?"

Maruch's face darkened, all traces of hesitation vanishing into freshly kindled pride-driven rage. Eyes on Ravagin, he raised his sword high and took a step toward Danae—

Cursing under his breath, Ravagin leaped forward and to the side, raising his hands chest high with palms together. Maruch clearly expected the move; changing direction in mid step, he turned to face Ravagin, his blade beginning its downswing directly toward Ravagin's head—

And the coiled tentacle on the scorpion glove snapped out like a whip, slapping Maruch's wrist with a loud *crack*.

The other howled, his stroke going wild as he tried with limited success to hold onto his weapon. Ravagin sidestepped with ease, coiling the tentacle again and then snapping it out a second time to strike at the blade itself. The sword went flying, barely missing one of Maruch's companions before it clattered to the paving stones.

Someone in the crowd gasped . . . but what Maruch's companions lacked in manners one of them, at least, made up in cunning. Even as Ravagin stepped back, coiling the whip again, the man on the left raised his own weapon and shouted, "Sorcerer! Black magic! Help us, citizens, against this Power of Darkness!"

The crowd stirred, clearly unsure of what to do. Ravagin gritted his teeth, his full attention by necessity on the two men cautiously moving in on him. Snapping the whip out again, he held it extended in a stiff z-shape between him and his attackers. One of them slashed at it; he pulled it back slightly and the blow missed. *At least they've only got regular swords*, he thought, counting one of the few blessings available at the moment. A spark-sword would cut through a scorpion glove whip with ease if it connected; with ordinary swords it would take half a dozen solid blows to do the same.

Which gave him an idea . . .

Easing the defensive line back toward himself, he took a

slow couple of steps to the right. His opponents shifted in response, the sword tips easing closer toward him as the whip withdrew. Almost in position . . . and as one of them started to lunge, Ravagin braced his feet and snapped the whip out in a converging helix around both swords.

One of the men yelped as the tightening coil slammed the two blades—and their sword hands—together, but it was already too late for either to fight back. Bracing his palms together, Ravagin yanked hard, and an instant later both swords stood at his feet, securely tangled in four meters of whip, their points grounded against the stones.

For a long minute all three of the disarmed men just stood or crouched there, looking dumfounded at Ravagin. "Now," Ravagin said softly, "the noblelady and I will be on our way."

"Not quite yet, outlander," an authoritative voice came from the crowd. Ravagin turned to see an old man dressed in purple and gold step forward, the half-scepter of a justice official held before him. Beside him, a similarly garbed younger man held a sword at the ready position, its vaguely indistinct blade pointed in Ravagin's direction.

A spark-sword.

Chapter 7

The Kelaine City way house was one of a couple of dozen that the government of the Twenty Worlds had quietly set up in Triplet, their purpose to provide both travelers' aid and relatively permanent centers for a handful of continuing studies. A large house situated in the northwest part of the city, it had a permanent staff of four and could provide overnight lodging for a party of up to six more. Ravagin hadn't planned to stay that long; but under the circumstances, he'd had little choice in the matter.

"So what did our esteemed justice officials say?" Pornish Essen asked as his two visitors settled into chairs in the way house's spacious conversation area.

Ravagin shrugged, automatically taking an estimate of the way house's director. He'd never met Essen before—way house directors generally served terms of one to two years in a given location, but Ravagin had seldom visited Kelaine City in the past few years. Still, the man seemed at first impression to be competent enough. "Fortunately, one of them had seen a scorpion glove before and could confirm that it wasn't black sorcery," he continued. "There was some question about whether I'd attacked first—the official hadn't gotten there in time for his half-scepter to record how things started—but they apparently knew the three *carhrats* well enough to believe my story."

"The woman wouldn't testify for you?"

Ravagin glanced over at Danae, noting the lines of barely

concealed anger still in evidence on her face. "The woman apparently cut out on her own sometime after Danae and I took the center of attention away from her."

Essen shrugged. "I can't say I'm surprised."

"I'm not, either, but it could have made things damned awkward. But as I said, the city seems to have tangled with those idiots before. Anyway, they dithered around for awhile trying to find her and probably consulting the town's crystal eye for anything other cities or protectorates might have on us. Finally decided they wouldn't lay any punishment against us if we would agree to leave the city."

"So you came here instead?" Essen's eyebrows went up politely. "Wonderful."

"Relax—I talked them into letting us spend the night since it was getting so late. We're to meet one of the officials at a sky-plane landing area a few streets north of here tomorrow and he'll watch us leave. Until then, we're your guests."

"And honored am I to have you, too," the other replied, the sarcasm of the words blunted by the twinkle in his eye. "This assignment is certainly turning out to be a caseload of thrills—just last week we had a traveler come through with a case of ymaricc fever and had to petition to use the Dreya's Womb."

"I thought Dreya's Wombs were supposed to be accessible to anyone," Danae spoke up from deep in her chair.

"Anyone who's a citizen, yes," Essen told her. "But outlanders don't have any such automatic rights. Fortunately, Kelaine is fairly relaxed about such things and we basically just had to go through the motions to get permission."

Ravagin nodded. Outside, it was becoming dark enough for the first faint stars to appear; in a few minutes the globe atop the Giantsword to the southeast would begin to glow, supplementing the pale moonlight overhead.

Essen had apparently followed his gaze. "Could I interest either of you in sampling Kelaine's night life?" he asked.

"Not me," Danae said before Ravagin could reply. "I've had my fill of Kelaine for one day, thank you. I'd rather just go to bed early and get started for Karyx as soon as possible in the morning."

"Ah." Essen shrugged, "To each their own, I suppose. Personally, I find Shamsheer a much more fascinating and potentially useful world than Karyx. However . . . Ravagin, if you'd be interested in accompanying me there'll be others here to look after Ms. Panya."

"Thanks, but I'll pass, too," Ravagin shook his head. Shamsheer's entertainment facilities showed the same sharp contrast as everything else on the world, and while it could be interesting and sometimes even fun, it had a tendency to depress him. "As Ms. Panya said, we want to get an early start tomorrow. I think we'll just get some dinner and settle in."

"Up to you," Essen said, levering himself out of his chair. "If you'll excuse me, then, I need to go get ready for the evening's festivities. I'll leave instructions about dinner, and I'll try to get up in time to see you off in the morning." Nodding at each of them in turn, he strode from the room.

For a moment Ravagin and Danae sat in silence. Out the window, the Giantsword light was beginning to glow; a city's traditional demarcation between the work of day and the relaxation of evening.

"Certainly doesn't seem to be a hardship post, does it?" Danae muttered. "Housesit all day, party all night."

Ravagin shrugged. "He's new here. Give him a few more months and he'll be as frustrated as every other person from the Twenty Worlds that spends much time on Shamsheer."

"Frustrated how? By the laws?"

He shook his head. "By the technology."

"Come again?"

Abruptly, Ravagin stood up and headed for the stairs. "Come on, let's go sit outside on the balcony."

Danae's face was suddenly wary. "Why?"

"Why not? It's a nice night . . . and besides, it'll give you a good chance to see part of the answer to your question."

She followed silently as he climbed the steps to the second floor and found the doors leading out to the wide balcony facing out onto the street. Essen and his staff clearly spent a good deal of time here themselves: the furniture included both stuffed chairs and meal-size tables, and the guardrail was equipped with a spindly sort of device that Ravagin recognized as a minor bit of magic called a rainstopper. Choosing a chair near the rail, he sat down.

"Well?" Danae asked, looking around.

"Have a little patience," Ravagin advised her. "The pace of life on Shamsheer is slower than you're probably used to. Sit down and listen to the sounds of Kelaine at night."

"I said I wasn't interested in Kelaine at night," she grumbled, but pulled a second chair up to the rail anyway and sank into it. From somewhere down the street the sounds of musicians warming up could be heard, as well as the rising rumble of conversation as the locals began gathering.

"What's that, a bar or something down the street?" Danae asked, craning her neck to look toward the sound.

"That, or a private party. Though 'private party' is something of a misnomer—most of them are open to anyone who wants to drop in."

"Sounds like a typical university party."

"Mm. I think you'd find one of them interesting, but if you really don't want to go—there," he interrupted himself, pointing southward into the sky.

"What?" Danae asked, turning to look.

"The sky-planes—see them?"

"Yes. Huh. Where are they all going at this time of night?"

"Eastward, to Forj Tower. Carrying all the gadgets that broke in Kelaine City today."

"The—? Oh. *Oh.*" She watched in silence for another minute, until the aerial caravan was out of sight, then turned back to Ravagin. "I counted at least twenty sky-planes. And all the stuff they're carrying will be repaired overnight?"

"That, or else replacements will be sent back before morning. We're not quite sure which, or whether it's the same in all cases."

"Why don't you try marking one of them?" she asked.

"Or better yet, why not get someone inside the—did you call it *Forj?*"

"It's the local Dark Tower," Ravagin explained. " 'Forj' comes from the initials of the four protectorates surrounding it. Actually, we *have* tried marking some of the repair jobs—the results have been inconclusive. As for getting into Forj—" He shrugged. "Well, the getting in part is possible, or so say the legends. The problem is that all the actual repair work is done in sealed modules within the Tower itself, and trying to break into one gets you escorted out by a set of trolls in double-quick time."

"And *that's* what frustrates everyone? The fact that you can't watch the magic technology being repaired?"

"And can't seem to disassemble any of it without ruining it; *and* can't find any equipment outside the Dark Towers to analyze it with anyway; *and* therefore can't bring a single scrap of this technology out to the Twenty Worlds. And for most people, the more they see of Shamsheer, the more the fact that this stuff's beyond their reach gnaws the hell out of them."

She snorted gently. "Pure, unadulterated greed."

Ravagin flicked an irritated glance at her. "Greed, yes. Unadulterated, no."

"Perhaps."

They sat in silence for a few more minutes. From the other end of the street a second party added counterpoint to the sounds of the first, and pedestrian traffic in front of the way house picked up as people began traveling back and forth between the two foci of entertainment. One of the fascinations this culture held for sociologists, Ravagin knew, was that of a still largely medieval setting where even the peasant class had real quantities of leisure time.

"Would you really have let that jerkface hit me?"

Ravagin brought his mind back. "Yes," he told her honestly. "If he'd chosen to exercise that right it would have been the simplest and safest way out of that mess. And don't think it wasn't a mess—we could have gotten into serious trouble out there."

Danae's face twisted into an irritated grimace as she stared straight out over the rail. "And since I'd gotten us into it in the first place I needed the lesson anyway?" she growled. "Maybe; but I'm not sorry I did it. Maybe you could sit by and watch that woman get hurt, but I couldn't."

"Which proves all by itself you didn't really understand what was going on," Ravagin countered, fighting against his own irritation. "If they'd gone so far as to actually hurt her, *they* would have been the ones in trouble. And they knew it. Shamsheer law is strongly set up along the eye-for-an-eye philosophy, applied evenly to all people. Especially in the Tween cities, which are generally at least a little more democratic than the protectorates."

Danae pondered that for a moment in silence. "Well . . . maybe I did go off a little prematurely," she admitted.

"Prematurely, hell," he told her bluntly. "You could have gotten us both killed out there. And it is *not* going to happen again, or I'll abort this trip and take you straight back to Threshold. Understood?"

She glared at him. "You don't have to beat it to death," she said icily. "I was wrong, I admit it, and I promise to stay fully on track from now on. Happy?"

"Ecstatically." He hadn't really intended to bring this up quite so soon, but after that thickheaded play this afternoon the more caution he could plant in her the better. "I'd be even happier if you'd explain why you've got a professional bodyguard trailing along behind you."

She jerked, actually spinning to look over her shoulder. "What—? *Damn* him. It's Hart, right? Where is he?" she growled, facing Ravagin again.

"If my instructions have been listened to, he's still back on Threshold. But some of my colleagues may have more trouble than I did turning down the cash dripping off his fingers."

"Damn. But he can't find us here . . . can he?"

"Not as far as I know. Are you saying he's a danger to you?"

"Not a danger, no. But definitely an annoyance." She sighed and seemed to slump in her chair. "He's been dogging my every move ever since I left home, watching out for nonexistent danger and smoothing my road for me whenever he could."

"So why don't you send him away?"

"Because I'm not the one paying his salary. That comes

from my father—and Daddy Dear sees monsters underneath every bush."

"Maybe he knows something you don't," Ravagin grunted.

"Like . . . ?"

"Like maybe something new has come up. Some reason he suddenly didn't want you here alone."

Danae snorted. "Daddy Dear's a chronic worrier, and paranoid on top of it. And if you listen to him—" She broke off suddenly. "Anyway, just because Hart's here doesn't mean there's anything in particular to worry about. Especially while we're on this side of the Tunnel."

Ravagin pondered for a moment. She was right, of course—whether her father was afraid of kidnappers or assassins or God knew what else, there was little chance such dangers could reach into the Hidden Worlds. And yet . . . "You're probably right," he admitted after a moment. "But I think we should take some extra precautions anyway, just in case. Hart's veiled warnings may have been just talk, but he may have known something he didn't want to tell me."

"The bottom line being . . . ?"

"The bottom line being that we're going to cut short this part of the trip. Instead of the two-day tour of Missia City and the Feymar Protectorate I'd planned, we're instead going to head directly to Darcane Forest and the Tunnel to Karyx."

Danae shrugged. "Fine with me—like I said, I've had all of Shamsheer that I want."

"I hope you can keep that attitude," Ravagin warned. "In a lot of ways the laws and customs of Karyx are harder and more violent than those of Shamsheer."

"Perhaps—but at least there I won't have the problem of being unarmed in an armed society." She glanced pointedly at the scorpion glove dangling from his belt and got to her feet. "Well, if that's all you wanted to talk about, I'm going to go get something to eat."

Ravagin felt his lip twitch as he looked up at her. "Help yourself," he nodded. "I'm going to stay here a bit longer, I think. Remember that we'll be heading out early in the morning, so don't get to bed too late."

"Not likely," she said dryly; and with a brief nod she was gone.

Ravagin sighed as he settled back into his chair. So she wouldn't be unarmed in an armed society, would she? He'd lost track of all the people he'd escorted to Karyx who'd started with that same confident—hell, *arrogant*—attitude. Who'd truly believed that their brief training had properly prepared them to command the spirits of that world.

She'd learn. Eventually, they all did.

Closing his eyes, he listened to the sounds of Kelaine City at play . . . and wondered how music and laughter could be so depressing.

Chapter 8

They left just after dawn the next morning, under the dour eye of one of the city's justice officials, and headed eastward into the sun and a day that was promising to be as clear as the previous one had been. Again, Danae experienced a mild case of acrophobia as their sky-plane flew in and out of wispy clouds and the occasional flock of birds; but within a short time the fear left her, and she was even able to lean her forehead against the invisible edge barrier and gaze at the landscape below.

It was, for the most part, fairly unremarkable. With Kelaine City behind them and the borders of Ordarl Protectorate still ahead, the area they were passing over was sparsely inhabited. There were occasional villages—most, Danae noted, equipped with stone or sharpened tree trunk walls to discourage robber gangs—each one surrounded by areas of cultivated land. But most of what she could see was the same type of undeveloped landscape that had been around the Tunnel exit. "Hard to believe they've been living here for four thousand years or more," she commented.

"Hm?" Ravagin glanced over where she was looking. "Who?—oh; Shamsheer's people? Well, I'd take that number with a cautionary footnote, if I were you."

"Why? You think they haven't been here that long?"

"I have no idea how long they've been here," he shrugged. "Neither does anyone else, no matter how confidently they throw figures back and forth in the journals. Certainly there's never been any physical evidence found, and if the people themselves have legends about their arrival, I've never heard them."

"But it *is* certain they were brought here from Earth, isn't it?" she persisted. "I've read that they *are* true humans, not some close copycat alien race."

Ravagin turned a patient look on her. "Danae, one of the first things you need to learn is that we don't know nearly as much about the Hidden Worlds as we pretend we do. *Yes*, the people of both seem human enough; *yes*, all their organs and nerve centers are in the right places; *yes*, a Dreya's Womb seems to work as well on someone from the Twenty Worlds as it does on a Shamsheer native. But the definition of human boils down to genetic structure, and the only way we're ever going to find that out for sure will be to kidnap someone and drag him naked and screaming through the Tunnel for a complete DNA scan. At the moment that's what's called an unacceptable procedure."

"Even if you drugged him so that he didn't realize he'd been anywhere? That way—"

"Drugged him with what?"

"With—" She snapped her mouth firmly shut. "Right. Damn; I keep forgetting about the telefold."

"Everyone does. Don't worry about it." Ravagin nodded ahead at the row of jagged peaks cutting across their path. "Those are the Ordarl Mountains up there—we'll be crossing the western border of Ordarl Protectorate as we pass over the foothills and skating just inside the northwest edge of the hexagon for an hour or so."

Danae nodded; she'd already noticed that the foothills coincided with the abrupt return of civilization. Half a dozen small villages could be seen clustered along the line there, their inhabitants no longer needing to rely solely on numbers or barricades for defense against robber gangs from the Tweens. "It still seems like they should have been able to build up a bigger population than this after even a couple of thousand years. Especially with such advanced medical facilities as Dreya's Wombs available."

Ravagin snorted, his eyes giving the area around them a

slow sweep. "What is this, a two-person seminar on unanswerable questions? Do us both a favor and save them for the last chapter of your dissertation, all right? We're going to have enough practical questions to keep us busy."

Danae gritted her teeth against the sarcasm that wanted to get out. *Don't get mad girl*, she told herself firmly. *So he's lost whatever academic curiosity he ever had—file the fact and drop the subject*. "All right, then—let's hear one of these big practical questions of yours," she said.

"Let's start with how well you can imitate a demure Shamsheer-bred woman," he said. He had risen up on his knees and was gazing over her shoulder with a tight expression on his face. "Because in about half a minute you're going to have to be one."

Startled, she twisted around to follow his gaze. Behind them, two men on another sky-plane were rising swiftly up to intercept them.

Robbers! She inhaled sharply through clenched teeth, hands curling into impotent fists at her sides. "What are we going to do?"

"Whatever they say, of course," Ravagin told her. "Look at their tunics: blue/red/gold. They're soldiers from Castle Ordarleal."

"But—"

"No buts, Danae." He shifted his eyes back to her face. "And I meant what I said about being quiet and demure—especially the quiet part. Ordarl's castle-lord doesn't much care for strangers, female strangers in particular. You look like you're even thinking of butting against his authority and we're likely to wind up spending one or more nights in the castle's cells."

"But what the hell do they—?"

"Shh! Greetings, soldiers of Ordarl Protectorate," he called abruptly. Danae turned to look, a little shaken that the other sky-plane had made it within hailing range so quickly. Her first impulse—to urge Ravagin to try and outrun them—died stillborn.

"Greetings to you, travelers," one of the soldiers called across the narrowing gap. "We would be honored if you would accompany us to the ground."

"We would be pleased to comply," Ravagin answered,

raising one hand to point. "Sky-plane: follow the sky-plane at my mark: *mark.*"

Their carpet slowed abruptly, allowing the other to pass beneath it, and then settled into place a meter behind it. One of the soldiers turned back to the front of his sky-plane and murmured something; the second kept his full attention on his prisoners as both vehicles made a sharp turn and dropped toward the mountains below.

"May I inquire as to the purpose of this delay in our lawful trip?" Ravagin asked politely.

"Whether it is lawful or not is yet to be determined," the second soldier said. "I would be honored if you would place all weapons and magical devices before you on the sky-plane."

Ravagin sighed and began to unfasten the scorpion glove and knife from his belt. "You, too," he muttered to Danae. "Your firefly's considered a magical gadget."

Danae pursed her lips tightly, slid the ring off her finger and dropped it in front of her. "Has it occurred to you that once we land the force-field wall won't protect us anymore?"

"If you're suggesting we run for it, forget it," he murmured back. "They could have a dozen more sky-planes on top of us before we could get past the border . . . and there are ways for a group of sky-planes to force down a lone one. With or without leaving its passengers in good shape."

Danae gritted her teeth and shut up.

They landed minutes later in a grassy lea between two impressively craggy mountains. A handful of tents had been set up at one end and more of the liveried soldiers could be seen going about various tasks. "Looks like a semi-permanent base," Ravagin commented as the sky-planes came to rest and the two soldiers got to their feet and motioned the prisoners to do likewise. "I wonder if the castle-lord's been having trouble with raiders coming in through cover of the mountains."

"Maybe," Danae murmured back. "Does that help or hurt us?"

"I haven't the faintest idea."

"Greetings, travelers," a voice came from behind them, and they turned to find an older man clumping toward them from one of the tents. "What errand brings you over the Ordarl Protectorate?"

"We journey from Kelaine City to the Darcane Forest, sir," Ravagin told him with a courteous nod. "Is Ordarl Protectorate now forbidding travelers to fly over its land?"

"Ordarl Protectorate objects only to black sorcerers practicing evil within its territory," the other said grimly, eyes boring into Ravagin's. "What are your names and professions?"

"I am called Ravagin; I claim no city or protectorate as my home. My companion is named Danae. As to business, I do service as bearer of private messages between distant places."

The officer's eyebrows raised. "Indeed? Do your clients distrust the sanctity of the crystal eye?"

Ravagin shrugged. "My clients' thoughts and fears are their own. I merely provide a service to those who wish it."

The other's gaze shifted to Danae. "And you?"

"The lady is—"

"I am traveling to visit relatives in Darcane Forest," Danae interrupted him. "The man Ravagin consented to escort me, as none of my closer kin were interested in making the trip."

"Indeed." The older man's frown deepened slightly, his eyes flicking over her clothing. "Where is your home, noblelady?"

"In the Numant Protectorate, to the west of Castle Numanteal," Ravagin said, taking control of the conversation back from her. "May I ask what form this black sorcery takes?"

The other looked over Ravagin's shoulder. "What do you find?" he asked.

Danae glanced back to their sky-plane, where the two soldiers were examining the devices they'd left there. "Nothing out of the ordinary, O Captain," one said, holding up the scorpion glove. "Our Ravagin is indeed a far traveler; I have not seen one of these weapons in a long time."

The captain pursed his lips and returned his attention to Ravagin. "You do not seem to have the scent of black sorcery about you, I'll admit. Still, I would expect a careful messenger to carry stronger weaponry."

"Precisely what I expect others to think," Ravagin said calmly. "The best defense, I have found, is not to be attacked in the first place."

Surprisingly, a smile twitched at the old man's lips. "A subtle philosophy indeed, Ravagin. I do not believe I would trust it, myself."

Ravagin shrugged. "I *am* still alive."

"True." The other cocked an eyebrow. "It would be interesting to see how long you remain that way. But that is of no immediate concern. Tell me, are the magical devices in Numant Protectorate showing signs of sorcerous interference?"

The question seemed to take Ravagin by surprise. "I—am not sure what you mean. What sort of interference do you refer to?"

"Widespread failures, for the most part," the other said. "Devices, too, that appear to have ceased functioning but then are whole again without making the journey to the Dark Tower."

The memory of the automated aerial caravan from Kelaine City the previous night flashed into Danae's mind. *Widespread failure?* she wondered. *Or was that just the normal breakage rate?* A quick mental search of what she'd learned about Shamsheer gave her nothing either way.

Ravagin, too, seemed a bit uncertain and pondered the question for several seconds before answering. "I don't recall hearing word of such unusual failures," he said at last. "But you must understand that by the nature of my profession, I am seldom in any one place for long and do not talk to a great many people."

"But you *do* speak to people in widely scattered areas," the other pointed out.

"True, though with his crystal eye your castle-lord has an equally good ear for news from afar," Ravagin pointed out. "How long has the trouble been happening here?"

"A few weeks, although the worst seems to have passed." The captain seemed to make a decision, and again caught his men's eyes. "These may go. Resume your duties."

Ravagin bowed. "My thanks, sir. If I should come across

this problem elsewhere in my travels, would it be of use to your castle-lord for me to inform him?"

"It would be useful," the other nodded. "If you are nearby at the time you may bring word to any of these our castle-lord's outposts; if not, the news may be sent directly to Castle Ordarleal."

Ravagin nodded. "I hope you find this black sorcerer quickly," he said, taking Danae's arm and leading her back aboard their sky-plane. "Good day to you, O Captain. Sky-plane: to the southwest of Darcane Forest."

The carpet rose into the air . . . and Danae took a deep breath. "What in all Twenty Worlds was *that* all about?"

Ravagin handed her back her firefly, an oddly intense look on his face. "Probably nothing," he said. "These mythical black sorcerers tend to get blamed for anything that goes wrong on Shamsheer."

"I didn't mean that part. Do you think something could really be going wrong with the equipment in Ordarl?"

"Again, probably not. Random chance is occasionally lumpy, as the saying goes—these are probably nothing more than a bunch of malfunctions that just happen to have come up at the same time."

The words were confident enough . . . but there was something in his tone that made Danae slide forward on the carpet to take a good look at his face. "But you're not sure. Are you?"

The lines in his face smoothed slightly as he turned to find her looking at him. "Well, I can't be *absolutely* sure, of course, can I? But this sort of thing has happened before, and after a certain amount of fussing the probability curve smooths itself out and everyone's happy again."

"Uh-huh," Danae said, scooting back to her place again. Clearly, he wasn't going to confide any thoughts to her that he might feel would be upsetting to a paying client.

And yet . . .

Abruptly, the awareness of where they were flooded in on her. Flying high above the ground on a flimsy carpet-sized piece of alien machinery . . . a piece of machinery that could very well have been doing this for four thousand years or more. And good maintenance or no, she'd never yet heard of a machine that could run forever.

Could it be that Shamsheer's magical technology was finally starting to unravel?

Come on, Danae, she scoffed silently. *After all this time, you really think the whole marvelous machine would just happen to come apart while you were here to watch? Let's not let egocentrism run away with us, okay?*

Nevertheless, she found herself keeping well back from the sky-plane's edge for the rest of the flight . . . and concentrating on the blue sky overhead instead of the ground far below.

Chapter 9

They'd been flying two more hours when Ravagin called her attention to a dark, irregular mass of buildings spreading across the landscape to the southeast. "Missia City," he identified it. "Probably the largest city in this section of Shamsheer, though genuine population records aren't really kept. Look straight past it and you'll be able to see Forj Tower."

Danae squinted against the sunlight. Beyond the city was a section of open space—desert, she remembered from the maps—and beyond that a clump of something that could have been the dense forest she knew was also there. And rising out of the center of the forest—

"My God," she murmured. "That thing is *big*."

"Nearly a kilometer high," Ravagin agreed. "And something like seven hundred meters in circumference at the base."

"I've seen the numbers, thank you," Danae told him shortly. "It just looks bigger than that, somehow."

"Optical illusion, probably—most of the comparable buildings you've seen in the Twenty Worlds are surrounded by other buildings of similar height. Here it's just standing out there on its own."

Danae shaded her eyes. Details were impossible to pick out at this distance, but superimposed in her mind's eye were the drawings she'd seen: the secondary spires poking skyward from halfway up the main tower body; the intricate and unexplained relief patterns climbing like stone ivy from top to bottom; the windows in the upper third through which every bit of portable technology in this part of Shamsheer would eventually make its way. "I used to read fantasy books with Dark Towers in them when I was a girl," she commented, half to herself. "It was always where the chief villain lived."

"Here it's more like where the shoemaker's elves live," Ravagin said dryly. "Anyway, that's where it is. I thought you might like to see it."

She nodded silently, still looking at the dark mass of buildings of the city below. All those people, in Missia and other cities nearby, clustered around the Tower as if around a wizard's abode . . . "They really don't understand, do they?" she murmured.

Ravagin half turned. "You mean how all this operates? No, of course not. I thought we'd discussed that."

"Well, yes, but . . . oh, never mind."

"The scientific method isn't a basic component of the human psyche, Danae," Ravagin shrugged. "It's a relatively recent development, and it only caught on because it happens to work. On Shamsheer, it's not needed."

Danae grimaced. "So in exchange for all their marvelous voodoo technology they get locked into a totally stagnant society."

"Basically. Probably on purpose."

She looked at him sharply. "You're talking Vernescu's theory, aren't you? That Triplet was set up as a deliberate test of whether humans function best with magic, science, or a mixture of the two."

He glanced back at her. "I take it you disagree with him."

"I hate the whole idea," she snorted. "It's internally inconsistent, for one thing. Any beings so advanced they could build two entire worlds *and* possibly even the dimensions to hold them *and* the Tunnels to get between them surely would have had enough ethical sense not to play games like this with other sentient beings."

"Why?" Ravagin countered. "What makes you think the Builders even saw us as sentient beings, let alone cared about us? Maybe the human race started its existence as the white rats for their experiments and we just got out of hand after they went off and left us."

"I hate *that* theory, too."

He shrugged. "You're the one who was grousing about the lack of scientific curiosity on Shamsheer a minute ago. Why are you so upset by the possibility that Triplet itself is a massive monument to scientific curiosity?"

She glared at him for a moment, then turned away and glowered toward the Dark Tower fading into the horizon in their wake. There was no answer for that, unfortunately, which galled her to no end. She hated Vernescu's theory—hated the way it reduced human beings to pawns on someone else's chessboard—but she had no viable alternative to offer in its place.

Not yet, anyway. But that didn't mean there wasn't one . . . and if there was, she was damn well going to be the one to find it.

Pursing her lips, she glanced over her shoulder. Ravagin was again sitting facing front, his back to her. Nothing in his stance or posture indicated anger or hostility—almost certainly, the argument had been little more than a game to him. A way to slide salt under her skin without doing anything he could be reprimanded for. *Cynical; perhaps more than a little bitter*, she decided, playing back that last conversation in her mind. *A function of all his years of running people through here? Or is it just the way he's expressing the frustration he said everyone eventually suffers in Shamsheer?*

She didn't know. And for the moment, anyway, she didn't really care.

The sun had just passed zenith when they reached the western edge of Darcane Forest.

The forest was *huge*, and perhaps more than anything else Danae had seen it served to drive home on a viscereal level the strangeness of this world. All other forests she'd ever seen—whether on developed or relatively undeveloped worlds—had somehow carried about them a noticeable and in many ways comfortable aura of civilization. Not here. The trees stretching to the horizon below carpeted the ground completely, with no roadways or mono-

lines cutting artificially straight lines through the green-
ery. No roadways, no watchtowers, no tethered guidelights;
nothing down there but untouched, untamed, uncaring
wilderness. Abruptly, she shivered.

"Impressive, isn't it?"

She grimaced, annoyed that Ravagin had noticed her
reaction. "It's nice," she told him shortly. "Not a place I'd
want to spend the night."

"I don't blame you," he grunted. "There are some particularly nasty animals living down there—most of them,
fortunately, nocturnal. Sky-plane: follow my mark." He
pointed about forty-five degrees to the right of their current direction. "Mark."

The sky-plane obediently took up the new course, and
Ravagin glanced up at the sun. "We'll be at the way house
in about an hour. Do you want to wait until we get there,
or eat the lunch Essen packed us now?"

Danae hadn't even thought about food. "I'm not really
hungry at the moment. As a matter of fact, why do we
even have to stop at the way house? I thought you wanted
to get us to Karyx as soon as possible."

"Well . . ." Ravagin scratched thoughtfully at his cheek.
"It's occurred to me since we last talked about it that I
might be pushing things a bit much." He waved a hand
back toward the way they'd come. "After all, there's been
absolutely no indication that your pal Hart has even managed to get through to Shamsheer, let alone that he's right
behind us. I think it might be a good idea to spend one
more night here before tackling Karyx."

Danae frowned, visualizing the maps of Karyx she'd
learned. "I don't see the problem. We wouldn't be able to
get to Besak or Torralane Village before nightfall if we
went through now, but so what? There are supposed to be
inns along the road, or we could even camp out overnight."

He cocked an eyebrow. "You really *are* eager to get to
Karyx, aren't you? Has it occurred to you that the culture
shock you experienced in Shamsheer will be even worse
on the far side of *this* Tunnel?"

"Maybe not as bad as you'd think," she retorted coolly.
"At least there I won't have to worry about offending
someone without any way to defend myself."

"Oh, really?" Ravagin snorted. "All right, let's take a quick for-instance. We step out of the Tunnel, and you turn to find a *cintah* crouched to spring. What do you do?"

"I say *sa-trahist raooh* with the proper placement gesture and invoke a firebrat btween us and him," she said promptly.

"And if that particular spot happens to be where a clump of dried leaves has collected . . . ?"

"Then they catch on fire, I suppose."

"Right. So how do you put the fire out?"

Danae glared at him. "What's this supposed to prove, anyway?"

"I'm just trying to show that all you've got at the moment is tape-learning," Ravagin sighed. "Fine stuff, very useful, but hardly the full preparation you think it is. So either tell me how to put out that fire or we stay overnight at the way house here. It's up to you."

Danae gritted her teeth, stifling the urge to argue. Once again, damn him, he was right. . . . "All right," she growled. "I release the firebrat by saying *carash-carsheen* and then say *sakhe-khe fawkh* to invoke a nixie."

"Who will have a hell of a time bringing water to a fire in the Cairn Mounds," Ravagin cut in. "The nearest stream is over a kilometer from the Tunnel, and it's hardly a trickle at the best of times."

"So she can pull the water up from underground," Danae snapped. "Or condense it from the air if she has to. I know she can do both, so quit trying to mislead me."

"Agreed; but if you set her too hard a task you could wind up with a premature spontaneous release," Ravagin warned. "I don't suppose anyone thought to mention those to you?"

"No, I know about them, thank you," Danae ground out. "All right, then—let's hear how *you* would handle it."

"Oh, about the way you described," he shrugged. "But knowing how dry the Cairn Mounds are, I would have added a geas onto the nixie's invocation to put it more firmly under my control."

"I was told not to use a geas unless absolutely necessary," Danae said stiffly. "They said the spirits don't react well to them."

"No, they don't," Ravagin nodded. "But premature releases are usually worse—the damn thing can sometimes take a swipe at you before it vanishes."

"So how do you know which is the better risk?"

"Experience, of course. Which was the point I was trying to make in the first place."

She bristled. "Are you telling me that I'm not to use any spells unless you clear them in advance? Because if you are, you can just—"

"Whoa, Danae—take it easy," he cut in, holding his hands palm outward toward her. "I never said anything of the sort. All I'm trying to do is let you know that things on Karyx aren't nearly as laser cut as those little six-week fact-stuffing courses pretend. Karyx's spirit magic is every bit as layered and complex as Shamsheer's technological magic, with the added danger of the spirits turning on you if you aren't careful. You've already shown yourself willing to disobey orders you don't especially want to follow—I'm trying to impress upon you the fact that pulling that stunt here could literally get you burned alive."

"Consider me suitably impressed," Danae growled. "I suppose this means we're going to have to spend the night in the way house?"

"Oh, for—" Ravagin exhaled in thinly veiled disgust. "All right—the hell with it. You want to hit Karyx tonight, fine; we'll hit Karyx tonight. It'd serve you right if you had to go back to Threshold with a withered arm and explain how you asked for the most experienced Courier and then argued every damn decision with him."

Without waiting for a reply, he twisted back around. "Sky-plane: follow my mark. *Mark.*"

Behind him, Danae closed her eyes and let her mouth twist with some disgust of her own. He was right—she *was* giving him far too much of a hard time . . . and knowing *why* she was doing so was unfortunately no excuse. She was an adult, and was supposed to be able to suppress such childish reactions.

Still, the whole thing had shown her something new about Ravagin, too. He did indeed know he'd been specifically asked for . . . and it was abundantly clear that he wasn't feeling overly flattered by the request. *Well, then, to hell with him, too,* she grumbled to herself. If she had to show her father, Hart, *and* Ravagin too that she was capable of taking care of herself, then that was exactly what she would do.

And if they didn't like the consequences, then that was their hard luck.

An hour later, they reached the Tunnel.

From the outside it looked virtually the same as both the Threshold and Shamsheer ends of the first Tunnel had: a small leaf-carpeted clearing with several small hills grouped around a longer one containing the Tunnel. Grasses and small bushes grew on the secondary mounds, and the surrounding trees were tall enough to hide the clearing until one was almost on top of it. Fleetingly, Danae wondered how the early explorers to Shamsheer had ever managed to find the thing.

At Ravagin's command the sky-plane dropped down to hover a meter off the ground in front of the Tunnel mouth. "Want to make sure there's nothing nasty prowling around before we give up the edge barrier," he explained, eyes giving the forest a careful sweep. Palming his firefly carefully away from them, he pointed it into the Tunnel and ordered it to full power. Danae caught a glimpse of the familiar sloping floor and rough walls before Ravagin shut off the light with a satisfied grunt. With one last scan of the forest, he brought the sky-plane down.

Danae took a deep breath as she carefully stood up and eased the kinks out of her legs. The forest breezes—no longer held back now by the sky-plane's edge barrier—played about her hair, bringing along with them an unusual and tantalizing mixture of aromas. She sniffed cautiously, trying without success to identify them.

"Let's get moving," Ravagin said, and she turned to see him already a meter or so inside the Tunnel mouth. On his left hand his firefly was giving off a gentle glow; on his right, his scorpion glove was mute testimony to the fact that even on the threshold of another world Darcane Forest could be a dangerous place. Swallowing, she went to join him, fighting back the urge to look over her shoulder as she did so.

But no animals had taken up lodging in the Tunnel, and they reached the familiar set of camouflaged lockers without incident. "Okay, get those clothes off and let's get across," Ravagin said briskly as he laid his weapons on the top locker shelf and started unfastening his tunic.

"I know the routine," Danae growled. Her bodice's top fastener had broken that morning while she was dressing, and now her jury-rigged replacement was refusing to come loose. Gritting her teeth, she tugged at it, first gently, then with more and more force—

"Need any help?"

"I'll get it," she snapped. "It's just—*stuck*—a little . . ."

"Move your hands," he sighed. "Come on—move them."

She obeyed, a hot flush of embarrassment flooding her face as he brought the firefly near her chin and examined her handiwork. With a grunt, he retrieved his knife from the locker. "Hold real still," he said, teasing the knot delicately with the tip . . . and a moment later she felt it come open.

"Thanks," she muttered, turning her back on him and starting on the rest of the fastenings.

They finished the rest of their disrobing in silence. "Give me your hand," Ravagin said as he shut off the firefly's glow and closed the locker. "Come on, come on— it's not getting any earlier out there."

"I want to try it by myself this time," Danae told him shortly.

Even in total darkness she could practically see him grimacing. "All right," he sighed. "But stay close."

They set off around the curve, Danae following the slap of Ravagin's footsteps. The telefold, when they passed it, wasn't the surprise it had been the first time and she managed to keep her feet and most of her balance. "Well, that wasn't so bad—" she began.

And abruptly, a loud voice split the silence of the Tunnel. "*HAKLARAST!*" it shouted.

Chapter 10

It wasn't until the echoes of his shout were beginning to fade away and Ravagin heard Danae's startled gasp that he realized he'd forgotten to warn her he would be invoking a sprite as soon as they'd crossed the telefold into Karyx. "Sorry," he said over his shoulder. "I didn't mean to scare—"

He broke off as a flicker of glow-fire appeared in front of him. "I am here, as you summoned," it said in a squeaky, almost unintelligible voice.

"Scout down the Tunnel—that direction," Ravagin ordered the sprite, pointing ahead. "Examine both the Tunnel and the area for a hundred *varna* around its exit for other humans, wild beasts, or trapped spirits, and then return to me."

The glow-fire flared momentarily and vanished. "The lockers are over here," Ravagin told Danae, turning around and reaching out a hand to find her.

"You could have warned me before you shouted like that," her voice came from his right. Oddly enough, she didn't seem upset.

"Yeah. Sorry." Stepping to the Tunnel wall, he found the lockers and got one open. "You need some light?" he asked as he chose some clothing by feel and held hers out into the darkness.

"No," she said, almost too quickly. Her hand found his, took the clothes, and retreated. Keeping an eye out for the

71

sprite's return, Ravagin shook out the tunic and trousers to make sure no insects had taken up residence there and began to dress.

He was almost finished when the glow-fire reappeared. "There are no other humans, beasts, or spirits within the region," the squeaky voice reported.

Ravagin nodded. The exit into Karyx was usually clear, but it never hurt to make sure. "Good. Then I want you to take a message to a woman named Melentha living in a large house just to the west of Besak: that Ravagin and one other have come and will be arriving tomorrow. *Carash-mahst.*"

Again the sprite flared its understanding and vanished. "Whenever you're ready," Ravagin told Danae, fastening his last buckle and locating a short sword on the locker's weapons shelf. "I'd like to try and get a few kilometers toward Besak before nightfall."

"All set," Danae grunted, and he sensed her come to his side. "Do I get any weapons here, or don't women carry blades on Karyx either?"

"Many of them do," he said. Groping for her hand, he placed a sheathed dagger into it. "Your profile said you'd had some knife training, but just the same don't draw it unless you absolutely have to. Stick with your spirithandling spells, or better still just stand back and let me handle any trouble."

She snorted, but fastened the weapon to her side without comment. Ravagin debated invoking a dazzler, decided against it, and started along the Tunnel. They could make it through well enough without light, and once outside he could be a shade more discreet about making sure she had her outfit on straight, anyway. He'd stomped her toes enough this trip—though why he should give a damn about that he didn't know. After the shoddy way she'd pressured him into this trip in the first place he didn't owe her anything but guidance and protection and the most basic of courtesies.

They walked the rest of the way to the Tunnel mouth in silence. Ravagin gave Danae's garb a quick once-over as they started up the last ramp-like section, found she'd indeed managed to get all the primitive buckles and ties fastened properly. They stepped out into Karyx's more muted sunlight—

"Huh," Danae grunted, looking around. "Hardly worth invoking a sprite to check this place out."

Ravagin shrugged. She had a point—no animal in its right mind would live in the hilly wasteland that surrounded them on all sides. "It's worse just a few kilometers northwest of here," he commented. "The Cairn Waste is about as desolate as any place could be."

"So I'd heard. Site of some long-ago battle or something, wasn't it?"

"That's the legend. No one knows for sure."

"Couldn't you ask a spirit?"

"There are some things even a geas spell won't make them talk about," he shook his head. "The Illid ruins and Cairn Waste are one of them." He glanced around one last time, pointed toward the east. "The road between Besak and Torralane is about ten kilometers that way."

"Who is that woman you sent the message to?" Danae asked as they started off through the mounds.

"Melentha's the mistress of the Besak way house, like Essen was in Kelaine City," Ravagin explained. "It's standard procedure on Karyx to inform one of them when you're coming—travel here's a bit riskier than on Shamsheer and it's a good idea to have someone making sure you don't just disappear out in the wild somewhere."

He glanced at Danae, saw her swallow visibly. "I see," she said with forced calmness. "A shame we don't have sprites on call back home—seems a pretty efficient way to send messages."

"The novelty fades after a while," Ravagin told her dryly.

"I suppose so."

They walked in silence for several minutes more, and after a bit Ravagin noticed her throwing frowning glances at the sky and the landscape around them. "Anything wrong?" he prompted.

"I'm not sure," she said slowly. "The light seems . . . funny, somehow. Not bright enough or something."

He nodded, impressed in spite of himself. Most visitors noticed the anomaly eventually, but few picked up on it this quickly. "Karyx's sunlight is about ten percent dimmer than that of Shamsheer, which in turn is that much dimmer than sunlight on Threshold. Have you ever been to Earth or Ankh during a partial solar eclipse?"

"Ah—yes," she said, understanding flickering across her face. "You're right; that *is* what it's like—the sunlight's the right color and all, but not the right intensity."

"Yeah. Only it's not an eclipse in this case—the sun's just dimmer. Just one of the sizeable collection of things we don't understand about this place."

"But the stars *are* the same as you see from Threshold, aren't they?"

"As far as we can tell, bearing in mind we can't bring in the necessary instruments for an exact check. No, all three worlds *are* in the same place in the universe—every study anyone's ever invented has come to that tentative conclusion. But remember that there's no particular reason why the suns of the three have to be the same. Certainly the terrains of the worlds are different, so we're not just experiencing different dimensional manifestations of the same planet."

"How do you know?" she countered. "I mean, the equivalent spot on Shamsheer is covered with dense forest—how do you know it didn't have all these mounds, too, before the tree roots wore them down? And who knows *what* Threshold's landscape looked like before the original inhabitants blew it into the stratosphere?"

A pat answer rose to Ravagin's lips . . . and stayed there unvoiced. How *had* the savants and investigators come to that conclusion, come to think of it? "Well . . . there's a good-sized ocean inlet about seventy kilometers west of here at Citadel that definitely doesn't show up in either of the other worlds," he said slowly. "On the other hand . . . there've been some tremendously powerful spiritmasters in Citadel's history, and if one of them had decided he wanted the city to have ocean access, he might very well have been able to force an elemental to dig that inlet for him."

Danae shivered suddenly. "With an elemental he could probably have gotten the whole *ocean* dug for him. Unless their power's been exaggerated."

"It's hard to exaggerate elementals' power," Ravagin said, feeling his stomach tighten. "Almost as hard as imagining the kind of damn fool who would try invoking one of them in the first place. I don't even like working with demons and peris, personally." With an effort he forced his mind back to the original question. *Could* the worlds in fact be more identical than was generally conceded? With some difficulty he tried to imagine a superposition of the Shamsheer and Karyx maps . . .

"The Morax Forest east of here could be the same as the Darcane back on Shamsheer," Danae murmured. "Just receded to the east a hundred kilometers or so—maybe by whatever made the Cairn Waste. The South Fey River in Shamsheer would be somewhere in Citadel's inlet—that doesn't help us any. The North Fey River . . .-?"

"There *is* a river up there somewhere," Ravagin nodded. "But I'm not sure precisely where. Part of the problem is that we don't know all that much about Karyx's landscape—travel is by foot or horseback, and we rarely wind up going more than fifty or sixty kilometers from the Tunnel. Funny no one's thought of this before."

"Oh, they probably have," Danae shrugged. "And then rejected it for some perfectly good reason." She sighed. "Doesn't really matter, I suppose. Just theoretical brain-gaming."

"So what else is there here?" he said dryly. "It's not like studies of Karyx have any application to the real universe."

"You sound like Essen," she snorted. "I don't suppose it's occurred to you that the spirits we find here may not be unique to this place."

"If you're talking about all the Earth legends and stories—"

"*And* most religions, too," she cut in. "Virtually all of them make provision for spiritual beings."

"But spiritual beings that are different from those of Karyx."

"Who says?" she said hotly.

"Just take a minute and look at the facts," Ravagin said, feeling his temper beginning to slide out from under his control. He'd never much cared for people who couldn't have a discussion without turning it into an argument.

"The spirits here are easy to invoke, easy to control, interact directly with the physical universe, and their presence is *very* apparent. Contrast that to all the legends—*or* the religious stories, if you'd prefer—that you remember."

She clamped her jaw tightly, but he could see in her eyes that she was indeed thinking about it. "You think the legends are just that—legends?"

"I have no idea—I'm not a theologian. All I'm saying is that anything you learn about spirit characteristics and control here will have no direct application to life off Karyx because spirits like these don't seem to exist off Karyx."

"So you *do* agree with Essen's philosophy."

"There's no agreeing or disagreeing, damn it," Ravagin snarled. "There are no sides to be taken here—it isn't a contest or war or something. In many ways I happen to prefer Karyx to Shamsheer; so what? All Essen was saying is that Shamsheer's technology is at least based on scientific principles, and that if we can find out how it works there we can make it work in the Twenty Worlds, too."

"If science really *is* a universal." She held up her hand before he could reply. "Sorry—I'm not really trying to start any arguments."

"Could've fooled me," Ravagin muttered under his breath.

"What'd you say?"

"Nothing," he growled. "Let's step up the pace a little—I want to try for one of the inns a few kilometers down the road."

They kept on, but within another hour it was clear they weren't going to make it. Danae was trying—he could grudgingly admit that much—but her preparation for the trip had clearly not included building up her leg muscles for this kind of continual up-down climbing, and he was forced again and again to reduce the pace or risk leaving her behind. The latter idea had a certain nasty appeal—he could invoke a djinn to watch over her progress, after all—but it wasn't really a serious option. Keeping most of his attention on their surroundings, he began working on the problem.

They reached the last row of mounds about an hour before sunset, and there Ravagin called a halt. "There's no way we're going to make any of the inns tonight," he said, studying the strip of dirt and gravel through the lengthening shadows of the mounds that were slowly but steadily creeping over it. "We might as well find a good spot around here and set up a camp. Are you hungry?"

"A little," she admitted, gazing out over the road. "There's not much cover out here, though. Wouldn't we do better to head for that little grove of trees?" She pointed south along the road.

"The lack of cover isn't all that important," Ravagin told her. "The presence or absence of bandits is much more of a consideration, and I'd just as soon avoid such blatantly obvious places for travelers to stop."

"But we could invoke a lar to protect the camp, couldn't we?" Danae persisted.

"We could and we will," Ravagin nodded. "The problem is that any bandits we meet will have some knowledge of spirithandling, too. Spirit battles can be fun to watch, but not at close range. We'll do better to stay out of sight here—"

A scrape of two stones together was all the warning he got, but for anyone who'd survived as long as he had on Karyx it was enough. He spun around, snatching his short sword from its sheath, just in time to see a huge disheveled man doing his best to sneak up on them around the mound. With a hoarse battle roar, he abandoned his attempts at stealth and switched to a full, head-down charge.

"Get back!" Ravagin snapped at Danae, bringing his sword up into ready position. The other's blade was a full-sized one, and in addition he was sporting the small armguard/buckler favored by bandits who liked to be at least a little inconspicuous. Against them Ravagin's weapon was definitely a poor second . . . but fortunately, he didn't have to rely on steel alone. There were half a dozen ways for a good spirithandler to trip up the unwary—

"*Plazni-hy-ix!*" Danae shouted abruptly from the side. "Jinx arise!"

"Damn!" Ravagin snarled under his breath. A *jinx* invocation, of all the stupid things! A hazy brown cloud formed around the bandit; without so much as pausing, the thug plowed through it and swung his sword in a high overhand cut—

Sidestepping, Ravagin caught the blade on his sword's guard and deflected it away. The bandit's inertia kept him going for several steps before he was able to skid to a halt. Ravagin took advantage of the breather to move further up the mound where he would have at least a slight high-ground advantage. The brown cloud had meanwhile followed the bandit, positioning itself around him with the same lack of effect as before.

Danae obviously saw that, too. "Jinx—" she began.

"Get rid of it!" Ravagin shouted to her, spitting dust. The bandit was moving toward him again, an entirely too cunning expression on his face. "You hear me, Danae? Release the damned thing."

"But—all right. *Carash-hyeen.*"

The bandit was ready. "*Man-sy-hae orolontis!*" he shouted as the brown cloud faded. "Try your tricks *now*, sorceress."

Ravagin favored the other with a tight smile that was ninety percent bravado. "So you know how to do basic spirit protection, do you? Not surprising. Not very impressive, either."

"Talk while you're able," the bandit responded, giving Ravagin a broken-toothed grin of his own. He continued warily forward, sword held at the ready.

"*Sa-doora-na,*" Ravagin called. "*Sa-doora-na, sa-doora-na, sa-doora-na.*"

And abruptly there were four more of him standing there.

The bandit stopped in his tracks, eyes bulging. Ravagin had rather expected him to be taken by surprise; doppelganger invocations weren't especially common. No more than a temporary solution, of course, but it ought to at least buy him the time to try something more effective. With the bandit's spirit protection in place none of the usual frontal assaults would work fast enough to be of any real use . . . but Ravagin had always prefered more subtle approaches, anyway. "*Sa-khe-khe fawkh pieslahe*; bring a flood," he intoned . . . and a second later an instant artesian well appeared between him and the bandit as the nixie he'd invoked forced ground water to the surface in obedience to his command.

The bandit spat a curse as the flow reached him, washing around his ankles and rapidly turning his footing to slippery mud. "You will die painfully, spirithandler," he snarled. Stepping sideways, he moved toward the edge of the small river flowing around him . . . heading toward the spot where Danae was crouching.

Ravagin gritted his teeth. Almost ready. . . *Now.* "*Carash-kakh!*" he snapped, releasing the nixie. The water flow cut off, the bandit staggering momentarily as the current he'd been fighting against vanished. He glanced at Ravagin, grinning—"*Sa-trahist rassh!*" Ravagin called, making the placement gesture and then crossing his fingers. With a *whoosh* of flame a firebrat blazed into existence—

And as the heat hit the water, the hillside abruptly erupted with a dense cloud of steam.

The bandit bellowed with rage, but it was a rage rapidly turning to uneasiness as the steam swallowed up his intended prey. Ravagin didn't wait for him to regain his mental balance; dodging around the blazing firebrat, he dived into the cloud, senses alert. His hand brushed the other's arm and he ducked low, jabbing his sword toward where the bandit's ribcage ought to be. A swish of air over his head showed the other's last reflexive attempt to cut him in half—

His blade jarred against bone and slid past . . . and it was over.

Ravagin backed away from the body, soaked to the skin with sweat and steam and the splashed mud of the bandit's final landing. "*Carash-carsheen,*" he said with a sigh. The firebrat vanished, and a minute later the worst of the steam had blown away. "It's all over," he called to Danae, who was still in a half crouch a dozen meters away, knife in hand.

She straightened up, eyes still looking confused . . . "Oh, right," he nodded, glancing at the four doppelgangers still surrounding him. "*Carash-meena, carash-meena, carash-meena, carash-meena.*"

The images vanished. "Cute," Danae said stiffly, jamming her knife back into its sheath as he walked up to her. Her eyes drifted once to the bloody corpse, moved quickly away. "I suppose that's just one of the tricks you pick up after you've been here awhile."

"The doppelgangers or the fire and water?"

"Both." Her lips were pressed tightly together. "The lecture probably comes next; but before you begin, whatever happened with the jinx wasn't my fault. That was the invocation spell I was taught, and if it was wrong—"

"Relax," Ravagin sighed, sheathing his sword. "The spell was fine. It was the application that you fou—that was wrong."

"What do you mean? A jinx is a spirit of confusion, isn't it?"

"Sure, but it only works if you have two or more opponents there to confuse," Ravagin explained patiently. "It's not so much an internal confusion as an external one—it's supposed to foul up coordination between adversaries, get rid of their numerical advantage over you."

"Oh." Danae grimaced. "Well . . . I'm sorry. No one ever thought to make that clear to me."

Did you think to ask? Ravagin wondered; but he kept the sarcasm to himself. "Thanks anyway," he said instead. "In the future, though, I'd rather you'd just try to keep out of my way unless I ask for help."

"Yeah. Sure." Danae turned abruptly away from him and started climbing up the nearest mound. "Well, what are we waiting for?" she snapped back over her shoulder. "If we're going to camp here overnight we'll want to set up a shelter, won't we?"

Ravagin shook his head in tired disgust. It was precisely that kind of unthinking reaction to criticism that could make a Courier's life in Karyx a hell on wheels . . . and far too often got him killed.

Taking a deep breath, he set off after her, watching the surrounding mounds closely. In case the bandit hadn't been a loner.

Chapter 11

The cool night breeze drifted across Danae's face, and for the third time since nightfall she came awake with a start. For a long minute she lay still, heart pounding, fighting against the feeling of dread that had suddenly seized her. No sounds except those of occasional insects or small animals broke the silence of the night; certainly nothing to suggest there was anyone sneaking up on them. A meter to her right, Ravagin's breathing was steady in his own sleep—surely he would have come awake himself by now if anything was amiss. *Nerves, girl,* she chided herself. *That's all—just a case of nerves.*

That, and sleeping out on a bare hillside without even a blanket between her and the hard ground. Stifling a groan, she rolled from her side onto her back, easing the ache there. Directly above her, the stars were almost hurting in their brilliance. *I wonder if they're muted like the sunlight is,* she thought. Though the way they were blazing down it hardly seemed likely.

Lowering her eyes, she gazed at and through the barely visible haze surrounding them. The lar Ravagin had invoked, circling their camp like a soundless, spectral whirlwind. Supposedly a powerful first line of defense against anything that should choose to attack them . . . Moving as quietly as possible, Danae got to her feet and began walking toward the haze. There was no resistance, no evidence of anything between her and the rest of Karyx but fog or imagination; nothing that could be remotely considered a defense—

Abruptly, the fog thickened in front of her, condensing in on itself like a reversed film of an explosion. She stopped, stomach tightening with sudden nervousness as a three-meter piller of living smoke formed in her path. For a moment she looked at it, wondering what would happen if she tried to reach out and touch it. The lar *was* supposed to be on their side, after all . . . but on the other hand it was Ravagin, not her, who had invoked it. Carefully, she backed up toward her place on the hillside, watching as the lar gradually spread itself into a defensive circle again. By the time she lay back down there was again nothing between her and the rest of Karyx but a hazy fog.

Licking her lips, she closed her eyes. *We're perfectly safe here*, she told herself. *Perfectly safe*. Eventually, she convinced herself enough to fall asleep.

But the vague feeling of dread refused to go completely away, and her dreams were troubled ones.

"We should be able to rent a couple of horses at one of the inns down the road," Ravagin told her as they finished their breakfast. "At that point the trip to Besak will only take a couple of hours."

Danae nodded silently, taking one last mouthful of aromatic meat and tossing the bone aside. Ravagin had hunted down the small animal sometime before dawn, roasting it over a fire ignited by a firebrat he'd let her invoke. The fact that she'd done the spell flawlessly was a small nugget of satisfaction against the general malaise hanging over her this morning. The bad dreams and poor sleeping conditions of the previous night, she'd decided, perhaps coupled with a lingering remnant of culture shock. Once they reached Besak and she had a halfway-decent bed to sleep in this would all blow over.

"You haven't really told me what you're doing here," Ravagin commented as he got to his feet and wiped his hands on his pant legs. "What your project is, I mean. I can't very well advise you as to location and all if I don't know that."

"There was a complete writeup in my application," she

told him, standing up herself and wincing as she followed his example on cleaning the oils from her hands. Fastidious cleanliness wasn't a major characteristic of Karyx's culture, and it wouldn't do to stand out too blatantly from the rest of the population.

"I'm sure there was, but no one showed it to me," he told her shortly as he led the way through the last line of mounds toward the road below. "Maybe you'd be good enough to give me a brief summary?"

She pursed her lips . . . but there really wasn't any reason he couldn't know most of it. "I want to study the psychology of the people here, both Karyx natives and those from the Twenty Worlds manning the way houses. Try and determine the effect such easy access to spirits has had on them."

"Sounds really interesting," he said with a distinct lack of enthusiasm "I presume you don't care that it's been done before?"

"As you were so careful to point out before, there aren't a whole lot of ways studies of Karyx can be related to the Twenty Worlds," she said tartly, annoyed despite the fact she'd half expected that reaction. "One of the few is to measure how this system of basically free wishes has affected the human psyche here. Assuming, of course, that the people here *are* true humans."

He threw her a sidelong glance. "Not going to let that one go, are you? So tell me how this is supposed to relate to the Twenty Worlds—or are you going to suggest that Karyx adult development has been arrested at the adolescent level because they can get everything done for them by spirits?"

"I'm not starting with any preconceptions," she said. "Though I *have* heard that theory."

"It's total nonsense," he said flatly. They'd reached the road now, and he paused to gaze both directions before turning them south. "There's a lot more raw wish fulfillment on Shamsheer—a lot more, for that matter, on the Twenty Worlds—than there is here. The spirits don't *like* us, Danae—if you always remember one thing about Karyx remember that. The spirits don't like us, they don't especially like running errands for us, and they hate like hell when one of us traps them into a sword or mill wheel or something. When you invoke a spirit you're almost literally taking the same chance as fiddling with an appliance without throwing the breaker first: the possibility you're going to get kicked across the room. Or worse."

She walked in silence for a few steps, digesting that. It sounded paranoid in the extreme . . . but after last night she wasn't inclined to dismiss such feelings out of hand. "You think the spirits are . . . well, out to get us somehow?"

"How could they?" he countered with a shrug. "The spells we've got have been used for centuries—if they weren't adequate, don't you think the spirits would have made some countermove long ago? The demons certainly would have done something—I think they hate us more than all the other types of spirits put together."

How do you know they haven't taken over? she thought, but resisted the urge to throw the question at him. Her penchant for argument had always been one of her weak points, and now that they were in Karyx she had to be more careful about not antagonizing people unnecessarily. "Well . . . how exactly would they go about fighting back, assuming they wanted to? Can they affect the physical universe, for example, on their own volition and without a direct human order to do so?"

Ravagin pondered for a moment. "I don't know," he admitted at last. "I've never seen one do so, but that doesn't mean a lot. I suppose if you forgot to release a spirit after you were done with him he might be able to fiddle around on his own for awhile, but why he'd want to is another question entirely. Our physical universe isn't really their environment, and rumor has it they aren't very comfortable here. They don't see things the same way we do, for one thing—they mostly just sense the presence of life. The only possible reason they could have for messing around here would be to keep us from ordering them around—and the only way to do *that* would be to keep us from voicing commands."

"Which we'd see as a rash of speech impairments," Danae nodded, picking up on his logic. "I understand."

Ravagin nodded. "Or unnatural deaths. Depending on how permanent they wanted to shut us up."

Danae shivered. The lar last night . . . "How effective is that spirit-protection spell that bandit used yesterday?"

"Reasonably so, but there are better ones. I could—" He stopped abruptly, frowning off toward the road ahead of them.

Danae held her breath, feeling her teeth clench as she heard the faint sounds of approaching hooves. "Trouble?" she whispered.

"Probably not," he murmured, reaching down to loosen his sword in its sheath. "You get a little paranoid after you've traveled on Karyx enough. If any trouble starts, though, you're to get to the side of the road and invoke a lar around yourself—you remember the spell?"

She nodded. The dust of the approaching horses was visible now, obscuring any details of riders. "Should we do something like that before they get here? Just in case?"

He smiled tightly. "It's a fine point of Karyx etiquette that you don't want to be the first one to invoke a spirit, especially a defensive one like a lar. It would either be construed as an insult—that we don't trust them—or, worse, that we have something devious in mind ourselves. Just stay sharp and there'll be no problem."

Danae swallowed hard. There were three horses approaching—that much could be seen now. Of riders, only the one on the center horse was visible. Danae caught glimpses of dark hair and a blue cloak through the dust . . .

Beside her, Ravagin abruptly exhaled in relief. "Well," he said. "You see?—there *are* occasionally nice surprises on Karyx."

"What?" Danae frowned, glancing at him and back at the rider, who she could now see was indeed alone . . . and was a woman.

A woman? "Ravagin . . . ?"

"Don't worry," he told her. "It's a friend. Melentha, from the way house in Besak, here to give us a lift."

"Oh." Danae licked her lips. It certainly would beat walking . . . but as the party approached she couldn't help noticing that there was something odd about the two riderless horses flanking Melentha's. An unnatural intelligence or alertness about them, perhaps, beyond anything she could ever remember seeing in an animal. *Bio-*

enhanced? she wondered fleetingly before remembering where she was. Animals, bio-enhanced or ordinary, were incapable of passing the Tunnels' telefolds. But then . . . ?

"Well met, Ravagin," Melentha called as she reined to a halt a few meters before them. The other two animals likewise stopped, without any obvious command from the woman. "I didn't expect to have to come this far to find you. Did you have some trouble?"

"A little—ran into a bandit," Ravagin grunted, striding forward. "Melentha, this is Danae—she'll be here for a month or two doing some studies."

"Danae," Melentha nodded, eying Danae with cool politeness. "Are you a professor?"

"A student," Danae corrected evenly. Melentha was surely not trying to be condescending, after all. "I'm here for a field assignment—it's a psychological study—"

"That's nice." Melentha looked back at Ravagin. "Whenever you're ready. I'm sure you have better things to do than loiter along the Besak-Torralane road; I know *I* do."

"That's what everyone likes about you, Melentha—your devotion to duty and hearth," Ravagin said dryly. "We're ready any time . . . as soon as you turn the horses over to us."

"What?" Melentha glanced at the animals standing unnaturally still beside her. "Oh, come on, Ravagin—don't tell me you're getting squeemish in your old age."

Ravagin's face seemed to darken slightly. "Just humor me and do it, okay?"

"But—oh, all right." Shaking her head in disbelief, she rose up in her stirrups and looked down at the horses. "Ishnaki, Giaur: *carash-natasta, carash-natasta.*"

Danae inhaled sharply as, for just a second, both animals were abruptly sheathed in green auras. One of the horses whinnied as the auras coalesced above them into drifting humanoid figures, vanishing before they were fully formed. But from what had been visible of their faces . . . Danae shivered violently. "Ravagin—were those *demons?*" she whispered.

Ravagin's eyes were on Melentha, his expression stony. "They were indeed," he growled. "I don't suppose it's occurred to you that using a demon for trivial jobs like animal control is a damn fool thing to do."

Melentha cocked her head, making a snatch at the horses' reins as the animals, freed from their possession, began to paw the ground restlessly. "I consider it a rather smart idea, actually," she told Ravagin coolly. "It's pretty obvious you haven't tried this stunt with nothing but reins or ropes to keep the extra horses under control."

"As it happens, I have," he countered, stepping forward to take one of the ropes from her. "I also know that you can get by perfectly well with a djinn or sometimes even a sprite to keep them with you. Using a demon where it's not absolutely necessary is just plain stupid."

"I'm sorry you disapprove," Melentha said stiffly. "Try to bear in mind, though, that I don't have to answer to you or anyone else for how I run my life and way house." She looked at Danae, jerked her head toward the other horse. "Well, come on, Danae—get mounted and let's get out of here. They *did* give you some idea of how to ride, didn't they?"

"I know enough." Reaching up, Danae pulled herself smoothly into the saddle and took up the reins in the expert's grip she'd been taught in childhood back at the family estate. "Lead on—I'm anxious to get to work."

She had the satisfaction of seeing momentary surprise in each of the others' faces at her obvious equestrian experience. Then, with a slight shrug, Melentha turned her horse around and headed back south along the road. "Well, let's go, then," she called over her shoulder.

Danae swung her own mount around and followed, settling herself easily into the horse's rhythm. Ravagin pulled up alongside, and she glanced over to see him checking her technique. "Adequate?" she asked tartly.

"Oh, quite," he nodded, and dropped back behind her again into what was probably a standard rearguard position.

But before he did so she caught just the hint of a smile as it crossed his face. *Great*, she thought darkly. *Just great. He and Melentha have some sort of feud going, and I've just bought him a couple of points*. Well, that sort of nonsense was going to stop damn quick—she'd just escaped from her father's chess game and had no intention whatsoever in joining someone else's.

And yet . . .

It was the first time Ravagin had showed even a hint of approval toward her . . . and for some unknown reason it made her feel rather good.

Which in its way was more irritating even than Melentha's condescending attitude toward her. *I am* not *here to gain Ravagin's approval,* she told herself sternly; and repeated it several times until it was firmly set in her mind.

In a silence broken only by necessary conversation, the trio made their way down the road toward Besak.

Chapter 12

The village of Besak, or at least the part Danae saw as they rode toward the way house, was exactly as the Triplet information packet had painted it . . . which was, in Danae's opinion, a bad sign.

Her overwhelming first impression of the place was that it was *filthy*. The narrow streets that wound between the cottages were lined with piles of garbage, through which small half-seen animals burrowed. Some of the larger and fancier buildings had outhouses out back—or front—for their occupants' sanitary needs; how those in the smaller cottages managed she tried not to think about. Above it, a variety of odors rose and mingled to become a truly memorable stench.

The info packet had been right about the filth. It had also said Besak's inhabitants were rough, conniving, superstitious even by Karyx standards, and occasionally extremely violent.

For the moment, though, those more dangerous aspects of village life seemed to be dormant. All around them the main activity seemed to be the bustle of commerce, with no more violence in sight than occasional overloud haggling. Children ran and played in the streets, much as children anywhere in small towns in the Twenty Worlds would, their game shifting to a race around the newcomers' horses as Melentha led them along at a brisk walk. Adults, passing by them on various unknown errands, paused to bow their heads to Melentha, their eyes flicking briefly over Ravagin and Danae with obvious curiosity but no apparent hostility. No one seemed particularly clean . . . but as Danae got used to the grime, she noticed that no one seemed particularly unwell, either. *All the sick people are indoors, maybe?* But that was unlikely—people in primitive cultures could seldom afford to stay away from their work for the complete duration of an illness. *Spirit healing, then,* she concluded, the thought sending a shiver up her back. It was one thing to lie in a diagnostic chair in a spotless room with tailored biochips circulating through your body; it was something else entirely to have a living entity doing the probing.

She started abruptly as something hazily bright flashed past her face. "What—?"

"Just a sprite," Ravagin reassured her, bringing his horse up alongside hers.

She licked her lips and exhaled a ragged breath. "Good thing I wasn't galloping," she growled. "Running practically into my face like that—I could have fallen and broken my neck."

He eyed her oddly. "Yeah. Well . . . like I said, the spirits don't especially like us—"

"Nonsense," Melentha said, half turning. "There was no malace there—sprites just aren't smart enough to realize when they're doing something dangerous, that's all."

Danae looked back at Ravagin, saw the other's brief grimace, and decided to change the subject. "Strange how all these houses are built so close to each other," she commented, waving a hand toward them. "I'd think that with all the open space around for expansion they'd spread out a little more."

"You'll find most villages on Karyx are this tightly packed," he grunted. "There's a limit on how much area a single lar can protect."

"I know that, but what stops them from using more than one lar?"

"I really don't know," he frowned. "Tradition would be my first guess. Melentha, you have any ideas?"

"No," the dark-haired woman said. "But then, I haven't had all that much direct experience with lares on a village-sized scale. I know that some of the other classes of spirits don't get along well with each other—peris, especially, don't work well with other peris. Maybe that's part of it."

They passed by the edge of the village center a minute later, Melentha veering them west then onto the road that would eventually end at the riverport village of Findral some thirty kilometers away. Danae got only a brief look at Besak's central marketplace as they passed along its perimeter, but it seemed remarkably well stocked with everything from spirit-enhanced tools and weapons to the more mundane items of everyday life. *Except that spirit-enhanced items are part of everyday life here*, she had to remind herself. Though come to think of it—"Why is there a market here for bound-spirit items?" she called ahead to Melentha. "Can't the villagers do the binding part themselves and save the expense?"

"Binding any but the simplest spirits isn't as easy as your teachers probably implied," Melentha answered tartly. "*Really* binding one, I mean. Anyone can do a temporary lock, but that hardly counts."

"Actually, you'll see a lot more enhanced tools here than in most villages," Ravagin added. "There's a settlement about forty-five kilometers from here in the Morax Forest that specializes in them."

"Yes: Coven," Danae nodded. "I've heard of the place, though no one would say much about it."

"Mainly because we don't *know* much about it," Ravagin said dryly. "Coven guards its privacy closely."

"Hardly surprising when you consider that their binding spells are the local equivalent of trade secrets," Melentha said. "But that brings up another point. When you start browsing around the Besak marketplace you'll find two or three shops selling spells. Avoid them like the plague."

"Frauds?" Danae asked.

"Borderline incompetent. You're not going to get more than an eighty percent accuracy rate out of them, especially on anything really complicated, and I presume I don't have to tell you what *that* can mean. If you need to find a particular spell, ignore the locals—come to me and I'll get it for you."

"Thanks. I'll keep that in mind."

They were through the main part of town now, and within a few minutes the tight clustering of houses Danae had already noted gave abrupt way to farmland and wilderness. A few houses were visible outside the city limits, but they were far between and somehow gave Danae the feeling of small beleaguered fortresses. The bandit who'd accosted them the previous evening came to mind; surreptitiously, her hand drifted to her waist and the dagger sheathed there. "Why so far out of town?" she called ahead to Melentha.

"It's quieter," the other woman said. "Also more private—I have a lot of visitors, you know, and a single woman in this culture who has strange men dropping in on her for a few days at a time gains a poor name for herself."

Danae thought back to the reactions of the villagers they'd passed. "The townspeople seem to think highly enough of you," she pointed out.

Melentha threw her a vaguely annoyed look. "Like I said, they don't know too much about me."

Danae glanced at Ravagin, to see her own frown mirrored in his face. A small village whose inhabitants didn't know everything about everyone was almost a contradiction in terms. "I'd say they seemed more respectful than just—"

"Just drop it," Melentha cut her off. "Here we are—right through the trees here."

The trees mentioned were a double hedgerow sort of arrangement paralleling the road on their right, the rear line set into the spaces left by the first so that the view from the road was completely blocked. Melentha led them between two of the trees in the first line and around to a gap in the second . . . and Danae felt her mouth fall open.

After the unassuming way house in Kelaine City on Shamsheer she'd expected something equally modest here. It was a shock to find Melentha's "house" built more along the lines of a mansion. Three stories high, with a gleaming white exterior, it was surrounded by a large lawn in which squat green bushes and patches of brightly colored flowers had been laid out in a careful arrangement. More trees blocked the views from north and east; other trees grew in clumps elsewhere on the grounds. Surrounding the house

and most of the lawn was a rough square of posts set into
the ground perhaps five meters apart.

Danae had seen far larger and more impressive homes
before . . . but in the richer sections of her home world of
Arcadia they hadn't looked at all out of place. This one, in
the middle of Karyx, most emphatically did. "Nice place,"
she said cautiously. "A little—uh—ostentatious, though,
isn't it? I'd think it would draw bandits like moths."

"It can attract them all it wants," she said blandly.
"Actually, it's rather fun to watch a band of them trying to
get in."

Beside Danae, Ravagin swore under his breath. "The
post line. *Esporla-moonay.*"

Danae's teeth clamped tightly together. For just a second each post had been sheathed in green light . . . "Bound
demons," she breathed. "One in each post."

"Actually there's only a single demon," Melentha said,
pointing to the free-standing archway toward which they
were heading. "The ones in the rest of the pillars are his
parasite spirits. It's why I used a demon in the first place—
you can get a whole legion for the price of one entrap-
ment," she added, looking at Ravagin as if expecting another
lecture on the dangers of demon-binding.

But Ravagin merely nodded, his eyes on the archway.
Danae followed his gaze . . . and as they neared it she saw
what he'd already spotted: an evil caricature of a human
face carved into the keystone, its deep-set eyes watching
them with unnatural alertness.

Or perhaps it wasn't a carving at all. Perhaps it was the
actual visage of the trapped demon, impressed into the
stone as a side effect of the spell binding the spirit there.

Shuddering, Danae averted her eyes, and watched the
ground beneath them as they rode single file through the
arch. The unpleasant tingle she felt was almost certainly
just her imagination.

They left the horses at a small stable hidden within one
of the groups of trees and walked across the lawn toward
the main house. The flowers, Danae noted in passing,
were extremely delicate things, alive with buzzing insects,
while the squat bushes were rich in oddly shaped berries.

She wondered briefly if they were edible, decided that since the info packet hadn't mentioned them they probably weren't.

The interior of the house did nothing to spoil the majestic effect of its exterior. Here again Danae had seen better, but it was no less impressive even held against those memories. The main floor contained a library filled with rough leather-bound volumes, a kitchen that was spotless despite the primitive cooking implements, two large conversation rooms where scattered cushions seemed to serve as chairs, and—surely an oddity on Karyx—an inside bathroom. Another chamber, down the hall from the conversation rooms, was closed off. Melentha didn't offer to show that one; taking the hint, Danae didn't ask.

The guest bedrooms and a double bathroom were on the second floor. "This will be your room," Melentha told Danae, leading the way into an airy room on one of the front corners of the house. "I'm sorry I can't offer you one with a private bathroom, but I decided against building the house like that. You have to remember that even having the things indoors is somewhat radical here, and I can't afford to be *too* far out of step."

"Sure," Danae nodded, stepping to one of the south-facing windows and moving aside the gauze curtain. The lawn, with all its splashes of color, was visible below . . . as was the archway with the trapped demon. "This is fine—much nicer than I was expecting from Karyx, certainly. If I may ask, how in the worlds do you handle the, uh, mechanics of the bathrooms?"

"It's perfectly simple," Melentha shrugged. "I've got a couple of large water tanks on the third floor that feed into the showers—a bound nixie keeps them filled for me and there's a firebrat in one to heat it. I don't suppose you've ever seen an old-style flush toilet?—well, trust me, they're noisy but perfectly adequate. Another tank holds water for that purpose; the wastes run down pipes to an underground chamber where three firebrats under a djinn's control disintegrate it all into component atoms and dump everything into the ground water."

"Clever," Danae murmured.

"Straightforward, really," Melentha said. "There's a lot

you can accomplish on Karyx if you have even a vague conception of science to complement your spirithandling."

"As long as you don't let it run away with you," Ravagin spoke up from the other side of the room, where he was peering out one of the windows facing east. "Too much and you'll attract attention from the locals. How many of them are you employing here, incidentally?"

"Just four," Melentha said, face hardening again. "All but one leave at night, and the fourth has a small room off the kitchen. The rules *do* permit me to hire locals, you know."

Ravagin turned back to her. "I'm aware of that," he said mildly. "How many other visitors do you have at the moment?"

"One group; five men, two women. They're out at Findral at the moment, not due back until tomorrow, and then they're due to leave. No one else, though of course I can't ever be sure when someone will drop in."

Ravagin nodded and shifted his attention to Danae. "Will you be wanting to do your studies here in Besak, or would you prefer to pick a different village?"

It was surprisingly difficult for Danae to force her mind back onto what was by now a very familiar track. Such esoteric concepts as statistics and psychological comp/correlation seemed jarringly out of place in such a setting. "No, Besak will be fine," she managed. "Though I'd like to try working up a correlation of attitudes in Findral or Torralane Village, too, if we have the time."

"Thought about how you're going to go about it?" he asked.

"More or less." She looked at Melentha. "I plan to offer either a brand-new item or an improvement on an existing one to the merchants and people of Besak—I'll want to discuss with you later which of my possibilities would be best received."

Melentha frowned. "What do you expect to prove?"

"It should give me a measure of their receptiveness to new things; and since I'll also be offering a spirit-enhanced version of the same item, I'll get at least a preliminary reading on their feelings toward the use of bound spirits. I'll need your help for the binding spells, of course."

"Um," Melentha grunted, clearly not impressed. "Sure, all right, I'll give you whatever help you need."

"Thanks," Danae said, giving the other a tentative smile. Getting on better terms with the woman couldn't hurt, and would probably help in the long run. "When do you want to sit down and discuss it?"

"Tonight," Melentha said promptly. "I have some things that need to be done before sundown, and you ought to take some time to orient youself anyway. Maybe go into Besak and have a look around—I can give you one of my people as a guide if you want."

Danae glanced at Ravagin. "You know the way around Besak, don't you?"

"Well enough," he replied. "Though we might need one of Melentha's employees to get back in through the post line."

"Oh. Right." Danae shivered at the memory of that inhuman face.

But Melentha shook her head. "There'll be no problem with that. I'll just instruct the demon that you're my guests and have free access to the house and grounds. It's as simple as that." Stepping across the room, she opened a sliding panel to reveal a well-stocked closet. "If you're going to pass yourself off as a trader in bound-spirit goods, you'll need to change into something more appropriate to your station," she said, locating an intricately embroidered robe and holding it out for Danae's inspection. "This one will give you instant attention—I got it from a traderess from Coven, and it bears their emblem." She indicated a series of golden threads weaving in and out of the metallic red-and-blue pattern tracking diagonally across the robe's front.

Ravagin stepped to Melentha's side to take a closer look at the thread pattern. "That's Coven, all right," he agreed slowly. "Where did you get this, Melentha?"

She smiled slyly. "Suffice it to say no one's going to miss it."

"Uh-*huh*. And you want Danae to go walking around in broad daylight dressed in it? Forgive the bluntness, but that strikes me as rather stupid."

"Why?" Melentha countered. "Don't you think it would guarantee that no one in Besak would give her any trouble?"

"No one except possibly another Coven trader."

Melentha's expression turned patient. "Ravagin, you've become a real worlds-class worrier—anyone ever mention that to you? Why would a Coven trader care if she was dressed in a robe from his town?"

"Maybe because they don't like unauthorized people claiming Coven quality for their merchandise," Ravagin gritted. "That ever occur to you?"

"But this isn't an offical trader's robe," Melentha said blandly. "It was part of the traderess's sale stock. Didn't I mention that?"

No you certainly did not, Danae thought, eyes flicking between the other two. *Short-term memory damage? Or was she just baiting him?*

The latter, obviously. Melentha's expression—wide-eyed innocent, but with more than a hint of amusement showing through—made that clear. She'd planned to trap Ravagin into an argument and then pull the floor out from under him, and she'd succeeded.

And it was clear from *his* expression that he didn't like it at all. Danae didn't blame him; her own disagreements with him aside, the trick struck her as childish. "Thanks anyway, Melentha," she said into the brittle silence, "but if Ravagin doesn't think I should wear the robe—"

"When did I say that?" Ravagin snapped, shifting his glare to her. "You want to wear the damn thing, go ahead and wear it." With a last look at Melentha, he spun around and stalked toward the hallway door. "Let me know when you want to head out, Danae," he called over his shoulder as he disappeared down the hall. A moment later the floor vibrated slightly in time with the slamming of his door.

For a long moment the two women eyed each other in silence. "Any particular reason you did that to him?" Danae asked at last.

A flicker of something almost painful-looking passed over Melentha's face . . . but before Danae could read anything from it an almost arrogant calm had taken its place. "Not really," she said coolly. "Though perhaps he'll be less likely to criticize my methods now that he's aware he doesn't know everything." She walked forward and laid the robe across one edge of Danae's bed. "Why don't you take an hour or two to rest and then try the robe on. If Ravagin's still sulking after that, I'll have one of my people take you into Besak." Without pausing for an answer, she turned and glided out into the hall, shutting the door behind her.

Grimacing, Danae sat down on the other side of the bed, feeling the firmness of the mattress beneath the quilt. *So much for appealing to her better instincts*, she thought, a mild taste of disgust staining her tongue. *An effect of Karyx, or was she just that kind of malicious personality to begin with?*

Hard to tell . . . and at the moment she almost didn't care. It was slowly becoming apparent that they weren't especially wanted here, and for a minute she considered going to Ravagin and telling him she'd changed her mind, that she'd decided to move their operation to Torralane Village after all.

Her eyes fell on the robe. It was made of a soft, velvety material that promised its wearer comfort as the woven red and gold promised her elegance. A lovely garment . . . and if Melentha thought that sparking friction over it could force her guests to move out, she'd damn well better call for a recount.

Pushing the robe over, Danae stretched out on the bed and closed her eyes. Melentha had been right about one thing, anyway—a quick nap was just what she needed. An hour's sleep, no more, and she'd be ready to take on Besak and everyone in it.

And not until she was fully rested would she decide whether or not to wear the damn robe.

Moments later, she fell asleep, her fingers gradually ceasing their idle carressing of the robe as they came to rest on the almost too-soft material.

Chapter 13

The weapons dealer snorted with contempt as he glanced at the small bow in Danac's hands and then looked back down at the knife he was honing. "What you have there is a toy for children, my lady," he told her. "I deal in goods for real hunters, not those playing games in the streets. Take your business to someone more appropriate and save us both our time."

"You are indeed remarkable, tradesman," Danae said calmly, "to have the courage to so quickly dismiss Andros's claim that he shot an arrow over five hundred *varna* with this same bow."

The dealer looked up abruptly. "*This* is the one Andros did that with?" he asked cautiously. "I'm—I mean, I'd heard of that, of course, but. . . ."

He trailed off. Wordlessly, Danae held the bow out, and with a sour twitch of his lip the other took it and began to examine it. Slowly the last remnants of skepticism left his face, to be replaced by admiration and cautious interest. "I have never seen such a bow," he said at last, looking up. "What is the manner of its construction?"

"It's called a composite bow," Danae told him, tracing the sections with her fingers. "Five parts of wood are fastened together—here are the joints—with two pieces of bone extending from center to one of the ends and a layer of sinew backing the entire bow." It was the ancient bowmaking method of the Turks of Earth, and it had taken

Danae a solid week to track down the technique back at the university. But the aggravation all those computer hours had cost her was rapidly being paid back. Virtually all bows on Karyx were of the single-piece self bow type, and in the three days since she'd begun showing this new design around Besak the word was sweeping the village. The interest she'd hoped to generate was there in trumps; the only trick now would be to avoid getting herself talked into starting a composite bow factory to handle all the men who wanted to order one.

The dealer nodded slowly, looking closely at the points Danae had identified. "It must be an extremely strong glue, to be able to hold the pieces against the tension," he said. "Or is there a bound spirit within the bow for that purpose?"

"This one is indeed held together only by glue," she said, eyes and ears primed to pick up all the nuances of his reaction. "However, the same bow *is* available with a bound djinn for even greater strength."

The other nodded again, face thoughtful. *A brief hint of displeasure when I mentioned the bound djinn?* Danae wondered. Hard to tell. If the dealer had a preference one way or the other, it was a small one. "I see," he said. "With a corresponding difference in price, of course?"

"Of course."

"Um." He frowned, hands running over the bow, and she saw his eyes stray across her robe and the subtle Coven markings woven there. Ravagin continued to be less than pleased by her decision to wear the garment, but even he had had to admit that it had helped her get a hearing for her bow from Besak's business community.

A cloud seemed to pass across her eyes, darkening Karyx's already dim sunlight even further. Danae squeezed her eyes shut, and when she blinked them open her vision had cleared. That sort of thing had been happening more and more frequently to her lately, and she was starting to wonder if she was coming down with some kind of illness. She fervently hoped not; on Karyx the chief diagnostic method was to send a spirit into the patient's body to check things out, and the whole idea sent chills up her back.

"What are you asking for this bow, my lady?" the dealer asked, breaking in on her thoughts.

"This particular bow is not for sale," she told him, fighting to keep her annoyance at herself out of her voice. This tendency to woolgather at the wrong time was also becoming more and more of a habit. "I'm merely showing it to interested persons, to ascertain whether or not it would serve us to produce quantities of them."

The merchant's face registered surprise and some chagrin at the unusual procedure, quickly shifted to calculated slyness. "You wouldn't, I presume, be doing all the selling yourself," he said carefully. "Perhaps you'd be interested in striking a bargain whereby I would market your bows for you?"

Danae cocked an eyebrow thoughtfully, as if the plan had never before occurred to her. At least two other merchants and hunters had already presented her with this "authorized dealer" idea—a concept, according to Ravagin, that wasn't common to the culture. It was a tribute to Besak's sophistication and business acumen, and a warning to pay attention lest she get herself into a bargaining pit she couldn't get out of. "That's an interesting offer, tradesman," she said carefully, "but I fear that the making of such deals is still in the future. Should those who sent me choose to produce these bows for general sale, though, I will surely remember your suggestion. And your name."

The other bowed respectfully. "Thank you, my lady. I will look forward to dealing further with you in the future."

Danae nodded back and moved away from the other's booth. Ravagin was supposed to be loitering off to the side somewhere around here—

"How did it go?" his voice came from directly over her shoulder.

She jumped, twisting around to glare up at him. "I wish you'd break that habit of sneaking up on people," she growled. "It went okay, I suppose. We've certainly got another market outlet if Melentha ever wants to start making Turkish bows, if that's what you mean."

"Don't laugh—she's just the sort who might go ahead

and do it. Hold it a second," he added as she started to turn away.

"What is it?"

For a moment he didn't answer. Holding her head firmly between his hands, he gazed intently into her face . . . and as she returned his stare she noticed for the first time that the blue of his eyes was tinged with gray. It was a rather unusual combination, one she found oddly attractive . . . Pursing his lips, he released his grip on her head. "Nothing, I guess," he said. "I thought something looked funny about your pupils. But I guess I was wrong."

She licked her lips, thinking about her moments of faded vision. "There wasn't anything in the packet about unusual diseases here," she said.

"This isn't a real disease," he shook his head. "It's more of a—well, a syndrome, I guess—that I've noticed affecting some of the clients I've brought in. Come on, you wanted to talk to one more dealer today before we headed back, right?"

They started down the crowded pathway between dealers' stalls. "Only visitors?" Danae probed gently. "Not the way house keepers or other Couriers?"

He shot her a sidelong look. "I haven't had as much opportunity to observe either group," he said. "Is the next question why I haven't reported this?"

She felt her mouth tighten before she could stop it. "All right, why haven't you?"

"Because all the symptoms disappear before we get back to Threshold, of course. Even here it's more of an annoyance than anything else—certainly nothing life-threatening or even debilitating. Besides which, half the time the victim wasn't even aware anything was wrong with them."

"And so naturally resisted any suggestion that they let you get them out of Karyx immediately?"

He shrugged. "You can hardly blame them, considering what it costs to get in here in the first place. Eventually, I learned not to mention it unless they did."

"You broke the rule with me."

He smiled bitterly. "What're you going to do, get me fired? I was on my way to a leave of absence anyway when you and your moneycard father hijacked me."

"When we—what?" She frowned up at him. "What do you mean?"

"Never mind. The dealer we'll be talking to next is named—"

"Don't change the subject," she cut in. "If you think you can drop a line like that and expect me to ignore it, you've got the wrong lady. What do you mean, we hijacked you?"

Ravagin's jaw tightened momentarily, and he gave a slight shrug. "I don't suppose it really matters. You asked for the most experienced Courier on Triplet, which happened to be me. I wanted to turn it down, but the people above me decided they wouldn't take no for an answer. End of story."

Danae felt her stomach tighten. No wonder he was so antagonistic toward her. "Oh, hell. Ravagin—look, I'm sorry. I had no idea—I didn't think anyone would pull something that shabby."

"Of course you didn't," he grunted. "You've never shown *any* tendency to think out consequences in advance. And you know why?—because you've always had Hart or someone like him trailing along behind you to clean up any messes you make before you can see them."

"Oh?" she snapped back, loudly enough to attract brief attention from some of the passersby. "And *you*, of course, are one of those who have to clean up our messes, huh? Is *that* why you don't like me?"

"Keep your voice down," he growled, starting to walk again. "Unless you want to announce you're from somewhere no one here's ever heard of. And take any consequences."

Danae gritted her teeth, taking a few quick steps to catch up with him. *Primitive culture*, she reminded herself . . . and primitive cultures were not known for being open-armed toward strangers. "All right, all right," she muttered, pacing him again and forcing herself to cool down. "Where's this other dealer you had in mind for me to see?"

"This way." Ravagin gestured off toward their right. Danae nodded and followed as he turned off on a sidestreet. The cloud was trying to obscure her vision again. . . .

"Hey!"

She came to with a jerk to find Ravagin standing in front

of her, gripping her upper arms hard enough to hurt. "What do you think you're doing?" she asked, wondering how he'd gotten in front of her without her noticing the move.

His face was tight. "You started off in the wrong direction and ignored me when I called after you," he said. "Didn't you hear me?"

She licked her lips, something cold closing around her heart. "No. I don't—we had just finished our discussion and had . . . made a right turn toward the weapons dealer . . ." She stopped as his expression tightened a bit more. "All right, let's hear the bad news. How much did I miss?"

"About two minutes, I think," he told her grimly. "How do you feel?"

She paused, trying to take internal stock through the panic starting to simmer inside her. "Fine. Really. Except for being scared as hell."

"You sure you don't remember anything?" he asked. "You *do* have a tendency to get lost in your thoughts."

She thought to glance around before answering. No crowd had gathered; none of the passersby seemed to be paying them any attention. "I've had a full high-retention mnemonic treatment, remember? There ought to be *something* there—and there isn't. It's as if I'd been sound asleep."

Ravagin nodded. "Yeah. All right, let's get back to the horses and get the hell back to the way house." His eyes fell on the bow she still carried; without comment he reached down and plucked it from her grasp. "Probably nothing, but we'd better get it checked out, fast."

"Sure." Danae took a deep breath. "Ravagin . . . please hold me."

For an instant she was afraid he'd misinterpret; but he didn't. "Don't worry," he assured her, turning her gently and putting a firm arm around her shoulders as they started back to where they'd tied their horses. "I've never yet had a client wander away from me. I'm not going to start now."

Chapter 14

She lay quietly on the bed with her eyes closed, arms and legs spread slightly away from her body, a somewhat gauzy sheet from armpits to thighs her only covering. Under other circumstances, Ravagin thought vaguely, he might have had a hard time keeping his eyes and thoughts at professional levels. But as it was, he had far more serious things than Danae's body on his mind.

"*Esporla-meenay!*" Melentha intoned, her hands tracing out intricate contrapuntal patterns in front of her. "*Askhalon-mistoonla. Olratohin kailistahk!*"

Nothing. No momentary aura, no sparks or shimmers anywhere on or near Danae's body. Ravagin pursed his lips, stole a glance away from her across the bed to where Melentha stood. "Well?" he prompted.

Melentha shrugged, an annoyed frown creasing her forehead. "I'm afraid that's my whole repertoire of spirit-detection spells. If something's in there playing games with her, I can't coax it out."

"Are there any spiritmasters in Besak these days?" he asked, looking back at Danae. Her eyes were open now, looking up at him . . . and while she was putting on a good front, it was obvious she was still scared. "He'd know other spells to try, maybe even a general exorcism we wouldn't need a full identification for."

"We don't have anyone of that caliber in Besak," Melentha shook her head. "The nearest would probably be in Citadel, and there's no guarantee he'd have the time or inclination to look at her."

"What about Coven?" Danae asked. "Surely they have spiritmasters there—they make all those bound-spirit gadgets, after all."

Ravagin cocked an eyebrow at Melentha, though he was pretty sure he knew what her response would be. "Feasible?"

"I'd rather take my chances with Citadel," she said shortly. "I don't know anyone who's ever been to Coven—rumor has it that visitors are intensely discouraged."

"So what do we do?" Danae asked, a slight tremor creeping into her voice.

Melentha sat down on the edge of the bed and took Danae's wrist. "How do you feel?" she asked, fingers locating the pulse and resting there a moment.

Danae's eyes unfocused briefly, and for a second Ravagin thought she was fading out again. But then she shook her head and shrugged. "I feel fine, I guess. Nothing hurts anywhere, and I'm not lightheaded or dizzy. Vision hasn't slipped lately, either."

"Any family history of epilepsy?" Melentha asked.

"They wouldn't have let her come in with something like that," Ravagin put in.

"And there isn't any in my family, anyway," Danae confirmed.

"Just eliminating the obvious." Melentha paused, frowning. "I don't know what else to try. I'll check the bow, see if one of the spirits we used to help assemble the thing somehow got left in it. But the chances of that are really too small to worry about."

"While you're at it, you might also check out that robe," Ravagin told her, jerking his thumb at the garment hanging over a nearby chair.

"Oh, come on, Ravagin," Melentha snorted. "Let's at least be reasonable about this."

"What's unreasonable? The damn thing comes from Coven—who knows *what* they might have done to it?"

"But—oh, all right. If it'll make you happy." Standing up, Melentha circled the bed and scooped up the robe. "I'll be doing both of them up in my lab, where I can have them in a pentagram. Just in case. You'll want to watch, I presume?"

"Yeah." Ravagin eyed Danae, noted the tightness around her mouth. "Go ahead and get set up; I'll be up in a minute."

Melentha nodded and left the room. "How're you doing?" Ravagin asked, taking a step toward the bed.

"How many times are you two going to ask me that?" Danae said irritably. "When something changes I'll let you know. Would you get me some clothes?"

"Don't you think you ought to stay in bed a little longer?"

"You sound like Daddy Dear," she snorted. "I'm fine—and I want to watch Melentha run the bow and robe through that rinse cycle of hers. Look, either get me some clothes or turn your back and let me do it, huh?"

Ravagin considered pointing out he'd already seen her naked, decided that she probably wouldn't appreciate the reminder. Wordlessly, he stepped to the window and leaned his elbows on the sill. "Help yourself," he called over his shoulder.

A moment of silence, followed by the sounds of her getting off the bed and padding over to the closet. Outside, the sun was nearing the horizon, throwing long shadows from the trees and post line surrounding the house. Ravagin's eyes flicked to the free-standing gateway, his memory bringing up the unwelcome image of the trapped demon's face frozen into the keystone there. *Why the hell does she have to play around so much with demons?* he wondered blackly. *If she'd at least treat them like touchy high-explosives instead of household pets—*

"You've noticed the pentagram out there, I suppose," Danae commented from behind him.

"Pentagram?" he asked, almost turning around but catching himself in time. "Where?"

"Around the whole house," she said, her voice frowning. "At least, I *thought* it was a pentagram. It starts at the gateway, goes in to those bushes flanking the entryroad, then out to the clumps of trees to left and right—"

"Yeah, wait a second." He frowned, tracing the subtle lines she'd described and locating the others within his field of view. Keeping his back to the room's interior, he moved over to the east-facing window to see if the pattern continued to that side . . . and damned if she wasn't right. "Now *that* really takes first prize," he muttered. "What the hell does she think she'd doing?"

"It *is* a pentagram, then?"

"Oh, it's a pentagram, all right—the lines are too symmetrical to be accidental. Though I've never heard of one made using trees and shrubs this way."

"Could she have trapped spirits in them or something?"

"Who knows *what* she could have done?" he growled. "Personally, I'm more concerned at the moment about the *why* of it. Pentagrams don't play the same role on Karyx that they do in Earth mythology—they're more of a mental focuser than anything with real power. But you usually don't use them at all unless you're working a really complex spell—invoking a peri or better or binding something permanently."

"Well . . . there's the demon in the post line," Danae pointed out, coming up beside him to frown out the window herself. She'd put on a pale blue gown with attached cloak, a sideways glance showed him, and was working on getting its accompanying sash tied properly. "There're also the nixies and firebrats of her plumbing system, remember."

"She'll have bound them using the smaller pentagrams in her sanctum," he shook his head. "And once they're bound you don't need anything external to contain them." For a moment he thought hard, trying to come up with something else. But the effort drew him a complete blank. Melentha knew far more about spirithandling than he did, and the only way he was likely to find out what she was up to would be to ask her.

If he could then be sure he could believe her answer.

"Damn," he muttered under his breath. "I wish we'd gone to Torralane Village instead of here."

"You knew her well before, didn't you?" Danae asked quietly.

"Reasonably well. She's been here—I don't know how long now. We always got along together—" He cut off that line of thought abruptly. The past was the past, and not something to dwell on. "She was always highly competent at dealing with the oddities of this world," he said instead, "and no matter what happened she never lost an underlying sense of humor about it all. *And* she was never this flip about the dangers of using and binding demons. That's what bothers me the most."

Danae was silent for a moment. "So what happened?"

"I wish I knew. Most of my trips the last couple of years have been to either the Torralane region or Citadel. I guess that somehow, while my back was turned, something happened to change her."

"She scares me a little," Danae admitted. "I don't know why, exactly. There's a hard edge beneath the surface that never seems to let go—and there's no sense of humor anywhere in her that I can find, either." She hunched her shoulders as if with sudden chill. "I expected to find changes in people who'd been living here, but I think with her I got more than I bargained for."

"Hmm." Ravagin sighed and turned away from the window. "Well, we'd better get downstairs if we're going to watch her go through her paces—" He broke off suddenly as Danae's words seemed to sink in and trip just the right set of synapses. "Just a second. What did you mean about seeing changes in people who'd been living here?"

Danae's face suddenly went rigid. "Uh . . . well, you know—I told you I was here to study the psychological effects of Karyx on the people here—"

"On the *inhabitants* is what you told me." The faint suspicion was rapidly becoming a full-blown certainty . . . and he didn't like it a damn bit. "You're primarily here to study those of us from the Twenty Worlds, aren't you? Melentha, and me—*damn* you, anyway," he interrupted himself as the last bit fell into place. "*That's* why you asked for the Courier who'd spent the most time on Karyx, isn't it? I'm your chief laboratory rat, the one you've got time to do a leisurely dissection of. Aren't I?" In a rush all of it came back to him, to be seen anew in this freshly kindled light: her probing questions into his feelings and thoughts, her tendency to pick unnecessary arguments, even her infuriating habit of questioning the judgment of the man whose specific expertise she'd supposedly asked for. "Is that why you were always questioning my decisions?

—because you assumed fifteen years in the Hidden Worlds had singed my faculties?"

"Ravagin, listen—"

"You deny it?" He was almost trembling with anger now, hands aching with the desire to slap her across the room. "Go ahead—tell me I'm wrong. Go ahead."

Her face was twisted with anguish, her eyes bright with tears. "Ravagin, I didn't mean—yes, *yes*, that's why I asked for the most experienced Courier. But it's not the way you make it sound—"

"Of course not—my logic center's been damaged, too, hasn't it?" he snarled, perversely pleased at the way his words deepened the pain on her face. "Well, good luck to you and the trusty old scientific method. I hope you've got plenty of data tucked away, because it's all you're going to get."

Without waiting for a reply he shouldered past her and strode out of the room, resisting the urge to slam the door behind him. The way Melentha was acting these days she'd probably find his fury a source of private amusement, and he was damned if she was going to get any more of that out of him than she already had. *Everyone around me, people I've known and trusted—it's like a damn conspiracy.* Breathing deeply as he stomped down the hall, he headed for the stairs and Melentha's sanctum-cum-laboratory on the floor above.

She was waiting when he arrived, the composite bow centered in a blood-red pentagram inscribed on the floor. "I thought I was going to have to start without you," she said.

"Sorry I'm late," he said briefly. "Let's get to it."

She gave his face a speculative look, but turned back to the pentagram without comment and began the first spell. A few minutes later Danae quietly joined them, her face pale but otherwise composed. Ravagin ignored her, and she took the hint; and standing together they watched in silence as Melentha ran through her repertoire of detection spells, first on the bow and then on the Coven robe.

And in both cases found nothing.

Chapter 15

The way house had been quiet for over an hour by the time Karyx's moon rose that night, its fingernail-clipping crescent adding only token assistance to the dim starlight already illuminating the grounds. Sitting on the mansion's garret-floor widow's walk, his back against the door, Ravagin watched the moon drift above the trees to the east and listened to the silence of the night. And tried to decide what in blazes he was going to do.

There actually *were* precedents for this kind of situation; loose precedents, to be sure, and hushed up like crazy by the people upstairs in the Crosspoint Building, but precedents nonetheless. Every so often a Courier and his group would have such a mutual falling out that continuing on together was out of the question . . . and when that happened the Courier would often simply give notice and quit, leaving the responsibility for getting the party back to Threshold in the hands of the nearest way house staff. Triplet management ground their collective teeth when it happened, but they'd long ago come to the reluctant conclusion that clients were better off alone than with a Courier who no longer gave a damn about their safety.

And Ravagin wouldn't even have to endure the usual frothmouthed lecture that would be waiting when he got back. He was finished with the Corps, and those who'd bent his fingers into taking this trip had only themselves to blame for the results. He could leave a note with Melentha,

111

grab a horse, and be at the Cairn Mounds well before daylight. By the time Danae had finished sputtering, he'd have alerted the way house master in Feymar Protectorate on Shamsheer and be on a sky-plane over the Ordarl Mountains . . . and by the time she made it back through to Threshold and screamed for Hart and vengeance, he'd have picked up his last paychit, said bye-and-luck to Corah, and boarded a starship for points unknown.

He could do it. No one would do anything more than yell at him . . . and best of all, even Danae couldn't complain too loudly about it. After all, she'd only wanted him for a test subject, and his leaving her on Karyx would be a dandy data point to add to her collection. Ravagin, the great veteran Courier, actually deserting a client. Genuinely one for the record books.

Yes. He would do it. He would. Right now. He'd get up, go downstairs, and get the hell out of here.

Standing up, he gazed out at the moon . . . and slammed his fist in impotent fury on the low railing in front of him.

He couldn't do it.

"Damn," he muttered under his breath, clenching his jaw hard enough to hurt. "Damn, damn, *damn.*"

He hit the railing again and inhaled deeply, exhaling in a hissing sigh of anger and resignation. He couldn't do it. No matter what the justification—no matter that the punishment would be light or nonexistent—no matter even that others had done it without lasting stigma. He was a *professional*, damn it, and it was his job to stay with his clients no matter what happened.

Danae had wounded his pride. Deserting her, unfortunately, would hurt it far more deeply then she ever could.

In other words, a classic no-win situation. With him on the short end.

And it left him just two alternatives: continue his silent treatment toward Danae for the rest of the trip, or work through his anger enough to at least get back on civil terms with her. At the moment, neither choice was especially attractive.

Out in the grounds, a flicker of green caught his eye. He looked down, frowning, trying to locate the source.

Nothing was moving; nothing seemed out of place. Could there be something skulking in the clumps of trees, or perhaps even the shadows thrown by the bushes?

Or could something have tried to break through the post line?

Nothing was visible near the section of post line he could see. Cautiously, he began easing his way around the widow's walk, muttering a spirit-protection spell just to be on the safe side.

Still nothing. He'd reached the front of the house and was starting to continue past when a movement through the gap in the tree hedge across the grounds to the south caught his attention. He peered toward it . . . and a few seconds later it was repeated further east.

A horseman on the road toward Besak, most likely . . . except that Besak had long since been sealed up for the night by the village lar. And Karyx was not a place to casually indulge in nighttime travel. Whoever it was, he was either on an errand of dire emergency or else—

Or else hurrying away from an aborted attempt to break in through the post line?

Ravagin pursed his lips. *"Haklarast,"* he said. It was at least worth checking out.

The glow-fire of the sprite appeared before him. "I am here, as you summoned," it squeaked.

"There's a horse and human traveling on the road toward Besak just south of here," he told it. "Go to the human and ask why he rides so late. Return to me with his answer."

The sprite flared and was gone. Ravagin watched it dart off across the darkened landscape and then, for lack of anything better to do while he waited, continued his long-range inspection of the post line. Again he found nothing; and he was coming around to the front of the house again when the sprite returned. "What answer?" he asked it.

"None. The human is not awake."

"Are you sure?" Ravagin asked, frowning. He'd once learned the hard way about the hazards of sleeping on horseback—most Karyx natives weren't stupid enough to try it. "Really asleep, not injured?"

"I do not know."

Of course it wouldn't—spirits didn't see the world the way humans did. "Well . . . is he riding alone, or is there a spirit with him protecting him from falls?"

"There is a djinn present, though it is not keeping the human from falling. There is no danger of that."

And with a djinn along to—"What do you mean? Why isn't he going to fall?"

"The human is upright, in full control of the animal—"

"Wait a second," Ravagin cut it off. "You just told me he was asleep. How can he be controlling the horse?"

"The human is asleep," the sprite repeated, and Ravagin thought he could detect a touch of vexation in the squeaky voice. "It is in control of its animal."

"That's impossible," Ravagin growled. "He'd have to be—"

Sleepwalking.

"*Damn!*" he snarled, eyes darting toward the place where the rider had vanished, thoughts skidding with shock, chagrin, and a full-bellied rush of fear. *Danae*—

His mental wheels caught. "Follow the rider," he ordered the sprite. "Stay back where you won't be spotted by any other humans, but don't let her out of your sight. First give me your name, so I can locate you later. Come on, give—I haven't got time for games."

"I am Psskapsst," the sprite said reluctantly.

"Psskapsst, right. Now get after it—and *don't* communicate with that djinn."

The glow-fire flared and skittered off. Racing along the widow's walk, Ravagin reached the door and hurried inside. Danae's room was two flights down, on the second floor; on a hunch, he stopped first on the third floor and let himself into Melentha's sanctum.

The room wasn't much brighter than the starlit landscape outside, the bound dazzler having been muted down from its level of earlier that evening. The place had made Ravagin's skin crawl even with good lighting, and the dark shadows stretching around the room now didn't improve it a bit. Shivering reflexively, he stepped carefully around the central pentagram and over to the table where Melentha had put the bow and Coven robe when she'd finished her spirit search.

The robe was gone.

Swearing under his breath, he turned and hurried back to the door—and nearly ran into Melentha as she suddenly appeared outside in the hallway. "What are you doing in there?" she demanded, holding her robe closed with one hand and clutching a glowing dagger in the other.

"The Coven robe's gone," he told her, "and I think Danae's gone with it."

"What?" She backed up hastily to let him pass, then hurried to catch up with him. "When?"

"Just a little while ago—I think I saw her leaving on horseback from the roof. I just want to make sure—"

They reached Danae's room and Ravagin pushed open the door . . . and she was indeed gone.

"Well, this is just great," Melentha growled as Ravagin took a quick inventory of her possessions. "What the hell does she think—"

"She's not thinking," Ravagin cut her off. "That's the whole trouble. She's into that open-eyed sleepwalking thing again. *And* she's not alone—the sprite I sent to check her out said there was a djinn accompanying her. Probably from the robe."

"That's impossible," Melentha said flatly. "I checked it thoroughly—you watched me doing it."

"So someone on Karyx knows more about trapping and disguising spirits than you do," Ravagin snapped. "That come as a big surprise? Look, never mind *how* they did it for now—we've got to get her back before she winds up dead."

Melentha nodded and headed for the door. "I'll have a couple of horses prepared right away. You want any special equipment along?"

"Bring whatever stuff you'll need if we have to do a complete exorcism," Ravagin said, following her out and turning toward his own room. "Standard survival pack, if you have one made up. *And* a good bound-spirit sword, if you've got one. Doesn't look like Danae even took a change of clothing, let alone any sort of weapon."

"I've got a dazzler sword you can use—the mate to my dagger," Melentha called from the stairway. "Though if the bandits are smart, they'll leave her alone anyway."

Yeah. Maybe. Gritting his teeth, Ravagin ducked into his room to grab a few essentials of his own. Sleepwalking or not, Danae had a fair lead on them, and it could turn out to be a very long chase.

They were on her trail within fifteen minutes—a trail, it turned out, that was remarkably easy to follow. Every kilometer or so Melentha sent a sprite ahead to locate Psskapsst and confirm Danae's direction, and each time the messenger came back reporting her still headed in a northeastwardly direction. Circling Besak, clearly, and the giant lar silently enfolding the village . . . and Ravagin's stomach tightened at the obvious destination the direction implied.

His fears quickly proved to be correct. The trail passed around the northern edge of Besak and continued almost due east toward the dark mass of Morax Forest. Toward it and, an hour later, into it.

"Now what?" Melentha asked tightly as they reined in beneath the first row of trees.

"We go in after her, of course," Ravagin growled, glaring ahead in a futile attempt to pierce the darkness. "I do, anyway. You probably go back and see if you can find someone who knows exactly where in Morax this Coven is located—I'd rather not trust a sprite to scout out the territory if I don't have to. Any hard information you can locate would be appreciated, too."

"No one in Besak knows anything," Melentha shook her head. "I'd have heard."

"Then send sprites to the other way houses as soon as the nighttime lares are down," he snapped. "The one in Citadel, especially—*someone* on Karyx has to know something about the place."

"All right." Melentha twitched the reins, turning her horse back around toward Besak and home. "How do I find you?"

"I'll send out sprites periodically. Let me have that provision bag, huh?"

She tossed the double satchel over the back of his horse. "What if you can't send out any sprites?"

"Why wouldn't I—? Oh. Hell. Well . . . if they're interested in blocking even outgoing spirits, I'm in trouble anyway."

"Oh, that's a *fine* attitude," she snorted. "Nothing like walking up and putting your head on the block for them.'""

"All suggestions cheerfully received. You got one?"

"At least wait until morning to head in there." She tossed her head back toward the trees. "Forests aren't fun to travel through in total darkness even under normal conditions, which these certainly aren't. Besides which, who knows what sort of nocturnal eating machines live here?"

"I suppose I'll find out, won't I?" Ravagin gritted. "Look, Melentha, I don't have any choice in this. Danac's my client, and I have to do my damnedest to get her out before anything happens to her. You've never been a Courier; you wouldn't understand."

"I suppose not." Melentha sighed. "All right—I guess all I can do for now is wish you bye-and-luck. And suggest you try and avoid doing any more spirit invocation than you absolutely have to."

"Agreed. See you later."

She nodded and galloped away. Biting at his lip, Ravagin watched her go, then reached into his pack and pulled out a stone and a long, tightly wrapped cylinder. He'd been ridiculed more than once by his fellow Couriers for making and carrying such things around on a world where light and fire were there for the invoking . . . but maybe he was about to get the last laugh.

Assuming he survived this at all, of course.

The dazzler sword lit the forest up briefly as he drew it from its sheath. Advertising his presence to anyone who happened to be watching . . . Ignoring the knot in his gut, he swung the sword, striking the stone in his hand a grazing blow. A shower of sparks burst out and onto the tip of the cylinder, igniting the highly flammable resin saturating it there. The torch flared brightly for a few seconds, then settled down to a quieter, steadier glow.

Fire and light. With luck, maybe even animals who were used to the presence of firebrats and dazzlers would shy away from it in this form. With even more luck, whatever spirits Coven had protecting their forest wouldn't notice it.

Taking a deep breath, he sheathed the glowing sword and nudged his horse with his knees. Torch held firmly aloft, he headed into the forest.

Chapter 16

It was, at first, easier going than Ravagin had expected. The trees were large and well packed, with wide skirts of branches reaching out to pluck at the casual traveler, but whether by design or accident Danae had entered at a spot where a trail of sorts formed a twisted path around the worst of it. With the light from his torch pushing the darkness back a few meters, Ravagin was able to keep pretty much to the trail. Even with that mysterious djinn along to show her the way Danae was unlikely to make much better time, and urging his horse along at a fast walk Ravagin almost began to hope he'd catch up with her before they reached Coven.

Half an hour into the forest, the trail petered out.

"Damn," Ravagin muttered to himself. Drawing the sword Melentha had given him, he reluctantly dismounted, wishing like hell he could afford the time and risk of invoking a lar to encircle him. Karyx horses could be nasty fighters, and even a forest predator might think twice before tackling a man astride one. But a man down at ground level was something else again, and Ravagin had to force himself to wrench his eyes from the surrounding shadows to study the ground.

It was, fortunately, a quick job that took only a few seconds of his attention. Danae's horse had kicked up identifiable chunks of the forest mat on its way, and discerning the direction it had taken was practically child's play. A minute later Ravagin was back in pursuit, at a necessarily reduced pace.

He kept on steadily, stopping every few minutes to make sure he hadn't lost the spoor, and about two hours later came to a small clearing that was nevertheless large enough to have a circle of moonlight at its center. A safer spot for a break he wasn't likely to find for a long time. Reining up, he stopped his horse in the center of the pool of light and, with a careful look around, dismounted. Holding his dazzler sword low where its shimmer couldn't affect his night vision, he worked a stick of cured meat out of the survival pack and wearily took a bite.

"Good evening."

Ravagin jerked around, dropping the meat stick and reflexively bringing his sword into low guard position. Halfway across the clearing from him a dark human figure stood, its figure swathed in a long cloak, its face hidden from the moonlight by a wide-brimmed hat.

Ravagin swallowed, hard. The other didn't seem to be armed; but under the circumstances, that didn't mean a hell of a lot. For starters, there was no way he could have simply walked in here without Ravagin hearing him, and that implied damn good spirithandling. Or worse. "Hello," he managed.

"What brings you to Morax Forest at this time of night?" the other asked, ignoring the sword pointed in his direction.

"I'm following a friend." Ravagin told him, wishing he knew just who—or what—he was facing here. It could be a human, a doppelganger, or even a major spirit like a demon or peri. "She was brought into the forest against her will."

"What will you do when you find her?"

Ravagin licked his lips. "That depends partly on why she was brought here," he said cautiously. "Are you one who knows what that purpose is?"

"What will you do when you find her?" the figure repeated.

There was no way out of it. Not knowing which side—if any—the other was on, Ravagin couldn't guess what sort of answer would be safe and what sort would mean trouble. "I need to make sure she's safe," he said, trying to stay as neutral as possible. "She's my companion and partner—I can't just abandon her to whatever purpose she's been brought here for."

The floppy hat tilted slightly in the moonlight. "Her partner?" the figure asked. "Explain what you mean by that."

A response at last. "We travel together, she and I," Ravagin said carefully. "Uh . . . we work side by side—"

"You work with her? You aid in the creation of her goods?"

Did he know Danae had been showing her composite bow around Besak? A faint suspicion began to glimmer at the edge of Ravagin's mind. "We create our stock in trade together, yes. Why?—is Coven interested in buying our bow-making technique?"

The figure stood in silence a long moment . . . and then suddenly the hat and cloak were gone, and in the moonlight Ravagin saw the hazy figure of an impossibly perfect man. "The masters of Coven will wish to speak with you," he said, striding forward. His feet, Ravagin noted without surprise, made no noise against the fallen leaves beneath them. "You will accompany me to the village."

Ravagin swallowed. "The woman and I really wouldn't be very useful to you," he said. The glowing sword in his hand twitched around to track the peri's approach . . .

The peri smiled. *"Ahlahspereojihezrahilkma beriosparath—"*

The rest of the spell was cut off by Ravagin's gasp as a blaze of light erupted directly in front of his eyes.

Instinctively, he threw himself to the side, dimly aware that the light moved with him and that the sword in his hand had suddenly become icy cold. Twisting aside again, he hurled the weapon toward where he remembered the peri standing—

The light cut off abruptly, leaving not a trace of afterimage on his retinas to obscure his sight. The peri hadn't moved; the sword, its now dulled blade broken in two, lay at the spirit's feet. Both pieces were already thickly covered with frost, and a fog of cold air was swirling lazily around them.

For a long moment the clearing was silent. Then the peri turned and started off in the direction Ravagin had originally been going. "Come," it called back over its shoulder. "The masters of Coven will be anxious to see you."

"Yeah," Ravagin muttered under his breath. Fighting shaky knees, he climbed back onto his horse and twitched the reins to follow.

"Awaken," a disembodied voice said; and at its command, Danae did so.

Her first thought was that it was Melentha leaning over her bed; Melentha, wearing the Coven robe. An instant later her brain came more fully on track and she realized that this woman was someone else entirely, someone she'd never seen before. But the robe still looked like the one from—

Her stomach knotted in abrupt horror. Sitting bolt upright in bed, she sent her eyes flicking around the sunlit room.

Carved wood . . . textured glass in the windows . . . cured animal skin quilt-rug on the floor . . . she herself dressed in a copy of the other woman's Coven robe . . . Biting down hard on her lip, Danae looked again at the woman seated beside her bed. "So," she croaked. "I'm in Coven. Aren't I?"

The other nodded, a flicker of mild surprise crossing her face. "You're quick," she said, getting to her feet. "That's good. The others will be here soon to talk to you." Turning, she walked toward the door.

"Wait!" Danae called after her. "What do they want *me* for—?"

The firm closing of the door cut her off. "Well, *damn* it, then," Danae muttered to herself. Swinging her legs off the bed, she stood up, pausing as the abrupt change in position made her momentarily dizzy. Stepping to the window, she peered out.

Coven, without a doubt. A score or so of buildings in neat rows could be seen from her angle, most of them single-story houses of the Besak type but a few larger structures visible as well. Beyond the buildings she could see a solid wall of forest pushing in on the clearing in which the town was built. Pressing her face against the glass, she could see more of the town to either side, with the same wall of trees at the edge. The area immediately around her was deserted, but around the buildings near the edge of the clearing she could see a dozen identically robed people milling about.

Easing back from the view, she gnawed at her lip some more and tried to get her brain working. The last thing she remembered was going to bed after Melentha's failed attempts to find evidence of spirits in this robe she was wearing; right after that awkward scene with Ravagin . . .

Her stomach twisted with the memory of that argument. Ravagin had been furious with her . . . and looking at it from his point of view, she could hardly blame him. The big question now was whether he was so mad he wouldn't even bother to come after her once he found out she was missing.

No. The *real* question was whether he would be able to figure out where to start looking in the first place.

Easy, Danae, take it easy, she forced down the sudden burst of panic. Ravagin was smart—surely he and Melentha together would be able to piece two and two together and come to the logical conclusion. She was wearing the Coven robe, so they'd have the missing robe as a clue to her disappearance. So if they could just make it through Morax Forest, find Coven, and get her out from under the villagers' noses . . .

She took a deep, shuddering breath, trying without much success to force calm into her mind. For all intents and purposes, she could consider herself to be on her own.

Daddy Dear, if you could see me now, she thought sardonically. *Where are you, Hart, when I really need you?*

Stepping back from the window, she made a quick scan of the room and then walked over to the door. The first job in getting out of Coven, clearly, would be to get out of this room.

She'd expected to have to do a careful search of the room in hopes of finding some way out . . . and it was therefore something of an anticlimax to discover the door wasn't locked. Gritting her teeth, she opened it and peeked out. No one was in sight. *There has to be a catch to this*, the thought occurred to her; but there was no point standing around wondering what that catch might be. Taking a deep breath, she stepped out into the hallway—

And froze.

Insofar as sheer power was concerned, peris were generally placed above lares and one step below demons; and for that reason Ravagin made it a practice to have as little to do with them as possible. For every person like Melentha who professed perfect and casual command over the higher spirits, he'd heard a flipside story of someone who'd tried it and lost control. For him the odds weren't worth playing with.

He'd had enough interaction, though, to confirm the common belief that peris were as knowledgable as they were powerful—knowledgable about both the spirit and the physical worlds—and it was therefore something of a disappointment to discover how dull a traveling companion this particular peri was.

Presumably on purpose, of course. Whoever in Coven had set the peri up as a forest watchdog had clearly added a geas against talking too much. Ravagin's gentle probings about Coven and the Morax Forest in general were totally ignored, and eventually he gave up and concentrated instead on getting through the densely packed trees with a minimum of scratches.

They rode through the remainder of the night, and the early morning sunlight was filtering through the trees as they reached a huge clearing in the forest. "You may dismount," the peri announced.

Frowning, Ravagin reined in just past the last line of trees and looked around. A perfectly empty clearing, from the looks of it, with not even a stream or hillock to break up the flat-grass matting. "This is it?" he asked. "Coven? Where is it, underground?"

The peri turned to look at him, and for an instant Ravagin thought he could see surprise in the spirit's eyes. "Only soil and the dead are underground," the peri said. "Coven is here . . . but not yet for your eyes to perceive."

"Ah," Ravagin nodded. "We have a little blindness spell

operating here, do we? Are your masters going to lift it, or do they expect me to find the buildings by walking into them?"

"Why not try lifting it yourself?" a voice came from Ravagin's right.

Ravagin started, spinning to look at the young man gazing up at him from no more than ten meters away. *Another spirit*, was his immediate guess; but hard on the heels of that thought another possibility hit him: that the man had simply become visible by emerging from an invisible house. Certainly the figure was no peri—that much was evident from his pockmarked skin and slightly bent nose. "I greet you, sir," Ravagin said, bowing from his seat. "Do you represent the masters of Coven?"

"I am one of many," the other said with a shrug. "And you are . . . ?"

"I'm called Ravagin. Friend and co-worker of a woman named Danae, whom one of your enchanted robes brought here last night."

"Oh?" The man glanced at the silent peri. "I didn't realize we had newcomers. Well. Come with me, then. Your friend will have been taken to the center of Coven; let us go and see just what skills you possess that you have been chosen to join our community."

Ravagin paused halfway through the act of dismounting. "To . . . join you?"

"Of course. Why else do you think you've been brought here?"

Slowly, Ravagin finished his dismount. It wasn't exactly an unexpected development, but he'd rather hoped the man would at least be a bit more circumspect about it. Such an open and casual admission that he and Danae were prisoners was the sign of a great deal of power. "I don't suppose we get a choice in this?" he asked.

"Not really." The man looked at the peri. "He and the woman were the only ones?"

"I was told another human arrived with this one but left without entering the forest," the spirit replied. "I leave him in your charge, now, and will return." Without waiting for a reply, it turned and glided away, disappearing among the trees.

Ravagin watched him go and then returned his attention to the clearing. "I'm surprised you bother with blindness spells with guards like that peri all around you," he said.

"We like to be careful. Did you want to try lifting the blindness spell yourself?"

For a long moment Ravagin was tempted. He hadn't the faintest idea how to handle a blindness spell, of course . . . but with the man essentially offering him the chance to get one free spell out without being stopped . . .

He resisted the temptation. The man couldn't be that naive, and if this was a test of some kind he'd do better in the long run to establish himself as being as harmless as possible. "I don't know much about spells," he said instead. "Just enough to protect us on the road against bandits, really."

"I see. Well, no matter." The man took a deep breath. "*Myorlaineoul-meeklorestra!*" he shouted.

And with the barest flicker of light the clearing was suddenly no longer empty.

Ravagin clamped down hard on the expletive that tried to come out. Knowing what to expect hadn't entirely prepared him for the gut impact of the blindness spell's removal, but he was damned if he was going to ooh and aah for his captor's amusement. "Impressive," he said instead. "Redundant, as I said, but still impressive."

"We like it," the other shrugged. "This way."

They passed between several rows of buildings—houses, Ravagin decided, for the most part, though there were more than a normal village's share of craft shops intermixed as well. A few people were visible near the center of town, near a larger and more elaborate structure. "Town hall?" he hazarded. "Or is it a temple?"

"Neither," his guide told him. "Or both, depending on your point of view."

"Ah." *Must have learned his conversational technique from peris and demons*, Ravagin thought sardonically. *None of them can give straight answers, either.*

The passersby had all disappeared by the time he and the other man reached the building a few minutes later. Up close, Ravagin decided, the temple part of the design definitely won out. The high and elaborate multi-wood main doors alone put the place beyond the village hall classification, and the matching window frames meant some-one had gone to a great deal more effort than was usual in such cases.

Which probably meant that some very high-ranking spir-its were routinely being invoked in the place. Elementals, perhaps? Or even the highest of the spirit hierarchy, a demogorgon? The thought made him shiver.

"Come," the other man said, gesturing toward the doors. "The others will be waiting."

"Right." No one else was in sight near them . . . but across the way near the far edge of town more of the familiar robes could be seen going about their business. Grimacing, Ravagin squared his shoulders and pulled open the doors.

Chapter 17

It wasn't painful or even particularly uncomfortable, Danae found, to be standing frozen half in and half out of her room. The overwhelming sensation, in fact, during those first few seconds was that of utter humiliation.

Damn it all, she thought viciously, the last remnants of her spirit-induced sleep burning away like fog before hot sunlight. *I should have done a protection spell before I opened the door . . . or had a sprite check things out . . . or even done a spirit-detection, for God's sake. Damn, but I'm stupid.*

Carefully, putting all her strength into it, she managed to turn her head enough to get a clear look at the far end of the hallway. No one was visible; straining her ears, she couldn't hear any sounds of life. *Your standard mixed blessing*, she thought, anger fading as she realized she might have a second shot at this. If she'd called out a protection spell someone might very well have come running fast enough to intercept her. But now, if she had even a few minutes alone, she might just be able to figure out how to break this spell.

All right, Danae, think. *There has to be a way out. What sort of clues have we got as to what this flypaper is?*

It wasn't a sleep spell or fractional-possession spell of the type used to bring her here in the first place; of that much she was certain. It didn't seem to involve neural paralysis or synapse interruption, either. She'd had an experience once with an icegun as a little girl, and there was nothing of that sensation in this. On the other hand, there *did* seem to be a faint haze interfering with her vision. A haze that reminded her of something . . .

Aha! She smiled grimly. So *that* was all it was: a lar, set into a defensive circle barely big enough for her to stand in. Back on her first night on Karyx she'd wondered what would happen if she tried to push her way past a lar; now apparently, she had her answer.

Okay. So now what? She knew the release for a lar, of course, but release spells usually didn't work unless the user had invoked the spirit in the first place.

Or unless whoever had invoked this particular lar had added a manifold-geas to the spell so that others in Coven could also give it orders.

She bit at her lip, running through her mind the three manifold-geas spells she'd been taught. Unfortunately, only the most general of them gave total strangers like her any control whatsoever, and it was pretty unlikely that Coven would be using anything like that. Still, it couldn't hurt to try the appropriate release. "*Harkhonistrasmylikiheen,*" she muttered. "*Carash-melanasta.*"

Nothing happened. *Nice try, anyway,* she told herself, fighting down a surge of disappointment. *Now what?*

Well, when all else fails, try logic. The spirit protection spell was theorized to form a short-range barrier around a person which spirits couldn't penetrate; if it was coupled with a release spell, the combination might at least push the lar far enough back for her to slip past it.

Or else she'd get the same result as she'd just gotten with the geas-release combination: namely, nothing. But giving up now was to lose by default. Mentally crossing her fingers, she took as deep a breath as she could manage with the lar pressing in on her. "*Man-sy-hae orolontis; carash-melanasta—*"

And lost the rest of her breath in a strangled *whuff* as the intangible cocoon abruptly tightened, squeezing in on her like a padded vise.

There was no time to try anything else, even if she'd had anything else to try. She couldn't breathe . . . and as the faint haze before her eyes became mottled, she knew the lar was doing its best to squeeze the life out of her . . .

She awoke back in the room to find three figures standing over her: a man and a woman in the increasingly familiar Coven robes, and a second man—

"Ravagin!" she managed.

"You all right?" he asked, his wooden expression not giving way any hint of what he was thinking.

Which could be any of a dozen unpleasant things. Danae felt her face flush with embarrassment and shame. "Sure, I'm fine," she muttered. "I guess I got the spell wrong."

Ravagin looked at the Coven man. "I may have mentioned that we're not particularly good spirithandlers," he said. "Really, we're nothing more than craftsmen. I don't think we can be of much service to Coven."

The man shook his head. "You misunderstand both our purposes and our needs. Spirithandling isn't the problem— we have all that sort of knowledge we need. But your— what was it, some new style of bow? Yes—your bow shows you're exactly the sort people we're always in search of."

Ravagin's eyes flicked to Danae and back again. "So it's creative talent you're looking for, is it? And you pass out those enchanted robes to help in the hunt?"

The man smiled. "Exactly. Each has a spirit trapped— well, not *in* it, exactly; that would be too easy to detect. But the spirit is associated with it in a rather complicated manner."

"How do you make sure the robes get to the proper people?" Danae asked.

"Oh, we don't," the man shrugged. "Most of them disappear out there and we never hear of them again. But enough find their way to people we can use. You'd be amazed at how many peddlers will buy a robe that has the Coven emblem on it, almost as if our reputation for quality will reflect on them."

Danae felt her stomach tighten. The exact logic Melentha had used on her . . . and she'd fallen for the trick like a halfwit. "So is that all you dragged us here for?" she demanded. "My composite bow design?"

"Oh, the bow will only be the start," the woman said.

"We're extending you the rare privilege of joining the Coven community. In return, you'll be expected to create a steady stream of ingenious instruments and tools for us to market."

Danae looked at Ravagin, her mouth going dry. "Did you explain to our hosts that we really can't stay here—?"

"I've tried," Ravagin said. "I get the feeling the invitation isn't a matter of choice."

"You're beginning to understand—" The man broke off as the glow-fire of a sprite came through the wall and decelerated to a sudden stop. For a second it engulfed first his head, then the woman's, before heading away in a smooth curve through the half-open doorway.

"Excuse us, but we're needed elsewhere," the man said as he and the woman started toward the door. "You'll be comfortable here until we return. I suggest you discuss the situation and try to reconcile yourselves to it." They disappeared into the hallway, closing the heavy door behind them.

Ravagin exhaled in a long sigh and turned to eye Danae. "You all right?" he asked. "*Really* all right, I mean?"

"I'm as well as can be expected," Danae told him, sitting up on the bed. "Ravagin—I'm sorry about all of this. I don't know what happened—"

He waved the apology away. "Forget it. You heard the man: they've clearly got this snatching technique down to a science. Let's try and figure out a way out of here, shall we?"

"I tried the door," she grimaced. "You saw what happened."

"Sure did. What was that, anyway?—a fractional-possession spell?"

"No, I think it was a lar, circling me at *very* close orbit. I tried combining a release spell with—"

"A lar?" Ravagin frowned. "You sure?"

"I'm not sure of anything, but I don't know what else it could have been. Why?"

"Because that wasn't typical lar behavior." Ravagin gazed into space a minute. "No. You couldn't set a lar to form a tube around a person like that. You only get that kind of full circle as a large perimeter—it reforms as a localized column in front of anyone who gets too close."

Danae thought back to that first night on Karyx. Sure enough, that was how the lar had behaved. "You're right," she admitted. "But the haze and—well, the basic sensation—both felt more like a lar than anything else."

"Great." Ravagin sat down heavily on the edge of the bed. "Just great. You realize, of course, what it means if you're right."

"Coven's come up with some brand-new spells?" she hazarded.

"Bull's-eye. And not just new spells, but ones that create entirely different behavior patterns in the invoked spirits."

She thought that over for a minute. "But the old spells should still work, shouldn't they? I mean, they work *now*, and—well, relativity didn't negate the accuracy of classical mechanics, you know."

Ravagin looked her in astonishment. "What does relativity have to do with it?"

"I meant that in its proper sphere, classical mechan—"

"I know what you meant," he cut her off. "Look, Danae, in case you hadn't noticed, we're not dealing with electrons and frictionless sleds here—we're dealing with living, sentient beings. There are no guarantees here—we're damn lucky that someone in Karyx's past found *any* way of controlling these spirits. But the whole thing is strictly empirical; if there are basic laws governing the interaction of spells and spirits, no one's come up with them yet."

"I'm aware of that," Danae snapped, getting to her feet. "You're welcome to start work on that oversight right away—*I'm* going to find a way past that lar."

Stomping to the door, she opened it a crack. This time, knowing what to look for, she found she could see the faint haze between her and freedom. "You said you tried a standard release spell?" Ravagin called from behind her.

"Yes," she gritted, trying to summon up courage to try this again. The memory of being almost crushed to death . . .

"I'm surprised you were able to get any words out at all, given the way you looked when we found you."

"It didn't try to strangle me until after I said the release," she told him. Maybe if she used one of the other geas spells this time . . . Clenching her teeth, she inhaled deeply—

"It did *what*?" There was a creak from the bed, and a second later Ravagin was peering through the door over her shoulder. "A lar shouldn't react that way to a release spell from the wrong person."

"Well . . . I *did* try using the control spell for a manifold geas first," she admitted. "Maybe that—I don't know, sensitized it or put it on its guard or something."

"It shouldn't have," he said, shaking his head slowly. "With a manifold geas you're either in control or you aren't, and if you aren't the spirit's just supposed to ignore you. Certainly not attack you."

"If you're implying I said the spell wrong—"

"No, no, I'm sure you did it right." He exhaled thoughtfully between his teeth. "Damn. This gets worse and worse, Danae."

She twisted her head to look at him. "What do you mean? You *said* we were probably dealing with a new set of spells and spirit behavior here."

For a long moment he was silent. Then, reaching around behind her, he carefully pushed the door closed. "You don't want to try the release again?" she asked.

"I don't want to try *any* spells for a while," he said quietly. "There's something wrong here—something very wrong—only I can't put my finger on it."

Danae licked her lips. *The most experienced Courier in the Corps*, she reminded herself. *If he thinks something's off-key* . . . "You want to give me a for instance? Besides the overzealous lar in the hallway, I mean?"

Ravagin stepped over to the window and stood looking out, hands clasped behind his back. "It's just feelings so far," he said. "Something about Coven feels . . . empty, somehow. I mean aside from the two people we've talked to, everyone else in town's been keeping their distance." He nodded toward the glass. "There are some people over there now near where I left my horse, but they weren't there when I rode up."

Danae came up behind him and peered out. "Yes, I saw

them earlier—or another group; you can't really tell them apart with those robes."

"But why are they all over *there*?" he persisted. "When I was being escorted here I saw people milling around this building, too, but by the time I got here they were gone."

"Maybe they don't want us to get too good a look at them," she suggested. Now that he mentioned it, it *did* sound a little odd. "If they're all victims of this same recruitment scheme, it could be the village leaders don't want us to identify any of them."

"Which could mean they aren't yet sure they can keep us here," Ravagin said slowly. "If we were stuck in Coven for the duration, without any possibility of a way out, they shouldn't care if we know who they've snatched."

"Pretty flimsy logic," Danae muttered.

"I'll take what I can get at this stage," he shrugged, running his fingers experimentally along the window frame. "Probably a waste of time to try and get out this way, but for the moment it's about all we've got available." Reaching to the back of his belt, he pulled a dagger from beneath his tunic and dug the point in between the frame and glass.

"They didn't bother to disarm you?" Danae frowned.

"Oh, the peri in the forest disarmed me, but good," he grunted, working the knife back and forth. "Released the dazzler from the sword Melentha lent me. Lot of fireworks and frost—you'd have loved it. Melentha'll probably kill me for losing it."

"Why'd the peri do that? Couldn't it have handled you even with a bound-spirit sword?"

"Hell, it could have handled me with *two* bound-spirit swords," he told her frankly. "You have to remember that spirits aren't like a pack of idiot dogs or something panting eagerly for the chance to be dumped on by humans. Being entrapped is the equivalent of slavery for them, and they'll do practically anything to get out of it. It's probably the main reason that getting a binding spell wrong is so dangerous; the spirit knows what you were trying to do and lashes out in self-defense . . ."

He trailed off, and the knife in his hand came to a halt.

"What is it?" Danae asked, feeling the hairs rising on the back of her neck.

"Coven," he said slowly. "Danae . . . what is Coven's claim to fame on Karyx?"

She frowned, thinking. "You told me it was their trade goods. Well crafted, many of them spirit-enhanced—"

"Spirit-enhanced," he nodded. "Is it just me . . . or is there something wrong about a peri who's able to release spirits working for a place that routinely binds those same spirits?"

She opened her mouth, closed it again. "Maybe . . . could the peri be under a geas of some kind?"

Ravagin shook his head. "I don't think so. But there's more. When we got to the village itself . . . yes. The peri told the man that it was heading back to the forest. *Told* him. Didn't ask permission, didn't wait for orders of any kind. And the man accepted this as apparently normal behavior."

Danae gnawed thoughtfully at her lip. "Well, it at least indicates that that particular man isn't in control of that particular peri."

"Maybe," Ravagin said slowly, "it indicates that there aren't *any* men in control of the spirits here."

Danae moved up to where she could see Ravagin's face. If he'd been making a joke, it didn't show in his tight expression. "Are you suggesting the spirits could be in charge of Coven themselves?" she asked. "May I remind you that you just got done saying spirits don't like being bound?"

"I also said we're a long way from knowing what the rules are that govern them," he reminded her. "There could be a whole set of power struggles underway we know nothing about. Maybe the—I don't know—the demons, maybe, are perfectly willing to trap the weaker spirits in the hierarchy for their own purposes, while the peris generally release them whenever they can get away with it. Something like that."

"Or maybe all of the spirits in Coven are united against the rest of Karyx," Danae said quietly. "With the bound-spirit goods they sell as their version of a fifth column."

Ravagin turned away from the window to face her. "Are

you suggesting there might be a way for bound spirits to release themselves when they wanted to?"

"Or else that one of the great powers could release them all at once," Danae said, speaking slowly as it gradually crystallized in her mind. "Neither elementals nor demogorgons are supposed to be particularly localized. But even if the bound spirits never get out it might still pay an aggressor spirit to give them as wide a distribution as possible. Economically, bound-spirit items are the heart of what passes for technology on Karyx. The more the people here grow dependent on them, the more power the spirits have."

"The wolf hunter method," Ravagin nodded grimly. "Makes sense."

"The what?"

"Old story I once heard about a man who trapped a particularly cunning pack of wolves by setting out food for them every night for a few weeks while during the day he slowly built a fence around the area. By the time the fence was completed the wolves had become so accustomed to coming there for food they walked right into the enclosure and he simply closed the gate behind them. Moral was that you're vulnerable to the same extent that you're dependent. If this is what the spirits—or any subset of them— are doing, we've *definitely* got to get out of here and blow the whistle."

Danae looked at the spot where Ravagin had been digging with his dagger. It was hardly marked. "We're not going to break any speed records going at it this way."

"Yeah." Ravagin scowled at the window frame and jammed his knife back into its sheath. "The whole building's probably crawling with bound spirits. I wish to hell you'd been out there in the forest with me when that peri released the dazzler—with that high-retention memory treatment of yours you might have been able to remember the spell it used."

"I'm not sure I'd care to have a whole swarm of freshly released and possibly hostile spirits buzzing around me, anyway," Danae said, shivering. "Looks to me like all we have left is the direct approach. Through the door."

"With a spirit-protection spell around us?" Ravagin said doubtfully.

Danae gritted her teeth. "And the possibility that you at least might be able to get out while the lar's busy holding me."

"Forget it," Ravagin shook his head. "We leave together or not at all."

"This is no time for male overprotectiveness," Danae growled, tension draining away what little native patience she possessed.

"Don't flatter yourself," Ravagin shot back. "Male protectiveness is usually reserved for friends and lovers. But you're a client, and I'm a Courier, and I'll be damned if I'll chase you all the way to Coven just to turn around and desert you."

"Well, then, the hell with your Courier pride, too," she snapped. "This is just a shade more important—"

And without warning the door slammed back on its hinges.

Danae jumped, spinning around as the Coven-robed man strode into the room. *Damn*, she thought viciously. Possibly their last chance to get out of here, and they'd thrown it away arguing.

And then she caught the look in the man's eyes . . . and abruptly her stomach tightened within her.

Chapter 18

Ravagin tensed, muscles and senses automatically shifting into combat mode. If the man assaulted Danae he would have to intervene . . . But a moment later the wild eyes shifted instead to him. "You—Ravagin," he ground out. "The woman called you 'Courier.' I heard her. Who—*what*—are you?"

The sheer unexpectedness of the question threw Ravagin off stride for a couple of heartbeats. "What do you mean?" he asked, trying to gain time.

The man's face darkened, and his voice was suddenly harsh. "Don't play games with me, human. If you're a Courier from the other world, admit your identity."

Beside him, Ravagin felt Danae tense. "You're mistaken," she said, her voice trembling slightly. "I merely meant he was acting as my escort in Besak—"

"*Do not lie!*" the man screamed, taking a step toward her.

Danae jerked back; and as the man took another step forward, Ravagin moved to stand between them. "*Carashnatasta!*" he called.

The man jerked back as if stung, and for a second an expression of pure hatred suffused his face. Slowly it faded, to be replaced by a look of almost amused bitterness. "And what did you expect to accomplish by that?" he asked.

"It was mainly to get your attention," Ravagin said, hiding as best he could the knot growing in his gut. He

138

hadn't expected a simple demon-release spell to do any
good . . . but the other's startled reaction had confirmed
his suspicion that the man before him was indeed playing
host to something else. "I also thought it might help me
find out who I was talking to."

"I trust you are satisfied?"

"Reasonably." There was nothing to be gained, after all,
by groveling before the demon. Whatever it had planned
for them, maintaining his dignity couldn't make things any
worse. "I don't suppose you'd care to give me your name?"

The smile on the other's face was very inhuman. "I do
not insult your intelligence, human. Do not insult mine.
Now tell me where you are from."

Behind him, Danae gripped his upper arm warningly.
Ravagin pursed his lips . . . but there was really no point
in playing coy. For the demon to have picked up on the
word *Courier*—and then to have placed the proper significance on it—meant he would merely be confirming something the spirit already knew. Somehow. "We're from a
different world a long way from here," he admitted. Peripherally, he sensed Danae's surprise that he'd given in
so easily. Perhaps she didn't yet understand what they
were facing here.

The man—the man/demon combination, rather—gazed
at him for a long minute, an unreadable expression on his
face. "How did you arrive in Karyx?" he asked at last.

"I think you know," Ravagin told him, feeling the sweat
collecting on his forehead. Spirit possession was one of the
few facts of life on Karyx that he'd long since realized he
would never be able to accept. "If you're looking for the
location of the Tunnel, I can tell you right now you can't
get through it."

The man/demon hissed, exactly as a demon would, and
for another long minute there was silence in the room.
*Demon-powered or not, the carrier still has normal hu-
man weaknesses*, Ravagin reminded himself. A knife could
still mess him up badly—maybe even kill him and release
the demon back to wherever it was spirits came from . . .
if he could get close enough to use the weapon before the
other was able to stop him. He threw a sideways glance at
Danae, her face very close to his as she looked out from

behind him, one hand still with a death-grip on his left arm. If he could somehow cue her to create a diversion—finger-spelling, perhaps, behind his back? And if he could be sure of distracting the demon as well as its human host. . . .

"Get out of here."

Startled, Ravagin brought his full attention back to the man/demon. "What?"

"You heard me," it snarled. "Get out of Coven. *Ahlah-spereojihezrahilkma beriosparathmistrokiai—*"

Danae shrieked, and Ravagin spun around to find her clutching herself tightly, a look of shock on her face. "It . . . got heavier," she gasped.

"The djinn has been released from the robe," the man/demon said. "It will trouble you no further. Now *get out*. Before the offer is withdrawn."

Danae's fingers gripped Ravagin's arm again. "You think it's some kind of trick?" she whispered.

Of course it is, was his automatic response . . . but if it was, there had to be a hook somewhere, and nothing obvious lept to mind. Besides which—"Doesn't matter if it is," he murmured back. "If we don't take a chance on it we'll be stuck here for good, anyway. Come on." Taking her hand in his, he turned back to the man/demon. "We want our horses," he told him, wondering just how far he could push. "I have no intention of hiking back through Morax Forest."

The other spat, snarling something under his breath. Abruptly, two sprites appeared. "Send them," the man/demon growled.

Ravagin focused on the glow-fires. "Have whoever's holding our horses bring them to the front of this building," he instructed. "Quickly."

The sprites flared and shot from the room. "Would it be out of order for me to ask why the sudden benevolence?" Ravagin ventured. "It might help future groups who happen to stumble into this place—"

"If any more of your people come to Coven THEY WILL BE DESTROYED!"

The man/demon's abrupt shriek left Ravagin's ears ringing and his heart pounding. "Understood," he managed. "Come on, Danae—let's go."

Passing the man/demon was the worst part. But the creature made no move to stop them, and a minute later they emerged from the building to find their horses standing stiffly by the temple door. "Hold it," Ravagin warned as Danae hurried forward. "All right, spirits, we're here. Now get out of our horses."

For a second there was no response. Then, abruptly, both horses were sheathed in red lights which coalesced into vaguely human shapes before vanishing.

Ravagin expelled a deep breath. "Djinns," he identified them.

"Yeah, I know," Danae murmured. "At least they weren't demons. Can we get out of here now?"

"You bet."

They mounted and headed off between the houses at a fast trot. "Maybe that's why they never came too close to us," Danae said as they neared the forest. "They knew we might be allowed to leave."

Ravagin looked in the direction she was pointing and saw another group of robed figures in the distance. "I doubt that's the reason," he told her darkly. "I don't think there are more than a handful of real humans in Coven any more. I expect those are nothing more than disguised spirits—possibly doppelgangers—put there for the sole purpose of making the place look populated."

Danae muttered something under her breath. "God. Let's get the hell out of this place."

Ravagin glanced at the sun one last time to check their direction and then hunched down into his saddle. "I'm with you," he nodded . . . and felt a shiver run up his spine.

Up ahead, somewhere, would be the hook in whatever this trap was that the demons of Coven had set for them.

They rode steadily for almost three hours, following a route that Ravagin insisted was the way they'd both come the night before; and as they continued on with no sign of hindrance or trickery from Coven, Danae's dread slowly faded into a sort of mid-level tension. The sun was still climbing in the sky—somehow, it seemed incredible that their whole stay in Coven had ammounted to only about an hour—and the forest was alive around them with the chirps of birds and the scurrying sounds of small animals. Of the larger predators that Danae knew must live in Morax as well there was no sign.

"Aha," Ravagin said, his voice jerking her out of a nervous contemplation of the tree branches above them. "I told you this was the right path. Here's the clearing where I met the peri last night."

"Oh, great," Danae growled, looking around them with rekindled apprehension. "Let's move on before it comes back."

"And pass up what may be our best chance for a rest stop?" Ravagin rode to the middle of the clearing and swung down from his horse. "Come on, relax a little."

"Re*lax*? How can you even *think* of relaxing at a time—"

"Danae." Ravagin held up a hand as he took a few stiff-looking steps. "I don't understand what the hell's going on, either, but if they'd wanted to stop or kill us, they would have done so a long time ago. Whatever else they've got on their ethereal little minds, I think we really *are* being allowed to go. So come over here and get the kinks out of your muscles."

"But it doesn't make any sense," Danae grumbled, dismounting and leading her horse toward Ravagin's. He was right, she realized: her legs and rump felt awful. "Why let us go? Especially when we'd figured out their secret?"

"Maybe there's a higher principle involved," he shrugged. Moving a few meters to the side, he stooped over and reached down. "It could be that whatever they wanted to do to us doesn't work properly on non-Karyxites. Or maybe the demogorgon in charge of this part of the planet over-ruled the demon."

"Why should it? Demogorgons aren't supposed to pay much attention to what goes on in human society here. There aren't even any spells to invoke them."

"Sure there are." Ravagin straightened, holding two halves of a broken sword. "Who do you think you're invoking when you do a spirit-detection or protection spell or something?"

Danae frowned. "Those are handled by a demogorgon?"

"Or else by an elemental—I'm not sure anyone knows

which. But it's definitely one of the two great powers. How else do you think those spells work?—by magic or something?"

She looked sharply at him; but if he was ridiculing her he was hiding it well. "I thought all this *was* done by magic," she said stiffly.

He shook his head, turning the broken sword over in his hands. "One sword, shot completely to hell. Melentha's going to be furious. Magic, huh? Yeah, I suppose you could consider this magic if you wanted to. I've always found it works better to think of it as an automated voice-command system, with the network being composed of spirits instead of computers. The words by themselves don't have any real power behind them; it's the spirits who respond that do all the work."

He was right, of course. Danae swallowed her reflexive urge to continue what would only be a futile argument and glanced back in Coven's direction. "So why did they let us go?"

"Let's not talk about it until we're out of the forest, okay?" Ravagin said quietly.

She looked at him sharply. "You don't understand it either, do you?"

"I've already said I didn't. I also said I don't want to talk about it. You want me to repeat it in Standard and Shamahni?"

"Why?" she countered. "You think we'll reason out something they were afraid we would see there and bring them down on us?"

"The possibility *had* crossed my mind," he growled. "And considering what just nearly happened to you in there, I'd have thought you'd be showing a little more caution yourself."

"In other words you'd rather run from danger than try to understand it." She snorted. "Well, I'm sorry, but I'm the one who was kidnapped, and I'm not going to let it go that easily. Besides, what can they do to us here that they can't do just as easily in Besak or even in Melentha's fancy fortress? Hmm?"

Slowly, Ravagin looked up from his contemplation of the broken sword, and she swallowed hard at the ice in his eyes. "You're perhaps forgetting that I know about my place in your little psychological experiment," he said at last. "If this is part of it, I strongly suggest you back off. If it's not, then I'll tell you right now you're a fool. Whatever else the demons of Coven have going, we know enough already to make us a danger to them. Yes, they let us go; but maybe it was because they didn't realize how much we'd figured out. And even if they did, it may not take a hell of a lot to tip the balance back the other direction. If you want to consider it cowardly, that's your privilege . . . but try to keep in mind that I've brought over three hundred clients to Karyx over the past sixteen years *and* gotten them out safely. When you've got a record like that, let me know."

For a moment they stood facing each other in silence. Danae licked her lips once, but she couldn't find any words to say. "I'm sorry," she said. "I didn't mean to offend you."

He dropped his eyes. "Forget it." For another moment he gazed down at the broken sword in his hands. Then, abruptly, he hurled the shards violently into the trees across the clearing. "Mount up, and let's get moving."

Feeling the blood flooding into her face, Danae obeyed.

Once again, Ravagin had succeeded in making her feel like a child. This time, unfortunately, she'd deserved it.

Chapter 19

"Well," Melentha said when Danae had finished, "that's as interesting a story as I've heard on Karyx in a long while. You ever consider working Besak as a bard?"

Danae leaned hard on her temper. "It's true," she said, keeping her voice steady. "Every word of it." She turned to Ravagin, sitting silently off in a corner of the conversation room. "Come on, Ravagin, *say* something. Tell her I didn't make this up."

"Unfortunately, my dear," Melentha put in, "Ravagin knows enough about Karyx not to take everything he sees at full face value."

"What are you suggesting—that it was all an illusion?" Danae scoffed. "Give me a little more credit than *that*."

"Illusions on Karyx can be very convincing," Melentha shrugged. "You've seen at least one doppelganger since you've been here, and that's actually one of the simpler ones. Someone who knows what he's doing can make extremely elaborate illusions."

Ravagin stirred. "Only if he's willing to put forth a *lot* of effort."

"Well, of course—"

"So what was the purpose?"

Melentha frowned. "What do you mean?"

"Okay, let's assume the whole incident *was* an illusion," Ravagin said. "Fine; but we start with the robe, and the robe was unquestionably real—you had it here long before

145

we arrived. Ditto for the sleepwalker effect, unless you want to admit that someone can send spirits past your post line without causing even a ripple of reaction from your trapped demon. That means that Danae was kidnapped for some other purpose; and that someone with the necessary ability just happened to find out about it in time to side-track her to a fake Coven where he'd set up this grand illusion."

"The perpetrator didn't have to send spirits across the line," Melentha pointed out. "She's worn the robe out into Besak any number of times—maybe someone there put the djinn into it."

"Subtly enough that you couldn't spot it?" Danae put in.

Melentha threw her an annoyed look. "Believe it or not, there are people on Karyx who know more about spirit-handling than I do. I don't find that particularly significant."

"So again we're back to the question of *why*," Ravagin persisted.

"Maybe as a joke," Melentha suggested, getting to her feet with cat-like grace. "Maybe she offended someone. Or maybe she interested someone too much with her composite bow and he was hoping to scare her into reveal-ing the method of construction to him."

"So as far as you're concerned, it's over and done with?" Danae asked tartly.

Melentha's expression was almost excruciatingly conde-scending. "Whatever it was that happened to you—or whatever it was you *thought* happened to you—you got out all right, didn't you? If you want to dwell on it for the rest of your stay here, that's your privilege. But I don't see any point in it myself." She turned to Ravagin. "If you'll ex-cuse me, I have to recall some spirits before I get all the safe houses on Karyx into an uproar over nothing."

She glided from the room. Danae muttered a caustic epithet at the closed door, then turned on Ravagin. "A lot of help *you* were," she snapped. "You could at least have scorched that nonsense about the whole thing being a dream. You were there too, you know."

Ravagin grimaced. "Unfortunately, she had a point. Illu-sion on Karyx *can* be extremely real."

Danae stared at him. "You aren't serious. Ravagin, we were *there.*"

"Yes, I remember," he said dryly. "And if it helps, I don't really think there were any illusions involved. Aside from the one we'd already agreed on, I mean, the one about Coven being almost deserted."

"So why didn't you *say* anything to Melentha?"

"Because there's a slight possibility she was right," he admitted. "As she said, I *have* experienced the kind of illusion a genius spirithandler can create."

"So reality is up for grabs here—is that what you're saying? I don't buy that."

"No, it's not quite that bad. Full-sensory illusions are devilishly hard to maintain over any length of time, especially if there's more than one person involved or if the creator winds up having to improvise along the way. And they also don't seem to translate to long-term memory quite the same as real events."

Danae considered that. "So what you're saying is that maybe by the time we leave Karyx we'll know whether all of that really happened?"

"Something like that." He caught the look on her face and shrugged. "I'm sorry, Danae, but there's nothing more we can do about it at the moment." He stood up. "You'll have to excuse me; but unlike you, I didn't get any sleep at all last night. I'll see you in a few hours."

She pursed her lips. "Sure. Look . . . I'm sorry for all the trouble this caused you. I *do* appreciate your coming after me like you did."

"No extra charge," he said equably. "Besides, it was hardly your fault. I suggest that you stick around the house until I get up. We'll have time to go into Besak later today if you really want to, but I don't want you going there alone."

He left; and Danae let her lip twist into a grimace. *Don't go into the street, Danae. Don't make up stories, Danae.* "What's it going to be next?" she snarled into the empty room. " 'Play nice and don't get dirty, Danae?' "

Slapping the floor beside her cushion, she got up and strode to the window. A spotting of cumulus clouds had formed in the sky since their arrival back at Melentha's mansion, and occasional shadows could be seen skating across the lawn and post line toward Besak to the west. And beyond the village—

"It was *not* a dream," she said aloud. "It was real. *Real.* I *know* it was."

Then why are you so vehement about it? a small voice seemed to whisper in the back of her mind.

Because she really *wasn't* sure.

For a long minute she stood there, watching the clouds occult the unnaturally dim sunlight and thinking about what Melentha and Ravagin had said about Karyx's brand of illusion. Of short duration, incapable of reacting well to the bombshell that she and Ravagin were from another world, playing to a limited audience—the Coven experience fit the pattern they'd described all too well. And if Ravagin was right, she wouldn't know for a long time whether it had been real or not. If she ever found out at all.

"I do not accept that," she called out toward the post line. "You demons can be as clever as you want; you're not going to screw around with my head like that. You understand?"

There was no answer. *All right, Danae; enough of the tantrum, already. Think it out.* She had Melentha's statement that her own internal evidence was no good. An independent observer? But Ravagin had been the only one there, and he'd already disqualified himself as a judge. That left only the demon-possessed people of Coven themselves . . . and there was no way she would travel that road again, even if she were given a guarantee that she would again be allowed to leave. And that was it. All who'd been present accounted for.

Or was it?

Danae caught her breath as a new possibility suddenly hit her. Crazy . . . but it might just give her the answer.

At an unknown but possibly extreme risk to herself. She sobered at the thought, knowing what Ravagin would say if he knew what she was considering. And what Melentha would say.

That she was being childish.

Danae's teeth clamped tightly together. Well, then, she

was perfectly capable of doing all this without them. Of showing them both how the "child" could manage on her own.

Moving quietly, she walked to the door and eased it open. Melentha should still be busy with her spirit work; Ravagin would almost surely be asleep by now. With luck, she would be back before either of them missed her.

And then they'd *really* see something.

The man's name was Gartanis, and he was ancient.

Not just old. Old people weren't all that common in Besak, but Danae had seen enough during her visits to know what old age looked like on Karyx. Without the blunting of reconstructive surgery or biochip internal work, of course, the effects of aging were much more pronounced here than in the Twenty Worlds; but even given that, Gartanis was an oddity. Wrinkled, his vanishing hair gone snowy white, his vision and strength fading, he looked to Danae to be almost literally on his last legs.

All in all, not what she'd expected of the man alleged to be the most knowledgable spirithandler in Besak.

"So," he wheezed as he waved his gnarled stick toward a chair across the pentagram-inscribed table from him. "What can I do for you, my young lady?"

"My name is Danae," she told him. "I've been in the area for several days now, talking to various of the tradesmen in Besak about a new kind of bow I would like to market—"

"Ah," Gartanis's eyes seemed to light up briefly. "You're the one. I've heard tales of you from others in the village."

"Yes," Danae nodded, obscurely surprised that he kept up that much with current events. "As I said, I've been marketing a bow that can be used as is or with trapped-spirit enhancement, and it occurred to me that you might have spells for sale that I might be able to use in my work."

For a long minute he sat motionless in his seat, eying her in a way she was not at all certain she liked. "I was informed that you sold spirithandling spells here," she said as the silence lengthened. "If I was informed wrong—"

"*Olratohin kailistahk!*"

She jumped at the other's sudden shout. "What—?"

"Be silent," he rumbled. " . . . no. No, I was wrong—there are no spirits about you. But there is something else . . ."

He trailed off, and Danae swallowed painfully. She'd taken off the Coven robe as soon as they'd arrived back at Melentha's mansion and she hadn't come near the thing since . . . but there was no guarantee that something else hadn't been done to her. "Is it something bad?" she half whispered, afraid of breaking his concentration.

"I don't know for certain," he said slowly. "But . . . ah; that's it. Coven. You've been to Coven."

Her heart seemed to skip a beat. "How can you tell?" she managed to ask.

"Eh? Oh, I heard it from one of my sprites, of course. That spirithandler you've been staying with—Melentha—sent out the word early this morning."

Danae got her breathing going again. "Oh."

The old man's eyebrows seemed to twitch. "You seem troubled by something. Something about Coven?"

"It . . . has to do with Coven, yes," she said cautiously. "It's really what I came to see you for in the first place. I'd like to buy a spell for invoking a demogorgon."

There was no reaction beyond a tightening of the wrinkled skin around Gartanis's eyes . . . but when he finally spoke his voice was oddly hollow. "A demogorgon. You wish to invoke a demogorgon."

"Yes," Danae nodded, forcing her voice to remain calm as her heart began speeding up again. "Is there a problem? I was under the impression all spirits could be invoked."

The old man's eyes seemed to come back from somewhere else. "Oh, surely, traderess," he snorted. "All spirits can be invoked. And all animals can be captured, too. Tell that to the foolish hunter stalking a maddened *cintah*."

Cintahs had been mentioned in the original Triplet orientation sessions. Usually in conjunction with emergency defensive spells. "Are demogorgons *that* dangerous?"

"Dangerous? Not necessarily. Not even always." Gartanis's eyes bored into hers. "But they *are* unpredictable."

Danae licked her lips. "For instance?"

He was silent a long while. "How old do you think me?" he asked at last.

She considered, remembering to judge by Karyx standards. "Seventy years. Perhaps seventy-five."

He shook his head. "A hundred forty-seven."

"What?" she whispered, feeling her stomach tighten within her. Average life expectancy on Karyx was supposed to be only about fifty-eight . . .

"A hundred forty-seven," he repeated. "I was fifty when in my pride I traveled to the Illid ruins and invoked a demogorgon. This was the result."

"But to have gained nearly a hundred years of life—"

"Life?" he snapped. "You—in the prime of your youth—you would consider *this* life?"

She frowned. "But surely you weren't always like—" She caught her breath. "You *were* like . . . like you are now?"

Gartanis's eyes focused elsewhere again. "Yes. A high price for my arrogance."

Silence descended on the room. Danae felt her hands trembling in her lap, found her eyes tracing the deep valleys cutting through his cheeks. To be so old for so long . . . it sent chills up her back. "What . . . what else happened? Were you able to talk to the demogorgon?"

"What does it matter?" he murmured. "Whatever I may have learned wasn't worth the price."

"No. I don't suppose it was." She took a deep breath. "Well . . . would it be safer to try and contact an elemental?"

He looked at her sharply. "Explain to me this brash desire to commune with the great powers, traderess Danae. Is your pride then so terribly swollen?"

She sighed. "I was hoping to get some information. Something happened to me in Coven, something that made no sense. I want to understand it, and I can't think of any other way to get the answers."

"Perhaps a peri or demon could help. Their invocations are certainly safer."

"The peris and demons are already in it up to their necks," she shook her head, feeling her resolve draining away. "I don't think I could trust anything they would have to say on the subject. But I suppose it doesn't matter all that much." *Just like a child*, she thought bitterly. *Quitting when the cost gets too high.* But he was right. Whatever was happening in Coven wasn't worth risking this kind of twilight life over. "Thank you for your time, Master Gartanis," she continued, getting to her feet. "If you'll tell me what I owe you—"

She broke off at the expression on his face. "Demons and peris involved on their own?" he asked. "Not simply obeying orders from a human spirithandler?"

"It seemed that way, yes," she said cautiously. "Unless there was someone far in the background controlling things. I don't think the demon-possessed people we met had any real say as to what happened."

"The demons made decisions on their own?" Gartanis persisted. "They didn't simply go off somewhere and return with new orders?"

"Again, I think so. Why?—is it significant?"

Gartanis took a deep breath, his eyes glazed over. "When I was in communion with the demogorgon a hundred years ago . . . I remember some of it. A vision of—never mind. A corruption of the present, I thought at the time . . . but perhaps it was instead a vision of the future. Of now." Abruptly, his eyes came back; and gripping his stick, he worked himself out of his chair. "Come into the back room with me," he wheezed. "I'll get you the materials you'll need to invoke the demogorgon."

"Wait a second," Danae said, taking an automatic step backwards. "What's this vision thing you're talking about? And anyway, I'm not sure any more I *want* to know how to invoke a demogorgon."

Gartanis looked up at her, his eyes burning. "You will," he said softly. "You must."

"Why?" Danae persisted.

"Because you already know something of the danger. And because if you do not, all of Karyx will pay a heavy price . . . and you along with it."

But I won't even be on Karyx much longer. She left the thought unsaid, and for a long moment she and Gartanis stood facing each other. Then, carefully, the old man turned and hobbled back toward the rear of the house. "Follow me," he said.

Swallowing, she obeyed.

The knock on his door snapped Ravagin awake. "Come in," he growled, glancing through slitted eyelids at the curtains pulled across the windows. There was still light coming through the material, which meant it was probably late afternoon. He'd had several hours of sleep, though it sure didn't feel like it.

The door opened; but it was Melentha, not Danae, who came into the room. "Have you seen Danae?" she asked without preamble.

"Where, in my dreams?" he growled. "I've been asleep, in case you hadn't noticed. What do you want her for?"

"I don't *want* her for anything," Melentha snapped. "She and a horse are missing, and I want to know where she's gone."

"*Damn* her." Ravagin hissed an angry breath through his teeth. "Ten'll get you twenty she's gone off to Besak again." He sat up, started to swing his legs out of bed, and froze as a sudden thought struck him. "The Coven robe—where is *it*?"

"Still here," Melentha assured him. "Don't worry, even Danae's not dumb enough to get near *that* thing again. No, she's off somewhere on her own, getting into who knows what kind of trouble."

"Yeah." Ravagin got his legs out of bed, snared his tunic from the sidetable. "Can you get some sprites out looking for her?"

"Already done that. No results yet."

"Figures." Sprites were great for carrying out specific orders, but something open-ended like a general search was largely beyond their limited intelligence. "We might as well start with Besak. You have some horses ready?"

"They will be in a minute. Meet you downstairs." Melentha vanished, closing the door behind her.

Damn her, anyway. Pulling his boots on, Ravagin grabbed his short sword and jogged down the hallway. That was it—the very last straw. Danae had disobeyed a direct order; and when they found her this trip was going to be officially aborted. He was through putting up with her childish reactions and her half-thought schemes and most of all of her damn psychological experiments with him as white rat.

And whichever heading this latest stunt came under, it was her last. He and Melentha would find her, dust her off if necessary, and bring her back . . . and tomorrow morning they would be be on their way back to the Tunnel.

Chapter 20

The sun was nearing the western horizon by the time Danae returned to Melentha's mansion, and she was nearly to the archway in the post line before it registered that there were no lights showing in any of the windows.

She reined her horse to a halt, frowning as her eyes flicked over the grounds for signs of life. But no one was visible, at least not on this side of the house. Could everyone be in Melentha's inner sanctum, perhaps, working on God only knew what?

"Danae."

She jerked at the voice, spinning to look behind her. No one. "Who's there?" she called.

"Do not pry into matters that are none of your business."

She licked her lips, fighting down a surge of panic. Her eyes darted all around—

Came to rest on the carved demon face in the archway.

Oh, God, she thought, stomach tightening painfully as she automatically clutched the pouch Gartanis had given her. She'd had more than her fill of demons at Coven, and the last thing she wanted right now was a confrontation with another one. "What do you want?" she asked, fighting unsuccessfully against the trembling in her voice.

"Do not pry into matters that are none of your business," the demon repeated.

"Why isn't it my business? Your friends dragged me to

Coven and scared me half to death—I figure that *makes* it
my business."

The stone didn't change . . . but even as she watched,
the demon's eyes seemed to take on a fox-fire glow. "You
are not of this world. It is not your concern. You will not
interfere."

Danae licked her lips . . . but even as a new shiver of
fear ran up her back, an odd surge of determination flooded
in on top of it. She'd been right—there *was* something
going on in Coven—and the demon's attempt to scare her
was just one more bit of evidence that whatever it was was
important as well as nasty.

The demon's *futile* attempt to scare her, she remembered suddenly. Its limits had been well defined for it . . .
or at least had been so once. Mentally crossing her fingers,
she twitched the reins and started tentatively forward—

"You will not interfere!"

The horse shied violently, and it took all Danae's equestrian skill to bring it back under control . . . and by the
time she'd done so the last of her fear had been completely buried under a white haze of fury. "Forget it!" she
snarled at the demon. "You can just for*get* it. I'm a human
being—*I* give *you* the orders on Karyx. And in case you've
forgotten, I was right there watching when Melentha told
you to allow me free passage. So knock off the bluff-and-
scare tactics and let me through."

For a long moment she could feel the demon's resistance like an invisible balloon filling the archway. Then,
reluctantly, it collapsed into itself and faded away. Gripping the reins tightly, Danae guided her horse through,
fighting the urge to kick the animal to full gallop and get
the hell away from there. But she really *did* have nothing
to fear from the demon . . . and she was damned if she
would lose her dignity to a spirit trapped in a chunk of stone.

But still she couldn't resist taking a quick look behind
her as she started up toward the house . . . and so it was
she saw the green patch of haze detach itself from the post
line and skim off toward the southeast.

They had spent over an hour in Besak before they
finally found someone who remembered seeing Danae.

"Yes—the traderess with the fancy bow, true?" the hunter asked. "Yes, I saw her some time ago over on the Hawkers' Way."

"Was she talking to the weapons sellers?" Ravagin asked.

"Not when I saw her. She was already past most of their booths, heading toward the south."

Ravagin looked at Melentha. "Anything down that way she might have been interested in? Or anyone?"

Melentha shook her head slowly, forehead furrowed in thought. "Not that I can think of. How long ago was this?"

The hunter glanced at the setting sun. "Three hours at the least. Possibly longer."

"Well, whatever she wanted there shouldn't have taken this much time," Ravagin growled, feeling his jaw tighten. He'd been right; Danae was in some sort of trouble again. "We'd better get down there and see if we can pick up her trail."

"She could just be browse shopping," Melentha suggested slowly.

"Or perhaps gone to see Gartanis," the hunter suggested.

"Who is—?" Ravagin began.

"DAMN!" Melentha exploded. "Of *course*—that damn idiot's gone to Gartanis to buy a spell."

"Who's Gartanis?" Ravagin asked, fighting against the infectious emotion almost visibly radiating from Melentha. "Is he a fraud or something?"

"He's a spiritmaster who came here from Torralane Village a few months ago," Melentha bit out. "And, no, he's not a fraud. At least not a deliberate one."

"Well, let's go talk to him, then," Ravagin suggested, wheeling his horse around. "Danae might even still be there."

"It may not do any—AHH!"

Ravagin twisted his head around. "What?" he snapped.

Melentha's eyes were wide and unfocused. "She's at the house," she breathed. "She's . . . gone inside."

Ravagin felt the tension beginning to drain from his muscles. "Well, great," he sighed. "Then at least she's safe—"

"No, no, no. Don't you understand? She's been to

Gartanis. She has the incense for a new spell—surely she's going to want to try it out."

"Oh, hell." An untried spell, from a spiritmaster . . . in the hands of an amateur. Would Danae really be foolish enough to try something like that alone?

Of course she would, he thought viciously. "Well, what are we waiting for? Let's get back, try and stop her."

"You go." Melentha's eyes turned to Ravagin, and he was startled to see anger building into genuine fury there. "I'm going to Gartanis—find out what spell he gave her. And then deal with him."

"You—? Hey, *wait*!"

But Melentha was already galloping off through the narrow streets, oblivious to the pedestrians scattering frantically before her mad rush. "What the hell?" Ravagin muttered as he watched her go. Like a woman possessed . . . and come to think of it, how had she known Danae was back at the house? There hadn't been any messengers, at least none he'd seen.

But there was no time to wonder now. Whatever Danae was up to this time, she was likely to get herself hurt in the process, and it was his job to get her out of it. Again.

Turning his horse savagely, he started back through Besak.

The sky was already growing dark as he passed under the post line archway at full gallop and reined to a halt in front of the mansion. The windows were also dark; if Danae was in fact back, she hadn't put on any lights.

Or else was in Melentha's windowless sanctum. Swallowing a curse, he slid off his horse and sprinted through the high doors.

Inside, it was pitch black. "*Sa-minskisk tooboosn,*" he snapped, throwing the placement gesture over his shoulder to set the invoked dazzler's location back out of his eyes. The room blazed with light; his shadow a dark mass angling sharply off to the side, Ravagin headed toward the stairway.

She was there, all right, seated cross-legged in the middle of the sanctum's large pentagram with tendrils of smoke curling up from a crucible set on the floor before her. "Danae?" Ravagin called tentatively.

There was no response. "Danae!" he called again, sharper this time. "Come on, snap out of it."

No response. Gritting his teeth, Ravagin moved to the edge of the pentagram and sniffed cautiously. Incense, all right, presumably one of the many varieties spirithandlers sometimes used to help clear and focus their minds for particularly touchy invocations. Interfering with her invocation could get them both fried to crisps; but if she wasn't too far along, there might yet be time to safely stop her. Certainly whatever spirit she was trying for hadn't yet made an appearance.

And then his eyes fell on the floor beside her . . . and he bit down hard on his tongue.

Sitting full in the light from his dazzler, she had no shadow.

He thought about that for nearly a minute. Then, with a sigh, he moved back and sat down against the wall near the door. *Well, she's done it,* he thought wearily. *She's finally managed to get herself into a situation I haven't a snowflake's chance of getting her out of. Great job, Danae.* All he could do for her now was wait. And hope like hell that the spirit she was working on didn't eat her alive.

The wait seemed to go on forever, but it was probably no more than twenty minutes. His first warning was the quiet fading in of her shadow; a moment later she suddenly shook and began gasping for breath. Her eyes fluttered open, squeezed shut again against the dazzler's light. "Who—?" she breathed.

"It's Ravagin," he told her, rolling back to his feet and hurrying to her side. The smell of the incense, he noted peripherally, had disappeared; a quick glance into the crucible showed it to be as as empty as if it had been scoured. "You all right?"

She took another few deep breaths and allowed him to help her to her feet before replying. "I think so. I guess—I think I got off easy."

"Got off easy doing what?" Ravagin asked.

She raised a hand to shade her eyes and squinted back in the dazzler's general direction. "Is there any way to turn that thing down? I don't think my eyes have come all the way back yet."

Suppressing his impatience with an effort, Ravagin released the dazzler. The darkness closed in, and he felt Danae stiffen beside him. "Wait a second," he grunted, guiding her to the wall and sitting her down against it. Groping around in the dark, he located the flat dish of a fireplate on Melentha's table and invoked a firebrat over it. The gentler reddish light flickered into existence, and he made his way back to Danae.

"Thanks," she said, taking a shuddering breath. "I guess I wasn't ready for total darkness, either."

"That's okay," Ravagin said, squatting beside her and giving her face a quick once-over. Tight, strained, but with no signs of injury or serious trauma. "What happened?" he asked, taking one of her hands between his. It was, he noted uneasily, icy cold.

She licked her lips. "I invoked a demogorgon."

He felt his stomach tighten. "You *what?*"

Her eyes flashed. "Don't snap at me! All right, so it was stupid—" She broke off and closed her eyes. "Ravagin . . . you have no idea what it was like."

"Can't argue with that one. So tell me."

She opened her eyes and looked around the room. "An entire world, in its own little universe—that's what Karyx is, isn't it? And Shamsheer too, of course. Triplet: three worlds for the price of one. Only it's not."

"What do you mean?" Ravagin asked cautiously.

She gave him a brittle smile. "There are actually *four* worlds here. The fourth one populated only by spirits. And I was there."

And abruptly, the smile vanished, and she turned her face into Ravagin's shirt and began sobbing.

Chapter 21

The crying jag lasted only a few minutes, and Ravagin's faint discomfort was more than matched by Danae's own embarrassment over the incident. "I'm sorry," she said for the third or fourth time as he found her a handkerchief to wipe her nose with. "I don't know what happened."

"Just forget it," he told her. Also for the third or fourth time. "Your psyche's been through one hell of a shock, and you can't just shrug that sort of thing off. Burying it wouldn't do you any good in the long run."

She sniffed one final time and handed the handkerchief back. "I'm okay now," she said.

"Good. Look, if you feel up to it, it might help to run through the whole contact out loud. Sort of—you know—flush the emotion out of it."

A tentative smile played at the corners of her lips. "Besides which, you're curious?"

"Of course I am. If what you saw was real, this is something none of us has ever stumbled on before."

For a moment he held his breath, cursing his verbal slip and wondering if she'd take offense at the implication that she might have been hallucinating. But she merely nodded. "It sure *felt* real. But I suppose you're right. Anyway, I got this spell from a spiritmaster in Besak named Gartanis—"

"Yeah, we heard. I thought Melentha warned you not to buy spells from the locals."

Danae snorted. "Oh, sure. I was supposed to go to her to ask for help proving what happened in Coven wasn't an illusion?"

Ravagin felt his jaw tighten. "Is *that* what all this was over? Pardon the bluntness, but that was a damn fool thing to risk your neck over."

"Yeah, I know." She shivered. "And I was going to back out, too, until Gartanis suddenly seemed to think it was very important that I go through with it."

"I'm sure he did," Ravagin growled. "Especially at the overinflated prices he probably charged you—"

"He gave me the spell for free."

Ravagin's tongue froze in midsentence. "He did—he gave you a demogorgon invocation for *free*?"

"That's unusual?"

"A spell like that ought to go for half the price of this house," Ravagin told her bluntly.

She rubbed her forehead. "Yeah, I sort of got that impression. But he wouldn't take anything for it. Anyway, I tried the invocation, but it didn't work out the way I expected. Instead of bringing the demogorgon here, it seemed like he took me *there*. Sounds crazy, but that's the only way I can describe it."

Ravagin thought about her shadowless form in the center of the pentagram. "No, I think you can assume you really were taken off somewhere. What gave you the impression it was a separate world, though?"

She shook her head. "I don't know. Lots of little things, I suppose. The terrain—well, no, it wasn't really *terrain*, at least not in the usual sense. Call it *background*, maybe— the background had a completeness about it that seemed to go with a complete world rather than just a different way of looking at Karyx. There was even a sky of sorts. And there were *lots* of spirits."

"Doing what?"

"Moving around, mostly, on whatever business spirits have in their own world. But I also saw several of them disappear; that was the part that interested me the most."

"Disappear . . . as in being invoked by people in Karyx?" Ravagin hazarded.

"That's the feeling I got at the time." She shivered

again. "And I saw a—well, it was a fight. Pure and simple.
I saw a demon attack a lar."

"And . . . ?" he prompted.

"And destroy it."

A bad taste rose into Ravagin's mouth. "You realize," he
said slowly, "that what you're implying is a level of spirit-
spirit interaction no one's ever seen before."

"In other words, I'm going to be accused of having
hallucinations?" she snorted. "I've already heard that argument once today, and I'm getting tired of it."

"Take it easy—*I'm* not the one you're going to have to
defend this against. Any idea where this fight might have
taken place?"

"I told you: in the fourth world—"

"I mean did it have any relationship to Karyx? Did any
part of the fight take place here, in other words?"

She pondered. "I don't know. Distances didn't seem to
be the same as they are in a physical world. And there
weren't really any reference points I could hold onto."

"Yeah." He took a deep breath, exhaled it thoughtfully
with a glance toward the pentagram. "Well . . . if you're
right, the scholars are going to hate you. Just think of the
trouble they're going to have to go through, changing every
Triplet in the literature to *Quadruplet*."

There was no response, and he looked back to find her
frowning off into space. "Danae? You still there?"

"More or less. Ravagin . . . why would the demogorgon
have shown me all that? I mean, why *me* specifically?
Other people have invoked great powers before—Gartanis,
for one. Why didn't any of *them* see this?"

"Maybe they did," Ravagin shrugged. "You have to
remember that everyone else who's tried this has been a
Karyx native, and none of them know about Triplet's
nature."

"No, it's more than that," she shook her head slowly.
"Gartanis seemed to think the demogorgon *wanted* to talk
to me; that he'd even foreseen some of this a hundred
years ago. Though maybe it wasn't about me specifically . . ."

"Look, Danae, you have to remember not to take everything you hear on Karyx at a hundred percent face value."

"This is different." She looked at him sharply. "The

demogorgon *was* trying to tell me something—I can feel it. Maybe if I do the invocation again and ask more directly—"

"Whoa!" he said, grabbing her shoulders as she started to get to her feet. "You are *not* going to try that again, Danae: period, lockdown."

"But—"

"No buts about it. You want an interesting form of suicide, you can do it back in the Twenty Worlds on someone else's responsibility."

Her eyes flashed. "You just saw me invoke the demogorgon and not get hurt—"

"And if your friend Gartanis wasn't a total fraud he must have warned you that the great powers are totally unpredictable," Ravagin shot back. "At any rate, you're not going to do it."

"Ravagin—"

"Besides which, you're not going to have time. Tomorrow we're heading back to the Tunnel and home."

Her jaw dropped as utter astonishment pushed all other emotion from her face. "We're *what*?" she whispered.

"You heard me: we're heading home," he said doggedly, ignoring with an effort the look of betrayal on her face. "Doing something as insane as invoking a great power without my knowledge is perfectly adequate grounds for me to abort the trip. We'll leave at sunup; I suggest you get to sleep early tonight." Ignoring the protests from his knees, he straightened back to a standing position and offered her a hand up. "And we'd better get out of here before Melentha gets back—she'd be furious to find you'd fiddled around with her stuff."

For a minute Danae just stared up at him. Then, ignoring the proffered hand, she got awkwardly to her feet. Turning her back, she strode unsteadily over to the door and left the sanctum.

Ignore it, Ravagin told himself, glaring at the empty doorway. *It's just another of her little tantrums. I'm right on this one; and for once we're going to do things around here* my *way.*

Turning his head, he snarled the release spell for the firebrat, and walked in darkness to the door. And tried to blot out the strange ache her expression had left in his chest.

"A *demogorgon*?" Melentha shook her head. "Crazy child. She could have gotten herself killed."

"I think we're all agreed on that," Ravagin said shortly. "We're also agreed—you and I are, anyway—that we can't give her another chance to do it again. Tomorrow at dawn we're heading for the Tunnel."

"And you'll be wanting an escort, I suppose?"

"Not necessarily," Ravagin told her, forcing down his annoyance at the breezy condescension in her tone. "Actually, all I need from you is a strengthing of your post line so that Danae won't be able to sneak out tonight if she gets the urge to do so."

Melentha's eyebrows raised slightly. "Yes, I suppose you ought to expect something like that from her."

"Under similar circumstances, I'd expect something like that from *you*, too," he said.

Her face seemed to harden. "I do my job," she bit out. "And I obey orders."

Ravagin sighed. He was getting sick and tired of constantly finding himself swimming upstream. "I meant it as a compliment to your spirit," he told her. "If you want to take it as an insult, that's your business. So can you seal this place up a little more or not?"

She nodded. "Oh, yes," she said softly. "Don't worry, Ravagin; no one will be getting out of here tonight."

Chapter 22

Damn him. Damn her. For that matter, damn this whole stupid planet. Flopping over under her blanket onto her back, her brain fighting stubbornly against the sleep the rest of her body wanted, Danae stared at the starlight filtering through the curtains onto her ceiling. It wasn't fair for Ravagin to pull the rug out from under her like this—it just wasn't *fair*.

It wasn't her fault. None of it. Not the demogorgon invocation—Gartanis had all but pushed that on her, what with his talk of fated contacts and future apocalypses and all. Not the friction with Melentha, either, which she suspected was a factor in Ravagin's decision—it had been Melentha who'd been riding *her* all this time, not the other way around. And certainly not the whole mess with Coven—it had been the demons there who'd been pulling all of those strings. *Damn the demons, too.*

The demons.

Danae frowned at the ceiling, her mind jumping back to her evening arrival from Besak and the confrontation with Melentha's pet demon. There hadn't been anything like that before today, not in all the trips she'd made in and out of that gateway since arriving on Karyx.

What had made that one trip different? The fact that she'd been to Coven and dealt with the powers there? No—the demon hadn't even twitched when she and Ravagin had returned together from Coven that morning. Alternatively, could it be the fact that she'd just learned the demogorgon-invocation spell and was carrying Gartanis's incense focuser? That was probably more reasonable . . . except how had the demon known about it?

Communication with all those other spirits, perhaps? The Twenty Worlds' sketchy understanding of spirithandling seemed to take as a basic assumption that each spirit operated basically as a free agent, interacting little except where ordered to do so. But her experience with Triplet's fourth world now put that assumption on extremely shaky ground. Was there, in fact, an entire spirit society, operating perhaps along hierarchical lines, that included such lines of communication as the post line demon's knowledge had implied? Then that green patch she'd seen leave the post line after she'd passed it could have been one of the demon's parasite spirits, sent by the demon himself to alert Melentha that Danae was back at the house. Ravagin had implied he knew she'd been to Gartanis before she told him about the trip. Presumably Melentha's demon had learned about it from another spirit from Besak, perhaps another parasite spirit under his control but not trapped into the post line. It opened up all sorts of new possibilities; if spirits were in fact being summoned from a separate world instead of from some vague sort of limbo, an information exchange would be almost inevitable once they were released back into their own world.

Into their own world . . .

Danae stared at the ceiling, almost feeling the blood draining out of her face as a horrible thought struck her. *Into their own world* . . .

Quietly, she rolled out of bed and fumbled for her clothes, hands shaking with sudden dread as she fought in the dark to get dressed. It abruptly made sense now: their sudden expulsion from Coven, the vision that Gartanis had tried to describe to her—

And why the demon in the post line had tried to stop her from finding out about the fourth world's existence.

The hallway was dark and silent as Danae slipped out of her room. Hardly daring to breathe, she hugged the wall as she tiptoed to the next door and carefully opened it.

Inside, she made her way toward the bed, a vague shape in the starlight. "Ravagin?" she whispered tentatively.

"What is it?" his soft voice answered instantly. "Danae?"

"Yes," she whispered back, finding the edge of the bed and sitting down on it. "I've got to talk to you right away. I think I know why we were thrown out of Coven."

There was the sound of shifting blankets as Ravagin's dim form elbowed itself to a sitting position in front of her. "Why?"

She hesitated, her dread giving way slightly before the fear that this was going to sound crazy. "Remember first of all that it was only when they realized we were out-worlders that they froze up and kicked us out. We wondered at the time whether that meant they didn't have some power or authority over us that they needed."

"I remember," Ravagin said, the first hint of impatience creeping into his voice. "This couldn't have waited until morning?"

Danae licked her lips. "No, I don't think so. You see, we were exactly backwards. It wasn't that they couldn't do something to us. It was instead that we could have done something to *them*. Or rather, that the rest of the Twenty Worlds could."

"Danae, would you kindly refrain from mentioning—"

"Look, Ravagin," she hurried on, "what would happen if the two of us disappeared on Karyx? They'd stop sending people in, wouldn't they, at least until they had some idea what had happened?"

"Not necessarily. We've lost people here before."

"Lost them dead, yes, but not totally missing. Right?"

"All right," he sighed. "For sake of argument, let's say they'd close down travel here until they found us. So why should Coven care about that?"

Danae took a deep breath. "Because they don't want access to the Tunnel cut off. *Because they're using it to get into Shamsheer.*"

"That's ridiculous," Ravagin snorted. "Spirits can't pass through the Tunnel."

"Why not?"

"Because they're not humans, and only humans can pass through the Tunnel."

"That's an assumption," she pointed out, shaking her head. "An assumption based on the belief that Triplet is only three worlds. But we know now that there are really *four* here."

"So what does the number have to do with anything?"

"It tells us that when we invoke spirits we're bringing them across a world-world boundary. Which says immediately that under certain conditions spirits can pass between worlds."

"Well . . . all right, maybe *here* they can. But the Shamsheer-Karyx boundary is different."

"Why?"

He was silent for nearly a minute. "It still doesn't make sense," he said at last. "Spirits *can't* get into Shamsheer—otherwise the place would be crawling with them."

"How do you know it isn't—?"

"*And* furthermore," he cut her off, "why would they bother? What does it gain them?"

"Maybe it's an extension of what they're going for here: control of the human society."

"Oh, come on, Danae—aren't you letting your imagination run away with you just a little?"

"We agreed that the Karyxites are growing ever more dependent on spirithandling and spirit-enhanced items, didn't we?" she countered doggedly. "Isn't Coven proof enough for you that that dependency is being deliberately pushed by the spirits themselves?"

He exhaled slowly. "Yeah. Coven. Demons in charge of a spirit-trapping operation. It *is* a pretty strong indicator, I'll admit—but only insofar as Karyx is concerned. I don't buy the Shamsheer invasion bit. For starters, there simply isn't a good mechanism for them to get across the teleport."

"Why can't they just drift across?" she suggested. "They're noncorporeal, after all. Or even come out melded with a traveler, maybe in a fractional-possession state."

"Nope," he shook his head. "The early explorers to Karyx did some careful experiments along those lines and pulled a straight zero. The telefold treats spirits like local objects and won't pass them. Period."

"Or at least it didn't back then," she argued. "Doesn't prove the spirits haven't come up with a new approach that *does* work. What about that sleepwalking syndrome you mentioned—God, was that only *yesterday?* You'll recall that Melentha's fractional-possession checks didn't turn up anything, but I was sure under *some* sort of influence."

Ravagin hissed thoughtfully between his teeth. "You sure were," he admitted. "I suppose it's possible. But it's hard to believe the telefold could be fooled like that."

"Why not? We know even less about the telefold than we do about Karyx's spirits. Besides, if there's no invasion under way, we're back to not knowing why Coven let us go in the first place."

"So how's that different from where we were this morning?" he said dryly. "Get off the bed, will you?"

"What are you doing?" she asked as she stood up and took a step back.

"Getting dressed, of course," he grunted. His dim figure swung its legs out of bed, and there was the sound of rustling cloth. "You *are* suggesting we head out to the Tunnel right away, aren't you?"

She opened her mouth, closed it again as all the warnings she'd heard about nighttime travel on Karyx flashed through her mind. "Uh . . . no, not necessarily. I mean, it would be dangerous. Wouldn't it?"

"Sure it would. But if you're right about all this, the demons are likely going to wish they'd kept us in Coven after all . . . and the longer we stick around, the longer they've got to find out about it and correct their mistake."

A shiver went up Danae's back. "God. You're right. Come on, let's get moving."

"I'm glad you agree," Ravagin said. " . . . Oh, hell."

"What?"

"Damn. Well, it's just that I had Melentha double-secure the house tonight in case you decided to contest my decision by skating out on us. We'll have to get her to ungimmick it."

Danae felt her stomach knot up. "Can't you do it by yourself? I know there are spells to release spirits you didn't personally trap."

"Yeah; and most of them are tricky beyond belief, either in execution or in consequences if you don't do it exactly right. I'd rather just wake her up and tell her we're leaving early. We don't have to tell her why." He stood up, reached to the nighttable for his short sword. "Come on; let's go." Taking her arm, he started toward the door—

And abruptly the room blazed with green light.

Ravagin had the faster reflexes. "*Man-sy-hae orlantis!*" he shouted before Danae could do more than throw her arm up to shield her eyes against the sudden glare.

But to no avail. The green light remained steady . . . and as Danae's eyes adjusted she realized with a gut-wrenching feeling that it was coming from a ring of glowing green shapes spaced along the walls surrounding them.

Green *demon* shapes. "*Ravagin—*" she gasped in horror.

The slamming open of the room's door cut her off. "Fool," a deep, mocking voice came from the hallway. "Did you really think a simple spirit-protection spell would avail against *me?*"

Danae caught her breath as that voice clicked in her mind. "Ravagin—that's the demon-possessed man who talked to us in Coven—!"

And Melentha walked into the room.

Chapter 23

It was, a distant part of Ravagin's mind seemed to whisper, like a replay of Coven. Danae standing half behind him, hostile spirits all around them, a demon-possessed enemy in front of them.

Except that this time the enemy was Melentha. Who should have been a friend.

Melentha, how could you have let this happen?

"Ravagin," Danae breathed tightly in his ear. "How did it get *here?*—and through all her defenses, too?"

"It's a different demon, Danae," Ravagin told her in a low voice. "And unfortunately, it was probably invited. Stay calm and let me do the talking, okay?"

Melentha glided to a stop facing them, an amused smile tugging at the corners of her mouth. "You were right, Ravagin; it *was* a good idea to double-safe the house. One never knows about these things, does one?"

"I guess one doesn't," Ravagin said, forcing his voice to remain steady. For the moment, at least, it was still a battle of wits, and the last thing he could afford was to panic. "So now what? The reasons behind your friends' decision back at Coven still hold, you know—you still risk a whole pack of trouble if you keep us here."

"True," Melentha nodded. "But now the risks of letting you leave are even stronger."

"What risks?" Ravagin scoffed. "Danae was just speculating through her hat on this—we know it, and you know

172

it. The only thing we've got at all is that you're trying to make the human population of Karyx dependent on you; and if that's news to anyone at the Crosspoint Building they deserve to be surprised. The indications have been there for a long time; you can ask Melentha if you don't believe me."

Melentha's eyebrows raised slightly. "You *are* naive about these things, aren't you? You think one partner or the other has to be submerged in this type of symbiosis?" She shook her head. "You've been influenced by the old Earth scare-legends of spirit possession, I'm afraid."

"Sorry if I offended you—either of you," Ravagin amended. "So it's a symbiosis, is it? Interesting. Clear enough what the demon gets out of the relationship— mobility on Karyx, a clearer view of the physical world, and access to human information. What exactly does Melentha get out of it?"

"Much the same sorts of things as the demon does," she said. "Immediate and continuous access to the spirit world, mainly."

"And *that's* worth giving up your freedom over?" Danae put in harshly.

Melentha turned glittering eyes onto her. "I would suggest," she bit out, "that you stay out of conversations you don't understand. You don't even have Ravagin's pitiful access to the spirit world—how could you possibly imagine the depth of *my* knowledge and ability?"

"Oh, maybe she can imagine it a *little*," Ravagin shrugged. "After all, she's been in communication with a great power, and I'd wager that's something *you* haven't done."

For just an instant an inhuman fury filled Melentha's face. "Yes, the demogorgon," she bit out, her expression turning to stone. "We'll deal properly with it some other time. But thank you for reminding me. That contact of hers gives me that much more reason to prevent your return to Threshold."

Ravagin felt his mouth go dry. That hadn't been the reaction he'd been trying for . . . "Uh-*huh*. Again, I suggest that keeping us here will open more of a hornets' nest than you can really handle at this point."

"Why? Because an experienced Courier gets himself

and his client killed on Karyx? Come, now, Ravagin—that happens often enough. No one's going to get into a major loop over it."

"But perhaps Cowan mal ce Taeger of Arcadia will," Danae said.

"Who?" Ravagin frowned.

"He's a billionaire politician/industrialist or something," Melentha said off-handedly. "All right, little girl, tell me: why would someone like that even notice, let alone care, if Ravagin turns up dead?"

"I'm his daughter."

Ravagin twisted his head around to stare at her. "You're *what?*"

"His daughter." Danae kept her gaze on Melentha. "Ravagin's right, Melentha—you can't just make us go away like a pair of unknown tourists."

Melentha's eyes flicked to Ravagin, back to Danae, and her tongue snaked out to flick at her upper lip. "You're bluffing," she said at last. "You aren't any relation to mal ce Taeger—you just read his name somewhere and made all this up."

"There's always one way to find out," Ravagin told her. "It's the hard way, of course."

Melentha's gaze returned to him . . . and this time there was no mistaking the hesitation there. She was in a bind, and both she and her companion demon knew it. "I suppose we'd better talk about this, then, hadn't we? Come with me. You—" she looked at Danae—"will stay here."

Turning abruptly, she strode from the room. As if on unspoken signal, the ring of demons shifted position, sweeping inward to form two sides of an aisle between Ravagin and the door. "Okay," Ravagin said, turning back to Danae. "Try to relax—maybe get some sleep if you can."

She clung to his arm. "Wait—you can't go with her. She might—who knows *what* she'll do to you?"

Gently, he disengaged her hand. "If she'd decided to kill us, she wouldn't be wasting time with talk," he reassured her. "They've just finally realized they've bitten off more than they bargained for, and I think they're going to try and negotiate themselves out of the corner. So just kick back and free-float; I'll be back as soon as I can."

Without warning, her arms looped around his neck, pulling his head down for a brief but intense kiss. "Be careful," she whispered as she reluctantly let go.

"You bet. You, too."

Turning, he headed off between the lines of demons, trying to walk boldly despite the slight trembling of his knees. Beneath his tunic, his skin prickled at the spirits' close and deadly presense; deeper within him, his stomach was tight with the anticipation of the delicate negotiations facing him. And on his lips, he could feel the lingering impression of Danae's unexpected kiss.

Gritting his teeth, he concentrated on the memory of that kiss.

The door closed, and Danae was alone.

No; not quite alone. A single green figure floated in the air between her and the door.

For a long moment she eyed the ghastly shape, wondering what her chances were of dashing past it and out the door to freedom . . .

The demon gazed straight back at her. Swallowing hard, she turned away and stepped over to the window.

The demon didn't follow, nor did he try to stop her as she lifted the edge of the curtain and looked out. Not that that was any real surprise. The post line below was hard to see in the dim starlight, but the shadows the posts cast were clear and sharply defined. "*Esporla-meenay*," she called on sudden impulse, and was rewarded by a pair of flashes from the post line: one green, one red.

The red was new. "I see Melentha's added some djinns to the post line," she commented over her shoulder. "You suppose that means she doesn't trust your fellow demon out there to keep us in?"

The demon at the door didn't respond. *All right, Danae: calm down, stop babbling, and think,* she berated herself. *What do you know about spirithandling in general and demons in particular?*

Precious little, she had to admit, and virtually nothing that looked like it might be of any use in getting her out of this mess. Even if she somehow managed to get past her watchdog, getting through the post line would take more skill than she possessed. Possibly more skill than even Ravagin possessed.

Gartanis.

Carefully, Danae turned her head. The demon was still there, was still watching her with inhuman stillness. Turning back to the window, she licked suddenly dry lips. This could be dangerous . . . but Melentha had surely given the demon instructions not to hurt her, at least not until she'd made a decision as to their disposition. All in all, a risk worth taking. "*Haklarast*," she murmured, as softly as possible.

The glow-fire of a sprite appeared before her. "I am here, as you summoned," it squeaked.

"Go to Besak, to a man named Gartanis—"

And the demon pounced.

It was over almost before it began. One instant the hazy glow was hovering in front of her; the next instant the demon's swooping dive had intersected it and it was gone. Quick and bloodless . . .

Leaving nothing but a horrible wail that rang in her ears long after it had faded from the room.

Knees shaking, Danae groped her way over to the bed and collapsed onto it. "You will have no communication outside this place," a deep voice told her.

She looked at the door, half expecting to see Melentha standing there. But it was only the watchdog demon. Ravagin had been right; they *did* all sound alike. "Go back to hell," she told him tiredly, closing her eyes.

"I do not accept commands from you," he said.

She glanced back at him, wondering if he was being sarcastic. But if he was, it didn't show.

Snap out of it, girl. Getting back to her feet with an effort, she walked over to the window again. Posture affects attitude, her father had been fond of telling her, and she wasn't going to be able to work up much defiance while slouched back on a mattress.

For all the good defiance would do her. *All right.* The sprite incident had shown she would at least have time to do a simple invocation before the demon could interfere.

Invoke the demogorgon again, see if it could or would help her? No; it took far too much time—and besides, the incense she needed was back in her own room. The manifold geas that she'd tried back in Coven? Molontha had even less reason to make her spirits subject to outside commands, but still—"*Harkhonistrasmylikiheen!*" she called. "Move aside."

The demon didn't budge. *Well, that's twice now that hasn't worked,* she thought bitterly. Still, she could hardly have expected Melentha to have left that big a loophole in her spirit protection ring. Melentha was smart enough . . . but she was arrogant, too, and in Danae's experience arrogance usually led to carelessness. If she'd thought to close all the big loopholes, perhaps she'd accidentally left some of the little ones open.

Something simple, then. A dazzler or firebrat, perhaps? No; a demon couldn't care less about either of those. A doppelganger, then? It would depend on how demons perceived the physical universe, but it might be worth trying during a mad dash out of the house. At least it would slow down any of Melentha's human lackies if any were around tonight.

Except that between her and that mad dash was the demon. And the post line. And no allies but Ravagin, who wasn't any better off than she was.

With a sigh, she leaned on the window sill and stared dejectedly outside . . . and so happened to be gazing directly at the post line when it flickered again with its red and green lights.

Danae caught her breath, biting down on her tongue to keep silent. Red and green flashes . . . the sign that someone had just done a spirit-detection. *Ravagin?* But he was closeted with Melentha somewhere. And there was no one else in the house who would be likely to do that spell just for the hell of it.

Which meant that there was someone prowling around *out*side the house. Looking for a way in.

Gartanis! Her heart started beating faster, even while her brain reminded her how unlikely that really was. More probably it was a bandit or group of same looking for nighttime booty.

But it almost didn't matter. Unexpected company of any sort would force a change in Melentha's careful arrangement, and if Coven was any indication, demons weren't very good at handling the unexpected.

It was time to try her best shot. Taking a deep breath, she turned back to the demon. "You realize, I hope, that Melentha will be furious with you if anything should happen to me," she told him.

"You will not be harmed," the demon replied.

"Glad you've got such faith." Behind her back, Danae's hands fumbled with the window's clasp. "Because—*haklarast!*"

A sprite appeared between her and the demon. "I am here—" it began.

The demon shot over and engulfed it; and as that mournful wail split the air, Danae twisted around and shoved the window open.

It was a good five-meter drop down to the flagstones below, but she was counting on the demon to have faster reflexes than that. And she was right. Barely had she gotten one knee up on the sill when the view before her exploded with green light as the demon jumped into the window between her and freedom. The shock of its presence threw her backwards, reeling past the center of the room—

And without even pausing to regain her balance, she turned and sprinted all-out for the door.

She almost made it. She actually had a hand on the knob when the demon finally recovered and again dove in front of her. She pushed hard against him, trying to force her way past—

And without warning, a scream of rage split the air.

With a gasp, Danae fell back, her whole body tingling with the afterclap of that scream. Slowly, the tingling faded, and as it did so, she suddenly noticed that her entire left side was numb. *A stroke!* was her first, awful fear . . . but a second later she realized the symptoms weren't quite right for that. More likely, it was an effect of her close encounter with the demon.

The demon. He was still hovering in front of the door when she turned her attention back to him. For a moment they stared at each other . . . and then, abruptly, there was a second green shape in the room. "So one paltry human is too much for one demon to handle is that it?" she commented sarcastically, the words from her half numb mouth coming out oddly slurred. "Good idea—send for help. Not that it'll do you any good; I'm still going to get out of here."

Neither demon replied. Swallowing hard, Danae turned awkwardly back to the window, noting without surprise that the demon had closed it. *Well, you got what you wanted,* she reminded herself. *They've doubled the guard on you. Let's just hope that this whole crazy idea actually works.*

And hope, too, that the numbness in her left side was only temporary. Listening to her heart pounding in her ears, she gazed out the window and waited.

Chapter 24

The dazzler usually situated in one of the conversaton area's back corners was absent when Melentha and Ravagin arrived downstairs. The fireplate, too, was empty, leaving the room completely dark except for the faint light coming from outside through the uncurtained floor-to-ceiling windows. The effect was almost certainly intended to be unnerving; Ravagin found it more annoying than anything else. "Please sit down," Melentha told him, her shadowy figure gesturing to a large cushion as she took one opposite.

Ravagin did so. "You have something against light?"

"Does the darkness bother you?" she countered.

"Not really," he said, looking around. Somewhere along the way, he noted with mild surprise, they'd lost all but one of their demon escorts. The rest had probably been released to other duties, he knew, and could be called back at a moment's notice. Still, their absence gave him a badly needed psychological lift. An error on Melentha's part. "I just thought you might worry about me slipping out in the dark," he added.

Melentha snorted. "Demons don't see things the way humans do."

"And since you have a set of demon eyes to see through, you're all set. Right?"

"Something like that." She leaned forward slightly. "Now. What exactly are we going to do with you?"

"It's certainly going to be a problem for you," Ravagin

180

agreed. "Danae and I disappear here, and the minute we show up overdue you'll have people crawling all over Karyx looking for us. If I were you, I'd turn us loose and hope that no one will pay any serious attention to us."

Even in the dimness he could see the mockery in her smile. "Oh, certainly. I'd prefer something that requires a little less trust, if you don't mind."

He shrugged. "Well, you could always try turning us into demon-possessed zombies like you are."

Her eyes flashed and she half stood up before sinking back into her cushion. "Nice try, but you won't bait me that easily," she said coldly. "I also happen to know that you can't take even a symbiont spirit through the telefold, but nice try there, too. You have any other suggestions?"

"Not really," he admitted. "If you had the equipment and the skill you could easily play brain games with us—set up a psychological fence or maybe dub in selective amnesia; that sort of thing."

"And if the effects don't last past the telefold?"

"Then you're out of luck." And they probably wouldn't, he knew. Like the spirits themselves, spirit effects usually disappeared once the person reached Shamsheer. "I don't suppose you've bothered to study the local pharmacology for anything that might work that way."

"Pharmacology?" she snorted. "There isn't any pharmacology on Karyx. Nobody here has even the slightest idea of how the physical universe is put together."

And of course you who should have known better didn't bother to do any such studies yourself. She was right, of course: anything physics or chemistry could do, spirit-handling could do faster and easier. Clearly, Melentha had slipped into that philosophy . . . and it was now costing her. "Well, in that case I guess we're back to letting us go and hoping for the best. Aren't we."

"Or else we're back to killing you both and hoping for the best," Melentha retorted. "I still haven't decided which would be the riskier—"

She broke off as a patch of green haze abruptly shot in through one of the windows and entered her. " . . . *what*?" she whispered. "*Damn . . . yes, of course* let him in."

The green patch reappeared and went back outside. "Trouble?" Ravagin asked.

Melentha eyed him, what little he could see of her face looking very inhuman. " . . . no, he'd better stay. The other may know he's here, and if so it'll look suspicious if I didn't wake him up . . . oh, he certainly *will* behave. Or else."

Ravagin cleared his throat. "You know, talking to yourself is a bad habit to get into—"

"Shut up," she cut him off. "We've got company. I'm going to have to let you stay here; and you *will* behave yourself as the situation requires. Or Danae will pay heavily."

"I understand," Ravagin nodded, fighting against a sudden surge of adrenaline. Here it was: the chance he'd hoped for but hadn't really expected to get. An unplanned-for situation, one that would force Melentha and her ally demons to split their attention partly away from him and Danae. It would be their best shot. Possibly even their only shot.

Melentha took a deep breath and made a placement gesture toward the fireplate. "*Sa-trahist rassh!*" she commanded, and a firebrat burst into existence, flooding the room with a flickering glow. Ravagin squinted against the sudden light . . . and when he could see again, he almost gasped at the change that had taken place in Melentha. The cold hardness was gone, replaced by a softer, more human, demeanor.

It was the Melentha he'd once known, and for a second he wondered if the demon had pulled out completely in order to avoid their visitor. "Melentha—?"

"Shut up," she said calmly. "I'm still in charge here, and you're still covered." She nodded toward the fireplate . . . and Ravagin saw that, almost hidden in the glare of the firebrat, the green form of his guard demon was lurking there.

Which meant it wasn't just the demon who was running things here. Melentha truly *was* a willing partner in her own possession . . . and it ended for good any chance that he could persuade Melentha to turn back to their side.

Across the room a door swung open and a travel-stained

man strode in . . . and Ravagin felt his jaw drop. He'd expected it would be some local person— "Nordis!" he blurted.

"Yeah, hi, Ravagin," the other said with a tired nod. "Glad you're still here—I'm going to need your help. Hi, Melentha," he added, turning to her. "You're both really gonna love this one."

"Calm down and tell us what's wrong," Melentha said coolly. "Where are your clients, still outside?"

"Yeah, in a way." Nordis's lip twisted into a grimace. "I—ah—appear to have misplaced him."

"You *what*?" Melentha frowned. "What do you mean, misplaced him?"

"Just what I said. One minute we were in Besak, watching the booths closing down for the night, and the next minute he was gone. I don't know whether he made a wrong turn in the excitement and got lost or whether someone took advantage of all the crowds and kidnapped him, but somehow he just vanished."

"What excitement?" Ravagin asked.

"That thing with Gartanis this evening—you know."

"No, I don't," Ravagin told him, glancing at Melentha. Her face was going rigid again . . .

"Oh, his private lar had it out with something nasty tonight—a peri or demon, probably. I'm glad as hell we weren't actually there when it happened—there're scorched buildings for almost a block around his place."

Ravagin felt cold fingers playing along his spine. Melentha had headed off to "deal with Gartanis" . . . and Danae had claimed to see a demon and lar fighting in the fourth world. "What happened to Gartanis? Was he killed?"

"Not unless the dead can limp around picking up pieces of their houses on Karyx," Nordis said impatiently. "You suppose we could forget about Gartanis for a minute and get back to the more immediate problem? Melentha, do you know of any kidnapping rings that might be operating—"

He broke off abruptly as a faint scream floated into the room. "Good lord," Nordis said, jumping and looking uneasily around him. "What the hell was *that*?"

"Just a little trouble upstairs," Melentha growled. "Ignore it; it'll be dealt with." Her eyes flicked to the fireplate, and Ravagin caught a flash of green as the demon lurking there shot upward and vanished. Trouble upstairs . . . with Danae? Almost certainly. A fist seemed to close around his stomach; sternly, he forced the muscles there to relax. Whatever it was Danae had done—or tried to do—that had riled her own guard, the immediate result was that Ravagin now had only Melentha to deal with . . . and furthermore had an opening the size of a truck just waiting to be exploited.

And the sooner he grabbed it, the better the chances it would pay off. "Right, Nordis, let's get back to your missing client," he said briskly. "Was he experienced or armed or otherwise capable of handling Karyx at night?"

"Hardly. This was his first trip in, and you never saw a more useless person in your life. He couldn't ever figure anything out by himself; he was forever asking questions about everything imaginable. If he's just wandered off by himself, he's going to be in a pack of trouble."

"But if he disappeared in Besak, he should be all right there at least until morning," Melentha pointed out. "With the village lar enclosing it—"

"Hello, Melentha, wake up," Nordis cut her off, spreading his arms out to the sides. "Look; see?—I got out of Besak after dark. Besak's lar isn't there any more."

"What? How the hell—?"

"*I* don't know," he snarled. "Side effect of the attack on Gartanis's lar, maybe. Does it matter?"

"Not really," Ravagin agreed, standing up. "You're right, Nordis—we'd better get a search going right away."

"No!" Melentha snapped, scrambling to her feet as well. "No—I won't hear of it. It's too dangerous."

"If it's dangerous for *us*, what do you think it is for *him*?" Nordis growled. "Yeah, come on, Ravagin. Melentha, can you scare us up a couple of spare horses?—mine's pretty worn out."

Melentha's jaw tightened, then relaxed. "Yes, of course. *Haklarast!*" A sprite appeared. "Have three horses prepared immediately," Melentha instructed the spirit.

"Three?" Ravagin asked as the glow-fire darted out of the room.

"Three of us will stand a better chance out there than

two," she said calmly. "Nordis, you have anything better than the knife you're wearing?"

" 'Fraid not. The selection you get in the Tunnel isn't oxactly the best."

"Yes, I know. There's a sword cabinet down the hall to your left—go and pick yourself out something."

"Thanks." Nordis strode to the door and out into the hall.

Ravagin eyed Melentha. "What did you do to Gartanis?" he asked quietly.

It was the deeper demon voice which answered him. "Less than I'd hoped to, it seems," it said. "His defenses were skillfully prepared, with the lar only one of them. But he won't be in Besak long."

"You think one lousy demon attack's going to scare him into running?" Ravagin snorted.

"Not at all—it'll be the leaders of Besak who ask him to leave. They won't risk losing their lar again."

"Ah-ha," Ravagin said, nodding. "Side effect, nothing—you took out Besak's lar deliberately. Is Gartanis that much of a threat to you?"

Abruptly, Melentha stood up. "I trust, Ravagin, that you won't try anything foolish while we're out looking for this wayward fool of Nordis's. Remember that Danae will still be here."

Ravagin felt his stomach muscles tighten. "Don't worry," he said softly. "I'll remember."

Five minutes later they were mounted and riding out from the house.

"*Esporla-meenay,*" Ravagin murmured as they reached the post line, felt his jaw tighten as he noted the red flash accompanying the green. So Melentha had added djinns to the demon already trapped there. Great.

"We'll start at Besak, see if we can pick up his trail," Melentha said as they turned eastward. "This guy have a name, Nordis?"

"Rax Andresson," the other supplied. "I tried using a djinn to track him down, but the thing couldn't make contact."

"You'd have done better to use a demon," Melentha

said shortly. "Djinns aren't much use for that sort of thing."

Riding a few meters off Melentha's left, Ravagin listened to the shop talk with half an ear and tried to think. Out here, far from Melentha's demon-infested house and grounds, getting away would be an almost trivial exercise. Getting back to the house afterwards and rescuing Danae, on the other hand, would be essentially impossible.

Damn it all. What am I supposed to do?

A Courier's primary responsibility is to protect his clients, the standard policy ran through his mind. Fine; so what did that policy require here?

He could escape. Possibly even escape to the Tunnel and out of range of this spirit conspiracy they'd stumbled into. He could bring back assistance . . .

And would find that in the meantime Danae had disappeared.

Or he could cooperate with Melentha and walk meekly back into his prison once they'd rescued this Andresson idiot . . . and the odds still were that Danae would be killed. Along with him.

There wasn't any third option . . . and unfortunately, he knew what his choice had to be.

He would have to walk back into the lion's den with Melentha. Go back and do what he could to at least win freedom for his client.

And if that effort failed, to be prepared to die there with her.

Chapter 25

From the window, Danae watched the three figures ride away from the house. Another flicker of red and green came from the post line just before they reached it—one of them checking on the spirits there?—and then they were past and riding off across the outer grounds in the direction of Besak.

She took a deep breath. For Melentha to send anyone out at this time of night was ominous in the extreme . . . but on the other hand, it meant that for a while at least there were going to be three fewer obstacles between her and freedom.

Would Ravagin read it that way, too? There was no way to know—no way to know, for that matter, if he even was aware that anyone had left. But it almost didn't matter. *One* of them had to get out if the Twenty Worlds were to be alerted to the threat sitting here across the Tunnels. If she could get Ravagin out too, they'd have a much better chance . . . but if she couldn't, she would just have to go it alone.

And right now was the best chance she'd ever have to make her play. It was time to close her carefully laid trap . . . and hope like hell she did indeed know what she was doing.

Turning from the window, she stepped over to the bed, surreptitiously testing the feeling in the fingers of her left hand. Still a little clumsy, but enough of the numbness had worn off. She'd just have to hope that her feet would behave properly when the time came.

"Your mistress will be furious with you if anything happens to me without her orders," she said, looking in turn at the demons hovering by the door and over the window she'd just left. "You realize that, don't you?"

There was no response. Licking her lips, Danae climbed to a precarious stance on top of the bed. This was it. The demons began drifting closer, sensing perhaps that she was up to something. . . .

"*Sa-trahist rassh!*" she snapped abruptly, gesturing. A firebrat burst into existence in front of her on the bed—

And an instant later black smoke billowed up from the mattress.

A flash of green exploded before Danae's eyes, and she felt herself falling backwards as the demon forced her away from the flames. *Now!*— "*Plazni-hy-ix!*" she snapped. Bending sideways, she slid away from the demon and rolled off onto the floor. Scrambling to her feet, she ran awkwardly for the door.

Nothing moved to intercept her. She got the door open; and as she slipped through it she threw a glance behind her at the flaming bed and the two demons swirling in furious activity around it.

Furious, yet oddly impotent activity. Closing the door gently, Danae permitted herself a grim smile as she hurried down the hall toward her own room. Ravagin had been right about it requiring two or more opponents; but she suspected even he was going to be surprised to learn that the confusion of a jinx spell worked against other spirits as well as human foes.

She just hoped they both lived long enough for her to tell him about it.

The hallway was deserted, both of people and spirits. Nor was anything lying in wait in her room as she ducked in and hurriedly scooped up the bag of incense Gartanis had given her. Cautiously, pressing against the stairwell wall, she tiptoed down the stairs, her heartbeat sounding like thunder in her ears. Somewhere along here Melentha would certainly have set up a second line of defense against escape. . . .

But she reached the first floor without incident. The conversation area door was open, the flickering light of a firebrat spilling out into the hall. Gritting her teeth, Danae eased over to the door and peeked in.

Empty.

The knot in Danae's stomach tightened a couple of turns as she flattened herself against the wall and looked quickly around her. There would be no time for her to search the whole house for Ravagin—the demons upstairs might blow the jinx away any time now, and when they did so they'd be after her like a pair of furies. "Ravagin!" she stage-whispered, straining her ears for any kind of a reply.

Nothing. "Damn," she muttered. "*Haklarast.*"

A sprite materialized before her. "I am here—"

"Where is the human called Ravagin?" she interrupted it.

"I do not know."

She gritted her teeth. She had to get *out* of here . . . . "Find him," she ordered. "He should be in this house somewhere. Tell him—wait five minutes and then tell him that Danae has gone. Tell him—" *I'm sorry.* The apology stuck to her tongue. "Just tell him that."

The sprite flared and vanished. Taking another look around her, Danae pushed off the wall and headed for the front door.

Again, no spirits appeared to challenge her, and a minute later she was outside. Ahead was nothing but starlit ground . . . and the deceptively innocent post line.

And behind her was nothing but demons. Gritting her teeth, she kept moving.

She was five meters from the line when a green glow began to form on the two nearest posts. "*Man-sy-hae orlontis,*" she intoned between dry lips; and as if in response, the intensity of the green light suddenly increased. Steeling herself, Danae started forward—

And the green lights suddenly detached themselves from their posts and shot directly toward her.

Gasping, she fell back a step. The lights combined into one in midair, then abruptly split apart again half a meter in front of her as if bouncing from an invisible bubble surrounding her. She held her breath; coming around in tight circles, the parasite spirits recombined and swooped back for a second attack. This time they struck the invisible barrier a few centimeters closer to her. The next time they made it even closer . . . the next time closer still . . .

"*Man-sy-hae orlontis!*" Danae called again, fighting against the panic she could hear bubbling up into her voice. They were almost upon her . . . !

But with one protection spell still in place, a second invocation was useless. The parasite spirits chipped again and again at the spell until, suddenly, it was gone. She braced herself—

And the spirits vanished back into their posts.

Biting down hard on her tongue, Danae took a shuddering breath. She should have expected this, she realized as the panic abated enough for her brain to function again. Melentha had set this defense up . . . Melentha the sadistic bitch, who'd mentioned once how amusing it was to watch people trying to break into her house. She wouldn't let her post line kill attackers on their first try.

Okay, Danae, settle down, she told herself. *You're safe, at least for now. So now what the hell do I do?* There were at least two other spirit-protection spells that she knew, but neither was supposed to be all that much stronger than the one the demon had just casually shattered. A lar would be stronger, but a lar was stationary and couldn't be made to move with her across the post line.

Unless . . .

It was a gamble, but gambles were about all she had left. Gritting her teeth, she started forward.

It wasn't easy. She'd seen a lot of demons here—had seen what they were capable of doing—and each step was a struggle between will power and the panic again starting to simmer just below the surface. The green glow brightened with each laborious step; with each step her eyes involuntarily squinted against the possibility that *this* time the parasite spirits would again burst forth to attack her. Four steps . . . five . . . six . . . the post line was no more than two meters away, and Danae's whole body was shaking with fear and dread. Forcing moisture into her dry mouth, she filled her lungs. "*Sa-preenhala minnistulri*," she gasped—

And fell backwards as a crack of thunder seemed to explode inside her skull. The ground came up and slammed into her back and head—

And then there was silence.

Groggily, she forced herself up on her elbows. Ahead, the entire post line was alive with flashes of green ribbon, looking for all the world like green high-voltage current arcing across inadequate insulation. Between her and the nearest posts . . .

Cautiously, she got to her feet. She'd never seen a lar in trouble before, but she had no doubt that that was exactly what she was witnessing. The clean spectral whirlwind she'd seen her first night on Karyx had changed into the dirt-laden funnel of a tornado, its muddy blackness shot through with angry flickers of color as the lar struggled to establish itself where she had invoked it against the resistance of the demon.

And the demon was winning.

Danae's muscles felt like they'd just been through two hours of hard exercise. Choking back a groan, she forced herself to her feet. She had no way of knowing how long the lar would last, but until it was defeated she should be able to move right up to its far edge without danger. That was the theory, anyway, and she hoped desperately it was correct . . . because as she started forward, she saw that the lar's far edge had indeed fallen where she'd hoped it would: a meter *past* the post line.

Her skin began to tingle as she dragged herself toward the silent combat. The number and brightness of the green flashes intensified, and as her eyes adjusted she could see that the high-voltage sparks were actually the demon's parasite spirits flicking in and out of their posts as they threw themselves against the lar. Steeling herself, she stepped boldly between the posts—

It was probably only a few seconds before her vision and mind cleared and she found herself beyond the post line leaning up against the lar's far edge. To both sides of her the fight was continuing; ahead of her the muddy edge of the lar had become transparent enough to see stars through.

The lar was about to collapse.

Danae took a shuddering breath, then another, trying to

drive the cobwebs of that passage from her brain. When the lar vanished, she had to be ready to move away from the post line as quickly as she could, before the demon could reach out. Invoking another lar would give her a chance to get her muscles back in order again; licking her lips, she took a deep breath and braced herself.

And all at once the lar was gone.

She hadn't realized she was still leaning against it until she toppled face-first onto the ground. "*Sa-preenhala minnis—*" she began.

And was interrupted by a crack of thunder as a flash of green shot out of the post line and ricocheted from her face . . . and she found her tongue frozen.

With her lar invocation unfinished.

There was nothing she could do. Dimly, she remembered having heard that there were spells that could be done with hand and body movements alone; but nothing that specialized had ever been given to her. Without her voice, she was completely helpless; open to whatever the demon decided to do to her. The green glow flared again—

"*Sa-preenhala minnistulri!*"

Danae jerked at the unexpected voice from behind her, and for a heartbeat wondered if it had been a product of her own desperate imagination. But there was nothing imaginary about the flashes of green high-voltage that were again arcing about a dark but no longer muddy lar . . .

A pair of hands gripped her shoulders as she started to twist around in the grass where she still lay. "You all right?" a voice whispered.

"Ahhh—" Danae worked moisture into her mouth. "Ahh . . . yes, I think so. Where—how—?"

"Let's hold off on any conversation until after we're away from here, all right?" She found herself being half lifted, half dragged to her feet. "I tried a little spell that's supposed to bind trapped spirits a little tighter," he added, "but I don't know how much range the demon there had in the first place, so I don't know whether it'll help us much."

His arm supporting her, they started away ..om the post line, and it wasn't until then that Danae realized how big the lar surrounding them actually was. "We go to the

edge, you release this one and immediately invoke another?" she hazarded. "Cute."

"Thank you. Your trick back there was pretty good, too.
I'd wager your friend Melentha never thought of someone
getting through her post line like that."

Danae felt her heart skip a beat. "Melentha! Damn!—I
forgot about her. She'll be after us any second now—"

"She'll have to hear the news and get back first," the
other said calmly. "She, Ravagin, and a man named Nordis
left the house a few minutes before you came out."

"You mean—?" Danae clamped her teeth together as it
suddenly clicked. No wonder there'd been no demons in
the halls or on the grounds to stop her: the system had
been set up for the demons to take their orders directly
from Melentha, and in her absence there was no way for
unexpected events like Danae's escape to be taken into
account. For the moment, at least, they had a little breathing space.

But only for the moment. Even if the demons themselves wouldn't or couldn't leave the house without new
orders, they would certainly have already sent word via
their parasite spirits, and Melentha would soon be galloping back to start the hunt.

"You must have been skulking around here for quite
awhile, then," she commented as they reached the far
edge of the lar's protection.

"Not that long, really," he shrugged. "I spent most of
the time I had studying the defenses. Get ready: *carash-
melanasta—sa-preenhala minnistulri.*"

The lar flicked out and a new one appeared to take its
place. "I'm glad you found your way out before I had to
find my way in," he added.

"I don't blame you," she sighed as they started off again.
"You know, I wondered if it might be you when I realized
that someone out here was testing the post line for spirits.
But I figured it was more likely bandits or something. Can
I assume it was more of your finagling that was behind
Melentha's sudden departure, too?"

"Oddly enough, it was, though totally accidentally. My
horse is tethered over behind the trees there—are your legs
doing any better?"

"I should be able to walk in a minute or two." Danae clenched her teeth and threw him a sideways glance. "I never thought I'd live to say this . . . but I'm sure as hell glad to see you."

A slight smile creased Hart's face. "I'm glad I was here when you needed me, Ms. mal ce Taeger," he said.

Chapter 26

"I'll tell you one thing—Andresson damn well *better* be in trouble," Nordis growled. "If he's just off sight-seeing somewhere I'll skin him alive."

"Shut up and keep your eyes open," Melentha snapped. "If you'd handled this right in the first place, the trail wouldn't have had time to get this cold."

Nordis subsided, and in the darkness Ravagin grimaced. Nordis was an old hand, with nearly ten years of service to the Corps on his file. Professional pride was probably behind his time-consuming efforts to locate Andresson by himself instead of immediately sending a message to the way house—pride, and maybe more than a little conceit. Still, there was no call for Melentha to jump all over him about it.

But then, Nordis had no idea of how his unexpected appearance had fouled up Melentha's plans.

They were in sight of Besak's lar now—or, rather, in sight of the place where the lar should have been visible. Ravagin felt his hands clench around the reins at the sheer *power* the lar's destruction implied. Could Melentha have done all that herself? If so, then any plan he could possibly come up with to escape with Danae was so much wasted effort.

Perhaps there was a way to find out. "Tell me, Melentha," he called across to her, "if someone wanted to take out a lar of this size, how would he or she go about doing so?"

"Hold it a second," she said shortly as a pair of sprites shot across the landscape and came to a hovering halt in front of her. She held a brief and inaudible conversation with them, and a minute later they flitted off again. "No sign of anyone on the Besak-Findral road," she reported. "What was the question again?"

"I was asking how you'd go about destroying Besak's lar."

"Afraid you'd have to ask someone with a little more spirit knowledge," she replied calmly. "Gartanis, for instance."

"Same thing I told Andresson when *he* asked that question," Nordis commented. "I've never seen a client nag your leg off with questions like that."

"You *told* him about Gartanis?" Ravagin frowned. "Maybe that's where he went, then."

"Give me a *little* credit, will you, Ravagin?" the other said. "That was the first place I checked."

Unless Gartanis had lied about Andresson's presence there . . . but why would he bother? "What exactly was Andresson's field of study?" he asked instead. "If he wandered off on his own, it might give us a clue as to where he might be."

"He didn't have one," Nordis snorted. "He was a tourist, here to see the sights. If you can believe that."

"What in the world does Besak have in the way of sights?" Ravagin frowned.

"Damned if I know," Nordis said frankly. "Or Torralane Village, either, for that matter. That's where we started this trip—we only came down yesterday."

"You were here *yesterday?*" Melentha put in. "Why the hell didn't you check in then?"

"He didn't want to," Nordis told her. "Said he wanted to live native-style, not in some transplanted part of the Twenty Worlds."

"You're not supposed to let *clients* dictate safety rules to you," Melentha snapped.

"Listen, Melentha, when we find him, *you* can try arguing with him," Nordis shot back. "This guy gets what he wants, and you get bowled over if you get in his way."

"He sounds like one of those rich fools who've inherited

all their money and can't find enough useful ways to spend it," Ravagin suggested.

"Probably is," Nordis agreed. "Then again, maybe he just thought he was being polite. We found out in town that you and your client were already staying at the way house, and he was pretty adamant about not wanting to intrude."

"Did you bother to explain to him how big the house is?" Melentha growled.

Nordis said something in reply . . . but Ravagin didn't hear it. A rich man playing tourist . . . who didn't seem afraid to stray from his host even in the dead of a Karyx night . . .

And who didn't want to run into Ravagin and Danae.

Hart.

And in the space of a few seconds the whole mess had abruptly been turned on its head. The bodyguard hired by Cowan mal ce Taeger of Arcadia to protect his daughter would hardly have gotten lost or even kidnapped. Somehow, for some reason, he'd deliberately deserted his Courier.

Of course. Hart knew about Gartanis . . . and Gartanis knew about Danae.

Beyond Nordis, three more sprites had converged on Melentha. Biting at his lip, Ravagin eased his horse into a slightly diverging path from that of the others. There was no time for any further questioning of Nordis; no time to consider the chances that his hunch was correct, or to consider what might happen if he was wrong. If there was even a chance that Hart was at the way house trying to get Danae out, it was absolutely vital that someone keep Melentha's attention occupied out here where she'd be out of the fight. And that someone had to be him.

A flicker of glow-fire appeared beside him. "You are the human named Ravagin?" the sprite asked.

"Yes," Ravagin nodded, frowning. He'd assumed that Melentha would make sure all the searching sprites would report directly to her—

"I bring a message: Danae tells you she has left."

Ravagin's heart skipped a beat. "What do you mean, *left*?" He threw a glance over at Melentha—

Just in time to see the green of a demon's parasite spirit vanish into her.

And the balloon had just gone up for good. Without a second's hesitation, Ravagin twisted his horse's head hard to the side—

And jerked in his saddle as an unearthly shriek split the air.

"*Man-sy-hae orolontis!*" he snapped—and an instant later a dozen green parasite spirits burst from nowhere to break like a tidal wave over him.

Beneath him, the horse whinnied and reared. Ravagin tugged hard on the reins, struggling to get the animal under control and to get the hell away from there. The spirit-protection spell he'd set up wouldn't last a minute under the kind of furious assault it was getting; less time even than that if Melentha was willing to reveal her possession to Nordis by sending her demon to take a direct hand in the fray.

Melentha.

She was, Ravagin realized, his best—possibly his only— chance. "*Sa-trahist rassh!*" he shouted against the green flashes buzzing like angry insects around him. "*Sa-trahist rassh, sa-trahist rassh, sa-trahist rassh!*"

And between him and Melentha four firebrats burst into flame.

Nordis shouted something, but his expletive was swallowed by another shriek from Melentha. Shifting to a one-hand grip on the reins, Ravagin waved the other hand toward Melentha in a placement gesture. "*Haklismeen-taetre!*" he called. "*Sudamentra markreforex pinchaila!*"

Beyond the flames, he caught just a hint of red as the invoked djinn responded to the fractional-possession spell and vanished into Melentha's horse. The animal reared in violent reaction to the spirit's sudden presence, and abruptly Melentha's scream took on a startled note. "*Sa-khe-khe fawkh!*" Ravagin called, making the same placement gesture—

And the horse twisted and fought for footing as the nixie's fountain of water erupted beneath it.

Almost enough. The swarm of parasite spirits was deserting Ravagin now, converging on Melentha to help fight off the zoo he'd thrown at her before their relatively fragile human link with the physical world could be hurt. For the moment, at least, the unstoppuble demon within her had his hands full elsewhere . . . and it was time for Ravagin to make a break for it. "*Sa-doora-na, sa-doora-na, sa-doora-na, sa-doora-na, sa-doora-na,*" he called.

And with his five invoked doppelgangers each heading in a different direction, he twisted the horse's reins around and kicked the animal into full gallop back toward the west.

He was free. At least for the moment.

The tree above Danae swayed slightly under its burden, sending a handful of leaves fluttering down around her. Her horse snorted gently, and she patted its neck in reassurance. "Anything happening?" she called softly up into the tree.

"The flames seem to be dying," Hart's voice replied. "Looks like the fog's starting to dissipate, too."

Danae sighed and returned to her attempts to massage away her latest leg cramp. "It's steam, not fog," she said. "That's Ravagin, all right—he pulled that same fire-and-water stunt our first night here."

"Did it work then?" Hart asked, dropping lightly back to the ground beside her.

"Well enough. You think he got away?"

Hart's silhouette shrugged. "No way to tell. He didn't escape without a fight, though—I saw a lot of what looked like demon parasite spirits swarming around the area."

Danae clenched her teeth hard enough to hurt. "So what do we do? Try and find him?"

Hart was silent for a moment. "Whatever precipitated that duel out there, it should be obvious to him that something's gone wrong with Melentha's hold on you," he said at last. "If the sprite you said you sent was actually able to find him, he knows you've escaped; otherwise, all he knows is that the demons watching you sent a message to Melentha that probably threw her into a panic. Either way he'll be on his way back to the way house to check."

"But if he knows I'm free—"

"You might have been recaptured," Hart pointed out. "Regardless, he'll try to come by and check for sure."

"Why?"

"Because that's the kind of person he is," Hart said simply.

Danae felt her lip twitch. "Yeah."

Stepping to the edge of the copse that concealed them, Hart peered out. "Yes . . . if he heads back in anything approaching a straight line, we should be able to spot him from here," he told Danae. "I think it's worth waiting a few minutes to see if he makes it."

Danae nodded, grimacing, as her earlier thoughts returned to shame her. She'd been all set to just go ahead and desert Ravagin—and here was Hart with his ice-filled circulatory system willing to take risks to keep the other from riding back to his death.

"If he does," Hart continued into Danae's thoughts, "we'll have a much better chance of making it back to the Tunnel. He knows the territory, possibly even better than Melentha does."

Danae snorted softly to herself. So much for Hart's newfound compassion . . . but the lesson to her was still applicable. "You seem to have picked up a lot of the territory yourself," she said. "That spell you mentioned, for instance, the one you used to bind the demon closer to his posts. I've never even heard of that one."

"I can't really claim any credit for it," Hart shrugged. "After I left Nordis, I went back to Gartanis to find out just what had happened. When he found out I was here to watch after you, he gave me some specialized spells he thought might help me get you out. Having seen the place, I'm glad I didn't have to use them."

Danae shook her head in wonder. "I'd have thought that after being attacked by demons himself he'd have wanted to wash his hands of me."

"Just the opposite, actually. He was mad as a fury over what Melentha's demons did to his house and lar." Abruptly, Hart stopped, cocking his head sideways. "Hoofbeats," he murmured.

Danae licked her lips and nodded silently, feeling painfully naked out here without any protection at all. A quick lar invocation, perhaps . . . but if it was Melentha out there, calling up a spirit would be about as clever as setting the whole copse on fire. "How are we going to attract his attention?" she whispered.

"We don't; I do. You'll stay here while I ride out and check."

Silently, Danae slid off the horse, thinking furiously. There had to be a way . . . "Wait a second," she said suddenly as Hart reached up to pull himself up. "If it's Ravagin he'll be alone . . . *plazni-hy-ix!*"

"What—? Oh; a jinx spell."

"Right." Holding her breath, Danae watched as the almost invisible cloud faded off toward the distant hoof-beats in response to her placement gesture. If it *was* Ravagin out there, he would hopefully notice the spell and come to the proper conclusion. If it was Melentha and her demonic entourage, the spell should at least buy her and Hart some time to get away.

Abruptly, the hoofbeats faltered and came to a halt.

Unconsciously, Danae's hands curled into fists, aware of the gamble she was taking. A jinx wasn't nearly as conspic-uous as a lar, but even so Melentha's demons would probably be able to trace it back to the point of invocation in nothing flat . . .

The hoofbeats began again. Coming closer.

Silently, Hart squeezed Danae's arm and moved a short distance to the side. Danae gritted her teeth as the shadow of a mounted rider loomed against the dimly lit landscape—

"Danae? Hart? Anyone there?"

Danae exhaled in relief, the tension draining out of her body along with the air. "We're here, Ravagin, in the trees," she called out softly.

"You both all right?" he called. The pace of the hoof-beats picked up, but remained somehow oddly cautious.

"Yes," she told him. "How'd you get away from Melentha?"

"With great difficulty, and only temporarily unless we get the hell out of the area."

"Well, then, let's go," she said, stepping to their horse and climbing up. "Hart? Come *on*."

The shadow that was Hart didn't move. "It might be a good idea first," he said calmly, "for our friend here to prove he's really Ravagin and not some illusion created to smoke us out."

Danae's mouth suddenly went dry as the memory of Coven and the doppelgangers Ravagin had himself used came flooding back. "But . . . how do we—?"

"Danae, on Shamsheer you tried to rescue a woman who was being picked on by three of her relatives," Ravagin interrupted her. "I kept them off you with a scorpion glove and we got arrested for our trouble. Your turn."

"Oh—I see. All right. I had a bad case of acrophobia on our first sky-plane ride. I saw a castle-lord's bubble in the distance. And I was furious that you insisted on a low buzz over Castle Numanteal."

"You were that mad? I didn't realize that. Hart? Go ahead."

"I tried to bribe my way onto the trip with you the night before you left," Hart said. "You turned me down and had me taken away from the Crosspoint Building. The guard on duty that night was named Grey."

For a moment there was silence. "Well?" Danae asked at last. "Is that it? Can we get out of here now?"

"Sure," Ravagin said wearily, sliding off his horse. "Just as soon as we figure out where exactly we're going to go. And how we're going to get there alive."

Chapter 27

"What do you mean, where are we going?" Danae asked. "We're going to the Tunnel and getting the hell out of here."

Ravagin shook his head, peering into the darkness at her. The visibility was lousy; but even so, it was clear she was suffering badly from fatigue. Fatigue, or something worse. "The Tunnel's out of the question, at least for the moment," he said. "There'll be spirits on guard in the Cairn Mounds long before we could make it there."

"But if we hurry, Melentha at least won't be there in person to oppose us," Hart pointed out from the shadows to Ravagin's left. "I've been told it's difficult to manipulate spirits long-range."

"Agreed," Ravagin nodded. "Especially since they don't react well to situations outside the scope of their specific orders. And of course Melentha won't be able to have a demon sitting out there indefinitely waiting for us to show— there's a limit to how long a non-binding invocation lasts. But there are other things she can do."

"Such as?" Hart asked.

"Such as keep a dozen demons or so circulating between her and the Tunnel. She can invoke one, send it there with orders to attack us if we're there, and by the time it goes into spontaneous release she'll have the next one on the way."

"So we just time our escape to come between the waves—" Danae began.

"She may also have human allies she can call on for help—spirit-possessed or otherwise," Ravagin cut her off. "And some of them may live close enough to the Tunnel to get there first no matter how fast we ride."

"Given all of this," Hart said, "it still seems to me that the longer we delay, the more time she'll have to set up a water-tight barrier around the Tunnel. *And* the better the chances one of the spirits out searching for us will get lucky."

"*Will* they be able to identify us, though?" Danae asked. "I didn't think spirits saw us as faces."

"You'd have to ask Melentha exactly how it is spirits see us," Ravagin said grimly. "Unfortunately, Hart's got a point. Especially since they already have our names to work with."

"Our—oh." Danae inhaled sharply. "Damn. That *does* make a difference, doesn't it?"

"A big one," Ravagin nodded. "It's not quite as simple as when you send a sprite off with a message for a particular person, but even with the more advanced spirits there's some kind of coupling between name and image."

"So you're basically offering us no choices at all," Hart said quietly. "If we race to the Tunnel we'll be caught, and if we attempt to hide out somewhere we'll be caught. Unless you have some Courier's trick up your sleeve . . . ?"

"Courier training doesn't cover this type of situation," Ravagin shook his head. "But I *may* have an idea." He looked at Danae. "Do you still remember how to do that demogorgon invocation?"

From the corner of his eye he saw Hart stiffen. "I *had* a full mnemonic treatment, you know," Danae told him. "Of course I remember it."

"Do you think you could stand to try it again?"

There was the barest hesitation before she answered. "If it'll help get us out of here, I'll try anything."

"There aren't any guarantees, I'm afraid," he warned. "For that matter, I'm not even sure if the spell I want really exists. But if it does, a demogorgon will probably know it."

"And what would this possibly nonexistent spell do?" Hart asked.

Ravagin pursed his lips. "Make us invisible to spirits."

For a moment there was silence as the other two seemed to digest that. "Uh-*huh*," Hart said at last. "Interesting approach. If spirits can't see us, the majority of Melentha's spy network becomes effectively useless."

"Not only the spy network, but the bulk of her defenses, too," Ravagin pointed out. "One trick she'll probably use to get around the spontaneous release problem is to bind some of her spirits into wild animals and set them to prowling around the Tunnel. But since that kind of possession usually plays havoc with the animal's normal instincts and sensory apparatus, if the spirit itself can't detect us chances are good we'll be able to walk past even a *cintah* without being bothered."

"Sounds like a worthwhile gamble," Hart said with a nod. "Yes, we'll try it. Ms. mal ce Taeger, you'll need to tell me how to do this demogorgon spell—"

"Hold it!" Ravagin cut in. "What makes you think *you're* going to do the invocation?"

"I second the question," Danae growled.

Hart exhaled loudly. "I may not be as experienced as you are, Ravagin, with Karyx and its wonders, but I *do* know that the inherent dangers of an invocation increase as you go up the hierarchy. Invoking a demogorgon is about as dangerous as you can get, and I doubt that either of us wants Ms. mal ce Taeger to take that sort of risk."

Ravagin opened his mouth, but Danae beat him to the punch. "Hart, it's time to get a couple of things straight," she bit out. "First of all, from a purely practical standpoint, you can't do the invocation for the simple reason that I'm not going to give it to you."

"Ms. mal ce Taeger—"

"Danae! It's just Danae here, Hart—no one has that many names on Karyx. Second of all, you're not in charge of me here. Ravagin is, and if anyone had the right to take this invocation away from me it would be him—and I'm not going to give *him* the spell, either. And finally, if you'd turn down your loyalty to Daddy Dear by a few degrees, you'd realize I'm the one who's got the best chance of coming out of this safely, anyway. I've invoked the demogorgon before and he didn't hurt me then. So. Ravagin, where should we try this?"

"Not here," Ravagin said, stifling the automatic urge to argue with her. One successful pass at a demogorgon was no guarantee that a second wouldn't end in disaster . . . but it was abundantly clear that her mind was made up, and arguing would only waste precious time. "We're too close to Melentha and her house. I suggest we head southwest, cross the Besak-Findral road and the plains south of it and hide out in the marshes by the Davrahil River. That's nearly twenty kilometers in the wrong direction, and I doubt they'll get around to searching anywhere that far away for at least a few hours. Hart?"

"Makes sense," the other said promptly. "Let's get moving."

Ravagin had fully expected to run into at least one of Melentha's searching spirits, if not the demon-woman herself . . . but as the minutes turned to half an hour and they'd still encountered no trouble, he began to both breathe easier and wonder if his flailing attack had indeed done Melentha some real damage. Certainly she would have thought to scour the immediate area as well as to send everything else available in a mad dash for the Cairn Mounds and the Tunnel.

Unless long association with her demon had dulled her mind that much. It was possible; most scholars had long since come to the conclusion that, for all their power, Karyx's spirit world was severely lacking in anything resembling human imagination.

But whatever the reason, they reached and crossed the Besak-Findral road without trouble and headed cross-country toward the Davrahil River. Besak's surrounding landscape, never more than rolling to begin with, began to flatten out even more as the occasional patches of forest became rarer. Once he caught Hart looking around with an air of disapproval, and assured him that well before they reached the Davrahil they would find more than adequate cover.

An hour later, they did.

Ravagin had been to these marshes only once before, nearly seven years earlier, and the place had not noticeably improved since then. In the daylight, he knew, the predominant characteristics would be the incredibly colored plant life growing around and on the black-trunked trees, and the multitude of animal, bird, and insect sounds. Now, in the dead of night, the first thing Ravagin noticed was the rancid smell.

There weren't any real paths into the marshes, but for a couple of kilometers at least Ravagin knew the land would be reasonably passable. Dismounting, he led the way, checking with his feet for holes and soft spots that might endanger their horses and with his hands for the sort of dangerous thorn limbs that always seemed to find a traveler at the wrong moment. More that once he regretted having had to leave the way house without any of his home-made torches, but there was nothing for it now. Invoking a dazzler was, of course, completely out of the question.

They'd struggled their way about half a kilometer inside the marshes when he called it quits. A small tree-covered knoll provided them with at least a little grazing space for their horses and enough dry ground for Danae's needs. Fifteen minutes later, with the aroma of burning incense mixing oddly with the swampy odors, Danae began her invocation.

"How much longer is this going to take?" Hart asked softly.

Ravagin shifted his attention from Danae's motionless cross-legged form to the vaguely brightening sky overhead. She'd been sitting there in communion with the demogorgon for at least half an hour now. "No idea," he told Hart. "I came in on the middle the last time she did this, and I still had to wait for twenty minutes or so before she came out of it."

Hart hissed between his teeth. "I should have insisted she let me do this."

Ravagin eyed the other. "You been her bodyguard long?" he asked.

The other threw him a sharp look, shifted his eyes back to Danae. "Since she was seven. Fifteen years."

"Almost the same time I've been ferrying people in and out of the Hidden Worlds," Ravagin commented. "It's easy to get stuck in a frame of mind, isn't it."

Hart smiled lopsidedly. "If you're suggesting I take my job too seriously . . . don't. There isn't any way to take bodyguarding too seriously."

"Un-*huh*." Ravagin paused, casting around for another topic of conversation. "So. You mentioned earlier that you'd talked to Gartanis. Did he say anything about what happened to his lar?"

"Not really, but as I said earlier he was furious that Melentha would attack him so brazenly."

"So he knew Melentha was behind it?"

"Oh, certainly. I get the feeling he's at least suspected her involvement with demons for a long time. A pity we can't enlist him onto our side in fighting her."

"We tell a Karyxite about Shamsheer and Threshold and we'll be dog meat as far as Triplet Control is concerned," Ravagin told him.

"Yes, I understand the rules," Hart said. "I also don't give a damn about rules if breaking them will make a life-and-death difference."

Ravagin thought about the automatic penalties that accompanied the illegal disclosure laws. Penalties even Cowan mal ce Taeger might find himself helpless to alter . . . "Let's wait and see what Danae comes up with before we try anything that drastic, shall we? Besides, didn't you mention earlier that Gartanis had already given you some help?"

"Spells designed to break a path through Melentha's defenses," the other shrugged. "Useless, really, for the way the game's changed." He paused, an odd expression on his face. "These more elaborate spells—the spirit-protection ones and all—they're distance-oriented, aren't they? As in their effect decreases as distance from the spell-caster increases, I mean."

"Well . . ." Ravagin considered. "Yes, to some extent that's true. Why?"

Hart was silent a long moment. "If Danae is able to get this spirit invisibility thing . . . I want you to help me arrange things so that I'm only partially covered by it."

"There'll be no need for that," Ravagin assured him. "There won't be any trouble getting the spell to cover all of us equally well."

"I understand, but that's not what I meant. I intend to leave you two as soon as we're protected and make my own way back to the Tunnel, arriving—ideally—a day or so after you're already through. With only partial invisibility, I should be able to attract and thus draw off the bulk of Melentha's surveillance and attack."

It was something he should have expected, Ravagin realized in retrospect, but it still came as a shock. Only someone ignorant of the dangers of Karyx would even have thought up such a scheme, let alone suggested it. "Forget it," he said when he found his voice. "I'm not leaving you here as a moving target for whatever the hell the demons might decide to throw at you."

"Then you automatically expose Ms. mal ce Taeger to greater danger," Hart responded coolly. "Is that how conscientious Couriers do things?"

"And what if you get caught?"

"What of it? *I'm* not your responsibility; Danae is."

Ravagin felt his molars grinding together. "And you don't think it would endanger her for you to be caught and questioned?" he snapped.

"No," Hart said calmly. "I've been trained to resist that sort of interrogation—certainly for the few days it'll take you to get her to safety. Face facts, Ravagin: letting me draw off the pursuit is the best chance you've got, and you know it."

"Hart—damn." Ravagin sighed. "All right, you win. But you get yourself killed out there and you'll be in big trouble."

Hart smiled slightly. "I'll remember that." He nodded toward Danae. "Something's happening."

Ravagin shifted his attention. "She's coming out of it, I think," he said. "She's starting to cast shadows again . . ."

And with an abrupt gasp, Danae collapsed to the ground.

Ravagin and Hart reached her at about the same time.

"Danae?" Ravagin called tentatively, patting her cheek. "Danae? Come on, come on—*say* something."

"Not till you stop shouting and slapping me," she said hoarsely, her eyes still squeezed shut. "*Oh*, that's loud. What time is it, anyway, noon?"

"About dawn," Hart told her. "Are you having problems with your eyes?"

"You could say that. I don't think I can open them— it's too bright out there."

Hart threw Ravagin an odd look. "I'll shade them with my hand. Okay; try opening them a bit."

"No—no good," she said. "It's still too bright. God, I hope this isn't permanent."

"We'll just have to wait and see," Ravagin told her, fishing a handkerchief from his pocket. "Let's try a blind-fold, see if that at least cuts down the glare."

"Yes," she said slowly a minute later. "Yes, that helps. Everything else seems okay. I, uh—do I look okay otherwise?"

"Near as I can tell," Ravagin assured her. "So . . . what happened?"

"The demogorgon took me back to the fourth world. It's weird there, Ravagin—really weird. Oh, and I got the spell we need, too. But I can only use it once."

"Why?" Hart asked.

"The demogorgon said it would fade from my memory after I'd done it once."

"I take it you didn't mention your mnemonic training—"

"He already knew about it. Said it wouldn't make any difference. God, that's bright. Well; you ready to become invisible to spirits?"

Hart and Ravagin exchanged glances. "Whenever you're ready," Ravagin told her. "Any idea how long the spell's good for, by the way?"

"Not really. All he told me was that it would last long enough."

"I hope he knew what he was talking about," Hart muttered.

"Me, too," Danae nodded with a shiver. "Well . . . help me sit up a little."

Ravagin complied, sitting down next to her and putting

his arm around her shoulders to give her some support. Hart, he noted peripherially, had taken advantage of the distraction to quietly move a meter away from them.

"Ready?" Danae asked.

"Yes," Ravagin nodded.

"Okay. By the way, the demogorgon warned me this might hurt a little."

The demogorgon turned out to be right.

Chapter 28

"If it helps any," Ravagin's voice came, too loudly, in her ears, "it looks like a line of storm clouds will be blocking off the sun in a half-hour or less. If they don't dissipate too quickly, they ought to keep it under cover until sundown."

Danae didn't reply. She was thoroughly sick of this whole mess. Sick of the blinding white glare that continued to burn into her eyes through both eyelids and three wrappings of cloth, sick of the loud swish-thud of their horse's hooves in the tall grass, sick of the exaggerated rolling motion of the animal and of the oppressive pressure of Ravagin's body pressing against her back. The encounter with the demogorgon had effectively left her in a reverse sensory deprivation tank, and after nearly half a day of it she was ready to go insane.

She'd risked her life to buy them all a way to escape. A difficult, dangerous decision, one she'd made in a responsible, adult manner . . . and in return, Ravagin and Hart had once again chosen to treat her like a child.

Behind her, Ravagin cleared his throat—a loud, raspy sound. "Look, Danae, we're going to be arriving at Findral fairly soon, and I'd like to be back on speaking terms before we get there. I understand why you're mad, but Hart was determined to go ahead with it, the same way you were hell-bent on doing the demogorgon invocation yourself. You can hardly defend one example of bull-headedness and not the other, now, can you?"

Danae gritted her teeth hard enough to hurt. "Oh, you understand why I'm mad, do you? Well, maybe you *think* you do, but then your style of thinking has never been too good where my feelings have been concerned."

"So explain it to me. Come on—the silent treatment's gone on long enough."

She took a deep breath. "Did it ever occur to you that I just *might* like to have some input into a major decision like that? That as a thinking, rational part of this team I had a *right* to be in on it? No, of course it didn't. I'm just Danae, the brainless heiress who has to be taken care of like she was still eight years old."

Ravagin waited until she was finished, until the echoes of her voice had faded from her sensitized ears. "I suppose that's one way to look at it," he said. "It's not the way I intended it, but . . . Well, all right. Suppose you'd been consulted. What would you have said?"

"What difference does it make now?"

"Come on, humor me. Would you have agreed to let Hart risk his life drawing the pursuit away?"

"Agree to let him get himself killed, you mean? Of course I wouldn't have."

"But that's his job, isn't it? He's paid for taking this kind of risk for you—and for getting killed in the process, if it comes down to that. Right?"

"That is about as cold-blooded—"

"No, answer the question first. Isn't that his job?"

She tried forming three denials . . . but none of them made it past her lips, and eventually she gave up. "All right," she sighed. "Yes, I suppose that's how he sees it."

"All right, then. From his point of view, this decoy plan was the best way he could see to do his job. You wouldn't have been able to change his mind. All an argument would have accomplished would have been to make him wonder whether he should instead have stayed here at your side . . . and that kind of doubt would have been a handicap he might never have gotten rid of. Is that what you would have wanted, to have given him something else to have to fight?"

"No, of course not—"

"Fine. Then you're saying you'd have been able to sit here, hiding all of your doubts where he couldn't see them, and given him your permission to go off and get himself killed in your behalf?"

"You make it sound so damn brutal . . ." She trailed off as her brain suddenly registered something her ears had picked up. Something in Ravagin's voice . . . . "That *is* what happened, isn't it? Only with you doing it instead of me? *You* didn't like the plan, either."

"It's the best possible plan for our safety—yours and mine." Abruptly, Ravagin sounded very tired. "It's also the worst possible one for Hart."

For a long minute there was no sound but the swish-thud of the horse's hooves and the droning of wind and distant insects. "It's not a matter of being treated like a child, Danae," Ravagin said at last. "It's the simple fact that there are certain no-win situations in this universe— and a no-win situation requires a no-win decision. When you've lived through enough of them, the way Hart and I have, you begin to realize that sharing the guilt around with others doesn't make your piece of it any easier to carry."

He fell silent . . . and for that minute, at least, the quiet pain in his voice overshadowed the glare in Danae's eyes. Groping in front of her, she found Ravagin's hand on the horse's reins and held it. "I'm sorry," she whispered.

He didn't reply; but a moment later his free hand reached tentatively around her waist to hold her tightly against him. Almost painfully tightly . . . but she didn't mind.

If she couldn't help share his guilt, she could at least try and share some of his pain.

It was after sundown, and the white glare in her eyes had subsided to merely a dazzling gray, when Ravagin called a halt. "How do you feel?" he asked as he helped her off the horse.

"Like I just spent four hours riding a car with oval wheels," she grunted, wincing. The pins and needles in her legs and buttocks were almost painful in their intensity. "I never realized just how much horses bounce when they walk."

"No signs of this sensory stuff wearing off?"

"I can't tell. Where are we?"

"About a kilometer from the village of Findral. Or, rather, from where the edge of Findral's nighttime lar will be."

"We going to spend the night there?"

"That's what I'm currently trying to decide."

He was silent for a long minute, and Danae found that if she ignored the countryside sounds around her, she could actually hear the faint sounds of humanity from the direction of the village. "What's our other choice?" she asked. "Spend the night out here?"

"Under the circumstances, that's not really an option. The risk of bandits aside, we're in fairly desperate need of food and rest. No, our only other real choice would be to backtrack along the road toward Besak and find an isolated inn that has its own lar at night. Unfortunately, we have the same problem in either case."

"Me?"

He snorted gently. "Your eyes and ears, actually, but it boils down to the same thing. You're going to attract a lot of attention, and we can hardly pretend you got lost from a blindman's bluff squad."

"How about if we say I've got a severe head injury or something?" she suggested. "That way we could pass these off as bandages and also explain why I'm staying isolated in the room."

"And that we're on our way to Citadel to consult one of the master healers there? Yeah, that's the obvious explanation . . . except that if we try it in Findral someone's bound to suggest calling in one of the local healers."

And since healers invariably consulted with spirits . . . "So if we use that excuse we have to go for the isolated inn instead, right?"

"Right." He didn't sound very enthusiastic. "We unfortunately get the opposite problem there, that we'll have less of a crowd available to hide in. If Melentha's got human agents scouring the area yet . . . well, if one of them spots us, we'll just have to deal with him, that's all."

Danae shivered. Earlier, her sensitized ears had read pain in Ravagin's voice. Now, she could hear equally clearly the death there. "We'd better get going, shouldn't we? Before we create more of a stir by asking someone to take down their lar to let us in?"

"Point. Circulation all restored? Good. I'll give you a hand getting back up and we'll get going."

Locked in her blindness, Danae had no idea what the lay of the land was like, and so for the next several minutes she rode with the uncomfortable vision of riding through a vast wasteland with the nearest inn ten or more kilometers away. It was almost with a shock, then, when she suddenly noticed the sounds of life penetrating the cloths around her ears, and realized that Ravagin was guiding the horse off the road onto what felt like a dirt trail.

"Remember," Ravagin murmured into her ear, "you're very sick. No sudden, confident motions—in fact, let me lead or carry you as much as possible, okay?"

"Right," she muttered back . . . and a moment later they were there.

The attached stable was small—that much she could tell from the echoes—and a small stable implied a small inn. That wasn't unreasonable, she realized; this close to Findral, the inn's main business would be only those travelers who missed the evening cutoff for getting into the village itself. But the smells of the place bespoke at least an attempt at cleanliness, and as Ravagin set about discussing price with the innkeeper's wife she heard the faint hum of a protective lar being invoked. All in all, she decided, a not unreasonable place for fugitives to spend the night.

"Okay, try it now. But take it easy."

Reluctantly, Danae began untying the bandages. The blackness that had finally settled in in front of her eyes was as welcome as cold water on a steaming day, and she hated to give up that relief so soon after gaining it. But Ravagin had a point . . . and besides, she as yet had no proof that her eyes were still functional. Eventually, she would have to try this, and it might just as well be now.

Setting her teeth firmly together, she lifted the cloths away and opened her eyes.

They worked. The room itself was still quite adequately bright—the cracks around the window shutters almost hurtingly so—but she could see perfectly well.

Perhaps too well. In the lines of Ravagin's face she could detect a quiet dread that he probably thought was better hidden. "Well, go ahead," she said. "Aren't you going to hold up some fingers or something for me to count?"

Some of the tension went out of Ravagin's face, and he exhaled with obvious relief. "Whoof. Good. I don't mind telling you—well, never mind. How bright is it?"

"Like maybe mid-morning on a clear day. What've we got, just the light seeping in from outside?"

"Yeah—and there's not a hell of a lot of it. A firebrat tethered around the corner of the building by the road, looks like. Okay. You feel up to taking care of yourself for a few minutes while I head downstairs to get us some food?"

She found the grace not to say anything sarcastic. Hart's single-minded concern for her safety—and its consequences—were too fresh in her mind for her to find fault with Ravagin's version of that same concern. "No, I'll be fine. Get going, I'm starving."

"Okay." He groped in the—for him—darkness for her hand, gave her the short sword Hart had left them before he took off on his own. "Remember, if anyone should come in, you've only got the advantage until he gets a light started. If it's not me or the innkeeper with a tray, kill him fast."

"I understand."

The tension was back on his face, but he rose and left without another word. She remembered to shade her eyes as he opened the door, but whatever the inn was using for hallway illumination wasn't too bad and it was no more than a few seconds before the faint purple blob faded completely from before her eyes.

With a sigh, she put the sword down on the bed beside her and stretched out, closing her eyes. *So here we are,* she thought tiredly. *The ones who are going to shatter whatever the hell the demons are up to on Karyx and*

*beyond. One aging Courier, and one complete and total
dead weight.*

Dead weight.

The words echoed painfully around her head. *Dead
weight.* Worse even than just useless. With her eyes and
other senses like this she couldn't run or fight or do
anything else to help get them through Melentha's gauntlet and back to the Tunnel. Ravagin would have to lead,
guide, or carry her everywhere they went until she recovered from the effects of that demogorgon contact.

If she ever did. Gartanis hadn't done so.

Unbidden, tears came to her eyes. *Child*, she flung the
word at herself like an epithet. *So, you wanted a chance to
make the hard decisions, huh? Well, great, because here's
a beaut of one all ready for you.*

And there really wasn't any question as to which way
the decision should go. Ravagin knew as much as she did
about what the spirits were up to . . . and Ravagin stood a
far better chance of getting back through the Tunnel on
his own. Hart had made his own sacrifice to get the word
through. Now it was her turn.

And if she was going to desert Ravagin, she would never
have a better chance than right now.

Rolling off the bed and onto her feet, she stepped to the
window, squinting against the light coming in around the
worn shutters. Theoretically, the inn's lar defined her
boundaries for her . . . but there was nothing that said a
lar would or even could block anything it couldn't detect.
And there was certainly nothing to be lost by trying.

Except perhaps their only weapon against the searching
spirits.

She stopped, hand on the window sash, and swore
under her breath. But there was no way around it. Half
the advantage of being invisible was the fact that the
searching spirits didn't yet know about it. If the lar couldn't
detect her, it would surely notice that *something* had
passed through its protective ring . . . and when it reported that fact, either Melentha or someone else would
surely come to the proper conclusion.

She couldn't risk it, not even to give Ravagin a clear
shot at the Tunnel.

Or in other words, she was in the clear. She didn't have to sacrifice herself. Didn't have to make the hard decision.

As, somehow, things had always seemed to work out for her. How many of the hard decisions along the way, she wondered suddenly, had yielded to that same kind of logic? And how much of that logic had been little more than rationalization? She opened her mouth again, searching her memory for the most vile word in her vocabulary . . . and paused.

Somewhere, she could hear a faint hissing.

The lar, was her first, hopeful thought. But that hum had been different, and she could in fact still hear it beneath this louder and closer sound.

Louder and closer . . .

Carefully, she lowered her hands from the window back to her sides and turned around. Nothing was visible . . . but facing this direction, the hiss was definitely louder. She licked her lips, heart beginning to beat loudly in her ears. An uncomfortable tingle raised the hairs on her arms . . .

And through the thick wooden door a red shape floated.

Danae bit down hard on her tongue. *A djinn*, a small bit of rationality in her brain seemed to whisper. *Only a djinn*. But the rest of her brain wanted to scream.

She'd never seen a djinn like this. Never seen *any* spirit with the sheer and horrible detail with which she was seeing this one. The spindly physique, like an emaciated mockery of the human form; the grotesquely misshapen head with its pointed jaw and gaunt cheekbones; the eyes—

The eyes. Redder than the rest of the creature, they sparkled with intelligence and hatred as they swept the room. Danae watched it drift slowly through the air, hardly daring to breathe as those terrible eyes swept the room. It couldn't see her—somehow, even in the rising swell of panic, there was never even a shadow of doubt in her mind about that. But the spirit was indeed searching for something—that much, too, was certain. And if it happened to touch her . . . or even heard her . . .

She bit down on her tongue again . . . and as the djinn circled over toward the bed a glint of reflected light there caught her eye. The short sword Ravagin hd left her.

Carefully, eyes on the djinn, she moved slowly toward

the bed. Djinns were about the most powerful spirits that could be permanently trapped in a tool or weapon, and the necessary spell was correspondingly tricky. But once bound in the sword, the creature should be incapable of hurting them.

Would it still be able to communicate with the rest of the spirit world? There was no way to know.

The djinn moved away from the bed, and Danae froze in mid-step. It drifted toward her . . . not quite on a direct line . . . she held her breath . . .

Concentrating on the djinn, she didn't notice the approaching footsteps until it was too late to do anything. The door came open; and as she threw her arm up to shield her eyes, she caught just a glimpse of a figure silhouetted against the glare from the hallway.

Chapter 29

She tensed as the footsteps continued on into the room. One long step would take her to the bed—get her to the sword lying there—but with the light from the hall blinding her, using the weapon competently would be another matter entirely. But if her attacker didn't notice her standing here by the window before he closed the door . . .

The door swung to a crack. Another second or two—

"Danae?" Ravagin called tentatively. "Where are you?"

Relief flooded into her—and was followed instantly by more tension. "Shh!" she hissed. "A *djinn*."

The door seemed to her ears to slam shut. "What?" he hissed. "Where?"

She lowered her arm and looked around. The djinn was nowhere in sight. "But . . . it was here a second ago," she whispered. "Searching around for us—I'm sure of it."

"Great. Just what we needed." Carefully, Ravagin groped his way to the bed, set down the covered tray he was carrying, and picked up the sword. "Was it moving quickly, like sprites when they've got a message to deliver?" he asked, buckling the weapon around his waist.

"No, it was going pretty slowly. Sort of like a bee hunting around a clover field for the best flower to go for."

Ravagin grunted. "Hmm. Well, it could be worse, I suppose. Did you hear anyone poking around out in the hallway while the djinn was here?"

"Uh . . . no, I don't think so. Should I have?"

"If you didn't then, you probably will eventually. The djinn almost certainly means one of Melentha's agents is around somewhere."

Danae felt her stomach knot up. "You mean *here*? In the *inn*?"

"Uh-huh. The lar out there's been in place too long for an unbound djinn to have been floating around since before it was invoked, and we'd sure as hell have known if someone had sent it through the lar from the outside. QED, and all that."

"Oh, that's just terrific news. How in the worlds did Melentha track us here?"

"I don't think she did, actually," Ravagin shook his head. "My guess is that when we didn't make a mad run for the Tunnel, she just got all the people together that she could beg, borrow, or steal and scattered them around in hopes of spotting us whenever we finally surfaced."

"So when whoever it is spotted us, he invoked the djinn to check us out?"

Ravagin was silent a moment. "My guess is that he isn't actually on to us yet. If he was, the djinn ought to have been flying more purposefully, and have left right away when it didn't find you here."

"But we're now stuck here with him until dawn," Danae pointed out, suppressing a shudder.

"Right." Ravagin drew the short sword, checked its edge, and resheathed it. "Which means we've got to identify him before he identifies us. And eliminate him."

Danae's heart skipped a beat. "You mean . . . kill him? But if he's not on to us—"

She stopped abruptly at the expression on his face. "Look, Danae," he said quietly, "in the first place, if I could be sure he wouldn't identify us, I'd be more than happy to leave him alone. But we don't have any such guarantee. And if there's going to be any confrontation, I want it to be on my terms and timing, not his. Understand?"

"Yes," she said, bending the truth only a little. "All right. What can I do to help?"

"Stay here," he said promptly, moving toward the door. "You'll be as safe here as anywhere else. Use that chair there to wedge the door and don't open it to anyone but

me. I'll identify myself by calling you the name with which
we were first introduced. Got that?"

Danae Panya. It almost startled her to remember. The
name seemed to come from a distant past, or from a life
not her own. "Got it," she told him. "Please be careful,
Ravagin."

"You bet," he grunted. "Watch your eyes . . ."

She shielded them, and in a flare of light from the hall
he was gone.

Pushing the heavy wooden chair over to the door and
wedging it under the latch took only a couple of minutes—
far more time, she thought grimly, than it would take a
determined attacker to break it down. She spent a few
minutes more searching for a better way to secure the
door, but aside from the armchair, bed, a couple of blankets, and a fireplate, the room was totally devoid of fur-
nishings. The ceiling was composed of rough-hewn boards,
each thick enough to make a good brace, but they were
solidly nailed in place and without tools there would be no
chance of getting one loose.

Eventually, she gave up and sat back down on the bed.
The sight of the food Ravagin had brought made her
stomach growl, reminding her that even with this new
threat having shot her appetite all to hell, her body still
needed to eat. Sighing, she tore off a piece of meat and
began gnawing at it. And tried to think.

Somewhere along the line, she knew, she was almost
certain to be attacked. Ravagin could probably not identify
and kill the spy without the other catching on as to who he
was, as well, and even a dying invocation could spell
trouble for them. And if Ravagin wasn't able to kill him
right away, the spy might even come up here in person to
try and find her.

She shivered at the thought. She'd been attacked by
spirits before, and had no interest whatsoever in repeating
the experience. But at least she had the partial protection
of invisibility where the spirits were concerned. She had
no such advantage over the spy . . . and the chance that
she might wind up being used as a shield or bargaining
chip by a demon-influenced human was about as horrible a
situation as she could imagine.

Which meant that that was the situation she should concentrate on resisting.

Slowly, she swept her eyes around the room, trying to think. If the spy identified them, he would surely remember the bandages around her face. Would he correctly guess their purpose and realize that even moderate light was a weapon he could use against her? Or would he think she was simply trying to disguise her features?

The latter, almost certainly. Gartanis had implied that contacts with demogorgons were rare, and that the physical effects in each of those cases were different. Ravagin had seemed taken aback by the sensory enhancement she'd suffered; she could take that as an indication that the spy wouldn't expect it, either.

So as far as he was concerned, she was a normal person hiding out in a darkened inn room. Given that, what sort of attack would he be likely to use?

She thought it through several times, but unfortunately the same answer kept coming up. When attacking someone whose eyes had grown accustomed to darkness, the first and most obvious thing to do would be to turn on the lights.

All right, she told herself fiercely. *So that's exactly what you* don't *want. So figure out a way to take advantage of it.*

Her eyes fell on the tray beside her . . . on the blankets lying rumpled next to it. Would he invoke a dazzler or a firebrat? Dazzler, most likely; there shouldn't be any need for him to burn down the inn. And if he weren't a complete idiot, he would invoke it somewhere behind him where the light wouldn't get in his own eyes. But not too far behind him, or he would have to come a few steps into the room on his own before the spirit made it in, too. So just behind him. Practically right there on his shoulder . . .

Slowly, an idea came to her. Undoubtedly the stupidest idea she'd ever heard in her life . . . but for now it was all she had.

Getting the necessary splinters from the window shutter was the hardest part, especially with nothing but the edge of the fireplate to pry them out with. But eventually she had enough. The blankets were single-thread woven; working with one of the splinters at the edge, she managed to unravel several meters of the yarn. Gathering it up with the other blanket and the splinters, she got to work.

It took her nearly half an hour, but at last she was finished. Then, picking up the heavy chair by its arms, she moved it a couple of meters back from the door and sat down nervously to wait.

She waited a long time, through many false alarms as the inn's other guests began to leave the common room below and tromp down the hallway in search of their beds. Once, she thought she heard the hissing of a spirit again, but if that was indeed what it was, it didn't enter her room.

The minutes dragged by, and as her adrenaline-fueled alertness began to yield to fatigue, she began to wonder if she'd been perhaps a bit premature in this . . . and to wonder what Ravagin would say if he walked into her trap first . . .

And abruptly her back stiffened. From out in the hall came the spirit-hiss again . . . but this time it was accompanied by a set of unnaturally quiet footsteps. Accompanied by, and coming nearer at the same pace as the footsteps . . .

She was out of the chair in an instant, stepping around behind it and grabbing for its arms. Lifting it up, holding it like a shield in front of her, she held her breath . . . and then the door was flung open to slam against the wall, and everything happened at once.

"*Su-trahist rassh!*" the man bellowed as he leaped into the room. Danae moved at the same time, ramming forward toward the silhouetted intruder with the chair. Through her narrowed eyes she caught just a glimpse of the sword in his hand—and of the ceiling falling in on him—and then the chair caught him squarely in the chest to jerk him backwards—

Directly into the firebrat that erupted into existence behind him.

His scream of rage and pain seemed to explode inside Danae's skull as she dropped the chair and fell back into the room, arms and hands trying to protect both her ears and eyes from the agonizing assaults on them.

"Danae!"

The voice was Ravagin's, coinciding with the sprinting footsteps coming down the hallway toward the room. Dimly, through the screams, she could hear the fury and fear in the voice—

"I'm all right!" she shouted back, knowing in that instant that if her attacker was not in fact incapacitated the sound of her voice would bring him instantly down on her.

But the other's screams had turned from rage to terror . . . and even as Ravagin's footsteps arrived she could hear a new sound adding to the mixture. The sound of burning cloth . . .

"Danae!"

"Over here, Ravagin," she called. A horrible smell was beginning to flood into her nose . . . "Help me!"

A strong hand closed around her free arm, and she caught a suddenly strong whiff of scorched hair. "The door's blocked—we'll have to use the window," he panted. "Come on—"

She stumbled along behind him. The screams from the doorway had faded to silence now, but the nauseating smell of burning meat was getting stronger. As were the light and heat . . .

From ahead of her came the sound of a window being flung open, followed by that of stressed wood as he slammed open the shutters. "Come on—I'll give you a hand—"

"Wait a second," she protested as he pulled her toward the sudden breeze. "Shouldn't we do something about that firebrat?"

"Like what?—the guy who invoked it is already dead or on his way there."

"But the inn will burn do—"

"Oh, all right. *Sa-khe-khe fawkh*; *simar-kaia*! Now come *on*!"

She had just enough time to identify the new sound as that of water gushing across the burning floor; and then she was being pushed to a sitting position on the sill, Ravagin was squeezing through beside her and jumping to the ground below—

"Okay—jump!" he called up.

Gritting her teeth, she pushed off the sill, and a heart-stopping second later landed in his arms. "Okay," he said, the frantic tension in his voice fading into a trembling relief. "It's okay. We're safe now."

And for the first time in minutes Danae found she was able to breathe again. And able to cry.

Chapter 30

"I didn't mean to kill him," Danae sniffed from Ravagin's arms when she was able to talk again. "Not that way. I thought he would invoke a dazzler, not a firebrat. I really did."

Ravagin nodded silently, wincing a bit as the movement rubbed his singed cheek against Danae's hair. They'd been sitting here together by this shed near the stable for nearly a quarter hour now, and if there were any words that would help her work through the horror and guilt she was feeling, he'd about given up finding them. *At least she never actually had to see him burning to death*, he thought. Unfortunately, he had, and the memory made him shudder.

"Ravagin?" Danae asked, holding him a bit closer. "You okay? You shivered."

"I'm fine. Look, Danae . . . it wasn't your fault. It really wasn't. You had no way of knowing I was only half a hallway behind him and that he would put that firebrat in the doorway to try and block my approach."

She inhaled suddenly. "You—it was right in the *doorway*? You didn't tell me that before."

"It's okay," he hastened to assure her. "I only got a little scorched. Probably got off a lot easier than I would have in a straight fight with him. Try remembering that, if it helps—he didn't just come in for a friendly chat. He was there to kill us."

"I know, and I'll be all right in a minute. It's just that
. . . I've never had a hand in killing anyone before."

He nodded understanding. "Just keep remembering that
everything you did was in self-defense. You're damned
lucky he didn't skewer you when you threw that blanket
over his head."

"I didn't throw it." She sniffed again, but her trembling
had eased and it was clear she was starting to regain
control of herself. "I wedged its corners into cracks in the
ceiling with splinters from the window shutters, with threads
from the other blanket set to pull it down when the door
opened. Sort of like a homeowner's security tangler net,
you know? I thought he'd invoke a dazzler behind him,
and that when I pushed him back with the chair he'd wind
up with it under the blanket and right in his eyes and then
he'd be as blind as I was—" She broke off, took a deep
breath. "We've been through all this, haven't we? Sorry.
What's happening out there? It sounds like the crowd's
breaking up."

Ravagin leaned forward to look around the shed at the
inn's main door. "You're right. Looks like some of the
guests have already gone back inside. The—oops, there's
the innkeeper . . . I think he's telling the rest it's safe
enough to go back inside. Must have gotten a fireplate
under the firebrat."

"And gotten the water shut off? What was that extra
phrase you added to the nixie invocation, anyway?"

"A time limit. If I'd done a normal invocation I'd either
have had to go in and personally release it or it would have
stayed there pumping water into the room for the next five
hours. With the ten-minute limit I gave it—well, it's already long gone."

"Um. They didn't teach us that one."

"They never do. It's assumed you won't need it."

For a minute the only sounds were the faint commotion
still coming from the direction of the inn and the even
fainter hum of the lar sweeping its protective circle at
their backs. *Protection*; and the word brought a sour taste
to Ravagin's mouth. He'd promised to protect Danae—had
told her explicitly that he would find the spy and kill him.

She'd believed him . . . and had wound up having to take the brunt of the attack anyway.

And the brunt of the guilt for the way things had turned out. *I should have let Hart stay with her while I played decoy*, he thought bitterly. *He's the one trained for this sort of thing, not me. I wish to hell I'd thought to suggest it to him . . .*

"I think he was spirit-possessed," Danae broke into his thoughts.

"He—? Oh. Why do you think that?"

"There was the same sort of hissing when he was walking down the hall that I heard when the djinn was flying around. Unless the djinn was with him?"

Ravagin shook his head, the knot in his stomach tightening another half turn. So *that* was why . . . "No, there weren't any spirits in sight, at least not when I could see him." He hesitated; but the knowledge might make her conscience rest a little easier. "But that might explain why he just stood there and let himself be burned to death instead of rolling away from the firebrat."

"You mean the demon had his brain so fogged he couldn't think even *that* well?"

"No. I mean that the spirit held him there. Deliberately."

He felt her stiffen beside him. "You can't be *serious*. Why would it do something like that?"

"To get away. If the spirit had just left him, the situation would have been as if it'd been freshly invoked, and it would have been stuck around here for anything up to several hours."

"And could have continued the attack on us."

"Unless it'd finally tumbled to the fact that we were invisible to it. In that case, it would do better to get back to the spirit world as quickly as possible and blow the whistle on us."

A shudder went through Danae's body. "Oh, God," she whispered. "If you kill an animal that has a spirit bound to it . . . the spirit's released. Are you saying—? Oh, God, that's *horrible*."

He nodded and held her a little more tightly. "They want us, Danae. They want us so badly they're willing to sacrifice major parts of their own conquest machine to get us."

"But *why*? What is it we know that's got them so frightened?"

"I don't know," Ravagin sighed. "The only thing that makes sense is that idea you had that they've found a way to get past the Tunnel and are trying to invade Shamsheer."

"But there isn't any way for them to *do* that. We already decided that, remember?"

"Yes, well, it's starting to look more and more like we were wrong. But we can discuss that later. For now, our more immediate problem is to stay alive."

Danae took a deep breath. "Agreed. So what do we do next? How soon will Melentha know about our invisibility?"

"Depends on how communication works in the fourth world, I guess," he shrugged. "If the spirit who just left here can pass the message on to any of the other spirits, then as soon as Melentha invokes one of them the word'll be out. If she has to invoke this particular spirit—which would require that she knows what its name is—we could be sipping drinks on Threshold before she catches on."

"I don't think I'd bet on that last one."

"Me neither." Ravagin took a moment to study the sky. Another four or five hours until dawn; well within a hard ride from the Besak way house. "I wish we had a real choice, but I'm afraid we don't. The spirits can't get to us without someone around to invoke them, but once Melentha knows where we are she can probably get her agents here before the inn's lar is released. Ergo, we need to leave before that."

A sound that was half laugh and half bark escaped Danae's lips. "I almost tried that on my own, earlier tonight. Deja vu strikes again. I'm game for it—Karyx at night can't be any worse than what Melentha will be throwing at us. You know any ways to get past a lar?"

"Depends on whether it has to detect us to stop us. In this case, though, there's an easier way. If we can risk using it." Ravagin bit at his lip, thinking. "Yeah, the benefits outweigh the risks. How are your eyes doing?"

"About the same as before. I don't . . . I don't know if I can stand another day out in the sunlight, Ravagin."

He pursed his lips. "Well, if we can cover enough distance before dawn, I think I can find a way to keep you under cover for most of tomorrow. Stay here; I'll be right back."

She nodded—too weary, he thought, to even be afraid of further attacks. Disengaging his arm from around her, he got to his feet and headed over to the inn.

The innkeeper was still outside the door, talking in low tones to two of the guests. All three looked at Ravagin as he approached, the innkeeper with a wary sort of anger in his expression. He opened his mouth, presumably to demand an explanation—

"Innkeeper," Ravagin nodded shortly. "Am I to assume it is common practice in these parts for the master of an inn to permit one of his guests to attack another?"

The innkeeper's eyes bulged, whatever he was about to say dying halfway out. But he recovered fast. "If there is any death-blame to be had, sir, it seems to me that *you* are the one who still lives—"

"The man burned to death on his own firebrat," Ravagin interrupted harshly, "while he was attempting to murder my companion. Your door had no lock and no bar—"

"With the lar about the grounds—"

"The lar failed to keep him out, did it not? And furthermore, you had no provision for the danger of fire—without the nixie which *I* invoked your entire inn might have burned to the ground."

The innkeeper clamped his jaw closed. "If you expect gratitude, you are sorely mistaken," he bit out. "Whatever your quarrel with the dead man, you brought it upon yourselves. I have no doubt the magistrates of Findral will find it so when your grievance is laid before them."

Deliberately, Ravagin looked in turn at each of the two men listening to the debate. After a moment both seemed to take the hint and drifted off back into the inn. "Now, then," Ravagin said when he and the innkeeper were alone. "Between honest and fair-minded men there is surely no need to bring in magistrates."

The other snorted; but it was abundantly clear from his face that he wasn't nearly as certain of his case's merits as he'd claimed to be. "If you expect to extort unfair compensation from a poor man, the results will disappoint you."

"I seek no such extortion," Ravagin assured him. "Nor do I threaten you," he added as the other's eyes slipped momentarily to the short sword at Ravagin's waist. "I seek only your cooperation in what is already due me."

That elicited another snort. "What is due you, save lodging for the night?"

"*And* breakfast in the morning. I have already paid you for that, if you recall."

The other blinked in surprise. "Then what is this all about?" he demanded. "Breakfast will be served at sunup."

"Ah—and *that* is what this is all about. I would like my breakfast right now, packaged for travel."

"For—? And where do you propose to go traveling at this hour? The stable?"

"I propose to go out," Ravagin told him calmly. "For this you will need to release your lar."

The innkeeper had a lot of other things on his mind, but even so that one seemed to hit him right across the face. "You want *what*?" he all but shouted before he could catch himself and lower his voice. "I cannot do that!" he hissed. "My guests—the safety of my inn—"

"I have no time for an argument," Ravagin cut him off, putting an edge of icy steel into his tone. "This unwarranted attack has worsened my companion's condition, and I must ride out to seek aid for her. Or will your magistrates claim that forcing the ill to suffer unnecessarily is also within an innkeeper's rights?"

The other clamped his jaw tightly. "I will have the meal prepared immediately," he growled.

"Good. And I will need another room for my companion, at least until the firebrat in our old one vanishes. Without charge, of course."

For a moment it looked like the innkeeper was going to argue that one. But with a sharp nod he turned and disappeared into the inn.

Twenty minutes later, the packed provisions on his back, Ravagin sat astride his horse at the western edge of the protective circle. "All right," he said. "You may release the lar."

"Are you certain you wish to do this?" the innkeeper standing beside him asked nervously. "You will be unable to reach anyone in Findral until their own lar is released at dawn."

"Then I will have to bypass Findral and find aid from one of the spiritmasters who live alone beyond the village," Ravagin told him shortly. "Whatever I do, it is my business. *Your* only concern in this matter now is to make sure my companion is provided with the quiet and rest she needs. If you think that beyond your skills, tell me now and I will take her to someone who possesses such abilities."

It was impossible to tell in the dim light, but Ravagin thought the innkeeper's face went red. Turning stiffly toward the humming mist ahead, he held out a hand. "*Carash-melanasta!*" he snarled—

And the humming stopped.

"Farewell," Ravagin said, nudging his horse forward. The other didn't answer; he was already hurrying back toward the inn, where he needed to stand to ensure the lar he would be invoking would encircle the entire grounds. Smiling tightly, Ravagin continued on, heading back toward the Besak-Findral road. A short ways from the inn there was a slight rise; on the far side of it, out of sight from prying eyes, he reined to a halt.

And waited, sweating, for about a thousand years.

But finally, he heard the approaching footsteps, and a couple of minutes later Danae was back in the saddle with him. "Any trouble?" he asked her, kicking the horse into a fast trot.

She shook her head. "It was a longer drop from the window than I expected, though."

"Sorry. I couldn't think of a good excuse to lose the innkeeper for a minute to come around and catch you."

"Oh, that's okay." She paused. "You really think it'll fool them?"

"Probably not," he admitted. "On the other hand, we lost nothing by trying it. If they send a scout ahead of the main force, the innkeeper can honestly tell them that only one of us has left. Not a particularly opaque deception, but with Hart already having split off on his own, they may conclude that you and I have done the same thing. If it makes them concentrate some of their strength on the inn longer than they have to, we'll have gained a bit."

"And if they don't fall for it?"

He shrugged. "We reach the confrontation sooner. That's all there is to it."

She sighed and fell silent, and Ravagin settled back into the increasingly familiar pattern of riding and watching. Around them, Karyx was alive with the subtle sounds of night . . . the sounds of night, and all the dangers that accompanied them.

It was, he knew, going to be a long ride.

Chapter 31

The djinn hovered before her, its grotesque face barely centimeters from her own, its flame-red eyes glowing with hatred and dark satisfaction. *I see you*, it seemed to say, and though she couldn't hear it with her ears, the spirit's message was abundantly clear. *Your invisibility is gone. We will hunt you down and burn your thoughts with such pain as you have never before imagined.* It paused, as if waiting for her to plead for mercy. But her tongue was frozen to her mouth; and as the silence lengthened she saw to her horror that a new image had joined the first: the carved demon-face from Melentha's archway. Like the djinn, it glared at her; unlike the other spirit, there was an amusement to its gaze that chilled Danae's blood even more than the djinn's hatred had done . . .

"Danae!"

With a start, she woke up. "Ravagin?" she croaked through dry lips. The glow that had been seeping through her blindfold had changed to unmitigated black, and for a horrible second she wondered if she had gone blind. "Ravagin!"

"It's okay, Danae, I'm here," his voice came, tired but soothing. "Another bad dream?"

"Oh, God. Yes." She licked her lips, working moisture back into her mouth. "Ravagin . . . I can't see anything."

"It's okay—there isn't actually anything in here *to* see. The sun's gone down, about an hour ago."

"An *hour* ago?"

"That's right," he confirmed. "I hope you got some good rest for having slept the day away; I sure as hell didn't."

Danae grimaced. "I'm sorry—my fault; I kept waking you up, didn't I? I don't understand it—I haven't had nightmares like this since I was seven."

"Let's hope we never do again," he said, and this time she could hear the tension in his voice. "I suspect it's the locale, not anything internal to either of us."

"You had nightmares, too?" she asked, pushing herself to a sitting position.

"Yeah—watch your head."

"Right." She felt above her with one hand as she massaged the small of her back with the other. An undersized cave on the southern edge of Cairn Waste wasn't exactly the kind of accommodations she'd been hoping for when they fled from the inn, but it had been the best Ravagin had been able to come up with as dawn had begun coloring the eastern sky and her eyes had started screaming for some relief from the light. The place had certainly taken its toll; in addition to the terrifying dreams, a quick inventory showed that she had aches in a dozen places, souvenirs of the chill and damp and the hardness of the floor.

On the other hand, they'd survived the day without being found by either Melentha's gang or any of the more bestial predators of the region. All in all, a fair enough trade. "Have you gone outside at all since morning?" she asked.

"Once or twice. Mostly watching out for either of those gangs we outran on the way here, but we apparently gave them the slip."

She nodded, pulling off the blindfold and rubbing furiously where the cloth had made her skin itch. "I suppose it's only fair for the demogorgon's curse to be good for *something*."

"I'd say being able to spot trouble twice as far away as it can see you qualifies as good for something, yes," he said with a touch of the old Ravagin dryness. It was a part of his personality that Danae hadn't seen much of since the escape from Melentha's house. A part of him, she suddenly realized, she'd rather missed.

"I hope you left me something to eat," she asked, feeling a strange heat rushing into her cheeks.

"Yeah, but you may not like it much." He rummaged in the innkeeper's pack, pulled out two hand-sized loaves of bread. "I think the same thing that gave us all those wonderful dreams is also affecting our taste buds," he added, handing her one of the loaves. "Be prepared."

Cautiously, she tried a bite. Usually this style of bread loaf had a light, sweet taste to it bordering on her usual definition of pastry. This one was as insipid as packing material. "Yeych," she growled, forcing herself to chew and swallow. "No wonder no one lives in Cairn Waste anymore. What do you suppose is causing it?"

"I don't think anyone knows for sure," he shrugged. "But after what you've told me about the fourth world and all . . . my guess is that this may be a weak spot between that world and Karyx."

"Like a half-finished Tunnel, you mean?"

"Something like that. In fact, the builders may have planned to build a Tunnel somewhere around here and just never gotten around to doing it."

She thought about that. "So it's not enough of a Tunnel for them to actually break through, but they *can* get close enough to affect us?"

"It's just a guess." He took a bite of his own loaf, made a face. "Though I can tell you that if *I'd* been in charge of planning Triplet, I sure as hell wouldn't have let these damn spirits get even this close to me."

"We'll take that up with the appropriate authorities. If we ever find them." Danae hesitated. "You still want to try for the Tunnel tonight?"

Ravagin exhaled tiredly. "I don't see any point in delaying it. Unless you've come up with some new reasons I haven't heard yet?"

She grimaced, but he was right: all her arguments for a different day or time for their break had already been soundly scorched. The guards Melentha would have at the Tunnel would certainly be expecting them to move under cover of darkness, which might have argued for a daylight blitz . . . except that with Danae's eyes the way they were such a move was out of the question. And putting it off to another day did nothing but delay the inevitable. "No, you're right," she sighed. "We might as well go ahead and get it over with. If she gets us, she gets us—that's all there is to it."

"That's the spirit," Ravagin nodded, getting stiffly to his feet and walking stooped over toward the cave's mouth where their horse was tethered. "Half pessimism, half fatalism. Just remember, if she's still thinking at all straight, she's going to recall that killing us could be hazardous to her masters' plans. Or at least killing you could be."

"That's great comfort," Danae muttered, brushing the crumbs off her hands and standing up into a cautious crouch. "Come on, let's get going."

There was still a hint of afterglow in the western sky, which to Danae's affected eyes left the world almost as brightly lit as if it were noon. Seated in front of Ravagin on the horse, she again took up her previous night's role as lookout, watching and listening for anything that might mean trouble. In the Cairn Waste, she'd discovered yesterday, that largely boiled down to scanning the horizon for other riders or large animals. Cover here was virtually nonexistent, save for occasional large rock formations and—increasingly—a gradually rolling landscape as they headed southeast into the region of the Cairn Mounds. In those cases, where her eyes couldn't serve, her hearing had to; but the Cairn Waste had earned its name honestly, and they neither saw nor heard anyone as they made their way along.

It wasn't until they began picking their path around and between full-fledged mounds, barely half an hour after starting out, that Danae realized just how close to the Tunnel their cave had been. "Nothing like spending the day on the enemy's doorstep," she muttered as Ravagin called a halt and found a scraggly bush to loosely tether their horse to.

"Can you think of a better place to hide than right under their noses?" he whispered back. "Besides, who'd be crazy enough to spend a whole day in the Cairn Waste?"

"That's great logi—yeep!"

"What?" he hissed, swinging around with sword already half out of its sheath.

"Over there," she told him, nodding nervously toward the spot of green haze moving slowly across the mounds a hundred meters ahead.

Ravagin took a deep breath, easing the sword back down. "Nice to know we're in the right place. Can you see any detail, or is it just a green blob?"

"Uh . . . nothing. Though it *is* kind of far away."

He grunted. "Chances are good it's a parasite spirit, then, not a regular demon. Interesting. I'd have thought Melentha could have pulled enough firepower to have nothing but the highest-level demons and peris watching the place."

"Maybe with our invisibility she's given up on unbound spirits," Danae suggested.

"Or else it means Hart's doing a slapjack job of leading the goose chase," Ravagin grunted.

Danae bit at her lip. "Whatever Hart does, he does well," she said quietly. "That's all part of his job, as he's so fond of saying."

They stood there quietly for another minute, watching as the parasite spirit ahead continued on to eventually vanish between two mounds to their left. Then Ravagin took her hand and together they started forward.

It was harder than Danae had anticipated. Her sole previous experience with the Mounds had been during their walk from the Tunnel to the Besak-Torralane Village road at the beginning of the Karyx leg of their trip, and it rapidly became apparent that that had *not* been a representative section of the landscape. The mounds to the north of the Tunnel were at the same time more angularly rocky and more gravelly, making footing treacherous and the consequences of missteps painful. Danae's enhanced vision gave her surprisingly little advantage, not much more than Ravagin's experience and greater knowledge of the area gave him.

But there was nothing else to do but continue on. And so they did; walking, and slipping, and bumping knees and shins, and hissing curses they didn't dare express aloud, because there was no way to know when they would be within hearing of the guards at the Tunnel. It was, all in all, a miserable two hours.

Eventually, they made it to the mound Ravagin had chosen to make their first direct reconnoiter from. Carefully, thankful the long trek was over, Danae crawled on her belly to the top and eased her head up for a look.

"Well?" Ravagin whispered in her ear. "What do you see?"

She took a deep breath. "About a dozen men," she whispered back. "Sitting or standing just in front of the Tunnel entrance. All armed, looks like. And . . ." She squinted. "I think I can see the haze of a lar around them."

"I'm sure you do," Ravagin grunted. "Probably backed up right against the entrance so that no one can get in."

She nodded, tears blurring her vision as all the tension and aggravation of the hike turned into frustration. Unreasonably, she knew, she'd still somehow clung to the hope that Melentha would have been foolish enough to entrust the Tunnel's defense to her spirit allies. But now, outnumbered six to one by armed men against whom their hard-won spirit invisibility was useless, the hopelessness of the situation abruptly threatened to overwhelm her . . .

"Hey! You okay?"

She licked her lips, sniffed once. "Of course I am. How could things possibly be better for us?"

Shuffling a few centimeters closer to her, Ravagin reached over to put an arm across her shoulders. "Come on, Danae— you can't let it get to you," he whispered urgently. "We've still got a chance, but not if you let fatigue and poor odds and all this damn spirit influence break you down. Come on—if your father could see you now—"

"Leave Daddy Dear out of this!" she hissed, fury erupting into the black depression threatening to bury her. "If you can't remember I'm more than just an extension of my father's money and personality and influence—get your arm *off* me, damn it, and concentrate on thinking up something clever."

Obediently, Ravagin removed his arm . . . but even as Danae swiped her fists at her eyes to dry them, she thought she saw a grimly satisfied smile tugging at the corners of his lips. "All right," he said calmly. "Now: look around—carefully—and see if you can see anyone standing watch farther out from the entrance."

Gritting her teeth, Danae again raised her head. *They can't see me*, she reminded herself firmly. *As far as they're concerned, it's pitch black out here . . . and I'm as invisible as if they were spirits.* She took a good look, then lowered herself back down. "I don't see anyone at all," she whispered. "Just the dozen or so down there."

Ravagin nodded. "Uh-*huh*. Interesting. Melentha's definitely lost her ability to think tactically."

"You could have fooled *me*," Danae growled back. "Besides blocking the only exit from this triple damned planet, they also just *happen* to be standing in the middle of a lar, which makes them impregnable from any attack we could possibly come up with."

"Impregnable?" Ravagin shook his head, a thoughtful look on his face. "Not even close—which is why I said Melentha's lost her touch. Tell me, what's the problem with sitting inside a lar circle?"

"Ravagin, this is no time for guessing games—"

"It's the fact that you're rooted to the spot there yourself, isn't it?" he continued as if she hadn't spoken. "Sure you're immune from any attack, at least for awhile . . . but if the attack keeps up, it'll eventually get through. And you're stuck there until it does."

"Great—except that we haven't the resources for that kind of attack," she pointed out.

"True, but maybe we can come up with something that looks like one. Quiet a minute, please, I have to think." He pursed his lips, gazing out into the darkness. "Okay," he said at last. "Okay, I see what she's got in mind. A small group, close in to the Tunnel, with no firebrats or dazzlers to tip us off . . . she's hoping we'll be lulled by the apparent inactivity all around and just walk right into their arms."

Frowning, Danae lifted her head again. They certainly *were* being unnaturally quiet for men on boring nighttime guard. On the other hand— "But then why aren't they waiting *inside* the cave where we wouldn't have had any chance at all of seeing them?"

"Partly because Melentha and the demons aren't too bright. Partly because the cave there is supposed to be even more haunted than the rest of the Cairn Mounds."

"Spirit-possessed men shouldn't care about ghost stories."

"Agreed," Ravagin nodded. "Which implies our little invisibility trick has forced her to give up using possessed people. Definitely a development in our favor."

Or else, Danae thought, *the spirit-possessed ones are hiding inside the cave.* But even she could see now that it didn't really matter. No matter who or what might be inside the Tunnel, she and Ravagin would still have no option but to go charging through and take their chances. "All right, I'm game," she sighed. "I guess. So how are you going to fake a major attack on their lair?"

"I'm not exactly sure yet," he admitted. "But I've got some ideas. You see, they may have all the numbers on their side; but we've got the one thing you can take between the worlds of Triplet."

"And that is . . . ?"

"Knowledge. Come on; let's move back a couple of mounds and see what resources we've got here to play with."

Chapter 32

The scraggly bushes dotting the region yielded branches which, though rough and gnarled, were surprisingly strong and flexible. Their own clothing yielded strips of cloth which, Ravagin hoped, would be both strong enough and flammable enough for their purposes. The mounds themselves yielded plenty of stones and gravel of various sizes, including a precious piece of flint.

And an hour of painstaking work with all of it yielded the centerpiece of Ravagin's plan: two small catapults.

"I don't know," Danae shook her head as he gave the baskets they'd made one final examination. "They don't look like they've got anywhere *near* the range we're going to need."

"They'll make it, all right," he assured her. "Or they will once I get them back on that mound overlooking the Tunnel. The only tricky part's going to be getting the delay timer to work right."

"I still wish we had one of my composite bows instead," Danae sighed. "But you're the expert here. You grab the baskets and sticks; I'll take the stones and pebbles."

"Hold it," Ravagin said as she reached down. "The rest of this is *my* job. Exclusively. *Your* job is to start circling over toward our breakaway point."

"Ravagin—"

"No argument," he interrupted her firmly. "If something goes wrong with the setting-up, the jackels down there will be all over this place. There's no point in letting them have both of us, now, is there?"

He realized the instant it was out of his mouth that he shouldn't have put it that way. Even in the faint starlight the sudden suspicion on her face was easy to see. "You're not saying," she said slowly, "that *that* was what your plan was all along, are you? To lure them up here and let me get away?"

"To let *us* get away," he corrected. "Come on, Danae— you've never before mistaken me for a martyr; kindly don't start doing it now. I fully intend to be there beside you when the balloon goes up—and if the Tunnel clears and you don't move, I may just run straight over you. Got that?"

She took a deep breath and the suspicion faded somewhat from her face. Though not entirely. "All right," she said with a sigh. "Now?"

"Now," he nodded. "Remember that you've got all the time in the world, so don't rush it." He hesitated. "And once you're in position behind the bush, it'd probably be a good idea for you to go ahead and get your clothes off."

He braced for an argument, found himself mildly surprised when she merely nodded. "I understand. Should I leave my shoes on?"

"Right—good idea. They'll make running easier, and you'll be able to kick them off easily enough when we reach the telefold. Okay; get going. And good luck."

She hesitated, then moved over to him and kissed him gently on the lips. "Be careful," she whispered, and was gone.

He stared after her for several seconds, the lingering feel of her lips on his both vivid and slightly unreal. It was the second time she'd kissed him . . . and the first time she also hadn't expected to ever see him again. . . .

Picking up one of the catapults with each hand, he eased himself to his feet and started cautiously back toward the Tunnel. Someday, he promised himself, he would have to see what it was like to kiss her without some deadly danger looming over their heads.

Just below the crown of his target mound, hidden from view from the Tunnel entrance below, was a ledge-like flat

spot formed by a jutting mass of stone. Setting up one of
the fulcrum stones, Ravagin placed a catapult arm across
it, tying one end down with a braided cloth strip around
part of the ledge. A small boulder went on the other end,
and he winced as the cloth strip tore a bit and the stick
creaked under the strain. But both held. A minute later
the second catapult was similarly in position.

And now, he thought, wiping sweat from his forehead,
comes the really *tricky part.*

Gathering his handful of pebbles together, he laid them
out in a neat row and cupped his hands over the first one.
He'd learned this combined invocation/binding spell a long
time ago but couldn't recall ever having used it . . . and if
it turned out that the spirit appeared even briefly before
disappearing into the pebble, he was going to bring the
guard down on him in double-quick time.

In which case . . . well, at least Danae ought to be able
to get away. He hoped she'd be smart and tough enough
to take advantage of it.

Licking his lips, he took a deep breath. "*Sa-trahist
rassh myst-tarukha-pharumasziakai,*" he whispered. For
an instant there was the faintest spark of red light beneath
his cupped hand, a spark that settled down into a dull red
glow . . .

A glow, he abruptly realized, that was coming from the
pebble. The firebrat had been successfully bound, and with
nothing the men down at the Tunnel could possibly have
spotted.

Ravagin let out his breath in a whoosh of relief. Carefully, he worked moisture back into his mouth and reached
his hand to the next pebble in line.

It took nearly fifteen minutes before all the stones were
glowing with trapped firebrats, and five minutes of scorch-
ing his fingers before they were all loaded into the little
cloth baskets on the ends of the catapult arms. Belatedly,
he hoped the pebbles' internal heat wouldn't burn through
the baskets before the catapults could be triggered, but it
was too late now to do more than worry about it. Careful
not to let it clang on the rocks around him, he pulled out
his sword and laid it down with its point next to the cloth
strips holding down the first catapult. Gritting his teeth—

the noise this might make could be as bad as he'd feared
the light from the firebat binding would be—he tapped
the sword firmly with his flint

It was louder than he'd anticipated, and for a dozen
heartbeats he froze, waiting for the landscape to light up
as the guards below invoked dazzlers and fanned out to
find the source of the noise. But the world remained
black, and after another moment he tried it again. And
again. And again.

Finally, on about the twentieth try, he got a spark that
actually settled into the cloth strip and began sending out
tendrils of smoke. The second catapult was easier; it only
took a couple of minutes and ten tries to start a smoldering
fire on the restraining strip there.

And now it boiled down to a simple race: whether he
could get around these mounds and into position with
Danae before the things went off. Easing back down the
mound, heart thudding in his ears, he resheathed his
sword and headed off.

Rather to his amazement, he made it.

Danae was waiting for him exactly where he'd told her
to, behind a bush a quarter of the way around the mound
from the Tunnel's entrance. She was also, as he'd ordered,
completely naked except for her shoes. And clearly not
enjoying it much.

"Well?" she breathed into his ear as he eased silently
behind the bush with her.

"As far as I could tell, it's ready to go," he whispered
back.

"You'd better get undressed, then, shouldn't you?"

He pursed his lips. "I don't think so, not right away. I
doubt they're going to be so stupid as to all rush out there
when the attack starts. Whatever guard they leave behind,
I'm going to have to deal with them." *And deal with them*,
he added silently to himself, *before one of them reinvokes
a lar and blocks the Tunnel again*.

"And what happens when they come charging back—"
She broke off abruptly. "There—the first one's just gone."

Ravagin hadn't heard it himself, but he knew by now
not to doubt her hearing. "Cover your eyes," he warned

her, and leaned cautiously around the bush. From there he could just see the faint haze of the lar's edge. . . .

And an instant later the haze exploded with flashes of light.

Someone around the corner barked a curse. "What the brizzling *hell*—?" someone else snapped.

"Firebrat attack," a third voice heavy with authority cut the others off. "Where'd the invocation come from?"

"Didn't hear one."

"Come on, there must have been seven firebrats there—they couldn't have come up by themselves."

"Damn it all, knock off the chatter," the authoritative voice ordered. "That won't be the last attack—listen for wherever the hell they're doing the invocation from."

The group fell silent. Ravagin gritted his teeth, sending up a quick prayer for the second catapult. If its restraint had stopped burning . . .

He counted ten heartbeats; and then the second salvo of pebbles hit, the confrontation between spirits as the trapped firebrats attempted to pass through the lar sending flares of light across the landscape. Easing his hand onto his sword hilt, Ravagin braced himself. If the leader reacted to the unheard attack with any intelligence at all . . .

He did. "*Carash-melanasta,*" the other snapped. "Everyone—get out there and find him."

"The lar—!"

"Shut up—you want to sit here and let him just break it down?" the leader snarled. "Spread out! Prilsift, Orlantin—you two stay here in case they try and slip past us. Everyone else, *move.*"

Ravagin froze in place as the dimly seen figures fanned rapidly out from in front of the mound. Sacrificial goats, if there had really been a spirithandler out there knowledgeable enough to have launched the attack they thought they'd just witnessed. The timing here was going to be critical . . .

The last searcher passed over the imaginary line he'd drawn . . . and Ravagin moved.

The closest of the two men flanking the Tunnel entrance never had a chance. He'd barely started to turn, responding perhaps to a flicker from his peripheral vision, when

Ravagin's short sword slashed viciously across his throat. The other swore and leaped away from the mound, bringing his sword to bear. Ravagin charged him, sensing Danae moving around the corner and into the Tunnel entrance—

"*Sa-trahist rassh!*" the guard shouted.

And a firebrat erupted directly in Ravagin's path.

He skidded to a hard halt, throwing up his left arm as the heat washed over him. "Run, Danae," he snapped. If the guard came around the firebrat now, while he was still blinded from its light, he was dead.

But no sword sliced toward him from the glare. Ducking past the flaming spirit, Ravagin turned toward the Tunnel, senses alert for the attack which still should be coming. Behind him, he could hear the sounds of running feet as the rest of the guards ran furiously to join the fight, and he realized that he had no choice. Clamping his jaw tightly, he lowered his head and charged, hoping that when the sword of his ambusher came for him he would at least survive the blow long enough to try and seal the Tunnel behind him.

Five long steps—a short eternity—and then his flickering shadow was looming over him on the Tunnel's ceiling, and he was inside. Without injury or attack . . . and Melentha's servants had just made their last mistake. He and Danae were inside, they were outside—

"*Sa-trahist rassh!*" he shouted, turning back to face the opening. "*Sa-trahist rassh, sa-trahist rassh!*"

And they were damn well going to *stay* outside. The three invoked firebrats flared up to block the Tunnel's entrance, cutting off his view of the men furiously running toward him around the firebrat their comrade had called up.

And Ravagin's blood froze.

He hadn't been attacked because there had been no one there to attack him. The other guard hadn't stayed around to fight after invoking his firebrat: *he'd followed Danae into the Tunnel*!

The others swearing and reaching for bow and arrow outside were instantly forgotten. Twisting around again with a speed that wrenched his back, Ravagin sprinted desperately down the Tunnel. Danae was alone, naked, unarmed—

He pushed the awful vision from his mind, putting everything he had into his legs. The light from outside was beginning to fade now with the distance; if Danae's extraordinary vision hadn't been blinded before she got into the Tunnel she would have the advantage over her pursuer when the path started to curve.

If she realized she *was* being pursued.

"Danae!" he called with all the breath he could spare from his running. "Behind you—watch out—get to the middle, fast!"

There was no response he could hear above his own pounding feet. *She'll make it*, he told himself over and over. *She'll make it*. But the words were small comfort. Gritting his teeth, he pushed his pace to the absolute limit.

And nearly wound up plastering himself against the wall as the Tunnel began its slow right-handed turn. "*Haklarast*," he panted. "Stay behind me," he added as the sprite appeared. The faint light from the glow-fire was just right. He kept on running—

The light faded around the turn as the sprite stayed where it had been invoked.

Damn. His spirit invisibility had unexpectedly played him false. Snatching his sword from its sheath, he stuck it out to the side, letting its point define the wall's position for him as he ran. It bounced back and forth across the roughness there, throwing off sparks as the indestructable Tunnel material tore microscopic bits of steel from it. But it gave him a clear track to follow, allowed him to run as fast as he could manage. Ahead, somewhere, his eyes told him that there was faint light; and as he came around the last stretch of curve—

They were there, both of them, and it was a shock to find out just how much of their lead he'd managed to close. Directly ahead of Ravagin, perhaps six meters away, was the guard, a sprite hovering at his shoulder giving off the glow Ravagin had seen as he rounded the bend. Farther ahead was Danae—

Ravagin's heart seemed to skip a beat. Danae was barely

two meters ahead of her pursuer. And he was visibly gaining.

"You want to fight someone, fight me!" Ravagin shouted. Or had intended to shout; it came out sounding more like a dying man's gasp. But it was enough. The guard twisted his head to look, slowing down in the process . . . and in the half-second breather it bought her, Danae reached down to half pull, half kick the shoes off her feet and sprinted the last three meters across the invisible telefold line to safety.

But the guard didn't know she was beyond his reach. Apparently satisfied that he was in no immediate danger, he turned back and continued on toward her, raising his sword as he saw her collapsed against the wall just ahead of him. Ravagin put on a burst of speed, knowing suddenly what he would have to do and how he would have to do it; skidded to a halt and spun a hundred eighty degrees around, sword braced straight out against his belt buckle. Behind him, the guard hit the telefold, reappeared the preordained five meters back—

And slammed headlong into Ravagin, impaling himself on Ravagin's sword.

The momentum of that rush bowled Ravagin over, the two of them toppling together onto the floor . . . and as the man on top of him rattled and died, a horrible, ululating scream split the air.

Dimly, through the ringing in his ears, Ravagin heard a voice. "Oh, God!" Danae was gasping. "*Ravagin!*"

"I'm all right," he panted, struggling for the leverage to push the bloody body off of him. He'd barely begun when Danae was kneeling beside him, taking the dead man's arm and helping Ravagin push. "Are you okay?" he added, looking up at her.

"I'm fine—he never touched me," she assured him distractedly, eyes widening at the sight of the blood matting his shirt. "But that *scream*—I thought you'd been killed.

"I don't think it was any human voice made *that* sound," he said, still trying to catch his breath. "Looks like the spirits hedged their bets a little, after all, and had something in here keeping an eye on things." In the glow of the sprite still riding the dead man's shoulder, Danae's sweat-sheened body fairly glowed; and it took a second for him to catch the significance of the way she was looking at him . . . "Your eyes!" he blurted suddenly. "They're all right?"

"I guess so," she said, helping him to his feet. "As soon as I crossed the telefold everything went dark."

"Everything—? Oh. Right." He took a deep breath, let it out slowly. "We made it. We actually made it."

"I never had any doubt we would," Danae said . . . and abruptly she was in his arms.

They held each other that way for a long minute . . . and when the trembling of mutually released fear and tension had finally worked its way out, Ravagin gently disengaged her arms. "Yeah," he said, "I thought we were as good as dead, too. Come on; let's shake the dust of Karyx off our feet and get the hell out of here."

Ravagin got undressed as quickly as fatigue and tired muscles permitted, stowing everything in the hidden lockers before crossing with Danae to the Shamsheer side of the Tunnel. He kept his ears cocked for sounds of further pursuit, but none of the guards they'd left behind had made an appearance by the time he and Danae were finishing dressing. "You think they've given up?" Danae asked, glancing nervously back down the Tunnel as he studied the weapons shelf in the glow of a firefly around his finger. "That spirit scream sounded like a battle call."

"It was probably just venting a load of futile anger," Ravagin shrugged. "The spirits must surely know we're beyond their reach now, and given that there's no real point in their wasting time sending men in after us. Damn, but I wish they'd keep these weapons lockers better stocked."

"If they came in naked—"

"I'd almost like to see them try it," he said grimly, removing his old scorpion glove and a dagger from the locker and securing them to his belt. "Here," he added, pulling out a second dagger and handing it to her.

She frowned a bit as she took it. "Last time we came through here you told me Shamsheer nobleladies didn't wear weapons."

"They don't, but for the moment I don't really care about the local customs."

She snorted gently. "And Melentha might just be desperate enough to send naked men after us?"

He sighed. Danae was getting altogether too good at reading his mind. "She wouldn't dare," he told her, not entirely honestly. "I just don't feel like taking unnecessary chances, that's all. Come on, let's go—I want to get a sky-plane and be somewhere civilized by breakfast."

The first light of dawn had driven away all but the westernmost stars as Ravagin emerged from the Tunnel and stepped a few meters into the forest clearing surrounding it. For a moment he listened, alert for any of the nighttime predators who might not yet have sought shelter and sleep. But only the sounds of awakening birds and insects reached his ears, and after making a careful visual scan of the area he turned back to the Tunnel and waved. "All clear," he called softly. She stepped out; and as he reached for the prayer stick at his belt, her eyes abruptly shifted skyward. He looked up, following her gaze—

And froze. Descending rapidly toward them was a sky-plane carrying the unmistakable figures of two trolls. Humanoid machines, programmed for defense of their Protectorate and castle-lord and totally incapable of moving even a meter outside their own boundaries . . . and yet they were *here*—at the Tunnel—over thirty kilometers from the nearest Protectorate.

"Oh, hell," Ravagin murmured, very softly.

The sky-plane came nearer . . . and from one of the trolls boomed a voice: "Stand where you are, trespassers on the soil of the Faymar Protectorate," it ordered. "You will submit to my command or be executed."

Chapter 33

This isn't fair, was the first, resentful, thought to cross Danae's mind as the sky-plane settled toward a landing. *We're tired and hungry, we've been hunted and harassed by an entire world and nearly killed in the process, and my eyes still hurt from what happened to them. And now this. Damn it all, it isn't fair.*

And then her fatigued mind caught up with her . . . and she felt her stomach muscles freeze. "Ravagin!" she hissed, "Those trolls—"

"Keep back," he said without turning around. "Something's very, very wrong here."

"They're not supposed to be this far out of their Protectorate, are they?"

"They're not supposed to be *anywhere* out of their Protectorate," he replied. "Stay back, Danae—if I have to fight them, I want to have room to maneuver."

Fight them? Danae shifted her eyes back to the sky-plane and the two figures rising to their feet there. Sophisticated machines—she knew that much from her Triplet orientation—but from less than twenty meters away she found it hard to accept that fact on a gut level. True, their barrel chests and tubular limbs showed too much curvature and too little muscular definition beneath their orange/black/yellow garb; and their almost non-existent necks, overlarge bald heads, and pale skin kept them from ever being mistaken for human beings. And yet, there was

254

something else about them—the ease and fluidity of their movements, perhaps—that seemed to belie their mechanical nature.

And in the midst of her sidetrack reverie, Danae's eyes fell on the crossbow pistol strapped to each troll's right thigh. *Fight them* . . . and she suddenly felt sick.

Ravagin let them get within ten meters of him and then raised his hand. "Hold, servants of Castle Feymareal," he called in a firm voice. "As a law-abiding citizen of Shamsheer, I am entitled to know the charges against me."

The first troll stopped; the second took another step before following suit. "You are trespassing on soil of the Feymar Protectorate," the first said.

"But the soil of all Protectorates is free to all lawabiders," Ravagin insisted. "What law-breaking charge is listed against me that my way may be interfered with?"

For the first time the troll seemed at a loss for words. "You will submit to my command or be executed," it said at last.

"Yes, you've already said that," Ravagin reminded him. "But if you cannot list any law-breaking charges you have no authority to detain me."

Again the trolls hesitated . . . and abruptly, the sense of aliveness that had been nagging at Danae's subconsciousness vanished. They were, really and truly, nothing more than machines—

"I think they're deciding how they're going to handle this," Ravagin said quietly over his shoulder, his voice tight. "Get ready to duck back into the Tunnel if this doesn't work."

"All right," she replied. The words felt odd in her mouth; abruptly, she realized Ravagin had spoken and she'd answered in Standard, not Shamahni.

The first troll seemed to make up its mind. "You will both return with us to Castle Feymareal," it said, its hand dropping down next to the crossbow at its thigh. "If you refuse—"

"You will leave me alone," Ravagin said suddenly, "or I will kill that woman." His hand swung back, his dagger flashing as he turned half around—

And sent the knife spinning toward Danae.

It was so unexpected she didn't even have time to gasp. Reflexively, she ducked, throwing up an arm in token defense as something only half seen darted in from the direction of the trolls. An instant later there was the crack of metal on metal and the dagger shot sideways off into the forest. Opening her eyes again—she didn't remember closing them—she saw the first troll standing with crossbow pistol at the ready, its string still visibly vibrating . . . and suddenly she understood what Ravagin had done. He'd forced the troll to move to her defense, and in doing so to waste its first shot.

And then she shifted her attention to Ravagin . . . and saw that the trick had been a waste of time. Even as Ravagin yanked his scorpion glove free and jammed his hand into it, the second troll was already bringing its crossbow to bear.

It was as if time had suddenly slowed to a crawl, freezing the tableau before her. She could almost see the slight damped-sine oscillations of the troll's arm as it corrected to its final aim; glimpsed the flat-tipped stun bolt which would be slamming into Ravagin's solar plexus in the trolls' normal so-called mercy shot . . . and when he was down and helpless before them . . .

And without any real thought of what she was doing, her sluggish brain finally reacted. *"Man-sy-hae orolontis!"* she screamed.

The troll seemed to start at the sound of her voice. Its bolt shot out—

And missed.

Danae felt her jaw drop. *No*, she thought wildly. *No—I didn't see that. I couldn't have; Shamsheer's trolls never miss. Never.* But it had . . .

And even as her peripheral vision recorded the fact that Ravagin, too, seemed to have frozen at the impossibility they'd just witnessed, both trolls lowered their crossbows and started forward.

Danae shot a quick glance at Ravagin, saw her own disbelief mirrored there. The trolls' casual manner could have only one reasonable interpretation: they were on their way to pick up what they clearly expected to be a gasping, helpless victim of their marksmanship. Not only had the computerized marksmanship failed, but they apparently weren't even aware that it had done so.

This isn't happening, Danae told herself again. *It's an illusion—some crazy dream left over from Karyx.* But the trolls looked solid enough . . . and they were still advancing on Ravagin.

Abruptly, they stopped. For an instant they just stood there, as if just noticing Ravagin still on his feet and startled by the sight. Then, in unison, each reached to the extra crossbow bolts strapped to its other thigh—

And with a snap, the whip from Ravagin's scorpion glove lashed out to yank the crossbow from the first troll's grip.

Danae half expected a bellow of pain, but the machine made no sound in response. Nor did it show any further interest in the crossbow as Ravagin sent the weapon flying over the trees. Reaching behind its back, it drew a short sword and continued to advance. Ravagin ignored it for the moment, sending the scorpion whip lashing out instead to wrap around the second troll's crossbow—

But whatever other problems the trolls were having, their capacity to learn was apparently still intact. The second troll had just seen what had happened to its companion; and with blinding speed its free hand darted up to grab the scorpion whip coiled around its weapon.

"Damn," Ravagin snarled, bracing his left palm against the right as he tried to pull the trapped whip free. "Danae! —distract it somehow!"

The fascinated paralysis freezing Danae in place snapped. Snatching out her dagger she slid one foot forward and dropped slightly into the position Hart had long ago taught her for target throwing. At this range the troll was far too big a target to miss—

But where the hell was she supposed to try and hit the damn thing? *All right: it's a machine, damn it—weak points ought to be joints, sensors, powerpack, power leads—*

"*Any*where!" Ravagin shouted as she hesitated in indecision. "Hit it anywhere!"

Gritting her teeth, she hurled the dagger with all the power and accuracy she could muster; and as it caromed off the troll's face near its eyes, Ravagin suddenly leaped into the air, twisted his body to bring tucked legs up toward the troll—

And was yanked horizontally through the air to slam feet first into the machine's chest and head as the untrapped part of the whip coiled back into place on the top of the glove.

They went down together, Ravagin managing to hold onto most of his balance and land on his feet. It took another second for him to extricate the end of his whip from the troll's loosened grasp, and then he was spinning to face the remaining troll, the whip snapping out into a defensive Z-shape in front of him.

The troll's blade arced down to catch the upper arm of the Z, the stiffened whip deflecting it just enough to send it wide of its intended mark. Ravagin countered instantly, slashing the whip hard across the troll's face. The machine staggered backward with the impact, waving its arms for balance—

And Ravagin coiled and snapped the whip out to wrap around the troll's legs. With a horrendous *thud* the machine slammed flat on its back.

And lay still.

Danae took a deep, shuddering breath. "Ravagin . . . ?"

"I think it's over," he said, wincing as he carefully massaged his right upper arm. "Come on."

Swallowing, she started tentatively forward, a wary eye on both inert trolls. If this was some sort of trick on their part . . .

But they remained motionless, not even stirring as Ravagin leaned over and relieved them both of their swords. "Well, at least we got some new weapons out of the deal," he remarked tiredly. "Too bad they're not spark-swords."

Danae shook her head. "I give up," she said. "What the hell just happened here?"

He frowned at her. "I thought you'd figured it out. *You're* the one who distracted them with that spirit-protection spell, after all."

"The—? Oh." She felt heat rising to her cheeks. "That wasn't really planned. It was just a reflex reaction, I guess, left over from too much time on Karyx."

"Yeah, well, reflex or not, it worked beautifully. Not really *worked*, of course, the way it would've on Karyx. But it did enough."

"Did enough *what*? Are you trying to tell me Shamsheer trolls can be that easily distracted by words in a language they've never even heard before—?"

"Not the trolls, Danae. The spirits."

She opened her mouth, closed it again. "If that was supposed to be an explanation, it didn't work. Try again?"

Rubbing the sweat off his forehead, Ravagin glanced skyward. "I just hope there aren't any more of them on their way . . . Look, you saw just as fast as I did that there was something seriously wrong with these trolls. Way out of their jurisdiction, though they thought they were still there, giving the wrong responses, having to stop and think their way through what should have been a pretty standard challenge and rebuttal session—the whole thing was cockeyed."

"I caught the jurisdiction part, anyway. *All* of that was wrong?"

"Uh-huh. And then, when they finally attacked, they couldn't seem to handle all of their systems at once—they could shoot but not simultaneously process incoming sensory information, to the point where it took an incredible amount of time for them to even notice that they'd missed me. And for that spell to have distracted them the way it did—" he shook his head. "That was the last bit of proof."

"Proof for *what*?"

"Proof that you were right. Some of Karyx's spirits have invaded Shamsheer."

An icy chill ran down Danae's back. "You mean . . . there were *spirits* controlling the trolls? How in the worlds could they *do* that?"

Ravagin shook his head, slipping his scorpion glove back onto his belt. "I don't know. But remember that on Karyx, anyway, the spirits are able to interact some with matter, especially on the microscopic level. Maybe that's how they're doing it here."

Danae thought back to the throbbing pain in her side that had been the result of her tangle with the demon in Melentha's mansion. "So instead of finagling synapse chemistry and neuron pathways like they do there, here they're fiddling with microfine circuits?"

"It seems reasonable enough. In fact, compared to what they handle on Karyx, pushing picoamps of current around must be a breeze."

"Oh, God." Danae felt her knees begin to shake, and let herself sink awkwardly to the ground. "You have any idea what this *means*?"

"In terms of our safety or Shamsheer's?"

"Either. Both."

"It's a hell of a mess for both of us." Ravagin took a deep breath. "Look, before we go looking for a place to give up in, let's see if there's a bright side we can look at. One: we don't know how many spirits are actually here—and if there're only a few of them we'll have a pretty good chance of getting through their cordon. Shamsheer is a mighty big place for two people to lose themselves in."

"Except that we eventually have to get to the other Tunnel."

"Yes, well, we'll cross that one when we get to it. And second: it's clear that these spirits, at least, were way in over their heads on this one. You and I and a dozen more shouldn't have been able to handle even one troll, let alone two. But apparently there're so many separate systems the spirits couldn't keep control of all of them. Which is what eventually tripped them up—they got sloppy and let the trolls realize where they were, which in turn tripped the deadman switch."

Danae looked down at the motionless trolls. "The what?"

"We call it the deadman switch. It prevents people from stealing trolls and transporting them out of their home Protectorate for illegal purposes. Basically puts them into a shutdown mode once they're a certain distance outside their boundaries. Once activated, it supposedly can't be lifted except back at their original castle and by their castle-lord."

"Not even by something inside with the circuitry?"

"Yeah. Well . . ." Ravagin looked down at the trolls and grimaced. "That *is* a point. Let's not hang around to find out. You as good with a crossbow as you are with a throwing knife?"

"I've never used a crossbow, but I'm pretty good with normal projectile guns. Hart made me learn all this stuff when I was younger."

"Good for him." Reaching down, Ravagin pried the crossbow pistol from the troll's grip and then collected both sets of spare bolts. "Take one of the swords, too," he said, handing the weapons to her. "I don't think we should take the time to go hunt for our daggers, if you don't mind. Come on—let's go."

"Wait a second," Danae growled as a horrible thought suddenly hit her. "You mean you *knew* they wouldn't be able to shoot straight and you *still* threw that dagger at me?"

He turned back, frowning. "I threw it to miss you. Didn't you notice?"

"No, I did *not* notice," she said stiffly. "And I'd appreciate it if next time you'd try and find a safer way to handle things."

"I'll do what I can. Come on; we'll try for the Darcane Forest way house, about ten kilometers due south."

She blinked. "We're going on *foot*? With a perfectly good sky-plane right over there?"

"You mean the sky-plane that brought the bewitched trolls here?" he asked pointedly.

"Yes, I mean—oh." Danae glanced back at the sky-plane, licked her lips. "Yeah. Okay; on foot it is."

"And stick close to me," he added over his shoulder as he started off toward the edge of the clearing. "A few of the forest's predators—not many, but a few—do hunt during the day."

Great. Gritting her teeth, Danae hefted the crossbow and followed.

Chapter 34

Two hours later, after struggling their way through perhaps a kilometer of the forest, Ravagin finally called it quits.

"This isn't going to work," he panted as he sank down beside Danae against a thick-boled tree and let his sap-stained sword sag to the ground between his feet.

"No argument from me," Danae sighed, her half-closed eyes showing slits of white as she kicked mechanically at the green frond wrapped loosely around her leg. "What are these vine things, anyway?"

"Berands fronds," he told her, slashing carefully at the offending plant. "They catch and eat the large slug-like things that move around under the dead leaves. They're not really strong enough to be dangerous to people, but normal walking pace is just slow enough for them to have time to react. If we were sitting still or riding horses there'd be no problem."

"I don't suppose there's any chance of that? Sitting still, I mean, and maybe getting in a couple of hours of sleep while we're at it?"

"Unfortunately, there are lots of things in the forest more dangerous than Berands fronds," he said, fumbling out his prayer stick and looking up. Overhead, the nearly-solid forest canopy showed a small patch of blue sky; just wide enough, he estimated, to let a sky-plane through.

"But you're right; we can't keep this up any longer. I pray thee, deliver unto me a sky-plane."

Danae pried her eyes open. "I thought you didn't want to use sky-planes."

"I don't," he admitted. "But it looks like we either risk it or we lie down and die here."

Danae nodded and closed her eyes again. *No argument on that one, either*, Ravagin thought, looking down at her. *She must* really *be tired*. Laying his sword down, he ground his knuckles into his eyes. *One* of them ought to stay awake until the transport came . . .

The *swish* of dead leaves and undergrowth as the sky-plane came to a soft landing in front of them startled him out of his light doze. Shaking his head to clear his eyes, he snatched up his sword and looked quickly around. No trolls, no predators. They'd been lucky. "Come on, Danae," he grunted, shaking her arm. "Time to go."

"Wha—? Oh. Already?"

"Yeah. Come on—a little effort now and you can be in a real bed in ten minutes."

"Sold," she murmured, getting to her feet with a sigh.

The trip to the forest way house took about five minutes, and Ravagin spent the entire time with his stomach tied in a tight knot. But the sky-plane performed with normal Shamsheer perfection, taking them exactly where he'd indicated and settling them down in front of the way house door without even a bump.

Danae had fallen asleep again during the trip, but she woke up enough to do most of her own walking as Ravagin guided her inside and to one of the bedrooms. "Where is everybody?" she mumbled once as he steered her past the kitchen/dining area and toward the bedroom wing.

"Probably no one else is here," he told her. "The place isn't manned full-time, like the way houses in the cities are."

"Mmm."

He took her to the first bedroom they reached and helped her make it to the bed. She flopped down across it, and was instantly asleep.

He took a deep breath, feeling his own fatigue washing up against the edges of his mind as he gazed down at her.

It was a large enough bed . . . for a long moment he was tempted to simply collapse there beside her and not bother finding a room of his own. But there were things he really ought to do before he could sleep, and with a sigh he went out, closing the door behind him.

A tour of the entire house came first, to make sure he and Danae were in fact alone. He took his time, trying to watch for anything that might look out of place. But the house was empty, and as nearly as he could tell everything was where it was supposed to be. *You're getting paranoid*, he chided himself as he headed for the kitchen. *You get a couple of renegade trolls, and you think the whole planet's out to get you.*

Though that *was* basically what had happened on Karyx . . .

He took a couple of minutes more to make sure the house's climate control was set at a good sleeping level, then used his prayer stick to have the kitchen prepare dinner for them in eight hours. Then, feet dragging noticeably, he headed back to the bedroom wing. Bypassing Danae's room, he opened the door next to it . . .

Renegade trolls.

He thought about it for a long minute. Then, sighing, he closed the door and retraced his steps back to Danae's room. She hadn't moved noticeably since he'd left her. Slipping the sword and scorpion glove from his belt, he laid them on the floor within easy reach from the bed and lay down next to her. Setting his mental alarm for eight hours, he dropped off to sleep.

Danae awoke with a gasp, the vivid dream of green-glowing trolls fading only slowly from in front of her eyes. For a long minute she just lay there on the bed, staring at the ceiling as she listened to her heart pounding and tried to break through her disorientation and remember where she was.

Something moved next to her—

She jumped violently, twisting her head in sudden fright, only to find that it was Ravagin moving in his sleep beside her. Taking a deep breath, she expelled it, and for another moment lay still, wondering if she should try and go back to sleep. But between the dream and the shock she'd just had, she was wide awake. Moving carefully, she eased her legs over the edge of the bed and sat up. Her scalp itched furiously, and as she scratched vigorously at it she realized her whole body felt more or less the same way. Small wonder—it'd been days since her last shower. Standing up, she made her way to the door and out into the hall.

The bathroom was a couple of doors further along down the wing. She spent the first minute taking care of her bladder; then, stripping down, she got into the shower, a good-sized booth designed to look like the area beneath a small waterfall. The water, coming over the top of a rock-like overhang in a wide sheet, completed the illusion, splashing into mist from the floor. It was also waterfall-chilly, though not as cold as she'd feared it might be—Ravagin must have neglected to get the heater started before coming to bed. Still, any clean water was welcome, and the chill helped drive the last bits of sleepiness from her brain. It was, she thought as the water cascaded down around her head and shoulders, almost impossible to feel demoralized as long as you were clean.

She'd finished scrubbing herself to a high gloss, and was standing beneath the radiant drier, when she first noticed the odor.

She sniffed cautiously, then more deeply, the cozy sense of well-being evaporating with the rest of the droplets on her skin. Even given all she didn't know about Shamsheer's smells, there was something wrong with this one. Something ominous . . . and it was getting stronger. Scooping up her clothes, she opened the bathroom door and stepped out into the hallway—

And straight into an inferno of smoke and fire.

"Ravagin!" she screamed, ducking halfway back into the bathroom and throwing a look down the hall. The flames running up the walls and flickering through patches of the floor, she saw with sudden horror, were heaviest directly outside the bedroom where Ravagin was still sleeping. *Oh, God, no*, she thought wildly. "*Ravagin!*" she shouted again.

"Danae!" his answering call came, almost inaudible

through the crackle of the flames. "Hang on—I'll be right there—"

"No!" she shouted back. "The hall's on fire."

Through the smoke she saw the door down the hall crack open. "Where are you?" he called.

"Over here, in the bathroom. There aren't any windows in here!"

"I know. Let me think."

For a few heartbeats there was no sound but the roar of flames, and for the first time Danae noticed an oddly strong wind blowing down the hallway toward Ravagin's room. *Must be an opening down that direction for the air to be coming in from,* she realized. "Ravagin? What's down the other direction?"

"More bedrooms and storage," he called. "Okay. Go back to the shower and turn it on as high as it'll go. Have you got anything that you can use to stuff into the drain?"

"Just my clothes."

"Use your bodice—you can afford to lose that. Soak the rest of your clothes and put them on. Keep the door closed while you do it."

"Right."

The operation seemed to take an eternity, but it was probably only a couple of minutes before she was dressed in the dripping clothes and easing the door open again. The water that had collected inside flowed gently out, adding steam to the smoke already there. It also snuffed the flames directly by her feet, and for a moment she dared to hope it would be enough to cut her a path back to the bedroom. But a quick look crumbled that hope completely. The entire ceiling and floor seemed to be ablaze now, creating a solid wall of flames in both directions.

And she was now thoroughly trapped.

"Ravagin?" she shouted, fighting to keep her rising panic out of her voice. There was no answer, and for a horrible second she wondered if he'd gone out the window. Deserted her . . . "*Ravagin!*"

"I'm right here," his voice came reassuringly through the roar—but from the wrong direction. Twisting around, she peered through the smoke the other way down the hall. Facing directly into the odd wind was a mistake, and in seconds her eyes were watering blindly with smoke and soot. But in that first second she'd been able to make out a dim figure beyond the flames. "I'm still here!" she shouted back, rubbing furiously at her stinging eyes. "Can I get through that way?"

"We don't have any choice. Are your clothes and shoes still wet?"

"Yes, and the water's still flowing around my feet."

"Okay. Go back and get your bodice; you'll want to put it over your head. Hurry—we haven't got much time."

She didn't need the urging. Ten seconds later she was back at the door, the sopping bodice wrapped around her face and hair. "Are you still there?" she called, feeling the panic rising again. "I can't see you."

"I know—I can barely see you. Grab hold of this."

And like magic a thin cord appeared through the flames in front of her. It wasn't until she'd grasped it and its tip curled firmly around her hand and wrist that she realized what it was: the whip of Ravagin's scorpion glove. "Got it," she called.

"Now make sure your eyes are covered, and then grab the whip with your other hand."

"Ready."

"Okay." He paused, and she could sense somehow that he was bracing himself. "On the count of three I want you to come around the corner and toward me like all of Melentha's demons were right on your tail. I'll help pull; you concentrate on keeping your feet under you. Ready? Okay: one, two, *three*."

Clamping her jaw tightly, Danae leaped out into the hallway—

A blast of hot air hit her square in the face, burningly hot even through the streaming bodice. Dimly, she felt her entire body blistering where she stood; but even as she took her first step, she found herself flying through the burning hallway. Her arms felt like they were being pulled out of their sockets; she stumbled once, her feet striking what felt like liquid lead—

And abruptly she slammed into something solid that caught her and half dragged, half led her into sudden coolness.

"Ravagin," she gasped, clutching him tightly.

His hand slid over her face, pulled the bodice free. "It's okay, Danae—you're safe now," he soothed her.

She took a shuddering breath, blinking enough of the tears out of her eyes to see that they were in another bedroom. Across the room a broken window was blowing a stiff breeze toward them. "I thought Shamsheer houses were more fireproof than this," she gasped.

"They also come with built-in detectors and fire-fighting systems," Ravagin growled. "Our little friends apparently figured out a way to shut them down."

"Our—?" Danae's stomach tightened into a knot. With the fire driving all other thoughts from her mind she hadn't even made the connection. "The spirits?" she whispered.

"Who else? Come on—let's get out of here before they come up with something else to try."

Together they headed over to the broken window, and Ravagin took a careful look outside. "Looks clear. I'll go first, you come down after me. Watch the broken glass."

It was indeed clear outside, and a moment later they were hurrying around toward the front of the house, keeping to the middle of the narrow grass strip between the house and the edge of the forest. Above them the roof of the house was beginning to crackle though there was remarkably little smoke and as yet no visible flame. "How did they do it?" she asked Ravagin. "I mean, even if they could knock out the anti-fire system, how did they get enough heat to start a fire in the first place?"

"They must have gotten into the central control system and found a way to overload the wiring throughout the house," he replied grimly. "*Damn* them, anyway. I never even thought they might do something like this."

They rounded the corner—and skidded to a halt.

Resting up against the front of the house was a huge, spindly circle sitting vertically on a wheeled base. A white haze filled its circumference, a haze that mixed with a billowing mass of black smoke streaming out its far end. "My God," Danae gasped. "What in the worlds is *that*?"

"It's a giant fan," Ravagin growled. "It's pulling the smoke out of the hallway, probably so as to give the fire a

good head start before we smelled anything and woke up.
Gives the fire a good air flow, too, of course."

Danae stared at the huge device. "But where did it
come from? You're not going to tell me they had something like that in storage here, are you?"

"Not hardly," he said grimly. "There's a Forge Beast out
back. I guess they got into that, too."

*Forge Beast: a computerized forge capable of designing
and making any desired metal object*, the definition from
her orientation came back to her. "They must have been
in the house for hours—maybe even since before we got
here."

"Maybe," Ravagin said slowly. "On the other hand . . .
well, it should be easy enough to test."

She watched, frowning, as he stepped to the nearest
tree and sliced a thick branch off with his sword. "What
are you going to do with that?" she asked.

"See just how strong this fan really is. Stay here."

"Ravagin—" She bit down on the protest. He surely
knew what he was doing. . . .

Carefully, he moved to within a few meters of the fan
and stood there for a moment studying it. Then, taking
hold of his branch with the whip of his scorpion glove, he
extended it as close to the fan as it would go—flipped it
into the blades—

And with a horrendous grinding of broken metal, the
blades shattered into shrapnel.

"Well, that settles that," Ravagin said as he walked back
to where Danae stood. "Extremely cheap construction,
probably thrown together in less than an hour. Which
means that it took them—" he glanced at the sun, glinting
now between the trees to the west—"eight or nine hours
to find us, get into the various systems and learn how to
use them, build the fan and get it into position, and
actually start the fire."

"That's pretty fast," Danae said, a sinking feeling tightening her stomach.

"Yeah," Ravagin nodded heavily. "But it could have
been worse. Such as if you hadn't woken up and taken that
shower."

Danae swallowed, remembering. "It was a bad dream

that woke me up. One where trolls had the green glow of demon possession."

Ravagin cocked an eyebrow at her. "Interesting. You may still have some spirit sensitivity left over from your demogorgon contact. Could prove useful."

"If we can get to civilization in one piece, you mean—" She jumped as a sudden crash came from the house beside them. "What—?"

"Part of the roof caving in, probably," Ravagin said.

She glared at him. "How can you be so damned *calm* about it?" she growled.

"Only because anger and panic won't gain us anything," he told her. "Like it or not, Danae, we've gotten ourselves tangled up in another battle of wits with spirits; and just like it was on Karyx, we're not going to be able to outfight them. So we're just going to have to outthink them."

Danae took a deep breath, fighting for some calm herself. She was only partially successful. "All right. So how do we outthink ourselves away from here without them catching on?"

"I've got an idea." Pulling the prayer stick from his belt, he raised it to his lips. "I pray thee, deliver unto me a skyplane."

"You think that's wise?" she asked as he returned the stick to its place. "The way this whole prayer stick network works implies there's a central dispatch somewhere. If they've gotten into that—"

"Actually, I think that network probably *was* the way they traced us here before," he admitted. "But our only other choice is to walk out, and with night coming on in a few hours I'd personally rather take my chances with the spirits. Besides, I've got an idea that might shake them off our trail, at least temporarily. Meanwhile—" he glanced over to the house, where flames were starting to flicker on the roof—"I tossed your crossbow and other stuff out the window earlier. I suggest we collect them and move a little further into the forest."

The sky-plane was nearly an hour in arriving, which Ravagin took to be a good sign. "It means the spirits didn't have a gimmicked one standing by near here," he explained, "which implies this one is clean."

To Danae it didn't imply nearly that much. "Suppose they just held it over behind the trees somethere for fifty minutes and then let it come?"

"Because any sky-plane that sat on the ground in response to a send-order would automatically be classified as damaged and power to it cut off until it was time for it to go to a Dark Tower for repair," he told her. "Sky-planes are notorious for being grounded when *anything* seems out of order."

She eyed the fringed carpet dubiously. "Well . . . maybe. It still doesn't get us out of here without the spirits knowing where we've gone."

"No," Ravagin agreed. "But this might." Stepping over to the sky-plane, he drew his sword and drove it straight down into the carpet's center.

"Ravagin!" Danae yelped. "What—?"

And suddenly she understood. "You've damaged it," she breathed. "That means . . . it'll have to go to the Dark Tower."

He took a deep breath and nodded. "And it'll go there without a prayer-stick call or anything else from us that can be traced. I hope."

Danae looked down at the carpet. "I guess we'll find out."

Chapter 35

A second sky-plane arrived shortly after sundown and proceeded to work its way underneath the one Ravagin had damaged. It was, Danae would have thought, a rather tricky maneuver, but the sky-planes carried it out deftly and with an almost miserly efficiency of movement. Barely a minute after the second sky-plane's arrival the piggy-backed carpets rose into the sky, apparently oblivious to their two unscheduled passengers, and headed southwest toward Forj Tower. Slowly, the ground vanished into the deepening darkness beneath them; and as stars and distant village lights came out together, Danae found herself lapsing into the hazy illusion that they were traveling out in deep space, far from unpredictable spirits and magical technology. Far from danger and trouble and decisions . . .

"That's the Tower ahead," Ravagin murmured.

She started, the warm sense of almost-security vanishing. Ahead, visible only as it blocked stars and distant lights, the Tower was a brooding shadow looming in their path. "That's it, all right," she agreed, feeling the tension begin to rise again within her. Ravagin had said once that there were trolls guarding the Dark Towers. . . . "We going to just ride it on in?"

"We don't have any choice," he said. "Sky-planes bringing in repair work are pre-programmed by our hypothetical central dispatch."

"I wish there was at least some way to knock first," she sighed. "Sneaking in like this makes me nervous."

"Yeah. Well . . . if it makes you feel any better, we've collected six or seven stories of people who got inside one or the other of the Towers, and none of them end with the person being killed."

She pursed her lips. "Though if someone just disappeared inside, you aren't nearly that likely to have heard about it."

"Point," he admitted. "Still, all the stories we *do* have agree that as long as we don't interfere with the Tower's work we should be okay."

The dark mass ahead of them rapidly grew larger, and within a few minutes they were close enough for Danae to pick out some of its details in the starlight. The secondary spires were well below them, the sky-plane clearly aiming for the windows near the structure's top. "A shame we can't take this tour in the daytime," she commented, striving for a light tone amid the tight silence. "I'd like to see the relief stone patterns further down."

"Maybe some day we can come back," Ravagin said. "Though if you want to see the patterns you'll do about as well to just stand at the bottom and look up. The internal programming that keeps sky-planes ten meters away from buildings also applies to the Towers. In fact, as far as I know these repair flights are the only exceptions to that rule."

The Tower filled the entire sky ahead of them now, and for the first time Danae could see the rows of windows as slightly lighter chunks of gray against the black background. She held her breath as one of the windows in the bottom row loomed straight ahead . . . instinctively ducked her head . . . and without any pause or hesitation the sky-plane slid neatly in through its center.

"Be light," Ravagin murmured, and the firefly ring on his hand began giving off its gentle glow. Danae had just enough time to notice that they were passing through what looked like a short hallway with gridded mesh for walls, ceiling, and floor when Ravagin suddenly grabbed her arm. "Come on!" he snapped, and half dragging her, rolled off the carpet.

He landed on his feet, throwing his free hand to the mesh wall on one side for balance. Danae wasn't nearly so graceful, losing her balance despite his steadying hand on her arm and dropping onto one knee. The mesh jammed painfully into her kneecap and she bit back an exclamation. "What is it?" she whispered tensely.

"Get a good grip on yourself," he said. "Be more lighted."

The firefly's glow brightened. Danae saw that they were barely two meters from the end of the mesh hallway . . . and beyond it—

Was nothing.

She gasped, clamping her teeth tightly together as the acrophobia from her first sky-plane ride suddenly flooded into her. Nothing—just black, empty space—as far as the light from the firefly could penetrate.

Dimly, she noticed that Ravagin, his hand still gripping her arm, was peering closely at her face. "I'm okay," she said with an effort.

"You sure?" he asked.

"Yeah," she breathed. "It just took me by surprise, that's all."

"Good. I'm going to go to the edge and see what we've got to work with here. You stay put, okay?"

She managed a nod. Releasing her arm, he straightened up and took a careful step toward the edge of the abyss. "Be full lighted," he ordered the firefly . . . and as its glow became searchlight-bright, she forced herself to look.

It wasn't as bad as she'd feared. In the brighter light the far side of the Tower was visible, perhaps fifty meters away, and she could see that it, too, had the same sort of short mesh corridors extending out from each window. Just beneath the meshwork, and continuing down the Tower as far as the light could show, were a series of hexagonal boxes that reminded her instantly of a giant honeycomb made up of private rooms. One of the hexes caught her eye as its door slid open, and she looked over in time to see their piggybacked sky-planes vanish inside. Once, Ravagin shined the light directly down; steeling herself, Danae looked through the mesh beneath her. To her vast relief the pattern of boxes across the way apparently repeated itself on this side of the Tower, too, and she could see the top of the nearest barely three meters away.

Ravagin stood motionless for several minutes, the firefly's light throwing sharp moire patterns around their end of the Tower whenever it happened to intersect part of the mesh. Finally, he shut the light back down to a dim glow and stepped back to her. "Okay, here's the deal," he said, his voice oddly tight. "These little individual corridors—" he waved a hand around at the mesh—"seem to be around every window in the place, all the way around the circumference of the Tower and all the way up. I don't know what they're for, but if this one is any indication, they seem sturdy enough to easily hold our weight. Also, since it looks like all the sky-planes bringing damaged merchandise come in through these windows, we should be able to hitch a ride out as easily as we got in."

"Sometime before dawn, right?" Danae put in.

"Several hours before, probably." He hesitated. "Now for the bad news. If ours was representative, it looks like the incoming sky-planes travel in pretty much a straight line from wherever they've come from through the windows and into their repair cubicles. If that pattern holds in reverse for the outgoing flights, it means we're going to have to get almost halfway around the circle if we want to pick up a sky-plane that's headed the direction we want to go."

Danae's mouth went dry. "Get across *how*?" she asked carefully, something deep in her stomach warning her she wasn't going to like the answer.

She didn't. "We go to the end of this corridor," Ravagin said, pointing, "hold onto the side mesh, and swing one leg at a time around into the next corridor. Cross the corridor and repeat."

She thought about that for a long moment, her memory bringing up the view across the Tower she'd had a minute ago . . . "The repair cubicles don't extend as far out toward the middle as these corridors do. Do they?"

He shook his head. "Afraid not."

"Which means . . . we'll be nearly a kilometer up over absolutely nothing when we do this."

"It won't be quite as bad as you're thinking," he assured

her. "We've got a safety strap available—the scorpion glove—and as I said before the mesh seems pretty sturdy."

"And very sharp," she said heavily. "I should know—I banged my knee on it a minute ago."

"Umm." Ravagin squatted down, felt the mesh gingerly, then repeated with the mesh of the walls. "Maybe a little. Remember you won't be hitting it with all your weight, either."

Danae took a deep breath. "There's no other way to do this?" she asked, just to make sure.

"I don't think so." He pursed his lips. "Look, Danae . . . I remember your trouble with the sky-planes. If you honestly don't think you can make it, we could probably stay here and try to pick up a sky-plane going back the way we came."

She snorted. "Back where?—toward Darcane Forest? We'd wind up at least five hundred kilometers from the Tunnel." Abruptly, she got to her feet. "Give me a little more light, will you?" He complied, and she turned toward the end of the hallway. *After all*, she told herself sternly, *you've been chased by demons, intruded into a world where you didn't belong, and gotten out of a burning house alive. What's a little gravity after that?*

The first one was the hardest. Gripping the mesh with her right hand, she leaned out just far enough to get her left hand around the wall and wedged into the mesh from that side. Then, concentrating on the reassuring pressure of the scorpion glove's whip against her back, she swung her left leg around and onto the floor of the next hallway over. A careful shift of weight . . . reaching over to get a grip further down . . . an easing of the other foot across . . .

She took a deep breath, moving automatically another step away from the edge before turning. "Well, come on," she told Ravagin. "We haven't got all night. Let's get this over with."

The hallways measured roughly three meters across each, and they wound up crossing twenty-one of them before Ravagin called a halt. "We're just past the southern edge of Missia City now—see the lights?" he said, pointing, as he knelt near the window. "That means we should be facing due west now."

"Uh-huh," Danae nodded, staying as close to the center of the hallway as she could. The window had no lip or sill, and had another equally long drop beyond it . . . Gritting her teeth, she concentrated on her mental map of Shamsheer. "Picking up a skyplane here is as likely to get us to Ordarl Protectorate as it is to Numant, though, isn't it?"

"Or it could take us to Kelaine City or anything else in the Tweens," he agreed, backing away carefully from the window. "Or even some distance beyond the Tunnel. We aren't going to get a whole lot of choice."

"That wasn't what I meant," she said. "Ordarl was where we were stopped on our way to Karyx, remember?"

"Oh, well, that won't be any problem. They released us, after all, so there aren't going to be any official grudges or anything being kept."

"That still isn't what I meant. Don't you remember? —they stopped us because they were having trouble with black sorcery and equipment malfunctions?"

"Yes—and I told you at the time that black sor—" He broke off abruptly. "Oh, bloody hell," he said, very softly.

She nodded, feeling a shiver go up her back. She'd just made the correlation a few minutes ago herself. "Which means the spirits have been in Shamsheer at least that long. And if their influence is centered in Ordarl . . ."

"We could wind up back in the hot seat again if we land there," Ravagin said heavily. "Or maybe even if we just fly over the place. Damn it all—we need to know more about what we're up against here."

"Couldn't we try some spirit-detection spells—?" She bit at her lip. "No, of course not—they need a demogorgon around to function."

Ravagin nodded "Right. Which is where the real crunch comes: we're having to fight these spirits without knowing which of the usual rules apply. If any of them."

"All right, then. In the absence of rules, let's try logic." Easing down carefully onto her back on the sharp mesh, Danae stared at the gridwork above her for a minute and then closed her eyes. She was considerably more tired than she'd realized, and it was an effort to try and think. "They were waiting for us the minute we got back to Shamsheer, and they challenged us without even stopping to ask who we were. Which implies—" *They're ready for an all-out war?* She shivered suddenly.

"Which implies," Ravagin picked up the thread, "that they knew we were coming and had to be stopped. Which means there's some sort of communication between Karyx and Shamsheer. Oh, sure—the spirit that cried out when we escaped across the telefold. Sound travels perfectly well across the thing; the Shamsheer contingent just has a messenger standing by in the Tunnel—"

"My God—that's it!" Danae interrupted, jerking bolt upright as it suddenly struck her. "That's *it*, Ravagin— that's how the spirits got here. All you need to do is bring a spirit into the Tunnel, leave him there while you cross the telefold, and then do a standard specific-name invocation. That affects only the called spirit, without the need for any demogorgon influence."

"But an invocation—" Ravagin broke off and swore viciously under his breath. "An invocation brings a spirit from the fourth world to Karyx. *Across a world boundary.* No wonder they tried to stop us—as soon as you know there's an entirely separate fourth world to Triplet, the rest follows immediately."

Danae swallowed as another thought occurred to her. "It also means that they've got at least one human ally here. The person who brought them across."

Ravagin rubbed thoughtfully at his cheek. "Yeah. Well . . . at least they're still not able to get across on their own. I guess that's something."

Danae shivered as images of Melentha's face, twisted by hatred and fury, floated up from her memory. To have to face something like that again . . . "I almost wish it were the other way around," she muttered.

"No, you don't," Ravagin shook his head. "Think about it a minute. The Ordarl soldiers said the malfunctions had been going on for—how long did they say?"

"Several weeks."

"Right. So if the spirits' human dupe were actively participating in a bid to conquer Shamsheer, he surely would have brought over enough of them to take control of every bit of machinery on the planet. Right?"

"Well . . . okay, I guess so."

"But they *haven't* done that—if they had, we would never have gotten this far. And several weeks should have given them enough time to make their move." Ravagin paused, forehead wrinkled in thought. "So they *haven't* got a whole army here. Which means their dupe very likely only brought over a limited number of them, for whatever damnfool reason of his own. In fact, he may not even realize yet that they've gotten out of his control."

It sounded reasonable enough, at least to Danae's increasingly foggy mind. "Okay. So then what?"

Ravagin hissed out a breath. "I don't know," he admitted. "If I were bringing over a spirit to test spells on, I wouldn't use anything more powerful than a sprite . . . but those trolls sure as hell weren't being controlled by something that limited. We could be dealing with djinns here—maybe even peris or demons. I just don't know."

Danae closed her eyes again. "I don't think I even care at the moment what we're up against. As long as they let us get some sleep."

"Point," he grunted with a tired sigh of his own, easing down onto the mesh beside her. "We've got at least a couple of hours before the sky-plane exodus starts. A little sleep'll do both of us good."

Not quite close enough to touch her . . . "Ravagin?" she asked tentatively. "If the spirits have gotten into the Tower with us . . . do you think they could send a sky-plane or a castle-lord's bubble in here to push us out?"

"I doubt it," he answered. "Towers seem to work under their own very specialized rules. If a spirit started monkeying with them, I think it would find itself pretty quickly cut out of whatever circuit it was in."

"Oh."

For another moment the faint background hum of the Tower was the only sound in Danae's ears. Then, with a rustle of clothing, Ravagin moved right up next to her. His arm slid across her stomach; his several-day growth of beard tickled lightly at her ear. "This what you wanted?" he murmured.

She felt blood rushing to her cheeks . . . but she'd gone through too much with Ravagin to hold onto false dignity now. "Yes," she admitted. "I'm not feeling all that brave at the moment."

His arm tightened comfortingly. "If it helps," he murmured, "neither am I."

Two hours later, they were again flying beneath the night sky, sharing their sky-plane with an oddly shaped piece of ribbed metal that Ravagin guessed was part of a rainstopper mechanism.

It was crowded aboard the carpet, but with reliable edge barriers between her and the rest of the universe, Danae almost didn't even care how close to the edge she had to sit. For a while she watched the stars overhead, but shortly after they passed over Castle Ordarleal the fatigue tugging at her eyelids again proved too much to handle. Stretching out as best she could, she again fell asleep.

"Danae!"

She snapped awake in an instant at his hiss, heart thudding as the horrible dream images faded reluctantly from before her eyes. "Ravagin?" she hissed back, twisting up into a sitting position and looking wildly around. Dawn was just beginning to break behind them to the east; ahead, Ravagin was kneeling at the sky-plane's front edge, peering at the ground below. Even in the dim light she could see that his body was tensed. "What is it?" she repeated, louder this time.

"We're coming down," he murmured over his shoulder. "Damn it all—we're coming down right inside Castle Numanteal."

"*What?*" she gasped, crawling over to his side. Sure enough, they were losing altitude . . . and the six-sided castle wall was directly ahead. "We can't land there. Can we?"

"Not without causing a stir," he said grimly. "No one's supposed to fly into a castle enclosure without permission. Damn. I hope Castle-lord Simrahi is in a good mood today."

Danae licked at dry lips. They were close enough now to see the trolls standing watch at the top of the wall. Automatically, her fingers sought the crossbow pistol at her side. If these trolls chose to shoot first and debrief later . . .

But the machines stood passively, giving no indication that they even saw the intruders, let alone cared about them. Of course the trolls weren't worried, she realized: in a few seconds the sky-plane would make a tight left-hand semicircle and settle down into the castle's landing area, and then the trolls could come down and examine them at their leisure. She braced herself; the sky-plane began to turn—

But to the *right*, not the left. Directly toward—

Danae gasped. "The *manor house*?"

"Damn!" Ravagin snarled. "Sky-plane: follow my mark. Mark. *Mark*, damn it, *mark*!"

It was no use. The sky-plane continued on unperturbed, straight toward the manor house. *At least*, Danae thought wildly, *we'll still be outside when we land. The ten-meter approach distance will keep it from taking us inside*—

And suddenly she knew what was about to happen. And why. "Ravagin!" she said. "My dream! I had another dream about demon-controlled trolls."

"Hell," he said, very quietly.

And as Danae watched with frozen impotence, the sky-plane slid neatly and impossibly through an open window and glided into the manor house.

Chapter 36

It was quite probably the most unusual sight the employees of Castle Numanteal had ever seen. And possibly, Ravagin thought grimly, one of the most subtly terrifying.

Certainly if the expressions of those setting out places at the long table were anything to go by. Frozen in place, some with the gilt-edged plates they were holding suspended above the table in motionless hands, the servitors all stared wide-eyed at the sky-plane as it slid through the window into the high-ceilinged dining room and floated across it. In the room's sudden silence the faint clatter of pots and pans and conversation from the kitchen beyond could be clearly heard, and Ravagin abruptly realized it was toward that noise that their rogue sky-plane was making a leisurely turn. Behind him, he could hear a hooting from the walls outside as the trolls there sounded the alarm; beside him, Danae's fingernails were digging into his arm. *Do something!* the grip seemed to say; but for the first time since their escape from Melentha he felt totally helpless. The sky-plane ducked down toward the floor as it aimed for the kitchen door—

Beside the table, someone screamed . . . and the frozen disbelief broke into total pandemonium.

"Keep down!" he snapped automatically to Danae as a handful of silverware flew up at them and scattered harmlessly away at the sky-plane's edge barrier. All around them, the servitors were making up for their earlier inactivity, either scurrying madly to get out of the sky-plane's path or else running toward it in an attempt to stop it; mixed in with the angry shouts and screams were calls for weapons and trolls. Another flight of silverware ricocheted off the barrier directly in front of Ravagin's face, making him flinch. From the corner of his eye he saw Danae unlimbering her crossbow— "Put that down!" he barked at her. "You can't use it anyway—you want us to look hostile to them?"

"You think we look peaceful the way we—"

She broke off with a gasp as, with a sudden jerk, the sky-plane came to a midair halt.

What the—? A horrible suspicion rose up into Ravagin's throat— "Sky-plane: follow my mark. *Mark.*"

And without any hesitation whatsoever, the machine curved smoothly away from the kitchen doors toward the direction he'd indicated.

"What are you doing?" Danae shouted in his ear.

"Trying to get us the hell out of here!" he snapped back. "The spirit's gone; I've got control again. Sky-plane: follow my mark, *mark.*"

The carpet swung around in a one-eighty-degree curve back toward the window they'd entered by . . . but even as it did so, Ravagin realized with a sinking feeling the spirit's sudden departure hadn't been a mistake. The window was directly ahead, perhaps fifteen meters away . . . and abruptly the sky-plane slowed and came to a gentle halt.

Ten meters from the wall.

"*Ravagin!*"

"Shut up, Danae," he snarled back, all his fury and tension and suffocating sense of helplessness welling up his throat and flooding out toward her. "I can't *do* anything, damn it all—the sky-plane thinks it's outside approaching a building."

The shouts around them had taken on a tone of triumph as the servitors saw the intruders apparently at a loss. A hundred plans flashed through Ravagin's mind . . . a hundred plans, each of which stood a good chance of getting them killed before they could even get out of the dining room. The precise fate, no doubt, that the spirit had planned for them.

There was no way out. Which meant there was only one chance left for survival.

He took a deep breath. "Sky-plane: land," he said, fumbling his sword and scorpion glove from his belt and pushing them up against the edge barrier. "Danae; get your hands away from that crossbow and put them on your head. We're surrendering."

The sky-plane landed, and in a moment they were surrounded by a ring of knife-wielding servitors who stood there menacingly, clearly at a loss as to what to do next. They were still sitting there quietly on their sky-plane when the trolls and human guards finally arrived.

For Ravagin, Castle-Lord Simrahi was something of a surprise.

He was young, for one thing, as castle-lords went: no more than forty-five, though in the full trappings of his rank he looked perhaps ten years older. The full trappings were a surprise all by themselves; they were seldom used except for formal protectorate events or when a castle-lord would be meeting with his peers. To see Simrahi dressed that way for what boiled down to a simple indictment hearing was more than a little unnerving.

As it was no doubt meant to be. Scanning the huge room as his flanking guards brought him forward, Ravagin noted with a sinking feeling that what appeared to be the full senior court were also present, including advisors, minor nobles of the protectorate, and even commoner observers. Clearly, Simrahi was determined to start his investigation with all the psychological weight on his side.

Making Ravagin and Danae sweat in the cells beneath the manor house for four hours while the event was being staged hadn't hurt, either.

The stir that had accompanied Ravagin's appearance had died down by the time he finished the long walk to the bar set a few meters before the castle-lord's chair. *Probably staged that, too*, he decided, giving the faces an unobtrusive once-over. The faces stared back, either blankly or with carefully measured hostility. A rubber-stamp crowd, almost certainly—here to applaud the castle-lord's decision.

Which was to be expected from a Shamsheer protector-ate, of course, and to some extent it actually made Ravagin's task easier. It meant there was only one man in this entire forbidding crowd whom he had to convince of his innocence.

A bearded advisor type standing beside Simrahi took a pace forward. "The court of Castle-lord Simrahi is now seated," he intoned. "The prisoner will first state his name and home."

So Simrahi wasn't much for flowery pronouncements, despite his fondness for the other trappings of office. *Doesn't want his time wasted unnecessarily?* Ravagin wondered. "I am called Ravagin," he said, keeping his voice respectful yet firm. "I call no land but Shamsheer my home."

The advisor wasn't to be put off. "Then state the land and village of your birth," he said.

"I was born somewhere inside the borders of the Trassp Protectorate, to parents who were also wanderers," Ravagin replied evenly. It was a story he'd used more than once before, and while a bit unusual it was also almost impossible to disprove. "Whether or not my parents registered my birth I do not know."

"A convenient tale," the bearded man said with barely hidden scorn. "And your companion?—does she also have no home?"

"She is a citizen of a small village named Arcadia in the depths of Darcane Forest," Ravagin said, working hard to keep his voice and expression steady. This one wasn't nearly as safe, but there was little he could do about it. If Simrahi bothered to cross-check with the soldiers who'd stopped them in Ordarl Protectorate he wanted the stories to mesh. At least this one would take time to disprove.

That thought was apparently on the advisor's mind, too. "A forest village far from any place with a crystal eye, ay?" He snorted. "How very convenient."

"Do you wish convenience or truth?" Ravagin countered. "Convenience would have all justice done away with."

"You speak of justice, do you?" the other spat. "You, who used black sorcery to defy the laws of magic and of the Castle-lord Simrahi's realm?"

"I've already told the guards and the cell-wardens that the behavior of that sky-plane was no doing of mine," Ravagin said, letting some heat creep into his voice.

"A story as totally without proof as that of your origin," the other said.

"But equally true," Ravagin shot back. "If you prefer another explanation, perhaps you can explain to the castle-lord and the assembled court why I chose to use these alleged powers to enter his manor house in the clear light of day. And why I would exhibit such power and clever-ness and yet fail to damage either him or his household."

"The burden of proof is not upon the castle-lord—"

"Enough," Simrahi said quietly.

The other bowed and stepped back into his place in line, where he glowered silently. Ravagin shifted his at-tention to the castle-lord, found him staring thoughtfully back. "You speak as one accustomed to courts and the presence of the lords of Shamsheer," he said, his voice smooth and cultured. "That by itself sets you apart from the common man of Shamsheer. And I will further admit your tale has much to commend it. Tell me, would it stand equally well against the scrutiny of my crystal eye?"

Ravagin felt his stomach muscles tighten. No, it damn well wouldn't, at least not if Simrahi was willing to put forth enough effort to really dig into it. "Of course it would, my lord. My companion and I have nothing to hide."

The other's thoughtful expression didn't change. "Of course not. Tell me, Ravagin, what is your profession?"

"I deliver private messages," Ravagin told him. "Those who wish to send such communications may hire me to travel the long distances—"

"Such as between traitors among my kitchen servitors and their allies outside?" Simrahi barked.

Ravagin blinked, thrown off balance by both the ques-tion and Simrahi's sudden change. "No, of course not, my lord."

"Then tell me why you used your black arts to bring your sky-plane into my house!" he thundered.

"My lord—" Ravagin spread his hands out helplessly. "I tell you again, it was none of my doing."

Beside the castle-lord, a hard-looking man in the tunic of a guard officer cleared his throat. "My lord," he said quietly, "even if there was such a message, he could hardly have drawn more attention to himself this way. Would he not have done better to wait until the day was fully born and then to arrive by horse or sky-plane in a lawful manner?"

"Perhaps." Simrahi's voice was controlled again, but his eyes still smoldered. "Perhaps this was simply part of the plot, though. Perhaps the black sorcerer's arrival was the signal to act—and what better way for the news to be spread quickly to any and all conspirators throughout the protectorate?" He glared up at the guard officer, then turned his eyes back to Ravagin. "You see, my innocent traveler, there is much about yourself you have failed to mention," he said, his voice calm but with an edge of iron to it. "I have spent part of the past few hours in the Shrine of Knowledge, seeking information of you through the crystal eye. Shall I tell the court that you were detained in Ordarl Protectorate less than a month ago on suspicion of being a black sorcerer?—and with the same companion that you travel with now, who claimed then to be on her way home? Or that you and this same companion attacked three men in Kelaine City shortly before that with weapons that bordered on the black arts? Or that the sky-plane you *claim* you were innocently riding had in fact come directly from the Dark Tower near Missia City?—which no normal person has ever entered?"

Ravagin had to work to get moisture back into his mouth. "My lord . . . all of those seemingly bizarre events can indeed be explained. The incident in Kelaine City—"

"Enough."

Ravagin swallowed hard. Simrahi's voice, barely louder than a purr, was infinitely more frightening than even his earlier shouting had been. It was the voice of a man who had already made his decision.

"You are accused of being a black sorcerer," Simrahi continued in the same soft voice, "possibly in league with forces attempting to overthrow my rule. In any case, you are a threat and a danger to the Numant Protectorate, and indeed all of Shamsheer, and you will remain in the cells of Castle Numanteal until I decide how to deal with you."

He rose to his feet, the signal that the hearing was over. The guards on either side of him took Ravagin's arms—"My lord!" he called over the buzz of conversation that had begun. "What about my companion? Surely she is blameless and can be released—"

"Your companion will remain in the cells with you," Simrahi said. "She who has shared in your activities will surely share in their consequences."

"But—"

"For that matter, I have not yet determined which of you is the actual wielder of the black sorcery." Simrahi shifted his eyes to Ravagin's guards. "Remove him."

They did so, none too gently. Apparently, Ravagin realized dimly as the blows began to fall about his face, speaking to a castle-lord out of turn was frowned upon.

Chapter 37

"There," Danae said, wringing out her cloth one final time into the cell's small washbasin. "How does that feel?"

"Probably about like it looks," Ravagin grunted, giving his fingertips a gingerly tour of his face. The largest cuts were still oozing blood; the bruises felt like they would like to.

"That bad, huh?" An attempt at a smile played briefly around Danae's lips as she came over and knelt down in front of the cot where he was half lying, half slouching. But even a show of humor was clearly too much of an effort, and the smile vanished quickly into the fear and tension lines that had been there since his unceremonious arrival back at the cell. "You *don't* look very good," she admitted. "I wish there was some way we could get you into the House of Healing and let a Dreya's Womb check you over."

"Fat chance," Ravagin said, peering at the traces of blood on his fingers before wiping them on his pants. "Unless you can convince someone that I'm going to die of infection before they get the chance to execute me."

"I wish you wouldn't talk like that," she said, her voice trembling. "It scares me."

He sighed; but she was right. There was no point in tearing down what little morale they had left. "Sorry," he apologized. "Look, my natural pessimism notwithstanding, there really *is* a chance that Simrahi will eventually let us go. Provided I can prove we are not involved either in black sorcery or any conspiracy his fevered mind has cooked up."

Danae licked her lips, her eyes flicking toward the massive door. "Perhaps you shouldn't, uh . . ."

"Insult the castle-lord in the hearing of his faithful cell-wardens?" Ravagin snorted. She was right, of course—the only reason for them to have been put into a common cell was in hopes that hidden listeners would glean something useful from their conversation. But for the moment he didn't give a damn about what anyone heard—or even what they made of it. Keeping Danae where he could watch over her was the all-important consideration now, and as long as they kept talking chances were fair that the cell-wardens would leave them together. "I don't care what they think, frankly. If he really believes someone's out to overthrow him he ought to be locked up in a Dreya's Womb under heavy sedation. Period."

"Why is it so hard to believe?" Danae demanded, eyes glinting with a spark of her old fire. "Palace revolutions are a great human tradition."

"Sure, but seldom work unless you can subvert or out-fight the castle-lord's personal bodyguard. In this case, you can't."

"Why—? Oh. Trolls?"

"You got it. A special cadre of them, programmed directly to the castle-lord's personal defense."

"Yes, but . . . there has to be a way to reprogram them. When the old castle-lord turns over control to his successor, for instance."

Ravagin shrugged, wincing as the movement sent a flash of pain up his side where one of the guards had kicked him. "I'm sure there is," he said, rubbing the spot carefully. "But I can practically guarantee that however it works you have to either *be* the outgoing castle-lord or else have free access to the castle-lord's private rooms to do it. There would be a whole layer cake of safeguards built in to keep anyone else from doing it."

"Like the safeguards built into sky-planes that keep them out of buildings?" Danae asked pointedly.

Ravagin gritted his teeth. "Damn. Yeah, just about exactly like that."

For a long moment there was silence. Then Danae stirred, looking down at the wet cloth still in her hand as if seeing it for the first time. Standing up again, she laid the cloth carefully over the edge of the sink. "Do you suppose," she said slowly, "that that's how they're planning to go about it? To cause or help with revolutions?"

Ravagin pursed his lips. "No, I don't think so. It would require them to work through people again—conspirators or whoever. Aside from the obvious difficulties they'd have in recruiting such a group, I doubt they really want to bother with people more than they absolutely have to. No, I think they came up with this sky-plane trick solely to get us in trouble with a castle-lord and just happened to find one who was certifiably paranoid already. An extra bonus." He shook his head. "The really frightening thing is how fast they're learning how to do combat on this side of the Tunnel. The head-on approach—with the bewitched trolls—didn't work, and they immediately switched to using the technology in a more indirect way, to try to burn us to death. When that one sank, too, they did an almost complete about-face and decided that the best ones to deal with humans were other humans. Ergo, they drop us in Castle Numanteal in a way guaranteed to scare the bejabbers out of the locals."

"You can call it intelligence if you want; I call it dumb luck," Danae said. Turning away from the basin, she stepped back over to him. Her eyes met his for a second, and with just the barest hesitation she lay down on the cot beside him, facing into his chest and pillowing her head on his left upper arm. "It seems to me that they're just flailing around and happened to get lucky."

Ravagin eased his left arm around her shoulder, pulling her comfortably against him. "Why do you say that?" he asked. *Keep her talking*, a small voice whispered inside his brain. *Keep her arguing; it'll help distract her from the mess you're in. . . .*

"Because they continue to do stupid things. Look at the trolls—they lost control of the things in a simple fight and couldn't figure out how to get it back. And at the way house they never even got around to shutting off the water to the shower."

Ravagin frowned. Now that she mentioned it, that *did* seem rather odd. The climate control electronics the spirits had overloaded *were* supposed to handle the water system, too. "You're sure that wasn't just so you would stay in the shower until the fire got going?"

"Positive. Remember?—you had me block the drain so that the water would go out into the hallway? And then when the sky-plane got us into the manor house, why didn't the spirits land it instead of just leaving the thing like it did? We were pretty invulnerable up there, with the edge barrier operating—wouldn't it have been to the spirit's advantage to get us killed or at least wounded in a kitchen riot instead of giving us the chance to surrender peacefully?"

"You're right," Ravagin admitted. "Letting us try and reason with the castle-lord was probably a mistake on its part." He bit gently at his lip. "Very interesting indeed. You see where this leads us, don't you?"

"Not really."

"Well, think about it a second. What kind of spirit could behave as if it's taking turns being brilliant and stupid? Or, I should say, what *group* of spirits?"

She twisted suddenly to look up at him. "A demon!" she gasped. "A demon and his parasite spirits."

"That's it," he nodded. "*And* it furthermore means that we were right about the demon's friend here being ignorant of what he's really up to. If the demon himself had been attacking us, we probably would have been stopped in short order. But it's clear that he's having to stick close to home—wherever that is—and just sending his parasites out against us." Ravagin felt a surge of excitement; for the first time in hours, it seemed, his brain was running at top speed again. The logical puzzle was unraveling right before his eyes. . . . "So the parasites come against us, can't handle the unexpected things we throw at them, and fall on their ectoplasmic faces. They head back—sure, it all makes sense. They head back and report and the demon comes up with a new plan, which they launch in a few hours or whenever they can get to us. If we analyze the time periods involved, in fact, we might even be able to isolate their home base area."

"Great," Danae said without noticeable enthusiasm. "So what does that mean for getting us out of here?"

Ravagin's growing excitement faded away. "Yeah," he said heavily. "You're right. How do we convince Simrahi that there are forces threatening all of Shamsheer, and further convince him that letting us go is the way to fight the attack?"

"He believes in magic, doesn't he? I mean, he *has* to believe in it, living on Shamsheer. And it sounds like he believes in black sorcery, too—"

"Convincing him that there's a threat wasn't the part I was worried about," Ravagin interrupted her gently. "He already believes that . . . and thinks we're part of it."

She sighed. "So it's up to us. Totally."

Ravagin eyed the bare walls around them. "I wish we were even that well off. Unfortunately, I don't see any way we can get ourselves out of this one. I'm afraid it's all up to your father now."

She tensed in his arms. "You mean the threat we made to Melentha? That if I disappeared, Daddy Dear would come looking for me?"

Something about the way she said that sent a quiet shiver up his back. "Yes," he said cautiously. "Why?—isn't it true?"

She took a deep breath. "Not really. In fact . . . I think he's probably already resigned himself to never seeing me again."

Ravagin felt his neck muscles tighten. "Are you suggesting," he said slowly, "that he poured money all over various Triplet officials . . . . *expecting* you to die here?"

"No, of course not. I don't think he realized until the last minute what I was really up to."

"Which was . . . ?"

She sighed. "Ravagin, I've been trying to run away from Daddy Dear for a long time. I've hated his money, hated the way everyone automatically fawned over me for no reason except the accident of history that I was his daughter. Hated the way they all treated me as if I was a cute little girl without any brains. Here—Triplet—was the only place I could find where his influence didn't penetrate. The only place where I could prove myself on my own, without Hart or someone like him showing up to grease my path. I started this trip eighty percent certain that I would run away from you at some point, to settle down and possibly spend the rest of my life here."

She stopped, and for a long minute there was silence. In his arms he could feel her body trembling, but he couldn't tell whether she was actually crying or just struggling hard to hold back the tears. Not that it mattered. "Well," he said at last, "it looks like you've done it. Proven yourself, I mean."

She sniffed. "Oh, sure. It takes a real capable adult to get both herself and a friend into a death cell."

"You're missing my point," he shook his head. "You know, Danae, you had the kind of life in front of you that most of the people I've known would have jumped at with all four feet. You could have allowed yourself to become a pampered parasite—let yourself be that little girl forever. But you didn't. You came to Triplet instead."

She sniffed again, reaching up with one hand to rub at her eyes, and when the hand came away he saw the moisture there. She had indeed been crying. "Nice to at least find it out before I die, isn't it."

He bit at his lip. "Danae . . ."

"No, please don't talk. What I really need . . . Ravagin, would you hold me?"

"I am holding you."

"No, I mean . . ." She took a ragged breath. "Hold me. Closer."

It took several heartbeats for him to finally realize what she meant . . . and several heartbeats after that to get his tongue unstuck. "Are you sure?" he asked awkwardly. "I mean . . . I'm hardly the sort of man . . . in, you know, normal circumstances, you wouldn't choose—"

She barked a laugh that was more than half sob. "You might be surprised. And since when are these normal circumstances, anyway? Unless you . . . don't want to, I mean . . ."

There was only one answer for that. Reaching over with his free hand, he turned her face gently upwards and kissed her. She twisted her body over toward him, arms snaking around his neck to press herself against him as she returned the kiss almost desperately. He let his hand drop lower, to her scorched, waterstained bodice . . .

It was only afterward, as she lay sleeping in his arms and he was dozing off himself, that the possibility they'd been observed occurred to him. An odd lapse, for him; even odder the fact that such a thought didn't even dent the sense of contentment filling him. It had been a long time since he'd felt this way . . .

Looking up at the ceiling, he sent it a half smile. *The hell with you*, he thought toward the hidden watchers. Closing his eyes, he fell asleep.

Chapter 38

The click of an opening lock jerked Ravagin awake, and he opened his eyes just as a tall, hard-looking man in a tight half-cloak stepped across the threshold into the cell. His eyes met Ravagin's, then flicked around the room, before he half turned to the shadowy figures waiting behind him in the corridor. "I will speak with them alone," he said in a voice Ravagin could tell was accustomed to giving orders. "No one is to listen in—is that clear?"

There was a muttered acknowledgment, and the man turned back and took a step into the cell. Behind him the door swung shut.

For a moment he simply looked at them. Propped up on one elbow, Ravagin looked back, matching the other's silence and—he hoped—his impassive expression. On her side in front of him, her back pressed against his chest, Danae was also motionless and silent, but Ravagin could feel the nervous twitches that told him she was also awake. Surreptitiously, he squeezed her hip, hoping she would take the gesture as one of reassurance. Though offhand, he couldn't see any reason for either of them to be reassured.

"Well," the man said at last, coming another step toward the cot. "You two look very cozy. I trust you've found a way to pass the time?"

Danae stiffened; Ravagin squeezed her hip again. "Indeed," he said, keeping his voice cool. "You don't need us to tell you that, of course."

The other smiled faintly. "Very good, Ravagin—you recognize me, then."

"You were dressed in a guard officer's tunic earlier," Ravagin told him. "Standing beside Castle-lord Simrahi at that farce of a hearing. What else could you be but a high-ranking member of the household guard?"

The other's expression didn't change. "You are indeed an observant man. Excellent. I am Habri; master of the Castle Numanteal guard. Does that name mean anything to you?"

"Not really. Should it?"

A flash of something—disappointment?—seemed to register briefly on Habri's face. But he recovered quickly. "No matter. So. Tell me, what do you think Castle-lord Simrahi is likely to do with you? You being black sorcerers and all, that is?"

"We're not black sorcerers," Danae said tiredly. "Isn't there any way we can convince you people of that?"

Habri smiled slyly. "After all that talk of demons between you? No, my good traveler Danae, I think your reputation is firmly established. Which brings me to the really important question: Why are you here?"

Ravagin opened his mouth . . . and closed it again as an icy shiver went up his back. A random, almost forgotten fact had clicked . . . "At the hearing," he said slowly, "you went out of your way to downplay the suggestion that we were messengers to plotters. Which means . . . there really *is* something going on here. Isn't there?"

"There are rumors—nothing more," Habri shrugged. But the intensity of his expression belied the casualness of the words.

Danae twisted her head to frown up at him. "But you said a revolt would be suicide."

"Yes, I did," Ravagin nodded, keeping his eyes on Habri. There was something else there . . . "And since Guard Master Habri here was eavesdropping on us he doesn't need me to repeat the reasons *why* it's suicide. Not to mention any extra reasons he knows that we don't. So why all the fuss?"

"You answer my question first," Habri said coldly. "Why are you here?"

"We're passing through; nothing more," Ravagin sighed. "We were being chased by agents of another power—the demons your people heard us speak of—and thought that a good way to put them off our trail would be to detour through the nearest Dark Tower. So we did. The skyplane we hitched a ride on came here—" he shrugged— "and its little sortie into the dining room you already know about."

"So you *do* admit, then, that you have certain unknown powers over magic? At least to the ability to reach into Dark Towers?"

Ravagin stared at him . . . and the last piece fell into place. "You're one of them, aren't you. One of those plotting to overthrow the castle-lord."

Habri's face had turned to stone. "You are indeed perceptive, Ravagin. Perhaps too much so."

Danae's hand gripped Ravagin's arm. "You wouldn't dare kill us," she stated firmly. Her tone startled Ravagin: it was as good an imitation of forceful contempt as he'd ever heard. "You wouldn't be here at all," she continued, "unless you wanted something from us, and wanted it badly. What?"

Habri took a step toward them, his eyes flashing fire at her as his right hand dipped beneath his cloak to grip a knife hilt there. "I need take no insolence from either of you, *woman*," he bit out. "Not from your protector, and certainly not from you."

"I wouldn't be quite so hasty if I were you," Ravagin spoke up, matching his own tone to Danae's cue. "Remember that you don't yet know which of us has whatever it is you need."

The other froze in place, his eyes darting back and forth between Danae and Ravagin. His lips parted once, closed; then, clenching his jaw, he dropped his hand from his weapon and moved back a pace. He took a deep breath, and inclined his head fractionally. "Your point," he acknowledged with passable aplomb. "My mistake, and my apologies. It is clear that neither of you is what you seem."

"Apology accepted," Danae said coolly. "For now, at any rate. So. Let us hear your request."

Habri's eyes settled on her. "I want you to get me into

the castle-lord's chambers, past the trolls guarding the door," he said bluntly. "Tonight."

The cell's tiny window had been showing the blackness of full night for several hours by the time Habri returned for them. "You have my weapons?" Ravagin whispered as the other eased open the door.

"Outside," Habri hissed back, gesturing impatiently as he stood in the doorway. "Quickly—the guards have been diverted, but they will be back soon."

Which meant Habri's rebellion wasn't nearly as widespread as he'd tried to imply that afternoon. For a second Ravagin toyed with the idea of flattening the traitor as he left the cell, decided against it. A good thing too; as he stepped past Habri and on into the corridor, he saw the other had brought three heavily armed men with him.

The guards fell into step behind him and Danae as Habri took the lead. Ravagin could feel the tension in Danae's hand as they walked, and he glanced over once to give her a reassuring smile. Whatever the deficiencies of Habri's organization, it was surely good enough to at least spring a couple of prisoners from the castle-lord's cells.

And it was. A minute later they emerged through a thick door into a hallway of the main manor house. A few turns later they reached what appeared to be the kitchen area; another heavy door took them into one of the four entrance hallways that led to the outside from the relatively narrow base of the manor house. A minute after that, they were out in the night air.

"Don't relax yet," Ravagin murmured as Danae gave a quiet sigh of relief. "We're still inside the castle walls, you know, and there are a lot of guards and trolls between us and the rest of Shamsheer."

"So let's use that fact," she whispered back. "Call the trolls down on us, expose Habri as a traitor—"

"His word against ours?"

"—and . . . oh. But—"

She broke off, and Ravagin looked around to see Habri step up to them. There was a glint in the other's eye that Ravagin didn't at all care for. "Well, sorcerer," Habri said, proffering Ravagin his scorpion glove. "The time is now.

My men are prepared; all that is lacking is a path into the castle-lord's chambers. So. Are you ready to open that path?"

"More or less," Ravagin nodded, taking the glove and slipping it on. The familiar tingle told him the weapon was ready . . . and for the first time in hours he felt somewhat less than naked. With a weapon again in his hand—

I could get both of us killed, he reminded himself sternly, forcing down the adrenaline rush. The only way they were going to get out of this was to play out the scheme he'd come up with in the hours since accepting Habri's offer. "I'll need some other devices first," he told the other. "A watchblade, prayer stick, firefly, and the sky-plane we arrived on."

Habri raised his eyebrows slightly. "You made no mention of any of this earlier," he pointed out.

"I didn't know earlier that I'd be needing it," Ravagin said tartly. "You want into Simrahi's chambers, or you want to stand here and argue?"

Habri pursed his lips, then nodded. "Wait here," he instructed, and turned away.

Ravagin took a step backward, letting his eyes drift casually around the area. The windows in the lower parts of the manor house still showed some lights, indicating that despite the late hour the day still hadn't ended for many of the castle-lord's servants. Above the overhang, where the slender tower of Simrahi's private section rose from the flat roof of the lower manor house like the stem from an inverted mushroom, all was dark. "What in the world do you want with that sky-plane?" Danae murmured at his side.

"I don't care about the sky-plane," he answered back. "What I want is the spirit inhabiting it."

A moment of silence. "I thought you said the spirit left it while we were flying around the dining room."

"I was wrong. I was concentrating so hard on the fact that the sky-plane had started avoiding walls again that I completely missed the fact that it was even flying at all."

"Aren't sky-planes supposed to work inside buildings—?" She broke off with a snort. "No, of course they're not. Damn—I missed it too."

"There wasn't all that much time for analytic thought," he reminded her. "You see the implication, though, don't you? If the spirit didn't leave the sky-plane at that point, maybe it wasn't able to leave at all."

He sensed Danae shake her head. "That doesn't necessarily follow," she said. "Besides, it clearly got *in* somehow. Shouldn't it be able to get out the same way?"

"Maybe; maybe not. Getting in *or* out could be a tedious process, and it's possible that once we were captured the spirit decided to stick around and make sure we were properly arrested and executed."

"All right, all right—suppose the thing *is* still there. Then what?"

Ravagin took a deep breath. With the danger of eavesdroppers hanging around their cell he hadn't dared discuss any of this with Danae earlier, and he was suddenly afraid that she would find a completely obvious flaw in the scheme that would leave it torn to shreds. Putting their chances for escape in roughly the same shape. "If the spirit is there, I think there's a chance I can take control of it," he told her. "There are special geas spells that allow control by people other than the one who invoked the spirit in the first place—"

"You mean the manifold geas?" Danae snorted. "I tried it at least twice back on Karyx without it doing me an atom of good."

"That's because the manifold geas requires the person who invoked the spirit to add a special addendum phrase at the time of the invocation. There's another one you can sometimes use for a short time whether the spirit's had any prior preparation or not."

"Oh, *is* there now? I wish someone had thought to teach that one to me."

"Actually, there were a couple of very good reasons no one did," he said. "One of them being that none of the Couriers want inexperienced clients taking over spirits and messing around with them." The other reason being considerably nastier . . . but it was still possible he wouldn't have to use it. With a little luck—and a little carelessness on Habri's part—they might still be able to fly out of here from under the would-be usurper's nose. "Anyway, if I can control the spirit, I may be able to get it to leave the sky-plane and enter the watchblade Habri's bringing me. I can then give it a transferance order and throw the watchblade at one of the trolls guarding the entrance to Simrahi's private tower." He spread his hands. "Presto, if I'm lucky: instant amok troll."

"And in the confusion Habri goes in and takes over?"

"In the confusion, you and I get the hell out of here on the freshly exorcised sky-plane," Ravagin corrected. "One troll out of however many Simrahi's got on his door isn't doing to do Habri a damn bit of good."

"What about the trolls and guards on the outer wall?"

"The trolls shouldn't stop an outgoing sky-plane, middle of the night or not. The other guards—" Ravagin shrugged helplessly. "We'll just have to risk it. The last thing I want is for us to be around here when Habri and Simrahi start at it in earnest."

A movement off to the side caught Ravagin's attention: four men lugging a limp sky-plane between them. "Looks like our transportation's arrived," he murmured to Danae. "Stick close to me and be ready to jump when I do."

Approaching from another direction, Habri arrived just as his men eased the sky-plane to the ground in front of Ravagin. "Ah—the sky-plane has arrived," he said with a nod. "Good. Here are the other items you requested."

Ravagin frowned at the firefly, prayer stick, and ordinary knife in the other's hand. "What about the watchblade?"

Habri smiled thinly. "I trust, Ravagin, that you don't consider me a fool. To give you a blade that will always find its mark when I'm not even certain you're fully on my side?" He shook his head. "No, my good sorcerer. If you have the black arts you claim, you can surely succeed without any such assistance. Just as you can surely succeed without the aid of your companion."

With a shock, Ravagin suddenly noticed that four large men had silently gathered around them while he and Habri had been talking. "What do you mean by that?" he asked carefully. "If you think I can do this without Danae's aid—"

"That is exactly what I mean," Habri said. He glanced over Ravagin's shoulder, and abruptly there was a white shimmering hovering between his head and Danae's. A spark-sword blade . . .

Danae made a sort of strangled gasp as hard hands gripped Ravagin's arm and pulled his hand away from hers. "You will open the path for us," Habri said flatly, his eyes on Ravagin's face as other hands took Danae's arms and moved her toward the shadows by the entrance hallway behind him. "Knowing your companion is back amid the attackers should strengthen your resolve, should it not?"

Ravagin took a deep breath. The temptation to use the scorpion glove, to wrap its whip around and around that face . . . "All right," he said through clenched teeth. "I'll try it alone. But the minute you have access to Simrahi's tower I want her released. You understand? Released, unharmed, and out here in the courtyard."

"So you can make your escape?" Habri shrugged. "Yes, I rather expected that was your chief goal in agreeing to help me. Well, no matter. As soon as I'm in the castle-lord's chambers I'll have no further need of you."

"The feeling is mutual." Ravagin looked down at the sky-plane lying at his feet. Now he had no choice; he *had* to get the traitors into Simrahi's tower. And that meant using the spell . . . "Get all your men back," he ordered Habri. "But keep them ready. When I open the way, you'll need to be ready."

The other nodded silently and stepped back . . . and Ravagin stepped forward onto the sky-plane.

The carpet didn't move as Ravagin walked to its center; didn't so much as quiver as he got down on his knees and gazed down into its decorated surface; didn't in any way indicate it might be anything more than just a normal part of Shamsheer's miracle technology. For a long moment Ravagin wondered if perhaps it *was* nothing more, wondered if the spirit that had betrayed them had perhaps already departed as Danae had suggested it might.

He could almost hope it had. If the spirit was gone he wouldn't have to do this thing he'd sworn never to do . . .

Licking his lips, he took a deep breath. There was nothing to be gained by hesitating now. If the spirit was there, he was already as prepared as he was going to be for what was ahead. Leaning forward, he brought his hands down onto the surface of the sky-plane. "*Mish-trasin-brikai,*" he said softly. "*Ormahi-insafay-biswer. Harkhonis-mirraim-suspakro.*"

And with a surge like a mild electric shock, Ravagin felt the spirit rise up through his hands.

And flood into him.

Chapter 39

He gasped . . . or, rather, sensed dimly that his body had gasped. Just as he sensed dimly that he was no longer attached to that same body.

He'd heard stories from others who'd done this, but none of them had prepared him for the sensations now flooding his mind. Or rather, for the lack of sensations. Being buried alive in cotton with a flaming torch in your face . . . drowning in spices, unable to breathe and yet with sharp odors jabbing into nose and brain . . . drifting on an intangible sky-plane with a drastically ingrown edge barrier locking all muscles in place—he'd heard all of those metaphors and others over the years. None of them even came close. All of mankind's most basic fears—falling, drowning, blindness—seemed to explode on him at once . . . and even as he fought to gain balance, to be able to think clearly amid the sudden panic, a flame seemed to burst beneath his unfelt feet, sweeping over him, buring his skin to a crisp blackness as the parasite spirit attacked and burned and fought to either control or destroy him—

Wait a second. I'm not even attached to my body at the moment—how can I feel like I'm on fire?

And with that single rational thought, the whole thing unraveled.

Ravagin took a shuddering breath—and then another, savoring the sense of being whole again. *Illusion—the whole thing was illusion. Wasn't it, my little companion?*

The parasite spirit didn't answer. Ravagin wasn't sure a parasite spirit even had enough intelligence *to* communicate . . . but whatever it lacked in intellectual capacity it more than made up in raw emotion. He could feel the hatred and rage of the creature as it swirled like a ghostly and impotent tornado through his mind—rage at being defeated and under Ravagin's control, hatred at some more basic and permanent level. It was the first time Ravagin had ever touched a spirit this deeply . . . the first time he'd ever realized how truly *alien* the spirit world was. A trickle of sweat ran down between his shoulderblades, and he was dimly aware that he was shivering violently. And not just because of the chilly night air.

Presently, the dark introspection faded, and the world around him began to reappear before his eyes. He was still kneeling on the sky-plane, his hands curled into fists pressed tightly against his abdomen. His shirt was soaked with sweat, his head ached fiercely, and there was oozing blood where his fingernails had dug into his palms; but all in all, it hadn't been as bad as he'd expected, even from something as relatively simple as a parasite spirit. *Lesson number one: spirits aren't nearly as strong on Shamsheer as they are on Karyx.* A damn good thing, too . . .

"Sky-plane—" He broke off, worked moisture into his mouth, and tried again. "Sky-plane: rise one *varn* and follow my mark: *mark.*"

He could feel the spirit resist . . . but for the moment, at least, it had no choice but to obey him. The sky-plane rose a meter and floated gently toward the entrance hallway Ravagin was pointing to.

"I was starting to think you had fallen asleep," a soft voice came from behind him.

Ravagin jerked as Habri stepped up to pace the sky-plane. "No one ever tell you not to sneak up behind people?" he growled.

Habri shrugged casually . . . but as Ravagin's sky-plane hesitated only a moment before crossing the ten-meter limit a touch of awe added brittleness to his features. "You were a long time casting your spell," he said after a brief pause. "But I can see that the results were worth the wait. If your other sorcerous powers are as potent—"

"What do you mean, a long time?" Ravagin interrupted him. "What was it, five minutes? Ten?"

Habri threw him an odd look. "Half an hour at the least. Perhaps a few minutes more."

Ravagin felt a new chill run up his sweat-soaked back as, for the first time, he noticed that the manor house was almost entirely dark now. The servants had finished their chores and retired for the night . . . and he'd lost thirty minutes of his life during that battle. "It took longer than I expected," he said to Habri through dry lips. Even to him the excuse sounded lame.

"Your companion seemed to think so, too," Habri said. "I think that fact was more worrisome to my men than the delay itself."

"She's never actually watched me do this spell before," he improvised. So Danae was being held nearby, somewhere where she could see the courtyard. He tucked the fact away for possible future reference.

Two of Habri's men were holding the doors to the entrance hallway by the time Ravagin reached them. Though not designed for sky-plane usage, the doorway was fortunately wide enough for the carpet to pass through without trouble. Behind him, Ravagin could hear soft noises as the rest of Habri's force fell in behind them. It was probably a good thing, he thought once as the parade trooped along the darkened corridors, that subduing the parasite spirit had taken as long as it had. The image of Habri trying to push his way past cleaning crews and the occasional butcher's assistant brought an unexpected giggle welling up from his throat.

He choked the laughter down. Did direct spirit contact always leave a person this giddy? *Like a narcotic drug*, he thought, fighting against the oddly euphoric feeling. *I wonder if that's why some people seem to like doing this kind of thing.*

I wonder if that's how Melentha got started.

It took them only a few minutes to reach the top floor of the lower manor house and the great chamber into which the stairs from below led . . . and it took Ravagin even less time than that to realize his plan was going to need drastic revision.

It was the same place where he'd had his all too brief hearing before the castle-lord a few hours earlier, though having been brought up from the cells by a different route he hadn't realized exactly where he was. As he'd noted then, it was a huge room . . . and the only ways into it were far from the fat pillar and ornate doors where four trolls stood motionless guard. Lying flat on the hovering sky-plane, his eyes barely above floor level, he tried to ignore the impatient rumblings from the men strung out down the stairs beneath him and made a quick estimate of both the horizontal distance and the height of the relatively low ceiling. The ballistic calculation was simple enough for him to do in his head . . . and there was absolutely no way he was going to reach any of the trolls with a thrown knife.

"Is that the way into the castle-lord's tower?" he whispered to Habri.

Crouched on the stairs beside the sky-plane, the other nodded. "That pillar contains the staircase up. The doors open directly onto it—allows for very commanding entrances." He shot Ravagin a frown. "You didn't know? I was under the impression all manor houses were exactly alike."

"Just checking," Ravagin said, eyes searching for some way to get closer to the trolls. But between their stairway and the pillar the room was completely open, without anything that would serve for cover. "Anyway, I needed to see what the guard situation was like here," he improvised. "So. Four trolls."

"I could have told you the castle-lord had four trolls on guard," Habri snorted. "The question now is how you intend to dispose of them."

A damn good question it was, too. Ravagin gnawed at his lip for a second without coming up with any good answers to it. "You and your men stay here," he told Habri at last. "I need to go back outside."

"You'll be back here for the attack, though, I presume?"

"If I'm not, you'll know when to move," Ravagin assured him.

For a long moment Habri's dark eyes bored into his. "Very well," he said at last. "I trust you aren't planning anything foolish. Your woman companion will be here with us, and if anything untoward should happen she will be the first to die."

"Understood," Ravagin said tightly. "You just make damn sure she's still in good shape when I deliver Simrahi's chambers to you. Or *you* will be the second one to die."

Habri nodded silently. Looking back down the stairs, he nodded to the man bringing up the rear. "You may go," he told Ravagin. "Whatever you have planned, you had best complete it quickly."

Ravagin licked his lips. "Sky-plane: follow my mark. Mark."

He reached the cool darkness of the castle courtyard a few minutes later without the slightest idea of what he was going to do there. "Sky-plane: rise slowly," he whispered. Perhaps as he looked over the castle grounds he would come up with some way to get rid of the trolls.

A spark of the parasite spirit's natural maliciousness leaked through, and Ravagin found himself drifting upwards so slowly that if the side of the manor house hadn't been right beside him to compare to, he would have sworn he was motionless. He felt a flash of annoyance, but said nothing. For the moment, anyway, speed was totally irrelevant.

What could he do? Off to his left, just inside the wall, the light from the castle Giantsword bathed the sky-plane landing area and the half dozen spare carpets scattered around it. Nothing there he could use. Over the top of the long entrance hallway extending out from the manor house the Shrine of Knowledge was coming into view; beyond that, the glowing knob at the top of the Giantsword itself was already visible. Send a message for help via the crystal eye in the Shrine? Or sabotage the Giantsword somehow to cut off the power broadcast? That would certainly incapacitate the trolls, if he could manage it, as well as knocking out the lights and every other bit of apparatus in the entire castle. On the other hand, he had no idea how to do such a thing . . . and there were probably few actions more guaranteed to bring trolls down on him than poking around the protectorate's power source.

Something above him caught his eye: the outward-curving manor house wall was coming down like a frozen wave toward him as he continued to rise. "Sky-plane: move ten *varna* away from the building and continue upward," he murmured. A slight hesitation as he sensed the parasite spirit repositioning itself amid the sky-plane's picocircuitry. Then it caught, and his slow vertical drift acquired an equally slow horizontal component. He watched for a moment to confirm he would miss the overhang, then turned his attention back to the problem at hand.

The House of Healing, directly behind the manor house, would be of no more use than the sky-plane landing area, though the thought of it made his bruises and cuts throb with new pain. The trolls had no need of the Dreya's Womb and other medical equipment there. Could he somehow persuade the guards that Castle-lord Simrahi was ill and had to be taken down? If they at least had to send someone in to check on Simrahi's condition, it would mean opening the door . . . but Habri wouldn't be stupid enough to consider that a practical opening for his attack.

And he wouldn't wait on that stairway forever.

Ravagin felt his stomach muscles tighten with the fresh reminder that he was on a dangerously tight schedule here. Danae was still Habri's prisoner . . . and whether the usurper really meant to release her after all this was over, it was a cinch that if Ravagin *didn't* come through he would kill her without a second thought.

The sky-plane reached the level of the lower manor house roof now, and the frozen breaker beside him gave abrupt way to a circular flatness. Ravagin's eyes moved to the darkened tower rising out of the center of the roof, and even preoccupied as he was he felt a surge of awe at the sight. He'd never seen a castle-lord's private section this close up, and he was struck by its resemblance to the Dark Tower he and Danae had spent the previous night in. *Got to hand it to the Builders*, he thought distantly as he took in the sight. *They sure knew how to keep thematic unity in this world of theirs.* The basic shape of the Dark Tower was there; so were the relief patterns climbing its lower part and the windows not limited to but concentrated in the upper third. Only the dome of the sky room at the very top made it more than just a miniature version of the Dark Tower—

He froze, sending his eyes searching frantically for what he thought he'd just seen. Imagination? Trick of lighting?

No. It was there. Almost exactly halfway up the tower. An open window.

Chapter 40

For a long moment he just stared at the open window, mind whirring with possibilities while at the same time half afraid it would all turn into a false alarm and evaporate before his eyes. The window hadn't simply been flung wide open, he could see now: there was a clearly visible gap between the two pieces of glass, but the gap was narrow and there was no guarantee that he could force them any further open. If they opened outward, in fact, as they almost certainly did, nudging the sky-plane up against the window would do nothing but push it shut. And if there were any alarms—or if whoever was nearest that window were even a light sleeper . . .

But all the caveats didn't really mean anything. If he didn't do something, Danae was dead. Pure and simple.

Carefully, he reached out to the side until he found the familiar wall of the sky-plane's edge barrier. "All right, spirit," he said, gritting his teeth unconsciously. "Remove the edge barrier."

Again he felt the sensation of the spirit shifting within the sky-plane . . . but this time nothing happened in response to that activity. "Remove the edge barrier," he repeated, sharpening his voice and mind against the spirit's unwillingness. Nothing. Apparently, even with a spirit in control, it really *was* impossible for a sky-plane to fly without an operating edge barrier. Ravagin thought back to all the cases of spirit animal control he'd seen on

312

Karyx—*So they're not just weaker in their contacts with humans*, he thought. Something to be grateful for, in general; in this particular case it was going to be damned awkward.

But there might be a way around it. Maybe. "All right. Sky-plane: land on the roof there, next to the central tower."

The carpet came smoothly to rest as ordered. Steeling himself against whatever the hell reaction this might cause, Ravagin let his scorpion glove whip uncoil until it extended beyond the sky-plane's fringe. "Sky-plane: go straight up," he said.

And without any fuss or argument the carpet rose into the air alongside the tower. Leaving the scorpion glove whip free outside the edge barrier.

They were at the open window a moment later; and as Ravagin had suspected, the two panes of glass did indeed open outward. The scorpion glove, he quickly discovered, had a markedly slower response time when operated through the edge barrier; but by forcing himself to take things slowly, he managed to swing both panes fully open without causing any noise.

Fully open, the window was about half the width of the sky-plane.

Ravagin swore viciously under his breath. Sky-planes on the ground could be rolled up just like ordinary carpets; once in the air, they were absolutely rigid. They also flew level to the combined gravitational and centrifugal vectors, which meant he couldn't bring up one side of the thing and slide in at an angle. For a minute he tried to come up with a way to make a tight banking curve that might do the trick . . . but even if he didn't smash both himself and the sky-plane flat against the room's far wall once he was inside, the kind of maneuver he'd need to accomplish it would almost certainly alert every guard and troll in the castle. And with the sky-plane's edge barrier in place, there was no way for Ravagin to simply climb in the window himself.

With the edge barrier in place . . .

Ravagin gritted his teeth. The scorpion glove whip was still hanging limply inside the open window; carefully, he wrapped it as tightly as possible around one of the small pillars supporting the edges of the window. To the best of his knowledge, scorpion gloves hadn't been designed to handle the kind of stress he'd been putting this one through for the past couple of days, and it occurred to him that eventually he was going to push it too far. But he'd pretty well run out of options. Looping the whip slightly to get a solid grip on it with his gloved right hand, he drew the knife Habri had given him with his left—

And with a convulsive motion jabbed it deeply into the carpet material at his knees.

The sky-plane dropped like a lasered bird. For an instant Ravagin fell with it; then the whip caught, and he found himself dangling along the wall with a twenty-meter drop beneath his feet.

There was no time to waste, and he wasted precious little of it. Even before the muffled thud of the sky-plane's crash reached his ears he'd jammed the knife back into its sheath and was holding on with both hands as the scorpion glove labored to pull him up. With what little of his concentration he could spare from the operation he listened tensely for signs that the movement or noise had attracted someone's attention. But there were no hooting alarms—no shouts or sudden lights—and a minute later he was sprawled on the floor inside the window.

He lay there quietly for a minute, waiting until the worst of the adrenaline reaction had passed and his arms were merely trembling instead of shaking. Then, licking his lips, he eased cautiously to his feet and looked around him. With the faint starlight filtering in from outside he could see that he was in a large bedroom . . . and as his eyes adjusted he discovered, to his complete lack of surprise, whose bedroom it was.

Fortunately, Simrahi and the woman in bed with him did not seem to be light sleepers. Both lay motionless beneath the blankets, their breathing steady and slow, neither giving the slightest impression that they'd been disturbed by Ravagin's unorthodox entrance to their room. *Uneasy lies the head that wears a crown*, Ravagin quoted to himself; but of course that hadn't been written about Shamsheer castle-lords with trolls guarding their bedrooms.

Trolls.

Ravagin gritted his teeth. He'd worked so damn hard getting into the tower he'd almost forgotten that getting behind the trolls downstairs was only the first step. A sneak attack at the back of a single troll might give him enough surprise advantage to beat out the machine's electronic reflexes . . . but with four of them down there that approach was an invitation to suicide. What he needed was a way to simultaneously take out *all* the trolls; to set a bomb off at the foot of the staircase, perhaps? But if there were any real explosives on Shamsheer, he'd never heard of them. What he needed was something heavy to push down the stairs . . .

What he needed was his sky-plane.

Carefully, with an eye on the sleepers in the bed, he moved back to the window and looked down. Below, the sky-plane was a slightly darker rectangle against the roof. *Spirit, I order you to rise*, he sent the mental command, trying to project the thought to the sky-plane. He hadn't felt the spirit's presence since knifing the carpet, and had no idea whether it could even hear him, let alone whether it was still obliged to follow his orders. *Spirit, I order you to rise*, he repeated. Nothing. Either the spirit was ignoring him, couldn't hear him, or simply couldn't move the damaged sky-plane. For Ravagin, it didn't much matter which.

Damn, he thought, turning back into the room as fresh sweat began to form on his forehead. Even in the dead of night, Habri's motly army couldn't hang around the stairs down there forever without being discovered. *Think, Ravagin, think. Here you are, right in the middle of a castle-lord's private chambers, with all the best of Shamsheer's magic machinery to draw on. There must be something you can use to take out a few trolls.*

Beneath the blanket, Simrahi moved in his sleep . . . and Ravagin smiled tightly.

There *was* something he could use.

He half expected to find a pair of trolls standing guard outside the royal bedroom, but apparently even Simrahi's suspicions hadn't pushed him that far. The hallway outside was deserted; quickly, Ravagin moved along it, searching for the stairway up. He found it, and began climbing, and a few minutes later reached the dome at the top of the tower. The sky room, it was called . . . and even after sixteen years of travel in the Hidden Worlds it was like a punch in the gut to discover there was still something on Shamsheer that could take his breath away.

Through the crystal dome arching over his head the stars blazed down.

Not the stars as seen from the middle of a Shamsheer castle surrounded by villages and lights; not even the stars as seen from a lonely field somewhere out in the Tweens. These stars were incredibly brilliant, shining with an intensity that seemed unnatural . . . and Ravagin stared in awe at them for several heartbeats before he finally realized why.

Around the edges of the dome, the top of the castle wall could be seen, as well as the tall hilt-shape of the Giantsword within it and the rolling Harrian Hills far beyond it to the west . . . but each of the shapes was a black shadow, lit only by the glow from the starlight above. None of the lights that had been shining anywhere outside were visible. On sudden impulse, he took a careful scan across the sky. The scattered clouds had apparently been filtered out, too.

He licked his lips and took a deep breath. The sheer technological ability the sky room implied . . . and yet, for those first few seconds, he was aware only of what the room said about its creators' souls. To have built something this sophisticated with no purpose except the enjoyment of beauty . . . For the first time in his life, Ravagin felt a flicker of true kinship with the Builders. Perhaps, for all their incredible power, they hadn't been all that different from human beings after all.

The moment faded, and the real world crowded back into Ravagin's mind, and he lowered his eyes and thoughts from the glorious display. The sky room was sparsely furnished—some comfortable chairs, a desk, a large bed in the room's center—and it took only a minute to find the crystaline throne he was seeking. The throne, he realized now, that Simrahi had been seated on during Ravagin's brief hearing.

The castle-lord's bubble.

The chair was large, clearly designed to accomodate heftier men than Ravagin. As solid-looking as glass, it nevertheless yielded like a soft cushion as he sank gingerly down into it. There was no reaction—no audible alarm, no attempt by the chair to throw him out—and Ravagin let out the breath he'd been holding. So far, so good. Now came the tricky part. He had no idea at all how the bubble worked, or even whether someone who wasn't a castle-lord could operate it, and there was no way to find out except the hard way. Taking a deep breath, he ran through the most obvious possibilities and chose one. "Bubble: rise," he said.

No response. "Bubble: ascend," he tried. "Bubble: activate. Bubble: be raised. Chair: rise. Chair: ascend. Throne: rise—"

The chair rose smoothly toward the dome above, Ravagin almost falling off the thing in surprise. "Throne: stop and hover," he managed, gripping the arms tightly.

The chair did so. Carefully, he reached out a hand, following it a minute later by the scorpion glove's whip . . . but both confirmed what his eyes had already told him: the bubble's spherical force-field was still off.

All right, don't panic, Ravagin ordered himself sternly. *Let's try thinking, instead.*

For starters, unlike the more proletarian sky-plane, the bubble had clearly been designed to be functionable indoors. A quick experiment showed it had none of the sky-plane's aversion to walls, either, which meant Ravagin should have no trouble getting it downstairs. But ramming doors and trolls without the force-field going wasn't exactly what he'd had in mind when he'd come up here. "Force-field on," he said. Nothing. "Bubble on. Bubble activate. Be bubbled. Uh . . . shield on. Simrahi: bubble on. Damn it all—" He broke off, thinking furiously. *All right: try changing perspective. How would a castle-lord refer to the force-field? As a shield? An aura?* "Aura on." *Or might the command be keyed to the more visible aspects of the field?* "Haze on. Sphere on. Golden on. Goldlight on."

And abruptly the room around him was filled with orange haze.

*   *   *

"I have the very bad feeling," Habri said tightly, "that your sorcerer friend has run out on us."

"He's not my friend," Danae said dully, keeping her eyes on Habri's feet. Habri's feet, and the feet of the two huge men sitting on the step on either side of her. There wasn't much to look at down there, but people who knew they were defeated seldom maintained eye contact with their conquerors. "He's just an acquaintance—and not even much of that, it seems," she added, letting a touch of bitterness seep into her voice.

Habri was silent a moment. All around them, she could sense that the growing nervousness in the men sitting on the stairway was dangerously close to the breaking point. How long would it be, she wondered, until Habri decided that Ravagin had indeed failed? And when that happened, what would they do?

They would retreat, of course, hoping to postpone their revolt to a more auspicious time. Retreat, taking her with them for Habri to vent his frustration and anger on.

And whatever had happened to Ravagin—whether he was dead or a prisoner—she couldn't count on him to get her out of this one. Swallowing hard, she licked her lips and let her shoulders slump a bit more where she sat. Only by being a weak, helpless female could she have any hope of survival.

"Apparently he valued his own skin more than he did yours," Habri said abruptly. "But I made a bargain—your help for your freedom—and if he has taken the freedom, you are still here to provide the help I want. Torlis, Carmum—bring her. Masmar, hold the men here until I give the signal."

And before she knew what was happening, Danae found herself yanked to her feet and half led, half dragged up the stairs. "Are you crazy?" she hissed at Habri. "You'll alert the trolls—"

"That is precisely what I intend to do," the other said grimly. He had his sword in his hand now; beside Danae, the guard he'd called Carmum had released her arm and similarly drawn his blade. "And I, not you, will do all the talking," Habri added, waving the tip of his sword near her throat. "Is that understood? Not a word, or Carmum and Torlis will vie for the privilege of killing you."

She managed to nod. *He's gone totally insane*, she thought desperately, heart pounding in her throat. *Good God, what do I do?*

Habri topped the stairs and headed straight across the room toward the trolls, Danae and Torlis close behind him as Carmum dropped back a pace. Habri made no attempt to be silent, and Danae saw with a sinking feeling that all four trolls had their crossbow pistols pointed before the intruders had taken their third step. "Ho, trolls of the Castle-lord Simrahi," Habri called across. "I bring news to the castle-lord that cannot wait until morning." He half gestured back to Danae and Torlis. "I have uncovered a traitorous plot to usurp the castle-lord's throne, with this sorcerous woman and this guard at the head."

Danae gasped in shock, shock that quickly turned to pain as Torlis squeezed her arm warningly. "The castle-lord is not to be disturbed until morning," one of the trolls called back, its flat voice sending a violent shiver up Danae's spine. Flashback to the confrontation outside the Tunnel . . . except that this time the trolls' electromechanical reflexes wouldn't be hampered by spirit meddling. Habri would get them to open the door—would attempt to gain entry to Simrahi's chambers—and the trolls would fight back.

And they would all die.

She clenched her teeth, then forced herself to relax them. With only one option left, the agony of decision making was gone, leaving an almost morbid peace in its place. *It's now or never, girl*, she told herself. *At least this way they won't get the door open. Who knows?—if you're fast enough, the trolls might even let whatever's left of you surrender to them.* Taking a deep breath, she eyed Torlis, chosing the best spot to hit him—

And behind the trolls, the doors exploded outward in an explosion of golden light.

The thunderous clamor as the heavy wood slammed the trolls to the floor almost but not quite drowned out Habri's startled expletive. But the traitor recovered fast. Danae's mind had barely had time to register the fact that the orange explosion was actually a chair and human figure encased in a glowing sphere when Habri gave a loud shout and charged toward the stairway now laid wide open before him. The grip on Danae's arm tightened as Torlis broke into a run behind his leader, forcing her to do likewise. Behind her, Carmum came past them on her other side, while a quick glance showed the rest of Habri's army streaming up into the room with swords drawn. Ahead, the orange sphere was slowing from its high-speed impact; the trolls were still struggling to get out from under the rubble of the shattered doors—

And planting one foot, Danae pulled sharply on her arm, yanking Torlis off balance, and drove her free fist hard into his armpit.

The other bellowed, letting go of her arm as if he'd been scalded. He spun around, his expression a mixture of pain and utter astonishment. *That's right, you scum*, Danae thought toward him with grim satisfaction. *The weak, helpless female is gone. As a matter of fact, she was never really here.*

His astonishment lasted only a second before he bellowed again and swung his sword in a vicious horizontal arc . . . but that one second was all she needed. Even as the sword slashed toward her side, she dropped to her left forearm and hip and kicked out with both feet directly at his knees.

The double *crack* was audible even over the war cries from behind and the troll alarms from ahead. Torlis toppled over backwards, screaming in agony, and Danae was free. Tucking her legs back under her, she rolled back to her feet—

Just in time to duck as a second sword whistled past her nose. Carmum, come back to help his comrade.

He'd caught her off guard, but the sword was already past her, and until he could stop its motion and bring it back around she would have the advantage. Giving a gut-tightening shriek, as Hart and her combat instructors had long ago taught her to do, she swung her empty hand up as if to throw something in Carmum's eyes. Empty or not, the other's blink reflex still cut in, and for a split second he was blind. Leaping toward him, Danae lowered one hand to block any backswing of the sword and swung the edge of the other toward his throat—

And dropped to the floor as, out of nowhere, the orange sphere rammed full into her opponent.

"Damn," she breathed, scrambling to her feet. The sphere came tightly around and abruptly the orange glow vanished. She took a long step, leaped upward to grab Ravagin's outstretched hand, and a second later was wedged beside him in the crystalline throne.

"Goldlight on" he snapped. The orange sphere reappeared, and suddenly his arms were around her, holding her tightly to him.

She hugged back with equal strength, feeling her arms beginning to tremble with reaction. "You okay?" he asked anxiously into her ear.

"I'm fine," she gasped back. "I was afraid you'd been captured. Where did you get this—my God, is this a *bubble*?"

"Sure is." Ravagin twisted partly away from her, freeing one hand while leaving the other still around her. "Throne: follow my mark; *mark*."

Danae turned her head to find they were moving toward the doorway Ravagin had just shattered. Beyond the golden glow, she could see some of Habri's men were already on the stairs and heading up. "Ravagin! Habri's past the trolls—"

"I know," he said grimly. "Throne: more speed; continual mark. Goldlight off."

And before she realized just what he was doing, the chair abruptly darted forward to follow his pointing hand through the doorway and up the stairs.

She inhaled sharply, stomach twisting with the sudden upward movement even as a spasm of claustrophobia tried to tie knots into it. "Ravagin!—the bubble—"

"Not enough room in here to use it," he barked. He was right on that count; between walls, ceiling, and running people, there wasn't a hell of a lot of room in the stairway. "I don't want to run anybody down."

"You don't want to run down *traitors*?"

"Nope—I want to save them for Simrahi."

They shot past the last of the climbers—Habri himself—reached the top of the stairs—

"Goldlight, on; throne, stop," Ravagin snapped; and with a hard deceleration that nearly threw Danae off the chair the orange glow reappeared and the throne came to a dead halt.

Neatly blocking the stairs.

Ravagin took a shuddering breath. "I'll be damned," he said, something midway between awe and disbelief in his voice. "It actually worked. Well . . . Throne: rotate one-half turn." Smoothly, the chair turned to face back down the stairs.

"You *carhrat!*" Habri spat at them, waving his sword impotently at the golden haze. "You spineless, lying bastard of a *carhrat!* I offered you your freedom and you repay me with treachery—"

Danae glanced at Ravagin, half expecting him to respond with invective of his own. But he just sat there, listening coolly as Habri continued to rave. A motion from the bottom of the stairs caught Danae's eye . . .

She barely had time to clamp her teeth before the troll fired its crossbow, and Habri's tirade was cut off in mid-word.

Closing her eyes, she let a shiver run up through her body. "Is it over now?" she asked, a sudden weariness washing over her. "Can we *please* get out of here now?"

"Not quite yet," a calm voice from behind them answered before Ravagin could speak. "Goldlight: off."

The golden glow vanished . . . and Danae turned to see Castle-lord Simrahi standing by the archway.

Flanked by six armed trolls.

Chapter 41

"If you have an explanation," Simrahi said calmly, "I will listen to it now."

Beside Danae, Ravagin slid forward and dropped off the chair onto the floor in front of the castle-lord. "I'd be happy to give you one," he said wearily, turning to offer Danae a hand. She came down beside him, keeping hold of his hand. "But I'm not sure what it would prove," he added, turning back to Simrahi. "As of yesterday you had already made up your mind about us. I doubt the events downstairs have changed that opinion any."

Simrahi simply cocked an eyebrow. "You may be surprised," he said, eyes flicking to the scorpion glove on Ravagin's hand. "Tell me, Ravagin, why did you join my treasonous guard master in his attempt to usurp my rule?"

Ravagin held his hands out, palms upward. "You had virtually condemned us to death, my lord, with no hope offered of reprieve. When one is offered freedom under such circumstances, one has no choice but to take it."

"Indeed. Then why did you turn against him at the end?"

It seemed to Danae that Ravagin stiffened slightly. "That question should need no answer."

"Why not? Neither of you are citizens of Numant Protectorate—you owe me neither loyalty nor love. For that matter, from what little I can learn about you it is unclear that you owe loyalty to *anyone* on Shamsheer."

"Perhaps one from whom no loyalty is demanded is more able to give it of his own free will," Ravagin said quietly.

"Perhaps." Simrahi's eyes flicked to Danae. "And you, Danae? Where does your loyalty lie?"

"With Ravagin, my lord," she said automatically. The words suddenly registered in her fatigued brain— "That is, in the way Ravagin has already said," she corrected, feeling blood rushing to her cheeks.

A touch of a smile flickered across the castle-lord's face. "I think perhaps you were correct the first time." His gaze returned to Ravagin and he sobered. "You entered my private tower through sorcerous means, yet did me no harm. You took my bubble unlawfully, yet used it in my defense. You allied yourself with treason, yet in the end used that alliance to expose and destroy it. Is this a fair summary of events?"

A shiver went up Danae's back as she realized what Simrahi's words and phrasing meant. They were on trial again; an informal trial, but no less real for that.

And it was clear that Ravagin recognized that, as well. "Only that our intentions remain as I stated them at my hearing yesterday, my lord," he said, matching the castle-lord's formal tone. "We wish merely to pass peacefully through Numant Protectorate and continue our journey."

"To where?"

"I am not permitted to say, my lord."

For a long moment Simrahi gazed at them in silence. Then, raising one hand, he tapped the nearest troll on its side. "You will escort Ravagin and Danae to the sky-plane landing area," he ordered it. "They are to be allowed to leave Castle Numanteal. They are not permitted to return. Ever."

"Acknowledged," the troll said, taking a step forward.

Ravagin bowed his head briefly. "Thank you, my lord. We will not betray your trust."

"No thanks needed," the other said. "And less trust than you may imagine. I need not rely totally on your statements; though you were apparently unaware of it, I have been following the events of this night ever since you entered my sky room and learned to command my bubble."

Ravagin's hand, gripping Danae's, suddenly tightened. "You—? But no trolls came to attack."

"I sent none. Like the trolls, the bubble is mine to take command of at any time." Simrahi's eyes bored into Ravagin's. "I confess that I felt a certain amount of curiosity as to your purposes, as well as your means of entry. And I was not disappointed. There is a great deal more to you than one would first imagine, Ravagin. To both of you," he amended, nodding courteously to Danae. "Someday I hope to discover just where it is people like you come from."

Danae held her breath . . . but Ravagin merely shrugged slightly. "It is not in my power to satisfy your curiosity, my lord."

"I thought not." The castle-lord took a deep breath. "At any rate . . . day will soon be here. If you wish your departure to be at all secretive, you had best take it quickly."

Ravagin again bowed his head. "Again we thank you, my lord." He hesitated a fraction of a second. "And we leave you with a warning: Habri's treason may not be the last such attempt on your rule. You had best be on your guard."

Simrahi's expression turned to flint. "I do not need outlanders to tell me how to defend the Numant Protectorate," he bit out. "Depart—now—and do not forget you are barred from ever returning to this castle. Do not forget; for the trolls will certainly not." Turning his back, he strode away from them, all but one of the trolls falling into a loose defensive pattern around him.

"You will go to the sky-plane landing area," the remaining troll said, taking another step forward.

"No argument," Ravagin sighed. Letting go of Danae's hand, he stepped closer to slip his arm around her waist, holding her tightly to him as they headed down the blood-stained stairway.

Fifteen minutes later they were seated on a sky-plane, soaring over the castle wall and heading southwest toward the Tunnel. Ten kilometers as the birdine flew, Danae remembered; perhaps ten or fifteen minutes by sky-plane.

We're going to make it, she thought. *This time we're really going to make it.*

Five minutes later, Ravagin brought them down in the middle of the Harrian Hills.

"All I know," Danae growled as he sent the carpet away, "is that you'd better have one damn good reason for this."

"*I* hope I don't, actually," he said, rubbing his forehead tiredly. "I hope like hell I'm being overcautious. But after everything that's happened, I'd rather err that way than the other. Come on—the Tunnel's this direction. We should be there in an hour or so."

"We'd better be," she said, setting off with a sigh. "In case you haven't noticed, we haven't had a lot of sleep in the past few days. I'm about dead on my feet—and we might get that way permanently if Simrahi catches us out here."

"He only told us not to come back to the castle," Ravagin reminded her.

"I somehow doubt he's going to be worried about the strict letter of the law," she shot back. "And we were getting along so well with him there at the end—why did you have to go out of your way to irritate him, anyway?"

"I didn't 'go out of my way,' " he growled, "and I don't think a little irritation really stacks up against life and death, do you?"

"Life and—?" She broke off. "You mean . . . the spirits?"

He shrugged uncomfortably. "It's one of the things I had in mind," he said. "What better place for them to take control of than the protectorate containing the Tunnel to Threshold?"

"Oh, God," she murmured. "You think Simrahi will be able to keep them back? He doesn't even know what it is he's up against."

"He can't stop them," he admitted. "Not for long, anyway. It's going to be up to us, Danae—us and whatever the Twenty Worlds can gather together to throw at the problem."

"Great." Something he'd said a minute ago . . . "Were there any other reasons you gave Simrahi that warning?"

"Yes. One."

"Care to enlighten me?"

"No. Not now, anyway. Suffice it to say that if what I was trying to do works, we'll hopefully never know it."

She had to be content with that.

An hour later they carefully topped the last hill and came within view of the Tunnel . . . to find four trolls standing guard at the entrance.

"Damn, damn, damn," Danae snarled, pressing her chin harder into the rocky ground of the hill as they lay there side by side. "*Damn* him. I *thought* he seemed to know too much about us, Ravagin—the way he called us outlanders and all. And now he's blocked the Tunnel—"

"I'm afraid it's worse than that," Ravagin interrupted her tightly. "Those trolls down there aren't Simrahi's."

"They're not—?" She caught her breath and took another look . . . and felt her hands curl into fists in front of her. The trolls' color scheme was green/white/violet, not Numant Protectorate's red/silver/black. Which meant—

Which meant the spirits had found the Tunnel . . . and after all they'd already been through, there was going to be yet one more battle to fight.

A battle she suddenly knew she couldn't face.

"God," she whispered, closing her eyes against it all. "I can't handle any more, Ravagin—I just can't."

Ravagin reached over to squeeze her hand. "I don't want to, either. But it looks like we won't have to."

"What?" she asked dully.

"Take a look."

Frowning, she opened her eyes and peered off in the direction he was pointing. In the distance, riding through a gap in the hills and clearly making for the Tunnel, were a half dozen men in the red/silver/black of Castle Numanteal. Accompanied by a half-dozen trolls. "I don't understand," she muttered. "What are they doing here?"

"Searching for trouble near the castle, of course," Ravagin said. Danae glanced at him, taken aback by the grim smile on his lips. "The other part of my reason for dropping veiled threats on Simrahi. Don't you see?—he's got his soldiers out sweeping the territory for possible trouble."

"And just happening to clear out our path for us in the

process." Danae looked back at the interloping trolls and shook her head, almost afraid to believe it. "I just hope this is going to be as one-sided as it looks."

It was even more so. Again, the trolls' complex and heavily layered battle/control/decision circuitry proved more than the spirits within them could handle efficiently under combat conditions. Within minutes of the Numant soldiers' first challenge, all four interlopers were laid out on the ground, frozen into immobility. A few minutes after that four sky-planes arrived and they were loaded aboard, presumably to be taken back to the castle. The sky-planes rose and vanished behind the hills to the east, the patrol continued on its way—

And Ravagin cautiously rose to his feet. "Let's go," he said, head turning back and forth as he made one final scan of the area. "Straight to the Tunnel, but remember not to go in right away. It's possible there might be someone skulking further in where the patrol couldn't see them, and we'll want to check things out carefully."

"If anyone's in there," Danae said grimly, "we'll kill him. Pure and simple."

There was; and they didn't.

He loomed out of the darkness just where the Tunnel began its curve toward the telefold, and for a moment they all stared at each other. "I was starting to think," the other said at last, "that I was going to have to tackle that reception committee out there all by myself."

Danae took a deep breath. "And you would have, wouldn't you. You blithering idiot."

Hart merely smiled. "Part of my job," he said. "Welcome home, Ms. mal ce Taeger."

Chapter 42

"Ah; Ravagin," Corah Lea said, looking up as he came in. "Sit down, please."

He took the proffered chair, noting with a sinking feeling that her face was a study in inscrutability. A bad sign.

"So." She arranged her forearms across her desk and tried without much success to smile. "Well. I have to say, first of all, that your report is the damnedest bit of high adventure I've ever seen come out of the Hidden Worlds. I hear the thing's been called up over eighty times in the past week alone—twenty of those requests coming from the the folks upstairs. You've really made a stir."

"It's nice to be noticed," he said. "You call me in here to get an autograph before the rush starts?"

She made another attempt at a smile, with even worse results. "I wish it was something that easy. Actually, you're here because—well, I've just gotten word down from the Directors' Council about your request to speak to them."

Ravagin felt his jaw tighten. "They turned me down?"

"Cold. I'm sorry, Ravagin. I can see how much this means to you."

"What it means to *me* isn't important—" He broke off, struggling to get his temper back under control. None of this was her fault, after all. "Did they *read* the petition? All of it?"

"Ravagin—" Lea spread her hands helplessly. "Look, *I* read your petition, too, and even knowing you as well as I

329

do I can't really blame them. You offer not a single shred of objective proof that anything's seriously wrong on Karyx or Shamsheer, and yet you want them to summarily close down both Tunnels—"

"No proof? my God, Corah, just what the hell do they think that report of mine *is*? Spirits openly attacking us on Karyx, spirit-controlled machinery on Shamsheer—"

"Nordis's report disputes your version of whatever it was happened on Karyx," Lea cut him off. "And as to Shamsheer, there's no direct, objective proof there were spirits involved in any of that."

"What about my contact with the sky-plane? Using a Karyx spell, I might add?"

"That could have been a psychological illusion," Lea shrugged. "Or maybe it *was* a real contact, but with the sky-plane itself—after all, the stuff *could* be semi-sentient."

"Oh, come *on* Corah—"

"I'm sorry, Ravagin, but you have to remember that the kind of spirit intrusion you're talking about is supposed to be impossible. You're bucking a hundred years of theory and experiment here, and with that kind of inertia behind it you need more than just a packet of fuzzy speculation."

"Inertia be damned," Ravagin snapped. "The theories are wrong."

"How, then? How did these spirits of yours manage to cross the telefold?"

And that *was* the crux of it all. He'd suspected—no, damn it, he'd *known*—that without that critical piece his report and recommendation would get exactly this kind of reaction. But to commit to the record the technique for calling spirits into Shamsheer or even Threshold itself . . .

"I don't know," he lied with a sigh. "But it's possible. It *has* to be. What happened to me—to all three of us—can't be explained any other way."

Lea licked her lips. "Ravagin . . . look, even if it *was* true, and you could prove that beyond a doubt . . . you can't seriously believe the Directors would actually shut Triplet down, let alone seal off the Tunnels. They'd be putting themselves out of prestigious jobs, and at the same time opening themselves up to a hell of a lot of ridicule. That's just not how the universe operates."

"Not even with the word and experience of their best Courier to go on? Not to mention the name *mal ce Taeger* on the report along with it?"

Lea grimaced. "And you'd be surprised at how much more important the latter seemed to them than the former," she said with a touch of bitterness. "But no, not even that was enough. Not even close. They're going to send an investigation team in to Karyx to get Melentha's side of the story, but I get the feeling it's more a *pro forma* response than a real expectation of gleaning any information out of it. She'll deny your accusations, of course, the investigators will funnel the report upstairs, and that'll probably be the end of it."

"Yeah." Ravagin exhaled between clenched teeth. Hart had been right, he thought bitterly; but he'd felt the direct approach would be worth the effort. And now it had cost them two weeks . . . "If that's all, then, I'll be going."

"Well, actually . . . no. There's more." She took a deep breath. "You remember that request for a leave of absence you filed a few months ago?"

He'd forgotten all about it, actually. "I do now, yes."

"Well . . . it's been approved. Starting immediately."

He stared down at her, an icy hand clutching at his heart. "Immediately?" he said slowly. "As in . . . when?"

Her eyes slipped away from his. "As in right now. As soon as you leave my office."

Or in other words, his attempt to do this the direct way had actually been worse than useless. He'd been branded a troublemaker—possibly even an unstable one—and they were countering by kicking him out of contact with the entire Triplet system until they could figure out whether that vacation should be made permanent. "Corah, they can't do this. I withdraw the application—"

"I'm sorry, Ravagin, but that won't do any good." She looked back at him with moisture in her eyes. "The decision's been made, and there's nothing I can do about it."

His hands tightened into fists, the pressure of his fingernails against the skin bringing back the memory of that lonely combat with the parasite spirit in the sky-plane. The spirit hadn't stopped him—all the spirits in Karyx hadn't stopped him—and he would not be stopped now.

Would *not* be stopped. "All right, Corah," he said at last. "I'm calling in all the favors you owe me—all the favors that anyone in the entire Courier Corps owes me. You understand?"

"Ravagin—"

"I'm not here," he interrupted her. "You haven't seen me—haven't been able to find me to give me this message—and therefore I cannot yet officially be barred from the Crosspoint Building or even the Hidden Worlds. You understand?"

"Ravagin, that's crazy," Lea snapped. "I can't just *forget* to give you an order like that."

"So you sent me the message to come here and I ignored it. Three days, Corah—just let me have three days. Please."

She stared up at him . . . and slowly, the tears dried and her mouth settled into hard lines. "Two days," she said at last. "I'll give you two days. I can't push it any farther."

He hesitated, then nodded. "Two days," he echoed. "Thanks, Corah."

"You've spent sixteen years earning it." She hesitated. "And I hope to God you're as wrong about this spirit invasion as they think you are upstairs."

There was nothing to say to that. So he said nothing, and left.

The Double Imperial restaurant in Gateway City was, from all appearances, one of the most expensive and exclusive eating places on Threshold—the kind, Ravagin thought only half humorously, where the salad vinegar was handled by the wine steward. The restaurant's walls and ceiling were covered with art objects from all over the Twenty Worlds; the tableware was hand carved from petrified ballisand bone; the flatware was white gold with yellow gold accents. It was an unlikely place for someone of Ravagin's station and income to find himself in, and he felt acutely uncomfortable as he waded through the deep carpet behind the maitre d', sending surreptitious glances at the other immaculately groomed diners they passed. It was a place of elegance, a place for those with sufficient wealth to enjoy spending some of it while immersed in the most civilized atmosphere Threshold had to offer.

It was, in short, a thoroughly unlikely place for a council of war. Which was presumably why Danae and Hart had chosen it.

They were waiting for him when he reached the table. "Well?" Danae asked as the maitre d' seated him and disappeared. "Any word?"

"Yes," he said grimly, "and all of it bad. You were right, Hart—the directors don't care for people who attempt to rock the boat. Not only was my petition turned down flat, but I've been kicked out of the Corps."

"You've been *what*?" Danae frowned. "But they can't do that . . . can they?"

Ravagin shrugged. "Officially, they're simply approving my request for a leave of absence—the one I filed months ago, the one they refused to grant then so that they could have me take you into the Hidden Worlds."

"A leave they can easily make more permanent once all the fuss you've raised has died down," Hart murmured, sipping at his wine. "A simple-minded approach, but usually effective for all that."

Danae reached across the table to squeeze Ravagin's hand. "So what happens now?"

The wine steward appeared at Ravagin's elbow before he could answer, filling his glass with a pale pink liquid. "I beat Corah's fingers into giving me two more days," he said when the steward had left. "But after that, I won't even be allowed into the Crosspoint Building, let alone the Tunnel."

"Two days," Danae murmured, shaking her head. "That's not much time."

"No." Ravagin focused on Hart. "Well, Hart, I guess this is where you get to show that same wonderful magic that got you out of the jail cell you were tossed into at the beginning of all this."

"Whatever contacts and skills I have are at Ms. mal ce Taeger's disposal," Hart said. "What exactly do you have in mind?"

"Sealing up the Tunnel, of course," Ravagin said grimly. "We'll need a few thousand cubic meters of exocrete, or something even more permanent if you can find it. We'll also need some kind of forged orders to get the stuff into the Dead Zone and on into—" He broke off at the expression on the other's face. "Objection?"

Hart cleared his throat. "Magic I can do, Ravagin; miracles are another matter entirely. Even setting aside the ethics of trapping a whole group of Twenty Worlds' citizens in there, you're talking about rolling an entire convoy of fully loaded reaction trucks through the Crosspoint Building. I'm not even sure there are any doors large enough to handle something that big. And you think no one will stop to question us, make a few phone calls—?"

"Okay; point taken," Ravagin growled. "Then plan B: we get a small tactical nuke, juice it up with cobalt or something equally dirty, and set it off inside the Tunnel near the telefold. The radiation ought to last—"

"Until they get teams in to scrape the residue off the walls," Hart interrupted. "Or were you expecting the bomb to irradiate the Tunnel walls themselves? Because there've been experiments done, and the walls won't accept radiation."

Ravagin stared across the table, annoyance at Hart's glacial calm beginning to edge toward anger. "Maybe you don't realize just what we're facing here," he bit out, hearing his voice tremble slightly as he fought to control it. "If that demon ever gets out onto Threshold the entire universe is up for grabs. That's not melodramatics; that's hard, cold reality."

"Ravagin—" Danae began.

"Let me finish," he cut her off. "We've already had a solid demonstration of how thoroughly spirits can invade and control electronic devices—that by itself would make them the worst threat the Twenty Worlds has ever faced. Add in the fact that they'll probably still be able to affect people's minds like they do on Karyx—and remember that none of the major control spells work here—and you've got an invasion that would be well-nigh unstoppable."

"Ravagin," Danae said quietly before he could continue, "we all realize what's at stake here. But getting mad at Hart just because he points out logical flaws isn't going to help any."

Ravagin clenched his teeth. "You're right," he admitted as the anger drained reluctantly away. "You're right. Sorry, Hart."

The other shrugged the apology away. "You're on the right track, though. Closing off the Tunnel is certainly the simplest way to keep the demon off Threshold."

"Except that it's impossible to do," Danae said.

"It's just a matter of finding the right way—"

"No: not *difficult*," she cut him off harshly. "*Impossible*. Mathematically impossible."

Both men looked at her. "What do you mean?" Ravagin asked, frowning.

She took a deep breath. "I've spent the past couple of days researching everything known or postulated about the spatial mathematics of Triplet and the Tunnels. If you run computer simulations, it turns out there *has* to be at least one selective passage between each of the dimensions. Tunnels, by any other name."

"Why?" Ravagin asked.

She shrugged helplessly. "I don't know. Maybe it's like a whorl—you know, the way a vector field has to contain at least one point whose vector has zero length."

He took a moment to digest that. "So what happens if the passage isn't there? Do the other dimensions just disappear?"

She shook her head. "On some models the passage simply reestablished itself in the same place, disintegrating whatever blockage I'd put there. On others the blockage stayed but the Tunnel popped out somewhere else. Somewhere completely random." She gazed across at him, her eyes aching. "I'm sorry. It's just not going to work."

Ravagin gazed back at her for a moment, then dropped his eyes to his wine glass, bitterness welling up in his throat. Everything he'd pushed for the past two weeks . . .

He took a deep breath. They had just two days left; he couldn't afford to waste any of it in self-pity. "All right, then. One more direct approach scrapped. What else have we got?"

Danae squeezed his hand, and seemed to let out a relieved breath. "I've been thinking about that, between computer runs," she said. "It seems to me that if we can't block off the Hidden Worlds, the next best thing would be to put things back the way they're supposed to be."

"Translation: get the spirits back to Karyx?" Ravagin chewed at his lip. "That's a tall order. We still don't know how any of the spirithandling rules work in Shamsheer."

"We know at least one of them does," Hart reminded him. "You used it against the sky-plane parasite spirit."

"Yeah—and I have no intention of ever doing it again," Ravagin told him, a shiver running up his back. "Especially since it's not the parasite spirits that are our problem. They have no power whatsoever without their attendant demon; and I am not, repeat *not*, making that kind of contact with a full demon."

"I wasn't suggesting you do so," Hart shook his head. "My point was that there clearly *are* rules that will work in Shamsheer. *We* may not know what they are; but there ought to be others elsewhere who do."

"Like on Karyx," Danae said thoughtfully. "Gartanis, maybe?"

"He's as likely to know something as any of the other spiritmasters," Ravagin shrugged. "Horribly illegal to take a Karyx native through to Shamsheer, of course."

Hart snorted gently. "You really care about that?"

"I stopped worrying about the legalities a long time ago."

From behind Danae a troop of waiters appeared and began setting out a dinner that the others must have ordered before Ravagin's arrival. It was, in retrospect, exactly the sort of meal Ravagin would have expected from a place like the Double Imperial: a large number of plates, each with modest to minuscule servings of elaborately sculpted food. The uncomfortable landed-fish sensation threatened to reappear, but he found that if he could ignore the surroundings and food design and look on it as just an ordinary sampler-style dinner, he could untie the stomach knots enough to relax and actually taste the food. Which, though far out of his experience, was generally pretty good.

For the most part they ate silently, both from an apparently mutual desire to concentrate on the food and also because the constant bustling to and fro of the waiters would have made coherent conversation difficult in any case. But after about forty-five minutes the steady stream of waiters carrying new plates ceased, and the dessert and caffitina were served, and they got back down to business.

"All right," Ravagin said, poking carefully with his fork at a stiff and astonishingly sturdy creation of cream and fruit flavoring. "It seems to me that before we can tackle the Shamsheer demon there are two or three basic hurdles we have to consider. First of all, in order to get any real control over him, we're almost certainly going to need to know his name. Second, to *get* that name we're going to have to find the damn fool who brought him into Shamsheer in the first place. And third, once we've *got* the name, we need to have some idea in mind as to exactly what we're going to do with it. That about cover it?"

"Covers it and a half," Danae snorted, shaking her head. "That's an awful lot of ground to cover in two days, Ravagin. Especially since we haven't got the faintest idea who this damn fool, as you called him, might be."

"Perhaps we can at least narrow down his location," Hart suggested. "You said someone in Ordarl Protectorate told you they'd been experiencing equipment problems?"

"Yes," Ravagin nodded. "And the trolls that first attacked us were from Feymar Protectorate, while the trolls that Simrahi's people cleared out from their territory were from Trassp Protectorate. Take your pick."

Hart made a face. "I see."

"Hang on, it's not quite that bad," Ravagin assured him. "We know that our target must have spent a good deal of time in Karyx to have had the knowledge and insight to pull this off in the first place. It's also pretty certain he's on Shamsheer at the moment; or if not, that he spent a fair amount of time there in the recent past."

"Why?" Danae asked around a mouthful of cream.

"Because whatever he intended to do with the demon—research or anything else—would have taken some time to accomplish," Ravagin told her. "That points to someone official, either a Courier or someone on staff at one of the way houses."

"Assuming you're right, what sort of numbers are we talking about?" Hart asked. "Ten possibilities? A thousand?"

Ravagin shrugged. "We're probably starting with something on the order of six or seven hundred altogether. We should be able to drastically narrow that down, though, by checking experience records."

"And med/psych records," Danae put in.

Ravagin frowned at her. "What do you mean?"

She gave him a tight smile. "Don't you. remember, Ravagin?—my official reason for going into the Hidden Worlds was to study their psychological effects on Couriers."

"Oh, right." He grimaced. "We seem to have lost that thread somewhere along the way."

"Yeah; but before we did I collected a fair amount of impressions on the subject. Particularly on how excessive spirit contact seems to affect the personality."

Ravagin studied the end of his fork, mentally leafing through his list of friends and acquaintances who'd spent time on Karyx. "Are you implying," he said slowly, "that it isn't so much absolute time on Karyx that matters, but how much contact you've had with the spirits there?"

"It seems to be a combination of the two." She hesitated. "And there isn't just one reaction to consider. For example . . . the emotional burnout you had seems to have been a direct result of *not* giving in to spirit influence. As if—"

"As if they couldn't control me, so they were working on driving me out?" Ravagin growled with a sudden flash of insight. "Why, those bastards. That *is* what they were doing, isn't it? Those ethereal little *bastards.*"

"It's just a theory—"

"But it sure as hell sounds reasonable." Ravagin jabbed his fork viciously into his dessert, trying to imagine a demon's face there. It seemed to help. "Okay; it sounds like a good approach," he told her. "The only catch in it is that med/psych records are on the restricted access list. I don't know any of the appropriate passkeys to get in."

"Can I phone into the computer from outside the Crosspoint Building?" Hart asked.

"No. It's a sealed system."

"How close is your phone to your terminal?"

"Oh—" Ravagin measured out half a meter between his hands. "About that far."

Hart nodded. "Then it can be done. I'll get you the appropriate gadget later this evening. You'll have to sneak it in and get it set up, I'm afraid, but it's a simple procedure and I'll include a set of instructions."

"What about the passkeys? Getting into the computer won't get you those."

Danae snorted. "That's the least of our worries," she said. "The system doesn't exist that Hart can't perk. I should know—he's been tracking me down through perk-proof systems for the past four years." She shot him a lopsided smile. "Funny how I never appreciated that talent before."

"My only real talent in such things lies in searching out the proper experts," Hart shrugged. "Fortunately, there are several such experts on Threshold."

"Whom you've already made contact with?" Danae suggested.

"Of course," he said equably. "Part of my job."

Chapter 43

Hart's "gadget" turned out to be something that looked like a standard computer record cube linked by a wide cable to a phone message disk. It arrived via special messenger at Ravagin's house at eleven in the evening, about an hour after he'd returned home from Danae's hotel suite and the continuation there of their council of war. Smuggling it into the Crosspoint Building was nerve-racking but otherwise uneventful, and just before midnight he called back to the hotel from his desk to report that the interface was in place.

The initial list of suspects came to eight hundred and sixty-four. Eliminating those who'd never been to Karyx dropped it to six hundred twenty-one; weeding out those whose last trip there had been over a year ago brought it to just under four hundred.

Sometime about three-thirty in the morning Hart's unnamed associate cracked the med/psych passkey, and while Ravagin dozed at his desk they copied all the relevant files over for Danae to study. By five o'clock, when Hart woke him up to remind him about disconnecting the interface before anyone else came in and caught him with it, she had the list down to fifteen.

By the time he'd packed up the interface, left the building, and driven to Gateway City and their hotel, it was down to one.

*　*　*

"Omaranjo Saban," Ravagin read out loud, settling tiredly into a chair and scanning the hard copy Danae had made of the man's files. Master of the way house in Feymar Protectorate, barely eighty-five kilometers from the Shamsheer/Karyx Tunnel for the past ten months; previous post had been four years at the way house in Citadel on Karyx. Personality profile . . .

"You know him?" Danae interrupted his reading from the chair where she was slumped, gazing blankly out the window at the reddening sky.

Ravagin shook his head. "Met him once in Karyx, I think, but our group didn't stay long and I don't remember anything about him. Four years—that's a long time to be on Karyx."

"About the same as Melentha," Hart spoke up from another corner of the room. "According to his file, he kept his post the same way she did, by simply requesting extensions of the original appointment."

Ravagin nodded grimly. "That's one of the things we're going to have to change about the way people are assigned. Danae, you really think he's the one?"

"I don't think there's any doubt," she said wearily, rubbing her eyes with her fists. "His personality changes are almost a parallel to Melentha's, and no one else even comes close."

"Hart?"

"I don't know anything about Ms. mal ce Taeger's psych study," the other said with a shrug. "But from a pure right place/right time analysis he certainly fits. Though I'd feel better if we could come up with a reasonable motive for him."

"Insanity," Danae murmured. "Too much time with demons on the brain and *poof*—" She spread her hands, sunburst fashion. "Instant psychological lobotomy."

"It may be even easier to explain than that," Ravagin said, skimming a part of the psych report. Saban's frustration level . . . "Anyway, it doesn't really matter. What matters now is stopping him and putting the cork back in the bottle."

"Yeah." Danae took a deep breath. "Okay. When do we start?"

Ravagin looked at Hart. "Can any of your specialized contacts get a pass for Danae to get into the Hidden Worlds?"

"No need," the other said. "I've already taken care of it."

"You have? When?"

"While I was on the computer, of course. It's all been filed and even properly approved. Though in all honesty the faster you get us in, the less chance there'll be of someone spotting it and making embarassing inquiries."

Ravagin gritted his teeth. Speed *was* indeed imperative . . . and yet, on the other hand, the farther away he got from the council of war and the plan they'd hatched during it, the more the second and third thoughts were beginning to crowd into his mind. "I've been thinking," he said slowly, "that maybe we've hammered this scheme out a little too quickly. For starters, maybe *I* should be the one to go into Karyx—"

"And leave Hart and me to confront Saban and his pet demon?" Danae asked, closing her eyes. "Come on, Ravagin—we hashed all the stuffing out of this earlier."

"You'll excuse me if I don't like the thought of sending you into danger again," Ravagin snapped.

She opened her eyes, and for a moment he thought she was going to snap back at him. The way she had when they first headed into the Hidden Worlds, when his chief concern was whether they'd still be on speaking terms by the time they got back to Threshold.

But those days were gone forever. "If it comes to that," she told him quietly, "I don't like the thought of *you* going into danger, either. And don't try to kid me; you'll be in at least as much of it in Shamsheer as I will be in Karyx. Believe me, I am *not* overly enthusiastic about going in there again—you show me a way we can all stay here and still stop the threat of spirit invasion and I'll take it."

"There's no reason for you to go into Karyx, Ms. mal ce Taeger," Hart spoke up. "I can do this just as well as you can."

"You know why we can't do that," Danae sighed. "I'm the one who spent all that time with Gartanis, remember? The one he taught dark spirithandling spells to? Not to

mention being Ravagin's companion during the mad dash
across Shamsheer."

"Yes, I remember all the arguments," Hart said. "I
don't recall it being mentioned during those arguments
that I met Gartanis, too."

"Under an alias," Danae sniffed. "Hardly the same cre-
dentials, all things considered."

"It may not make any difference—"

"But it might. Admit it; it might. And it's sure as hell
not something we can afford to take chances with."

Hart took a deep breath and sighed. "I unfortunately
can't argue with you, Ms. mal ce Taeger," Hart said. His
voice was one of resignation . . . and yet, in his eyes was a
glint that reminded Ravagin of something. "I suppose I
should consider myself lucky that you're at least not trying
to slip out on me this time."

Danae shivered slightly. "No, this time I'll be glad of all
the protection I can get."

"I'll do my best," he assured her. "I suppose that's
settled, then. Ravagin, when do you want to leave?"

Ravagin licked his lips briefly. "We'll all need to get some
sleep first," he said, bringing his mind back to the subject
with an effort. That glint in Hart's eye . . . "Eight hours at
the least. We've been up more or less all night, and under
the circumstances I think we should assume we'll need to
hit Shamsheer at a full sprint. Let's make it four this
afternoon at the Crosspoint Building."

"Isn't that a little late in the day?" Danae murmured,
clearly halfway to falling asleep right there in her chair.

"I'll tell them you want to fly over Kelaine City at
sunset. They'll buy it—clients are always making crazy
requests like that."

"Four o'clock, then," Hart nodded, getting to his feet.
"Ms. mal ce Taeger, I'll be right next door if you need me.
Ravagin, there's an extra bed in the other room if you'd
care to sleep here."

"No, thanks," Ravagin shook his head. "I'll sleep better
in my own house."

"Very well. Pleasant dreams, then."

Ravagin left; and it was as the suite door closed behind
him that he abruptly remembered where he'd seen that

glint before. In the early dawn in the marshlands of the
Davrahil River on Karyx . . . when Hart had made up his
mind to sacrifice his life for Danae.

They rendezvoused at the Crosspoint Building precisely
at four o'clock. No one questioned or tried to stop them as
they went through the checkout procedure, proving that
Corah Lea had indeed kept her promise to leave Ravagin's
name on the Courier Corps' duty roster.

Perhaps more surprising was the fact that there was
nothing waiting for them as they walked out of the Tunnel
into Shamsheer. Ravagin had half expected they would
have to talk their way past some of Castle-lord Simrahi's
soldiers, or even be forced to outfight another of those
commandeered trolls the spirits seemed determined to
throw at them. But the Tunnel entrance was clear, and the
sky-plane that came at their command took them to the tiny
village of Phamyr without any signs of hesitation.

At Phamyr they switched sky-planes and headed north-
east, and as night closed over them they reached the
southwest part of the Trassp Protectorate and the southern
shore of Lake Trassp. Fed by six rivers, with three thousand square kilometers of surface area, the lake served as
the major source of water for both the southern half of the
protectorate and also for the Tweens area immediately to
the west. From the sky an almost complete ring of village
lights could be seen hugging the lake's shore, a panorama
which some of Ravagin's clients in the past had found
interesting. At the moment, though, far more important
than scenery was the fact that Lake Trassp was the center
of an extensive fishing industry.

Most of which had already closed down for the night
. . . but with a little persistence Ravagin found what he
was looking for.

"What do you think?" Ravagin asked Hart as they all sat
around the small inn room they'd hired for the night.

The other shrugged, holding up one corner of the large
fishing net for a closer inspection and giving it a stiff tug.
"Well enough made, I suppose, as these things go. Certainly strong enough to handle any fish you might find in a

lake this size. But we're talking a lot more weight here than that of the average fish."

"My question was more aimed at whether you're going to be able to set it up in the first place," Ravagin said with a touch of asperity. "The net itself isn't going to last very long no matter how we slice it. So to speak."

Beside Ravagin, Danae shifted uncomfortably in her seat but said nothing. "Of course I can set it up," Hart said, folding the net and laying it aside. "You'll need to give me a few hours' head start, but the techniques are perfectly straightforward. The real question is whether you're going to live long enough for it to do any good."

"I wish to hell," Danae growled, "that for once in your life you'd try to be a little diplomatic."

"No, he's right," Ravagin shook his head. "But I should be safe enough. The Darcane Forest's pretty dense—Danae, you can attest to that—and once I'm in among the trees there shouldn't be any way for a sky-plane to get to me."

"Too dense for a sky-plane, but not too dense for a man on horseback?" Hart asked pointedly. "Perhaps; but you make the assumption that the demon will indeed come after you with a sky-plane. Suppose he merely commandeers a troll and chases you on foot?"

The same question had occurred to Ravagin. Often. "If he does, then I'm in trouble," he admitted. "But my guess is that he won't think to do that. He's presumably been on Shamsheer long enough to have become used to the convenience of sky-planes, and I think that by the time he realizes his mistake it'll be too late for him to backtrack. Anyway, I don't really have any choice. We know the parasite spirits can enter and exert limited control over sky-planes; weakened the way they seem to be here, I don't think they'll be able to do the same with horses. I'd rather take my chances with the forest and your skills with that—" he gestured to the net—"than wind up being flown somewhere nice and deserted where the demon can kill me at his leisure."

Danae took a shuddering breath. "Oh, God, I wish this were over."

Ravagin put his arm around her. "It will be soon," he promised, trying hard to sound convincing. "Tomorrow night.

Well—" his eyes flicked to Hart. "I guess there's nothing really left to say. I suppose we'd better get some rest; we'll want an early start in the morning."

"Yes," Hart nodded. For a second his eyes met Ravagin's. "Though I'm not particularly tired at the moment," he said, getting to his feet and heading for the door. "If you'll both excuse me, I think I'll go downstairs for awhile, check things out, then perhaps take a walk around the town. I've heard that Shamsheer's night life is worth sampling, and I didn't get the chance to try it the last trip in. See you in a couple of hours."

The door closed behind him, and for a moment Danae and Ravagin looked at each other. Then, without a word being spoken, they stood up and, holding each other tightly, walked to the bed. One final chance at a quiet moment before the storm . . . possibly the last chance they'd ever have. Briefly, one last stray thought flickered through Ravagin's mind, before all stray thoughts were crowded out: that perhaps Hart did indeed know how to be diplomatic, after all.

Chapter 44

Omaranjo Saban's way house was larger and more elegant than most Ravagin had seen on Shamsheer, its dimensions all the more pronounced when the modest size of the town of Horma over which it towered was taken into account. Horma, its outer buildings edging precariously close to the westernmost fringes of Darcane Forest in south-central Feymar Protectorate, was barely a tenth of the size of Kelaine City; yet Saban's way house was at least twice the size of the one Pornish Essen presided over there. But it wasn't just the size of the place that set Ravagin's teeth on edge. A sense of arrogant power seemed to permeate the house, from the harsh decor of the conversation area to the strained expression of the local servant girl who went to summon Saban. It evoked unpleasant comparisons with Melentha's mansion in Karyx, and Ravagin found his right hand curling his scorpion glove into a hard fist as he stood at the window and waited for Saban to appear.

"Yes?" a sharp voice came from behind Ravagin. "You wished to see me?"

Ravagin turned to face him . . . and in that first instant he knew beyond the shadow of a doubt that this man was indeed the one.

Not just because Saban's face, with its thinly tight mouth and hollow eyes fairly oozing hatred and impatience, reminded him so much of the demon face in Melentha's post line archway. Not even because of the hand twitching nervously at the hilt of the watchblade belted at his waist, a hand that, for all the arrogance of the man's voice and expression, proclaimed him to be deep in the grips of a full-bodied paranoia.

It was because of the way Ravagin's face seemed to register in those hate-filled eyes . . . and the way the man reacted. "Ravagin!" he whispered hoarsely. "But you were the one—he said you were gone—"

He broke off abruptly. "Sorry—talking to myself. Name's Ravagin, isn't it? I think we met once—"

"Too late, Saban," Ravagin shook his head. "Much too late. There's only one reason you could possibly have reacted to me the way you just did—you know it and I know it, so let's skip the wide-eyed innocence. Let's get down to the basics here; and you can start by telling me how many of them you brought over."

The hand by the knife hilt twitched a bit closer. "Who are you talking about?" Saban asked, clearly still struggling to regain his mental footing. "Listen, whatever you think you're doing here—"

"I know what *I'm* doing," Ravagin said softly. "The question is what the hell you think *you're* doing."

The shock was beginning to pass from Saban's face now . . . and in its place the hatred reappeared with renewed force. "What I'm doing is my business," he hissed. "And whether you hope to destroy it or to take it from me, you won't succeed. You hear? Because *I'm* the only one the demon obeys—the only one."

"Are you, now?" Ravagin said, keeping his voice as calm as possible. *Demon*, singular—confirmation at last that their guess about the number and type of spirits in Shamsheer had been correct. The best possible scenerio . . . and yet hardly a reason for optimism. All around him, an almost-felt whisper was beginning to breathe around the edges of his being: the demon and his parasite spirits, gathering their strength for battle. "Are you really in control of this demon of yours, or is it the other way around?" he asked Saban. "You really think that just because he tells you I'm a threat to your plans and humbly asks your permission to destroy me—you think that makes you the one in charge? Face reality, Saban. Without the demogorgon-based spells of Karyx to draw on, any hold you think you have over him is nothing but a wad of wrapping paper."

"Reality, is it? That's what you want, Ravagin; reality?" Saban strode across the room to a desk and yanked open a drawer. "Then take a look. *This* is reality—and after a century of trying and failing, *I'm* the one who found the key." He reached into the drawer and pulled out a sheaf of papers. "Feast your eyes, Ravagin, and let your gut devour itself with envy."

The papers were too far away for Ravagin to make out any real details, but he already knew what was there. Circuit diagrams. Mechanical layouts. Logic circuits, electrofluid control/decision algorithms, structural data—the secret technological magic of Shamsheer, ready to be memorized and taken across the telefold to the Twenty Worlds. "Impressive," he murmured.

" 'Impressive'; that's all you can say?" Saban gloated. "The complete—*complete*—circuit diagrams for a Dreya's Womb and a sky-plane, and 'impressive' is the best you can come up with? No mention of the sheer possibilities these papers contain?—nothing about the wealth, the fame and power? Your sour grapes are showing, Ravagin. Shamsheer is forever open to us now. Or, rather, open to *me* now."

He ended on a screech of triumph. "Oh, you found a key, all right," Ravagin bit out. "And I suppose Faust thought he was pretty clever, too, after he'd made *his* bargain with the devil. Did it ever occur to you that in having your pet demon trace out all this circuitry that he would pick up a hell of a lot of knowledge along the way as to how the stuff worked? And how he could bend it to his own ends?"

"His ends are defined for him by me—"

"No!" Ravagin snapped, patience breaking at last. "You're nothing but one of his tools, Saban—a damn stupid fool who let petty greed get the better of you. Just *look* at yourself—he's halfway to controlling you already. All right, fine; you've got your precious diagrams, and you're a big hero. So quit while you're ahead and help me get rid of him before it's too late."

"With so much of Shamsheer's magic left to uncover?" Saban snorted his contempt. "What sort of fool do you take me for?"

Ravagin sighed. "One who's going to get nothing but a footnote as the man who nearly brought destruction to Shamsheer before he was stopped."

Saban started to speak . . . and suddenly closed his mouth as the words seemed to register. "What do you mean, stopped?" he bit out coldly. "You can't stop us, not if you had five lives to do it in."

Ravagin stared at the man, an icy chill running up his back. *We*—the same word with the same inflection to it that Melentha had used . . . and like Melentha, it sealed away forever the last chance that Saban really was a relatively innocent dupe in schemes that had gone beyond him. Between occupational frustration with Shamsheer's elusive technology and the demon's steady emotional erosion, Saban was lost. Ravagin had hoped against hope that he could yet bring the other back, could turn him into an ally.

Now, instead, he would have to kill him.

"I won't need five lives to stop you," he told Saban, an almost infinite sadness welling up deep in his soul. "All I need to do that little chore is already on its way here. From Karyx."

Saban froze. "From . . . ? What do you mean?"

"Just what I said. Since I'm not sure how to deal with your demon, I'm bringing someone here who will. His name is Gartanis; I'd imagine your demon has heard of him."

The whisper at the edges of Ravagin's mind abruptly seemed to increase in intensity. "Yes, I see that he has," he said. "Good. Then perhaps you'll be able to persuade him that he might as well give up now and return peacefully to Karyx. And from there to the fourth world."

Saban inhaled; a shuddering, rasping sound. "You're bluffing," he all but whispered. "You're here—Gartanis is on Karyx—and between you and him are a thousand spirits to call on."

"Karyx spirits? Certainly . . . but I don't need to go to Karyx. Gartanis is already on his way here."

"Impossible. Across the telefold—" Saban bit at his lip.

"Across the telefold you can only communicate verbally?" Ravagin offered. "Don't worry, you're not giving away any state secrets; I know how you did it. A simple personalized invocation spell, with the name of your new spiritual master inserted into the proper place in the middle—"

"Astaroth is not my master—!" Abruptly, Saban gasped and doubled over, clutching at his stomach . . . and when he straightened up again he no longer looked human.

Ravagin felt his mouth go dry. The last bit of information he'd needed, tricked out of Saban as he'd hoped to do. But the price for that name was looking like it might be high indeed. "So; Astaroth, is it? You ready to give up and go back to Karyx now, Astaroth?"

"You cannot escape."

Within him, Ravagin's stomach tightened into a knot. Saban's mouth had moved . . . but the words had seemed to come from all around Ravagin. The memory of his battle with the parasite spirit flashed back, and for a brief, horrible moment he wondered if this sudden burst of unreality meant the demon had somehow taken control of his mind. Then the true explanation caught up with him and he began to breathe again. "Nice trick, Astaroth," he said as conversationally as he could manage. "So you've learned how to work a house's voice synthesizer, have you?"

"I will destroy you," the voice continued as if Ravagin hadn't spoken. "You and the female human will both die."

"I don't think so," Ravagin shook his head. "For starters, Danae—the female human, as you call her—is already out of your reach. Or hadn't I mentioned that she's the one who went into Karyx to bring Gartanis here? I doubt she'll have any trouble persuading him to come for such a—"

And without warning Saban snatched his watchblade from its hilt. "The human Ravagin!" the demon screamed, the knife's target to it in a voice that no human vocal cords could possibly have produced. Saban's arm cocked backward over his shoulder to throw—

And as his backswing reached its furthest point the

scorpion glove whip lashed out to strike him squarely on the wrist. There was the sharp *crack* of breaking bone and the knife clattered to the floor behind him. The walls screamed again in fury; without uttering a sound of his own, Saban lowered his head and charged.

As, simultaneously, the walls abruptly burst into flame.

Ravagin snarled a curse, sidestepping and throwing a kick into Saban's torso. In a single heartbeat whatever control he'd had in the situation had been snatched from him . . . and if he died now he would have no one to blame but himself. Saban *had* to be killed—Ravagin had suspected that for weeks, known it for minutes—and yet he'd hesitated, unable to strike the man down in cold blood. And now his scruples were going to cost him dearly.

Him, and possibly Danæ, too. If he died here, she would soon be following.

And with that thought the last shreds of hesitation vanished. Saban, chillingly oblivious to the flames threatening to bring his house down around him, had halted his mad rush, turning back to the attack with hands curled into talons aimed at Ravagin's face . . . and the scorpion glove lashed out one more time to wrap itself around the other's neck.

A single convulsive jerk, and it was over.

The demon couldn't cry out his fury through Saban, of course, with the man's neck broken; perhaps because the necessary circuitry was already ablaze he couldn't use the house's voice synthesizer, either. Whatever the reason, there was no sound as Saban collapsed to the floor except the increasing roar of the flames, and for Ravagin the silence was more unnerving than any further screams of hatred could possibly have been. Pausing only long enough to snatch the watchblade from the smoldering carpet and jam it into his belt, he scrambled back to the window, snatching up a chair and hurling it ahead of him in a single motion. The glass shattered; taking a long step, he dived head-first through the gap into the blessed coolness outside.

Only just in time. Even as he hit the ground and rolled, the second floor of the house caved in behind him.

"Give him aid!" someone shouted, and suddenly there were a half-dozen hands on Ravagin, pulling him to his feet and brushing bits of window glass from his tunic and palms. "What happened?" one of them shouted over the roar.

"No idea," he shouted back, looking around him. Surrounding the house at a safe distance, a crowd of onlookers had gathered, watching with horror and disbelief as the house collapsed inward on itself, sending a cloud of sparks into the pillar of smoke billowing upwards. "I was just standing there talking with Saban when the fire started."

"Impossible," someone insisted. "No house could simply catch on fire by itself—not like that, not all at once."

"What were you *really* doing in there?" another, more hostile voice demanded. "Was it some deadly spell of black sorcery?"

"Are you in league with Saban?" someone else added.

Ravagin gritted his teeth. So Saban's demon experiments hadn't gone unnoticed by his neighbors; and if they didn't know what exactly had been going on in the way house, they knew enough of the basics. And if they jumped to the conclusion that he was a part of it . . . "I know nothing about any black sorcery," he told his questioners. "I went to Saban in search of lodging, and as we were discussing terms the walls suddenly began to burn."

"Then what were the screams we heard?" the hostile voice demanded. "You trap yourself in lies, traveler."

Ravagin opened his mouth, thoughts spinning furiously . . . but before he could come up with anything to say his time suddenly ran out.

From the north, barely visible through the plume of smoke, a sky-plane could be seen flying rapidly toward them. A sky-plane, with a lone figure aboard it . . . and there was little doubt as to what that figure was.

"There is your black sorcery," he shouted, raising his right hand to point at the approaching sky-plane. The gesture brought his scorpion glove out from the confining press of bodies around him. "A troll, under the power of Saban's spell gone awry, coming here to complete the destruction he planned for you."

Someone in the crowd gasped an oath, and almost unconsciously the press around Ravagin eased as people began to draw back—

And, spinning around to face away from the fire, Ravagin sent the scorpion glove whip snapping out and down. The half dozen people in line with it jumped as if scalded at its touch, and for a handful of seconds the way through the crowd was clear.

Ravagin ran.

One of the men along the way tried to stop him, but a second crack of the whip was more than enough discouragement. All the rest, whether in fear or simply the normal paralysis of shock, stood by like statues as he sprinted through the corridor and out of the crowd. His horse was tethered nearly fifty meters away, a cautious distance that had successfully put it out of direct danger from the demon but which now could wind up costing him precious time. If the sky-plane caught up with him before he could get deeply enough into the forest at the town's edge—

"Stop him!" someone shouted from the crowd; and even as he glanced back over his shoulder, the mob surged forward.

Ravagin mouthed a curse and redoubled his speed. The horse was ten meters away now . . . six, five, four—the scorpion glove whip snapped out to slash the line tethering the animal to the post, saving him a few seconds—

And then he was there and in the saddle, grabbing up the reins as he kicked the horse into action. The leading edge of the crowd was angling toward his course in a clear attempt to cut him off; he sent the runners a warning crack from the scorpion glove and they veered off. A second later he was galloping down one of Horma's narrow and twisting streets, swerving back and forth as he tried to avoid running down any of the people hurrying toward the fire.

From far behind came a blood-chilling scream of rage: Astaroth and some of his parasite spirits, probably possessing both the sky-plane and the troll aboard it. Clamping his jaw tightly, Ravagin resisted the urge to look over his shoulder to see how close the carpet was getting, his full attention on controlling his horse. As long as the sky-plane was airborne, its edge barrier would keep the troll from using its crossbow, and once Ravagin got through the village there would be only about half a kilometer of grassland to cover before he reached the relative safety of the forest.

A block ahead, a carriage trundled out of a side street and stopped directly in his path.

"Hey!—you ahead!" Ravagin shouted, waving his arm toward the vehicle. "Get out of my way!"

The carriage didn't move. Cursing under his breath, Ravagin made a quick estimate and turned his horse's head to the right. Between the carriage and the nearest building on that side would be a tight squeeze, but he ought to make it—

And the carriage rolled a meter backward, sealing off the gap.

"Damn!" Ravagin snarled, yanking hard on the reins to slow his horse. "Damn you, get out of my *way!*" Rising up in his stirrups, he peered into the carriage, trying to catch the occupant's eye.

There wasn't any occupant.

A cold shiver went through the sweat on his back. Twisting the reins violently to the left, he swung the horse toward the front of the carriage, where a new gap had appeared. Again the vehicle moved to block him; waiting until the last second, Ravagin turned back to the right and kicked his horse back into a full gallop.

They barely made it through the gap, the ghost carriage's rear stand panel brushing the horse's flank as the vehicle moved backwards just a hair too slowly to cut them off. The horse whinnied at the touch, and it cost Ravagin a precious second to get the animal back under firm control. A scraping of wheels on stones came from behind, and he threw a quick glance over his shoulder

The carriage had swung around and was pursuing him.

Ravagin turned back to face forward, cursing under his breath. The grassland lying between village and forest was visible now, two or three streets ahead. If he could hang onto his lead long enough, the carriage's wheels would be at a disadvantage out in the grass—

A *whoosh* from his right was his only warning; and as he reflexively ducked something large shot past his head.

For a single, horrible second he thought he'd misjudged distance and speed and that the demon-possessed troll was upon him. But it wasn't a sky-plane that smashed with shattering force into the buildings across the street, but a heavy-looking metal ball with large protruding spikes. Throwing a glance to his right, Ravagin was just in time to see the catapult rolling down the side street toward him fire a second missile.

He ducked again as this ball struck the corner of a building and ricocheted back toward the ghost carriage behind. *Damn bastard demon*, he thought viciously, throat tight with the sinking realization that Astaroth had been smarter than he'd ever expected the demon to be. Belatedly, Ravagin remembered now the ease with which the Forge Beast at the Darcane Forest way house had been taken over to made a driving fan for the fire he'd started. It was now painfully obvious that Astaroth had learned far more about Shamsheer's "magic" than Ravagin had realized . . . and had prepared his own special version of that magic to defend his position here.

Behind Ravagin, the rumble of the carriage was growing louder. Digging his heels into his horse's flanks, Ravagin urged it into an extra burst of speed. One more cross street to pass . . .

And as he galloped toward it, a dozen alien machines rolled in from both directions.

Automated tumbleweeds, was Ravagin's immediate impression of the things. Roughly spherical in shape, perhaps a meter in diameter, they looked like they'd been constructed entirely of tangled wires and twisted tubes. Like a waste dealer's castoffs—which was, he thought grimly, probably exactly what the demon had intended them to look like. Harmless junk, not worth a second look by anyone . . .

It took the tumbleweeds bare seconds to get into final position, lined up in a solid row completely blocking the street, and as Ravagin galloped toward them he saw that each machine had three to five gently waving tendrils rising out from somewhere in its interior. Like faint echoes of the prehensile grabbing action of Darcane Forest's Berands fronds.

Or perhaps of scorpion glove whips . . .

Ravagin gritted his teeth. He had no choice at all: it was either make it over that barrier or else face the ghost carriage behind him and the even deadlier troll still on its way. And the only way to get his horse's legs past those waving tendrils would be to let them grab something else.

Jamming the reins into the crook of his left elbow, he reached over to his right wrist. The timing on this was going to be tight, with no margin for error. Eyes on the tumbleweeds, he made a quick calculation of the distance, adjusted his horse's stride for the jump. The barrier was seven meters ahead now; six; four—

And the scorpion glove whip lashed out and down, grazing the tops of the two tumbleweeds directly ahead.

The tendrils were fast, all right. Before Ravagin had even a chance to withdraw it, they had the whip thoroughly entangled. The end vanished into the center of one of the tumbleweeds, and abruptly the slack in the whip disappeared as something in the tumbleweed's center began reeling it in. Clenching his jaw, Ravagin fought for balance against the pull. The horse reached its take-off point, Ravagin kicked him into the jump—

And as they sailed unhindered over the barrier Ravagin tore open the wrist band holding the scorpion glove onto his right hand. With one final tug that threatened to pull him bodily off his mount, the glove was yanked off.

From behind came another scream of rage . . . of rage, but with an underlying coloring of frustration. Licking his lips, Ravagin took a ragged breath and permitted himself a grim smile. The edge of Horma flashed by, and a second later he was driving hard across open grass toward the forest beyond. From the sound of that scream the troll and sky-plane were still too far behind him to catch up before he reached the forest. He was going to make it . . .

Unless it occurred to Astaroth to put the sky-plane down within crossbow range of Ravagin's back. The smile vanished from Ravagin's lips, and he hunched down over the horse's neck, feeling the skin tightening between his shoulderblades.

But for once, the demon missed a bet. The sky-plane chased Ravagin right up to the edge of the forest, even attempting to force its way through the branches until its increasingly reduced speed seemed to finally persuade Astaroth that that approach wasn't going to work. The noise of it backing out through that same tangle of branches came as Ravagin, fighting hard to keep up his speed without running into a tree, shot on ahead. There was another scream—

And then there was silence.

Licking his lips, Ravagin fought the shaking in his hands and settled down for the long ride ahead. The die was cast; and in many ways what happened now was totally out of his hands. Riding as fast as a troll could hope to chase him on foot, with the forest's canopy sealing him off from any kind of aerial attack or landing, he was virtually assured of reaching the Tunnel some eighty-five kilometers away. The only question remaining was whether or not Astaroth would realize that his only hope of stopping Ravagin was to fly on ahead and wait for him at the Tunnel.

It was almost certain that he would.

Chapter 45

It was nearly sundown when Ravagin finally reached the clearing surrounding the Tunnel . . . to find the demon/troll waiting there for him.

"You have come," the mechanical voice boomed out as Ravagin cautiously approached the last line of trees on foot. "I have grown weary waiting for you."

"Translation: you hoped the forest animals would take care of me for you?" Ravagin called. The demon/troll was standing directly in front of the Tunnel's entrance, its feet half buried in an unusually thick leaf cover that seemed to have filled much of that part of the clearing. Cautiously, Ravagin eased around one tree, made for a second—

The demon/troll's hand snapped up, and a crossbow bolt sizzled past Ravagin's ear.

With a lunge, he dived into cover. That one had been far too close for comfort . . . "Still having trouble handling the auto-fire circuits, I see," he said, throwing a quick look around the tree. The demon/troll was making no attempt to move in. "Your dumb little parasite spirits had that same problem. I assumed a full-fledged demon would do somewhat better."

"Taunt me while you may," Astaroth retorted. "Your death is close and certain. I will kill you, and when the female human returns I will kill her, as well."

"Her name is Danae," Ravagin said, feeling sweat breaking out on his forehead as he studied the area all around

359

him in the fading light. Hart had said he would blaze the
tree where the trigger was set, but so far there was no sign
of any such mark. "Danae. I'd think you'd pay more attention to human names. Especially given how important your
spirit names are to you. Good thing I know yours now,
isn't it?"

A second crossbow bolt thudded into Ravagin's tree—a
wasted shot, clearly fired in pure anger. If the troll had
been carrying the usual complement of four sharp and two
blunted stun bolts when Astaroth took it over, that meant
two killing shots left. Getting him to expend those shots
would make things a hell of lot safer . . . "Do I take it
you're sensitive about your name, then?" he called. "Or
are you just mad about how easily we pitiful humans can
use those names for our own purposes?"

He held his breath; but the demon had apparently
regained his temper and no shot was fired. "You cannot
trick me into coming into the woods after you," Astaroth
snarled. "You may know my name, but neither Danae nor
Gartanis do, and without it they will have no true power
over me. I will not risk you passing me in the gloom of
night to deliver that knowledge to them. I will wait for you
here."

Translation, Ravagin thought, *he really is having trouble with the troll sensor circuitry. Otherwise there wouldn't
be a chance of me sneaking by him whether he came out
here or not.* Which was definitely to Ravagin's advantage;
or it would be if and when he ever found Hart's damn
blazed tree. Gritting his teeth, he gave the area another
careful scan; and then, on sudden impulse, looked above
him.

There, two meters up the trunk of his tree, was a neat
cut.

He smiled tightly. Good old Hart; reading Ravagin's own
tactical thoughts to the point of even anticipating the
direction and path he'd choose to approach the clearing.
Fumbling at his belt, Ravagin pulled out the watchblade
and explored beneath the leaves at the base of the trunk
with his free hand. There it was: the hard ridge of a thin
rope circling the tree. He eased an eye around the trunk
to confirm that Astaroth was indeed still standing in front

of the Tunnel. Taking a deep breath, he said a quick prayer for Hart's skill and slashed the edge of the watchblade into the cord—

From Ravagin's right came the crackle of breaking branches as a tree a dozen meters into the forest was abruptly released from its bindings and snapped back toward the vertical; and at the same instant, the ground beneath the demon/troll erupted in a flurry of dead leaves as the fishing net Hart had so carefully laid out there was yanked from its concealment. Leaning out from behind his tree, Ravagin watched as the demon/troll, firmly caught in the net, was hauled up and out into the nearby trees.

And to see a crossbow bolt thud into the ground barely a meter away from him.

He jumped, swallowing hard at the the sudden reminder that even with only partial control of the troll, Astaroth was a horribly deadly opponent. Gathering his legs under him, he sprinted for the Tunnel, shivering as the demon's scream of rage filtered down amid the crash of branches marking the end of the demon/troll's passage. Astaroth wouldn't be trapped for long, unfortunately—the troll's hands were strong enough by themselves to tear the net if there was no knife within easy reach. Within minutes, maybe even seconds, the demon/troll would be after him again . . . and Astaroth still had one lethal crossbow bolt left.

That last bolt remained unfired as Ravagin made it across the clearing to the relative safety of the Tunnel. Activating his firefly ring, he ran as quickly as the sloping floor and uncertain footing permitted. Barely halfway to the curved section the sudden sound of more breaking branches reached him. Swearing under his breath, he tried to pick up his pace . . . and just as he reached the curve and started around it there was a faint *twang* from far behind him and a crossbow bolt whistled past him to ricochet from the wall. Clamping his teeth hard, he kept running, resisting the impulse to shut down the firefly. With the curve between him and the demon/troll, darkness wouldn't give him any more protection and would only slow him down in the race ahead.

And it *was* going to be a race. Ravagin had seen trolls

run before, and it was only the fact that the curved path
slowed both of them down that gave him any chance at all
of beating the machine to the telefold. Even with that,
even with his head start and Astaroth's limited control
over the troll machinery, it was going to be close. If Danae
wasn't ready . . .

Another bolt ricocheted around the corner behind him,
jarring him out of his thoughts. Astaroth, shooting blind
with—Ravagin saw—one of the blunted stun bolts. Presumably the last one had been the other stun bolt, which
meant he was saving his remaining sharp one for last. For
right before the telefold.

Another fifty meters to go. The demon/troll's heavy
footsteps could be heard now, their echoes mixing with
those of Ravagin's to fill the Tunnel with rolling thunder.
A few more seconds. The center of Ravagin's back itched
with the thought of that last crossbow bolt—his breathing
sounded ragged in his ears above the pounding of his
heart—almost there—

He came around the last part of the curve . . . and
skidded to a halt at the sight that greeted him.

Danae was waiting for him, all right. Her nude body lay
stretched out against the wall directly ahead of him, her
eyes closed in the firefly's light, a dark bruise almost
visibly forming beneath her right ear. A half dozen meters
further ahead, facing him from the Karyx side of the
telefold—

"Astaroth," Ravagin gasped, dropping down beside Danae,
shielding her with his body from whatever was to come.
"His name . . . is *Astaroth*."

"Understood," Hart said, glacially calm. "I'm ready."
The tone of the thudding footsteps behind Ravagin suddenly changed, and he twisted his head around to see the
demon/troll come into sight, crossbow raised and tracking—

"*Hakleb*—!" Hart shouted.

In that instant Astaroth must have realized what was
about to happen. The demon/troll shifted its aim, instinctively firing its last bolt at this new and unexpected threat.
Reflexively, Hart ducked as the bolt came at him—and
came at him, and came at him, covering the teleport's five

meters over and over again until it struck the floor and finally lay still.

"—*Astaroth*—"

The demon screamed, one last welling up of hatred and fury. And perhaps of fear, for he knew now he was defeated, and Ravagin could only imagine what punishment the fourth world would order for that failure.

"—*mirraim!*"

And with the last part of the invocation spell Astaroth's wail suddenly changed its position, shifting in an instant from the troll behind Ravagin to the Karyx side of the telefold.

From Hart's side of the telefold. "Come on—move it!" Ravagin shouted at the other.

Hart needed no urging . . . but even as he leaped toward the telefold and the safety of Shamsheer an explosion of green flame abruptly enveloped his body. He gasped with pain, the sound mixing with the demon's own howling to set Ravagin's teeth on edge. A second later Hart was through the telefold; and as the corona vanished he collapsed to the ground in a smoking heap.

Ravagin was at his side in an instant. "Hart!" he snapped, fingers probing for the other's pulse. Weak, rapid, thready . . . "Come on, Hart, come on. You're safe now. Hang on—you can make it."

Slowly, the other opened his eyes. "The demon," he said with some effort. "Is he . . . ?"

"It worked," Ravagin assured him. "Exactly the way we thought it would. Of course he's across—who the hell do you think attacked you?"

"And . . . Ms. mal . . . co—"

"Danae's fine," he sighed. "You didn't hit her all that hard. For God's sake, Hart—"

He broke off, but Hart answered the unasked question anyway. "She wanted to do it," he whispered. "She insisted on . . . taking the same risk . . . you were taking. I . . . couldn't let her."

Ravagin gritted his teeth. "Danae!" he shouted, turning his head around. "Wake up, Danae—come on, damn it, I need you."

"Don't bother with me," Hart said, fingers clutching at

Ravagin's sleeve. "The shock alone . . . just get her out . . . and back home. Just . . . leave me here."

"The hell I will," Ravagin growled. "With air transport to a Dreya's Womb only a prayer stick call away? Sit tight, Hart—I'm going to go out a ways and call a sky-plane."

"Ravagin—"

"No argument, damn it. Just think of it as part of my job."

He wasn't sure . . . but as he stood up to go he thought he saw the faintest trace of a smile on the other's lips.

Chapter 46

It seemed fitting, somehow, for them to meet at the Double Imperial for their quiet celebration. Danae was late, and as she was led to the table she saw Ravagin was already there. "Sorry," she said as the maitre d' slid her chair in. "I stayed longer than I'd planned to at the hospital."

"No problem," Ravagin said, his eyes burning into hers. "How is he?"

She shook her head, feeling her throat tighten with the burden of memories. "They've found some more neural damage they have to try and track down. The right side of his face, this time. Aside from that . . . well, he's conscious and as calm as ever and . . . not in too much pain . . ." She broke off, blinking against sudden tears.

Ravagin nodded heavily. "Anything come of the suggestion that the doctors take him into Shamsheer and see if the Dreya's Wombs can do anything more for him?"

"They're afraid to move him," she said, wiping her eyes. "Especially since they can't take any support gear across with them." She took a deep breath. "I almost wish—"

She broke off, but too late, and she winced at the look of pain that appeared on Ravagin's face. "I'm sorry, Danae," he said in a low voice. "There just wasn't any way to get to Saban's circuit diagrams in time. I don't know—maybe I should have tried—"

"Hey," she cut him off softly, reaching across the table to grip his hand. "It's all right—really it is. Besides, what would we have told people when they asked us how we did it?" But even as she spoke, the thought of the diagrams rose, siren-like, before her. Perhaps if Ravagin could just have brought *one* of them out for her to memorize . . . With a supreme effort of will, she crushed the thought back down. "No, it's better this way," she sighed. "You saw what happened to Saban; those diagrams were his own private addiction. Even with just a taste of it—you think we could have held out against the temptation to go back and get just a *little* more? Especially since we know how to do it?"

"Yeah, you're right." He took a deep breath. "You're right. Let's get the hell off the subject before we blow Hart's whole sacrifice out of the water and replace Saban with one of us."

Hart's sacrifice. Unbidden, fresh tears formed in Danae's eyes. "It should have been me," she whispered.

Ravagin understood. "It was his choice, Danae," he reminded her gently. "He knew what he was risking when he took your place."

"I know. Just part of his job, he'd say," she said with a trace of bitterness.

"Yes, he would . . . and we both know how seriously he took that job. So don't feel guilty. Accept the debt, and make up your mind that you'll repay it in a thousand little ways to a thousand other people as you go through life. That's usually the only way we get to pay back something like this."

She nodded, dabbing at her eyes. It sounded so simple and so trite . . . but after two days of soul-searching she knew it was the best she was going to get. "Let's get off this subject, too, can we? Tell me how your own gauntlet went."

He shrugged, taking a sip of wine. "About as I expected. I'm officially out of the Courier Corps now."

"A flat dismissal?"

"A flat resignation," he corrected. "Quiet and peaceful, in exchange for them not pouring any heat onto Corah's head."

Danae bit at her lip, feeling more tears coming on.

Ravagin's career, gone to dust. Like Hart, another debt for her to shoulder.

"You all right?" Ravagin asked.

"Yeah. I just—" She sighed. "It wasn't supposed to work out this way."

"What way is that? Happily ever after, with all the spirits of Karyx seeing the error of their ways and turning over a new page? Come on, Danae—you know the real world doesn't work that way. Personally, I think all three of us getting out of this alive is a thoroughly rousing success."

"Hart's injuries and your unemployment notwithstanding?" she asked, a touch of bitterness creeping into her voice.

Ravagin reached across the table and took her hand. "We're all alive, and we've freed Shamsheer from the demon threat. Concentrate on that."

She took a deep breath. He was right, of course. "It still hurts. A lot."

He squeezed her hand tightly. "Learning how to hurt without giving up is part of what it means to be an adult."

She managed a smile. "That hurts, too."

A waiter appeared, and Danae realized she'd completely forgotten to look at the menu. No matter. "We were in here a few days ago," she told him. "We'll have the same meal, only for two this time."

The other bowed and left, and she turned back to Ravagin to see him cock an eyebrow at her. "Another council of war?" he asked.

"Is the war over?" she countered. "Really, I mean?"

He sighed. "I suppose not," he admitted. "We've won a battle, but the war still goes on. Whether we can do anything about *that* is open to question."

"We have no choice," she said. "That's why humanity was put here on Triplet—to control the spirits."

Ravagin frowned. "What do you mean?"

She nodded in the direction of the Tunnel. "I've been doing a lot of thinking, Ravagin. The Hidden Worlds aren't an experiment; they were a defense."

She hesitated, wondering if this was going to sound stupid. But Ravagin's eyes held no sign of ridicule. "A defense against the fourth world?" he asked quietly.

She licked her lips. "Yes. Karyx may even have been the original planet here, with some sort of weak spot between it and the spirits' dimension, before the builders created Shamsheer and Threshold to push it further back. The extra dimensions—and the way the Tunnels and telefolds were set up—put there as a barrier to keep them from flooding through to the universe as a whole."

Ravagin was staring out into space. "The sixes of Shamsheer," he said at last. "All those hexagons—the Builders weren't so much interested in six-sided figures as they were in a lack of _five_-sided figures."

Danae hadn't gotten around to the hexagons in her own speculations. But now that she thought about it . . . "You mean five-sided figures as in pentagrams?"

"Think about it for a moment. Pentagrams are part of the focusing process for a lot of the spells on Karyx. Giving the people of Shamsheer a mindset oriented to sixes would tend to keep them from placing any significance in fives— which would automatically limit the possibilities for spirithandling."

"Which means . . . the builders knew that spirits could get through the telefolds." She shivered. "And they went ahead and put people there anyway."

"To control the spirits that got through, maybe." Ravagin shook his head slowly. "But why us?"

"I don't know," Danae said. "Maybe it's some innate ability to control spirits; maybe some defensive mechanism in the human psyche that lets us interact with them with a minimum of damage."

"Or maybe it's because we're fighters," Ravagin said slowly. "And they knew we wouldn't just accept spirit domination without a hell of a struggle."

She looked at him. "Then you're not giving up." It was a statement, not a question.

"Who ever said I was? Just because I'm not a Courier any more doesn't mean we can't fight the fourth world from out here. We can push for changes in the way personnel are assigned, the way Couriers and way house people are to operate on Karyx—all sorts of things." He eyed her soberly. "That is, we can if you're willing to work with me.

And to accept the burdens you've worked so hard these past few years to get away from."

She smiled wanly. The burdens. The money, the family name, the influence—all the things she'd hated for not having earned them. But perhaps she could see them now in a new light. "They're not burdens," she said quietly. "They're tools. Tools there to be used."

Letting go of her hand, Ravagin picked up his wine glass. "Welcome to maturity," he said, raising it up.

"I'm an adult," she said, lifting her own glass and tapping his. "Maturity is just part of that job."

They drank.

Here is an excerpt from Vernor Vinge's new novel, Marooned in Realtime, *coming in June 1987 from Baen Books:*

The town nestled in the foothills of the Indonesian Alps, high enough so that equatorial heat and humidity was moderated to an almost uniform pleasantness. Here the Korolevs and their friends had finally assembled the rescued from all the ages. At the moment the population was less than two hundred, every living human being. They needed more; Yelén Korolev knew where to get one hundred more. She was determined to rescue them.

Steven Fraley, President of the Republic of New Mexico, was determined that those hundred remain unrescued. He was still arguing the case when Wil Brierson arrived. ". . . and you don't appreciate the history of our era, madam. The Peacers came near to exterminating the human race. Sure, saving this group will get you a few more warm bodies, but you risk the survival of our whole colony, of the entire human race, in doing so."

Yelén Korolev looked calm, but Wil knew her well enough to recognize the signs of an impending explosion: there were rosy patches on her cheeks, yet her features were otherwise even paler than usual. She ran a hand through her blond hair. "Mr. Fraley, I really do know the history of your era. Remember that almost all of us—no matter what our present age and experience—have our childhoods within a couple hundred years of one another. The Peace Authority"—her lips twitched in a quick smile at the name—"may have started the general war of 1997. They may even be responsible for the terrible plagues of the early twenty-first century. But as governments go, they were relatively benign. This group in Kampuchea"—she waved toward the north—"went into stasis in 2048, when the Peacers were overthrown. That was before decent health care was available. It's entirely possible that none of the original criminals are present."

Fraley opened and closed his mouth, but no words

came. Finally: "Haven't you heard of their 'Renaissance' scheme? In '48 they were ready to kill by the millions again. Those guys under Kampuchea probably got more hell-bombs than a dog has fleas. That basc was their secret ace in the hole. If they hadn't screwed up their stasis, they'd've come out in 2100 and blown us away. And you probably wouldn't even have been born—"

Yelén cut into the torrent. "Hell-bombs? Popguns. Even you know that. Mr. Fraley, getting another hundred people into our colony will make our settlement just big enough to survive. Marta and I haven't spent our lives setting this up just to see it die like the undermanned attempts of the past. The only reason we postponed the founding of Korolev till megayear fifty was so we could rescue those Peacers when their bobble bursts."

She turned to her partner. "Is everybody accounted for?"

Marta Korolev had sat through the argument in silence, her dark features relaxed, her eyes closed. Her headband put her in communication with the estate's autonomous devices. No doubt she had managed a half dozen fliers during the last half hour, scouring the countryside for any truant colonists the Korolev satellites had spotted. Now she opened her eyes. "Everybody's accounted for and safe. In fact"—she caught sight of Wil standing at the back of the amphitheater and grinned—"almost everyone is here on the castle grounds. I think we can provide you people with quite a show this afternoon." She either hadn't followed or—more likely—had chosen to ignore the dispute between Yelén and Fraley.

"Okay, let's get started." A rustle of anticipation passed through the audience. Many were from the twenty-first century, like Wil. But they'd seen enough of the advanced travelers to know that such a statement was more than enough signal for spectacular events to happen.

From his place at the top of the amphitheater, Wil

had a good view to the north. The forests of the higher elevations fell away to a gray-green blur that was the equatorial jungle. Beyond that, haze obscured even the existence of the Inland Sea. Even on the rare, clear day when the sea mists lifted, the Kampuchean Alps were hidden beyond the horizon. Nevertheless, the rescue should be visible; he was a bit surprised that the bluish white of the northern horizon was undisturbed.

"Things will get more exciting, I promise." Yelén's voice brought his eyes back to the stage. Two large displays floated behind her.

"As Mr. Fraley says, the Peacer bobble was supposed to be a secret. It was originally underground. It is much further underground now—somebody blundered. What was to be a fifty-year jump became something . . . longer. As near as we can figure, their bobble should burst sometime in the next few thousand years; they've been in stasis fifty million years. During that time, continents drifted and new rifts formed. Parts of Kampuchea slid deep beneath new mountains." The display behind her lit with a multicolored transect of the Kampuchean Alps. The surface crust appeared as blue, shading into yellow and orange at the greater depths. Right at the margin of orange and magma red was a tiny black disk—the Peacer bobble, afloat against the ceiling of hell.

Inside the bobble, time was stopped. Those within were as they'd been at that instant of a near-forgotten war when the losers decided to escape to the future. No force could affect a bobble's contents; no force could affect its duration—not the heart of a star, not the heart of a lover.

But when the bobble burst, when the stasis ended . . . The Peacers were about forty kilometers down. There would be a moment of noise and heat and pain as the magma swallowed them. One hundred men and women would die, and a certain endangered species would move one more step toward final extinction.

The Korolevs proposed to raise the bobble to the

surface, where it would be safe for the few remaining millennia of its duration. Yelén waved at the display. "This was taken just before we started the operation. Here's the ongoing view."

The picture flickered. The red magma boundary had risen thousands of meters above the bobble. Pinheads of white light flashed in the orange and yellow that represented the solid crust. In the place of each of those lights, red blossomed and spread, almost—Wil winced at the thought—like blood from a stab wound. "Each of those sparkles is a hundred-megaton bomb. In the last few seconds, we've released more energy than all mankind's wars put together."

The red spread as the wounds coalesced into a vast hemorrhage in the bosom of Kampuchea. The magma was still twenty kilometers below ground level. The bombs were timed so there was a constant sparkling just above the highest level of red, bringing the melt closer and closer to the surface. At the bottom of the display, the Peacer bobble floated, serene and untouched. On this scale, its motion towards the surface was imperceptible.

Wil pulled his attention from the display and looked beyond the amphitheater. There was no change: the northern horizon was still haze and pale blue. The rescue site was fifteen hundred kilometers away, but even so, he'd expected something spectacular.

The elapsed-time clock on the display showed almost four minutes. The Korolev pattern of bomb bursts was still thousands of meters short of the surface.

President Fraley rose from his seat. "Madame Korolev, please. There is still time to stop this. I know you've rescued all types, cranks, joyriders, criminals, victims. But these are *monsters*." For once, Wil thought he heard sincerity—perhaps even fear—in the New Mexican's voice. *And he might be right*. If the rumors were true, if the Peacers had created the plagues of the early twenty-first century, then they were responsible for the deaths of billions. If they had succeeded with their Renaissance Project, they would have killed most of the survivors.

Yelén Korolev glanced down at Fraley but didn't reply. The New Mexican stiffened, then waved abruptly to his people. One hundred men and women—most in NM fatigues—came quickly to their feet. It was a dramatic gesture, if nothing else: the amphitheater would be almost empty with them gone.

"Mr. President, I suggest you and the others sit back down." It was Marta Korolev. Her tone was as pleasant as ever, but the insult in the words brought a flush to Steve Fraley's face. He gestured angrily and turned to the stone steps that led from the theater.

The ground shock arrived an instant later.

320 pp. • 65647-3 • $3.50

To order any Baen Book by mail, send the cover price plus 75 cents for first-class postage and handling to: Baen Books, Dept. B, 260 Fifth Avenue, New York, N.Y. 10001.

*Here is an excerpt from IRON MASTER by Patrick Tilley,
to be published in July 1987 by Baen Books. It is the third
book in the "Amtrak Series," which also includes CLOUD
WARRIOR and THE FIRST FAMILY.*

PATRICK TILLEY
IRON MASTER

The five sleek craft, under the control of their
newly-trained samurai pilots, lifted off the grass and
thundered skywards, trailing thin blue ribbons of
smoke from their solid-fuel rocket tubes. Levelling
off at a thousand feet, they circled the field in a tight
arrowhead formation, then dived and pulled up into
a loop, rolling upright as they came down off the top
to go into a second—the maneuver once known as
the Immelmann turn.

There was a gasp from the crowd as the lines of
blue smoke were suddenly severed from the diving
aircraft. A tense, eerie silence descended. The first
rocket boosters had reached the end of their brief
lives. Time for the second burn. The machines
continued their downward plunge—then, with a
reassuring explosion of sound, a stabbing white-hot
finger of flame appeared beneath the cockpit pod of
the lead aircraft. Two, three, four—five!

The watching crowd of Iron Masters responded
with a deep-throated roar of approval. Cadillac, who
was positioned in front of the stand immediately
below his patrons, Yama-Shita and Min-Ota, swelled
with pride. These were the kind of people he could
identify with. Harsh, forbidding, and cruel, with
unbelieveably rigid social mores, they nevertheless
appreciated and placed great value on beautiful objects,

whether they be works of nature or some article fashioned by their craft-masters. Cadillac knew his flying machines appealed to the Iron Masters' aesthetic sensibilities. Like the proud horses of the domain lords, they were lithe and graceful, and the echoing thunder that marked their passage through the sky conveyed the same feeling of irresistible power as the hoofbeats of their galloping steeds. Here, in the Land of the Rising Sun, he had been taken seriously, had been given the opportunity to demonstrate his true capabilities, and had been accorded the praise and esteem Mr. Snow had always denied him. And his work here was only just beginning!

As the five aircraft nosed over the top of the second loop, leaving a blue curve of smoke behind them, their booster rockets exploded in rapid succession. Boooomm! Ba-ba-boom-boomm. Booom!

Cadillac, along with everyone else in the stand behind him, watched in speechless horror as each one was engulfed by a ball of flame. The slender silk-covered spruce wings were ripped to pieces and consumed. On the ground below, confusion reigned as the shower of burning debris spiralled down towards the packed review stand, preceded by the rag-doll bodies of the pilots.

Steve Brickman, gliding high above the lake some three miles to the south of the Heron Pool, saw the fireballs blossom and fall. It had worked. The rocket burn had ignited the explosive charge he, Jodi, and Kelso had packed with loving care into the second of the three canisters each aircraft carried beneath its belly. Now there could be no turning back. Steve caught himself invoking the name of Mo-Town— praying that everything would go according to plan.

General To-Shiba, seated on his left, was quite unaware of the disaster. Fascinated by the bird's-eye view of his large estate, the military governor's eyes were fixed on the small island in the middle of the lake two thousand feet below. It was here, in the summer house surrounded by trees and a beautiful rock garden, that Clearwater was held prisoner. The beautiful creature who was now his body-slave and who possessed that rarest of gifts—lustrous, sweet-smelling body hair. The thought of his next visit filled him with pleasurable anticipation. As a samurai, To-Shiba had no fear of death but, at that moment, he had no inkling his demise was now only minutes away. . . .

July 1987 • 416 pp. • 65338-5 • $3.95

TRAVIS SHELTON
LIKES BAEN BOOKS
BECAUSE THEY TASTE GOOD

Recently we received this letter from Travis Shelton of Dayton, Texas:

> *I have come to associate Baen Books with Del Monte. Now what is that supposed to mean? Well, if you're in a strange store with a lot of different labels, you pick Del Monte because the product will be consistent and will not disappoint.*
>
> *Something I have noticed about Baen Books is that the stories are always fast-paced, exciting, action-filled and seem to be published because of content instead of who wrote the book. I now find myself glancing to see who published the book instead of reading the back or intro. If it's a Baen Book it's going to be good and exciting and will capture your spare reading moments.*
>
> *Another discovery I have recently made is that I don't have any Baen Books in my unread stacks—and I read four to seven books a week, so that in itself is a meaningful statistic.*